P L KANE is the pseudonym of a number one bestselling and award-winning author and editor, who has had over a hundred books published in the fields of SF, YA and Horror/Dark Fantasy. In terms of crime fiction, previous books include the novel *Her Last Secret*, the collection *Nailbiters* and the anthology *Exit Wounds*, which contains stories by the likes of Lee Child, Dean Koontz, Val McDermid and Dennis Lehane. Kane has been a guest at many events and conventions, and has had work optioned and adapted for film and television (including by Lions Gate/NBC, for primetime US network TV). Several of Kane's stories have been turned into short movies and Loose Canon Films/Hydra Films have just adapted 'Men of the Cloth' into a feature, *The Colour of Madness*. Kane's audio drama work for places such as Bafflegab and Spiteful Puppet/ITV features the acting talents of people like Tom Meeten (*The Ghoul*), Neve McIntosh (*Doctor Who/Shetland*), Alice Lowe (*Prevenge*) and Ian Ogilvy (*Return of the Saint*). Visit www.plkane.com for more details.

Also by P L Kane

Her Last Secret

Praise for P L Kane

'Stunning suspense . . . You'll be turning those pages faster than you can say, "Didn't see that coming." Fabulous book. 5* from me.'
 — **Helen Fields, bestselling author of *Perfect Remains*, *Perfect Death* and *Perfect Kill*.**

'What are you doing to me, P L Kane? . . . I think my heart might be broken. Cracking thriller . . .'
 — **Jo Jakeman, bestselling author of *Sticks and Stones* and *Safe House*.**

'The character-driven plot is intelligent, clever and finely paced, and Jake Radcliffe is a flawed but compassionate protagonist. Exceptional.'
 — **M W Craven, bestselling author of *The Puppet Show* and *Black Summer*.**

'Riveting domestic thriller with a razor-edged twist, courtesy of a new top talent.'
 — **Paul Finch, *Sunday Times* bestselling author of *Strangers*, *Shadows* and *Stolen*.**

'A dark, twisty tale with an emotional heart.'
 — **Roz Watkins, bestselling author of *The Devil's Dice* and *Dead Man's Daughter*.**

'Tense and twisty! A few times I held my breath and raced through the pages to immerse myself in more of the story.'
 — **JA Andrews, author of *Mummy's Boy*.**

'Wow – what a great book! I was hooked from the start. The idea of a father trying to re-connect with his estranged murdered daughter was so poignant.'
 — **Liz Mistry, bestselling author of *Last Request* and *Broken Silence*.**

Her Husband's Grave

P L KANE

ONE PLACE. MANY STORIES

HQ
An imprint of HarperCollins*Publishers* Ltd
1 London Bridge Street
London SE1 9GF

First published by HQ Digital 2020

3

This edition published in Great Britain by
HQ, an imprint of HarperCollins*Publishers* Ltd 2020

ISBN: 9780008372248

MIX
Paper from
responsible sources
FSC® C007454

This book is produced from independently certified FSC™ paper
to ensure responsible forest management.

For more information visit: www.harpercollins.co.uk/green

Printed and bound in Great Britain by
CPI Group (UK) Ltd, Croydon CR0 4YY

For my cousins, Helen and Martin.

Prologue

He'd been looking for something else when he made the shocking discovery. The grisly, stomach-churning discovery that would change everything . . .

He had been walking along, here on the beach, looking for treasure no less – buried or otherwise – if you can believe such a thing. And he did, had done all his life. Believed the tales his father had told him about this place when he was young, about the smugglers and the pirates. Loved it when his old man had read *Treasure Island* to him at bedtime when he was little.

Jeremy Platt had only recently moved back to the area, partly to keep an eye on his ageing dad now that the man's wife, Jeremy's mum, had passed away; partly because his own marriage to Alice – who he'd met at college in the nearby town of Mantlethorpe – had fallen apart. Now, here they both were . . . alone, together.

They'd joke about it sometimes, over a pint in their local, or a game of dominoes, though their laughter would fade quite quickly. But at least they had each other, the roles reversed from when Jeremy had been little; now he had to read to his father because of his failing eyesight. Something that had put paid to the old bloke's hobby of amateur writing, and one of the reasons why he liked to stand at the window with those binoculars, looking out over the sea. Or had done, until a couple of days ago.

Until the heart attack.

Jeremy had been the one to make the discovery then too, calling round early because he couldn't reach him on the phone; all the while telling himself it was just lines down because of the storm. Instead, finding him collapsed on the floor, phone off the hook after clearly trying to reach it and ring for help. Jeremy had rung for an ambulance instead, straight away. They'd whisked him off to hospital, and there had followed an anxious few hours, waiting to hear the worst.

When the doctor came out and told Jeremy his dad had stabilised, he'd almost hugged the fellow. 'What he needs now, more than anything, is rest,' the physician had said to Jeremy, 'and time to recover.' He'd been allowed to sit by the bedside, even though Mr Platt Snr was still pretty out of it – wires running in and out of him, like some kind of robot. And Jeremy had cried, watching him, realising just how frail he was for the first time. How he might lose another parent before long.

To be honest, he'd come here today to give himself a break more than anything. The hospital had promised to call if there was any change and he could be back in no time.

So here he was, on said beach, looking for excitement, looking for treasure. Just like his old man had promised. All part of a hobby he'd taken up, something to occupy his time while he looked for – and had failed so far to find – work in the area. So, with what was left over from the redundancy package and his share of the marital savings, he'd treated himself to a metal detector.

Jeremy had often spotted people wandering up and down the sands, sweeping those things from left to right, and thought it looked like fun. Well, you never knew what you might find out there. The guy in the shop, that fellow with the beard and cargo trousers – front pockets bulging, so full Jeremy wondered how he walked without falling over – had done nothing to dissuade him. Had been a self-confessed expert on the subject, happy to give him lots of tips . . . Not to mention sell him the best detector on the market, or so he claimed: the Equinox 800 with the large coil, perfect for places like beaches.

It had continued to rain off and on since the storm, and that made for perfect conditions as far as detecting was concerned. 'When everything's wet,' the bloke from the shop had told him, 'it soaks into the ground and helps you spot anything that's deeper down. Ground's had a drink, see?'

He'd also advised Jeremy not to be in a rush, to expect lots of trash. 'Ninety-five per cent of what you'll find,' cargo guy had said, simultaneously showing him how to swing the machine – not too fast and not in great arcs, 'it'll be junk.'

He hadn't been wrong. In the months he'd been doing this, Jeremy had found enough bottle-tops to pebbledash a house, old-fashioned keys, the backs of watches, tin cans, safety pins, bits of shiny metal that looked like mirrors . . .

However, he'd also found enough to encourage him to carry on: toy cars (a couple of which had actually ended up being collectors' items); an old whistle once (which he hadn't dared blow, recalling an old ghost story he'd read in his teens); a few lighters; a couple of rings; and, though they weren't doubloons as such, quite a few pound coins that must have fallen out of wallets, purses or pockets. The point was, he had fun while he was doing it – and at the moment he needed that, needed to take his mind off things. Off his dad lying there in bed looking like C-3PO.

He stopped when the beeping in his earphones intensified. Jeremy stared at the screen in front of him: 12 . . . 13 . . . no, 14! A pretty good reading, he thought, pulling the 'phones from his ears to wear them around his neck. Bending and taking out his trowel from his pack, he placed the detector down and began digging in the spot it had indicated. What would it be this time – a gold chain perhaps? Down, down, and further down . . .

Jeremy stopped when he saw the metal, couldn't help grinning

3

to himself. The last few bits of sand he dug out with his gloved hands, fingers clawing, eager to see what it was he'd uncovered.

He stopped when he reached it, plucked the item out and held it up in front of him – where it glinted in the early morning sun. His smile faded. 'Just an old ring-pull,' he said to himself, the kind you wouldn't get these days because they were fixed to the lid. Sighing, he bagged it anyway, to stop another hunter from making the same mistake – and to keep those beaches clean, of course. They were a far cry from what they'd been when he was a kid, or indeed when his father had been a boy, and Jeremy wasn't even sure they deserved the name Golden Sands that had been given them now, their colour dull even when it hadn't been raining.

But it was as he'd contemplated this that he spotted it. Something in that dull sand, along the beach. Something not that well buried at all, sticking out in fact – just ripe for the taking. He looked around him, the beach deserted – though to be fair you wouldn't really get many tourists on this stretch of it anyway. They'd stick to the main beach for swimming and so they were closer to the pier and shops. Grabbing his stuff, he clambered to his feet and started over. He couldn't be sure what it was really, but it was glinting.

It was metal. It was gold . . . *Golden* at any rate.

Didn't even need his detector this time, which was real irony for you. All that sweeping, all that beeping. The closer he got the more he saw of it, some kind of strap . . . a watchstrap! Looked like it belonged to an expensive one, too. Just a bit of it sticking out, but there it was.

Jeremy got down again, started to uncover the find as he had done with the ring-pull. He hadn't been digging for long, perhaps only a few seconds, when he pulled back sharply. It was a watch-strap all right, with a watch attached. But there was skin there too.

And a wrist.

Swallowing dryly, he moved forward again. His imagination

surely, eyes playing tricks on him. He dug a little more, pulled back again.

There was a hand attached to that wrist. A human hand.

Jeremy hadn't uncovered much of it, but he could tell now – and though it was at an angle, it looked for all the world like a much dryer version of The Lady in the Lake's hand reaching up for Excalibur. Except there was no sword to catch. And this was no *lady's* hand.

He scrabbled backwards again, felt the bile rising in his mouth. That was a body, no doubt about it – and his mind flashed back to when he and his mum used to bury his dad when they went on the sands (*might be burying him for real soon,* a little voice whispered and he promptly ignored it). But surely nobody would have done that by accident? Left a relative here, especially in this isolated spot.

Jeremy frowned, then reached into his pocket for his mobile. Began to dial a number.

There you go, that same voice had told him, *you wanted excitement. An adventure.* He shook his head again, shook those thoughts away too.

'Yes, hello,' he said when the ringing at the other end stopped and a voice came on the line. Not asking for an ambulance this time, because it was far too late for that. Instead: 'Yes, could you give me the police please.'

Part One

Golden Sands acquired its name because the first people to settle there were struck by the colour of the beaches. The sands, a vibrant golden shade, remain some of the most impressive and cleanest in Britain. Located on the east coast, not too far from Dracula country and only a hop, skip and a jump from places like Redmarket and Granfield – which is why it remains a popular holiday destination with people who live in those localities – it is a family-orientated town (population of around 12,000, who live there the whole year round . . . lucky souls!).

For those history buffs among you, Golden Sands was once known as a smugglers' cove and notorious pirate haunt – you can still ride in the galleon that departs from the harbour at twelve o'clock, midday, and which will take you all around the bay area. Some also say that Golden Sands got its name because those same smugglers and pirates used to hide their treasure in caves or indeed on the beach itself, which is why it attracts its fair share of divers and treasure hunters, keen to uncover a welcome surprise.

Chapter 1

Why did she put herself through this, time and again?

She had no idea. No, that wasn't true. She knew exactly why she came here: to learn; to document; to look for hidden clues that might help with future cases. With hunting people like this – those who did so much harm. But that wasn't the main reason, was it? As Robyn Adams made her way down this corridor, having already gone through the various security checks so far, she thought once more about the why of it. The real reason.

And that reason was to see if she'd been right.

Robyn caught a glimpse of herself in some security glass as the guards escorted her, noting how tired she looked. Her blonde hair, which was streaked through with more and more silver these days, was yanked back into a bun, but that was still doing nothing to stretch and conceal the wrinkles that had appeared over the course of the last couple of years or so. Wrinkles that coincided with taking this job on, not that it was – had ever really been – her real job. More of an extra-curricular activity that the university allowed her to partake in, the kudos they got for having someone like her on their payroll more than compensation enough; all those mentions in the academic papers she had published, those stories in the newspapers. As long as she kept up with her lectures and marking, they were happy enough. And as long as she was helping the police to put away the bad guys, their government funding was also more or less assured.

It had been a total accident, how she'd ended up working for the cops. She'd been at a charity event to raise awareness for cancer research, representing their faculty, and due to her lack of a plus-one had been placed at the table for dinner next to a man who introduced himself only as Gordon, which for most of the evening she'd assumed was his first name rather than his last. He was about ten years older than her, but wore it well, even with the dyed hair – had aged better than she was doing recently, that was for sure – and at first she thought he was trying to chat her up. He'd asked about her work, taking more of an interest than she usually expected people to, especially at an event with free wine.

For a couple of hours or more, he'd quizzed her about various disorders and treatments, ranging from OCD to schizophrenia, and when it came time for them to say goodnight she realised she knew barely anything about the guy, aside from the fact he was a widower and a huge Bruce Springsteen fan.

'Well, it's been nice talking to you, Gordon,' Robyn had said, holding out her hand when their respective taxis arrived.

'You too, Doctor. I'm sorry I monopolised your time, but it was all genuinely fascinating . . . Oh, and please call me Peter. Or Pete if you prefer.'

Robyn had assumed that was that, because he didn't ask for her number or anything and didn't proffer his own. She didn't find out until a day or so later that she'd spent the entire evening talking to one Superintendent Peter Gordon (whose nickname in some quarters was 'The Commissioner' after that famous character in a certain comics series). He got in touch with Robyn through the uni and asked for her to come in to their local station at Hannerton. It had been weird seeing him out of context – the switch between dinner jacket and bow-tie to full dress uniform jarring – but he'd given her that same warm smile from the other night, then offered her a seat across from him as he settled down behind a huge, oak desk.

'Am . . . am I in trouble?' had been her first question to him, and he'd laughed.

'Far from it, Robyn. Far from it. Indeed, I think *we* might be ones in trouble and could really use your help.'

Over tea and biscuits, he'd told her about a case his people were working on that had stumped them all. A series of killings that had been in the news – young girls who'd been found dumped in various locations. Who'd been killed, bitten and partially eaten, then wrapped up in rope. 'Some kind of bondage thing, was our initial assessment,' Gordon informed her and Robyn had frowned. 'What?'

'I don't think the tying up is a sex thing, Superintendent.'

He shook his head and for a moment she thought he was disagreeing with her, but then he said, 'Peter, or Pete. Or plain old Gordon. Look, maybe it's best if I take you over and introduce you to some of the team working on this. Get you to have a look at what they've come up with so far . . .' He paused suddenly. 'If that's okay with you, of course?'

She'd nodded and that's exactly what Gordon had done: he introduced Robyn to people like DI Rick Cavendish and his loyal band of DS's and DC's, many of whom had worked together for ages. She hadn't exactly been welcomed with open arms by everyone, some saying that Gordon was too trusting and they didn't need a person like her – a psychologist – sticking her nose in. But once she was given access to the findings so far, the evidence they'd been sorting through, she'd come up with some theories, and even the naysayers had started to take notice.

Then, after she'd drafted a profile that helped them catch the person they were looking for, Robyn was definitely flavour of the month – especially when she insisted it be classed as a team effort. 'You guys had already done the legwork on this; it just needed a fresh set of eyes was all.'

Fresh eyes to see that the cannibalism was the key, that the person they were looking for – Adrian Nance – thought he could outdo Iranian serial killer 'The Spider', Saeed Hanaei. But Nance not only lured women back to his place like flies into a web, he also tied them up and ate bits of them, 'becoming' the arachnid he wanted to emulate. That extended to actually keeping spiders, the more exotic the better, and that was how they found him in the end: tracking anyone who'd bought such animals in the area.

So now, whenever Cavendish and his team needed those eyes of hers, she was called upon. In the time she'd spent with them, she'd helped with cases such as the so-called Postcode Killer, who was chopping up people who lived in a certain location; and Dennis Wilde, who some called The Baby, because he was leaving bodies in the foetal position . . . Right up to this last case she'd worked on, paying a personal price for his incarceration.

Kevin Sykes. The one who'd taken her prisoner, who'd almost killed her. The man she was on her way to see right now, today. Who was the reason she was hesitating, questioning why she was coming here in the first place and putting herself through all this.

Breathing in deeply, she just placed one foot in front of the other. The material of her trouser suit was swishing with each step, causing her to wince, every sound magnified in this place of echoes. Even her shoes – flats rather than heels (for one thing, the latter could be used as a weapon if any of the inmates got hold of them) – were still making clacking sounds, beating out the rhythm of her journey, matching her heartbeat that was quickening with each metre she covered in this place. The place they called Gateside. Located out in the middle of nowhere, this maximum-security facility for the criminally insane was definitely a misnomer, because it only had one gate – at the front, rather than on the sides – which was so heavily guarded that even if an inmate somehow reached it they would get no further.

Those who called Gordon 'The Commissioner' also referred to Gateside as Arkham, though once again they were totally wrong.

Far from the gothic monstrosity that asylum was, this was new and clean – all white walls and metal and toughened glass. None of which made her feel any better about being inside its walls. Because as much as she knew the science of how the people kept here ticked, as much as she'd studied things like nature versus nurture, behavioural patterns and brain scans showing whether people had shrunken amygdalae (the seat of emotion, of empathy, conscience and remorse) or not, when you got right down to it, the prisoners shut away in this place were just plain scary.

Robyn usually did her best to hide her fear, putting on a front as always, because showing it only made things worse. You'd get nothing out of subjects if they thought you were terrified; it would just make them want to 'play' with you more. Serial killers liked to be in control, liked that feeling. If Robyn was to find out anything during her visits to Gateside, she had to at least appear as if she was the one in the driving seat. Easier said than done, when the man you were facing had once towered above you and been ready to take your life.

All too soon she was there, at the final door. Robyn peered in through the square of glass in an otherwise solid metal barrier, seeing him handcuffed at the table there, attached to chains that ran through metal hooks welded to the table – which itself was bolted to the floor for added security. She would be safe enough, especially with the guards just outside the doors here. Sykes wasn't deemed as dangerous as some in Gateside, who you could only communicate with through bars or toughened glass, guards on either side ready to taser the person. She was at least allowed to sit in a room, sit down at a table with her . . . patient. A patient Robyn knew would never, ever be cured.

She swallowed again, sucked in another breath, and nodded at one of the guards who'd been with her since the inner door. He was dressed like something out of Judge Dredd, everything padded for his own protection, baton hanging from a belt at his waist – taser on the other side, looking for all the world like some kind of futuristic handgun. When he nodded back, helmet wobbling slightly, he reached out with gloved hands and undid the lock with a key-card, then held his hand out for Robyn to enter, like he was a butler at some kind of swish stately home.

Sykes barely looked up when she stepped inside the room, which was probably a good thing because the door slamming shut again made her start a little. Instead, he kept his head down, as if he was studying something in front of him on the table – though there was nothing there – bald patch on top clearly visible; premature for someone of his age. He wore the pale-yellow boiler-suit-style uniform of all the prisoners here, the theory being you wouldn't then confuse them with the guards who were in muted blues and greys. Here, yellow rather than orange was the new black, but then Robyn doubted any of them were concerned about fashion.

Only when she reached the table itself did Sykes acknowledge her presence, looking up slowly and regarding her with those penetrating eyes. The ones she'd gazed into when she thought she was about to die.

'Hello, Dr Adams,' he said with a smile that sent shivers down her spine. 'I wondered when I'd see you again.'

Chapter 2

Sykes' tone was even and considered; unemotional.

Yet it was as if he knew Robyn couldn't stay away, that she'd have to return and look again into those eyes, even though most people would have emigrated and spent the rest of their lives trying to forget the whole thing ever happened.

Not her. She was drawn back to this kind of thing again and again, and somehow Sykes knew that. Sensed it.

'I'm just sorry it took so long, Kevin,' she told him.

'Well,' he said, leaning back as best he could, 'you were recovering. How are the scars, Doctor?'

She flashed back then to the attack, brutal and unrelenting, before dismissing it from her mind. 'Pretty much healed,' she replied, which was true enough. The scars from the cuts had almost healed, the most you could see now were the white lines where they'd been. As for the emotional scars, that was something else entirely. Robyn pulled the chair out, unintentionally scraping the floor and causing Sykes to wince. Then she sat down, taking out her micro-recorder and placing it on the table. 'Do you mind if I . . .'

Sykes shrugged, then nodded to the cameras in the corners of the room behind her, which were scrutinising everything, as if to say: why bother?

'This is for my benefit,' Robyn explained. 'My own research.'

He smiled again. 'I see. If you're expecting my help to catch Buffalo Bill, though . . .'

Robyn gave a snort, thinking to herself: *Don't kid yourself, you're no Anthony Hopkins, mate.* 'Just hoping to talk to you, Kevin. That's all.'

'I would have thought you knew everything there is to know about me already, Doctor. How else would you have caught me? Oh, except you didn't actually catch me, did you. *I* caught *you* if anything.'

'And why did you do that, Kevin? It's not as if I fitted your usual pattern. I wasn't even the right sex, was I? Which was why, when it came right down to it, you couldn't—'

'I wanted to . . . to make you pay,' he cut in. 'For ruining everything.'

'For stopping you from ruining any more lives, from *taking* any more lives.' It was a statement rather than a question. 'Devastating other families, like the ones you've already destroyed. Children who will grow up now without fathers, because of you.'

Sykes spat on the floor and Robyn couldn't help herself, she instinctively sat back in her own chair, putting more distance between them both. It was a show of emotion she hadn't been expecting – usually killers like this were good at mimicking those, but lacked the capacity to feel them. Then again, she had just mentioned his trigger. The father figure.

Kevin Sykes had grown up in an environment where his father was definitely the one in control, who made it clear in no uncertain terms that he wanted Kevin to be a *real* man when he was older . . . tough and strong and as in command as that man was, especially when it came to ruling a household. Ruling over Kevin's mother, who couldn't do a thing to stop him. But no matter what he did, Kevin was always destined to fall short of the mark – and that constant abuse would eventually turn him into the killer he was destined to become.

'They're better off without their fathers,' Sykes told her then.

'I think they might disagree with you there, Kevin. Those men you kidnapped, took, on their way home from work . . . and then killed. They weren't like your own dad; they were loved. And they loved their children, took care of them.'

Sykes' lip curled. 'They're all the same. They deserved what they got.'

Robyn shook her head. 'No. No, they didn't. You were trying to punish your father, I realise that. He died before you could do what you wanted to do to him. But those men, they didn't deserve that kind of treatment.'

'What's deserve got to do with it?' snapped Sykes.

'Everything,' said Robyn sadly. 'No one deserved what you did. Not even your father.'

'You don't know . . . You think you understand, but . . .' Sykes shook his head.

Robyn understood enough. Had worked out from studying the case, a series of missing persons – all male, thirty-five to forty-something, all fathers – that whoever took them wanted to punish someone. Punish a father figure definitely, but also by association punish a wife and mother. Might also see it as freeing the children left behind somehow, like he was doing some good. From there, working with Cavendish and the team, they'd figured out how he was selecting the victims – how he had to have known enough about them to cherry-pick.

'Who do we give information like that to?' she'd said, thinking out loud one night in the station, Cavendish nearby and supplying her with cup after cup of coffee.

'The government, doctors, people in positions of power,' the DI had replied, leaning on a nearby desk, playing with that ponytail of his and narrowing his eyebrows.

'All positions of trust, yes. And of course that's how Shipman was able to do what he did. But . . . no, I don't think we're dealing with someone who'd spend years training to do all that. I think

17

he was quite eager to get started once he became an adult, those fantasies he dreamed of when he was young nagging at him more and more. Needing to move on from the Aura Phase to the Trolling Phase pretty quickly. From imagining it, to planning. These might not even be his first victims, Cav,' she'd told him, comfortable now using the name other members of his team called him by. 'He might have done this elsewhere; we just wouldn't have put it together.'

'So someone still quite young, you reckon?' he'd asked her, scratching his goatee beard now; combined with his hair, it made him look a bit like a Musketeer she always thought.

'Yeah, I think so. And what kind of jobs can young people walk into that give them access to that kind of information?' Robyn had tapped a pen against her mouth as she thought about it. 'Maybe even without any background checks . . . Telemarketing perhaps, or . . .' They'd both turned to each other at the same time and said it:

'Street marketing!'

The kind of people who annoy you by stopping you in the street, asking you questions. 'We never really ask for *their* credentials,' Robyn had continued. 'It might not even be his real job. Offer some kind of incentive, like a prize draw for a holiday or whatever, get them to fill in a form. He might even get them to post back a questionnaire, have a PO Box set up?'

'And Bob's your uncle,' Cavendish had said with a whistle. 'Instant victim database. He'd know if people had wives or not, kids . . .'

'Most importantly,' Robyn had said, 'he'd know their work and home addresses. He'd know just where to grab them between the two.'

'Christ. That's it! That's how we'll get him.'

And they had – almost. Teams had been organised to question the questionnaire people in the city of Hannerton and the neighbouring towns, asking for credentials. Only one person had bolted, led officers quite a merry chase before they lost him again. But in the process, he dropped his clipboard. Dropped the questionnaires he'd been handing out, complete with the PO Box people should send it back to in order to win a non-existent car. They traced the person who'd set it all up to a bedsit, a small apartment that had been searched thoroughly – with Robyn present. Kevin Sykes had fitted her profile almost exactly: mid-twenties and having lost his father a few years beforehand – his mother rotting away in some state-run home – he wasn't originally from the area.

'Now all we need to do is find him,' Cavendish said, though they were all painfully aware he could be anywhere now. Might be setting something similar up somewhere else, under a different name. There was nothing stopping him.

A week or two went by after that, and Robyn had been walking to her Citroën in the university's car park when she felt sure someone was following her. Racing to her vehicle she'd beeped it open and thrown herself inside, shrugging off her coat and pulling out her mobile, ready to report anything amiss. Only Sykes had been waiting inside the car for her, in the back seat, and the next thing she knew there was a handkerchief over her mouth and nose, the strong smell of chloroform assaulting her nostrils.

Then everything went black . . .

When she woke up again, everything was still black. Her eyelids fluttered, were definitely open, yet she couldn't see anything. Was she blind? Robyn also couldn't move very much, but realised that her hands were tied behind her back – felt like a plastic zip-tie – as were her legs, pulled together at the ankles. Her cheek kept brushing a cold, smooth surface, so she knew she was on the floor somewhere. Just didn't have a clue where. What's more, the police wouldn't have a clue either.

She had no idea how long she'd waited in there, but a sudden banging made her start. And when the place was flooded with light suddenly, Robyn knew whoever had taken her was back. Grateful – when she blinked once, twice, making out shapes – that she wasn't actually blind, her gratitude soon evaporated when she realised what was surrounding her. Or at least what little she could see from that floor.

The walls threw back her reflection . . . *reflections*, because they were covered in mirrors of all shapes and sizes; some with frames, others without. When she could tear her eyes away from them, Robyn saw that the room – which was no more than about fifteen feet by fifteen – seemingly had no way out. No, that wasn't correct: the door, which itself was covered in mirrors, was shut, locked, and there was someone else in the space with her now. Might have been there for some time before he put the lights on, who knows.

He was average build, hairline receding at the front, and dressed in a shirt and trousers. She found out later that Sykes' father had equated jeans with layabouts, always 'encouraging' his son to dress properly. Clean-shaven, the guy didn't even have sideburns, but those eyes . . . dear God, his eyes! He was also wearing latex gloves, and when she looked down Robyn understood why the floor was so smooth.

It was covered in plastic, pinned down tightly. The kind that would be easy to roll up and get rid of, getting rid of evidence at the same time.

She was in Sykes' murder room, the place he'd taken those men to kill them. The one bit of the puzzle they hadn't figured out yet. But where . . . where . . .

Suddenly, he was moving towards her – and he had a knife in his hand. 'Kevin. Kevin, wait!' Robyn shouted. She didn't bother calling out for help, figuring that if this was where he dispatched his prey it was bound to either be soundproofed or there was nobody around for miles. Couldn't risk being discovered, being interrupted in his work, whatever that was (they'd had no bodies to examine on that score, none of the missing men having been recovered – alive or dead – though it was probably safe to say they were no longer breathing).

Towering over her, he hadn't spoken a word, just lunged with the knife . . . To cut the plastic ties holding her ankles together. Then, moments later, she was on her feet – almost fell over sideways because legs that were practically dead were attempting to hold her weight. Robyn hoped the rest of her wasn't about to follow suit. 'Kevin, look, we can talk about this. I'm Dr Adams and—'

'I know who you are!' he'd said with a snarl. Of course he did, he'd been waiting for her in the car. Knew where she worked, knew that she'd been assisting the police to find him, and Lord knows what else. 'You're the reason I have to start again, move away!'

'I can help you, Kevin. Talk to me, tell me what you—'

'No talk,' he whispered in her ear, pulling them both around to face one of the mirrors. 'It's time to end this.'

But then he'd paused, as if he was used to doing something at this point with his victims. Used to saying or getting *them* to say something into the reflective surface. But he just hung his head, shook it. 'No . . . no.'

Robyn saw her window of opportunity, and seized it. 'What? What is it, Kevin? Something to do with your dad? Is that it? To do with mirrors and your dad?'

'No . . . *No!*'

'What? What is it you do with those men, *to* those men? To make you feel better, to make you feel like you're in charge? In contro—'

But she pushed it too far and Sykes grabbed her, shoving her back into one of the mirrors, which shattered behind her, showering her with glass. Robyn even felt one or two of the shards embedding themselves into her shoulder blades through the blouse she was wearing, having been relieved at some point of her jacket. He swung Robyn again and again into more of the mirrors that were clearly somehow significant to him and his practices, until she fell to her knees. Then he lowered the knife and held it to her throat.

This is it, thought Robyn. *After all these cases, after all the good I've done, this is the end for me.*

Except Sykes hadn't been able to do it. Hadn't been able to kill

21

her, as frustrating as that seemed to be for him. Then the sirens had come, the breaking open of the door and the men entering with their guns up and aiming at Sykes. Forcing him down, as Cavendish rushed over to Robyn – now on the floor again. Shouting for the paramedics, he'd freed her hands.

That was the last thing she remembered before waking up in the hospital, surrounded by Cav, Gordon and a few of her other colleagues, all with looks of huge relief on their faces. 'How . . . how did you . . .?' Robyn was aware she was slurring her words, on some kind of strong painkillers, but they understood what she was trying to ask.

'He'd registered a lock-up in his mother's name,' the DI told her. 'We didn't find out about it until after you'd been taken. Just sorry it took so long.'

Sorry it took so long . . . Her words to Sykes when she arrived, and it brought her back to the here and now, sitting across the table from the man they now knew had carved up all of those missing men and carried bits of them away in cases to dispose of, to bury. He'd told them happily after he was in custody where they could find them, was even proud of what he'd done. Oddly, he hadn't used the knife to take their lives, but rather had strangled his victims. More intimate, Robyn had informed Cavendish, and slower, giving him time to see the life leave them as they fought for breath.

'You weren't able to kill me, though, were you Kevin,' she said to him now, as their allotted hour drew to a close. 'Weren't able to do to me what you did to those men.'

'I did enough.'

Robyn shook her head. What he'd done, he'd done out of annoyance not out of revenge. 'You see, I think a part of you understood that your mother didn't have a choice. That she was frightened of your dad. It's why you've only killed men, only killed fathers.' The press had dubbed Sykes 'The Oedipus Killer' after the fact, but as with all things they totally misunderstood what he was about. Oedipus wanted to kill his father and sleep with his mother, while Sykes had simply wanted his father dead; had no interest in anything else. 'But why the mirrors, Kevin?'

'You tell me,' he said to her.

'I have my theories, but I'd rather hear it from you. What did your father used to do with them? Why were they significant?'

Sykes shrugged once more, as if he didn't see any reason to withhold it now. 'He . . . he would grab me by the neck, point to himself and say, "That's what a man looks like, boy!" Then he'd force me to look at myself and ask me what I saw.'

'And what did you say back?'

Sykes sneered at her.

She shook her head. 'All those families,' Robyn said again.

'They're better off,' Sykes repeated. 'Sometimes it's better to be by yourself.' He studied her. 'You disagree?'

Robyn said nothing. Then, without warning, 'I feel very sorry for you, Kevin. Even after everything you've done.' And she meant it.

'I feel more sorry for you,' he threw back.

'Why?'

'Because I'm alone by choice. You're not. Who do you have, Doctor? Not a boyfriend, or husband. I know that from following you.' That made Robyn shiver again, the thought that Sykes had been tailing her before he jumped her. 'You try and make up for it with your little police friends, but somehow that just doesn't cut it, does it? At least I had a family, as messed up as it was. Who do you have? Nobody, I think.'

Perhaps he was as perceptive as Lecter after all, she thought. Then she rose, switching off her recorder as she snatched it up. Robyn walked to the door as calmly as she could, rapping on it to be let out. But his words trailed her as she left Sykes behind in that room.

'Who do you have? Nobody you can turn to . . . nobody who'll ever really need you.'

* * *

23

Robyn made it to her car, sliding in behind the wheel again – checking the back seat first, as was her habit now – before the tears came.

She'd thought she was ready for this, had always been a big believer in facing your demons. They were, after all, stock in trade where her line of work was concerned. Both Cav and Gordon had warned her it was too soon, said that she really should talk to someone herself, but she'd wanted to prove them wrong she supposed. And it had at least proved some of those theories correct she'd had about Sykes, about his father, about the mirrors. But oh, the price she'd paid, back then and now.

He'd got inside her head. How had he done that? Was it purely because they'd spent that time together in the lock-up – how vulnerable that had made her, how scared Robyn had been that she was going to die? Or something more, the way he'd studied her almost like she studied people like him, like she'd come up with notions about his life . . . And hadn't he been proved just as correct back there?

Who do you have? Nobody.

Who *did* she have?

Your little police friends.

They'd accepted her, they needed her – didn't they? Robyn told herself they did, but Cav and his team had been solving crimes long before she came along. And some were still wary of having a psychologist around, weren't they? In case she saw something she shouldn't, was analysing them or whatever? Suspicious of her.

How many of them ever invite you to their houses, Robyn? she said to herself. They're your friends, like family – that's how you think of them anyway – and yet . . .

Then there was Cav. Happily married Cav.

Sometimes it's better to be by yourself . . .

Not a boyfriend, or husband.

Robyn began slamming the steering wheel, pounding it with the heels of her hands – so hard it rocked the car from side to side – and she screamed. Then she threw herself back into the seat, suddenly looking about her, worried that she might have drawn attention to herself, even though she'd deliberately parked all the way at the back of the facility's car park.

Nobody had seen her outburst, her tantrum as her late mother would have called it when she was little. Robyn's back ached, the soreness returning that she knew was just psychosomatic. Yet she found herself reaching into her pocket again for the painkillers, the ones they'd returned to her when she left the facility, along with anything else she wasn't allowed to take in with her.

She popped a couple into her mouth and held them there for a moment, relishing the sourness of their taste . . . before reaching into the glove compartment for the bottle of water there. She'd been signed off from the pills for a couple of weeks, but found that she couldn't really do without them. Had sourced some herself when her doctor wouldn't give her any more, said that she was worried Robyn might become addicted. If you knew the right people, however, and especially if you were in the profession, you could get hold of just about anything. She'd be the judge of when she needed to come off them! When the pain stopped, Robyn promised herself. When things didn't hurt quite so much. When she could sleep without relying on other pills, or alcohol.

Like mother, like—

The tinkling sound of her phone – which had also been recently returned to her – made her start again. It would be Gordon or Cav, seeing if she was okay after the visit.

Who do you have, Doctor?

Would be able to tell from her tone that she was far from all right, and would probably say, 'We told you so'. Robyn fished out the phone and for a moment thought about just switching it off, letting it go to voicemail, but that wouldn't really address the problem. Then she spotted the number, and frowned. It wasn't one she immediately recognised, certainly not one the phone recognised or a name would have flashed up on the screen.

Probably just a nuisance caller, someone trying to sell her insurance or going on about PPI. But something made her swipe the green symbol across to take the call.

'H-Hello?' said Robyn, trying to keep her voice steady and failing miserably.

'I . . . Hi, Robyn? Is that you?'

'Er . . . yes.' She vaguely recognised that voice, knew it from somewhere, but it sounded weird. Strange and strained, much worse than she herself was coming across.

'Robyn. Oh, *thank God!* I've been trying to get hold of you.'

'What . . . Who is . . .'

'It's Vicky.' There was a pause and Robyn thought she heard a faint intake of breath, maybe even the sound of this woman crying herself. 'I . . . I need you, Robyn. I know you're really busy and everything but . . . I didn't know who else to turn to. I'm . . . I'm sorry, but . . . Well, I really need you, Robs.'

Who do you have? Nobody you can turn to . . . nobody who'll ever really need you.

'What's happened?' Robyn asked.

'I . . . I'm . . .' Another pause. 'Look, would you be able to come? I wouldn't ask only . . . Robyn, I could really use your help.'

Chapter 3

With every mile that went by, it was as if she was travelling back in time.

As the concrete of tower blocks and huge industrial chimneys had given way to countryside, different shades of greens and yellows passing by, then finally the sea, the cliffs . . . The town spread out like a child's toy in front of her.

Golden Sands: the place where she'd spent every summer, growing up.

And suddenly she was on the high street, driving through it and taking in everything on either side, still slightly in a state of wonderment. The old place hadn't really altered massively in the last fifteen years or so: certain shops had changed hands by the looks of it, but still sold the same things, like postcards, a rack of which were outside the newsagents.

Robyn spotted a few knick-knack shops, a second-hand book place and a traditional seaside chippy, or so it claimed. But the real change was the pound shops that had cropped up, reflecting the current state of the economy. The offices of *The Torch* newspaper were still in the same location, she noted. And there was The Majestic hotel up ahead, which they hadn't really frequented as teens on a night out because it was too posh and expensive.

That was looking a little the worse for wear, but still practically the same, still standing. And not far away their old local, The Barnacle – though it looked like it had become part of a chain.

She checked the sat-nav to find that it had stopped working a while ago, especially now that she needed it and couldn't go from memory. She'd been warned in advance that parts of this place had that effect on technology, sent things a bit screwy. Back when she'd been here last, mobiles and the internet were still relatively new, definitely hadn't caught on here like they had now. Switching to a paper map instead, she eventually found the street she was searching for, complete with one or two news vans and a handful of disinterested reporters still scattered around.

Spotting the right number house, a new build, Robyn parked up, summoning the courage to get out and head up the path. To knock on the door.

The face that greeted her when it opened took her aback, made Robyn wonder if she'd got the right house after all. Framed by a mop of frizzy ginger hair – straight out of a bottle – that face sported more lines than Robyn needed to worry about, not to mention a pair of colourful glasses Dame Edna would have been proud of. She also hadn't expected the person to look so stern.

Robyn wasn't quite sure what to say at first, but managed: 'I . . . er . . . This is number 17?'

The woman nodded, expression still pretty severe. 'And you are?'

'I'm . . . My name's Robyn Adams, I'm Vic . . . Mrs Carter's—'

'Cousin!' she heard a voice say from behind the woman. 'She's my cousin.'

The woman with the frizz and glasses grudgingly stepped to one side, allowing Robyn to see past her. To see the woman standing there wearing a green trackie top and grey jogging bottoms. And though the face had definitely aged, it hadn't done so dramatically and was still recognisably Vicky's. The only real shock was that she'd had her hair cut short, getting rid of those raven locks that Robyn had been so envious of back when they were young.

'It's okay, Tracy, this is the lady I told you about,' confirmed Vicky. 'My cousin Robyn.'

The woman nodded, but still didn't move. Robyn cocked her head, waiting at least for an introduction, which the woman finally gave her. 'Oh, I'm Tracy Dobbs. I'm the FLO assigned to this case. That means—'

'Family Liaison Officer, yes I know.' She wished she didn't, and hadn't meant to say it in quite such an offhand way, but she was still getting some weird vibes from this woman and for some reason they were making her defensive. Obliterating that sense of belonging she'd been starting to feel again. 'Sorry,' said Robyn and stuck out her hand.

The woman's face relaxed slightly, but she didn't take the proffered hand. Robyn might have said the woman was in the wrong line of work, but Vicky explained she'd had to answer the door and fend off quite a number of reporters and 'well-wishers' recently – checking first whether Vicky knew them or not. It was bound to make you a bit tetchy. Or was it more than that? *How much* had this woman been told about her, and did that have something to do with the attitude? Nevertheless, Tracy offered to make some tea.

'That would be . . . er, thanks,' Robyn told her, not even sure she was included. 'Milk, no sugar,' she ventured anyway.

When Tracy wandered off to the kitchen and Robyn closed the front door behind her, Vicky finally approached. There was an awkward moment or two, when neither of them was quite sure what to do, then Vicky moved forward, wrapped her arms around Robyn and hugged her harder than she'd ever been hugged before. She winced a little at the pain from her back, but fought that down because Vicky needed this – probably more than she'd needed anything in her life. More even than any help Robyn could offer her. And so she bit back the discomfort and embraced her cousin too, rubbing her back and telling her it would be all right, even though she didn't believe that for a second. Things, for Vicky, would never be all right again.

When her cousin finally pulled away, there were tears in her eyes. Those same tears she'd heard her crying over the phone as she attempted to explain the situation. 'Robyn . . . Robs, I . . . Thanks so much for coming. I-I'm so glad you're here.'

'Me too,' said Robyn, then added: 'I mean, it's . . . I'm not glad to be here because of . . .' For someone who dealt with depression and grief as much as she did, and usually considered their words with care, she wasn't half making a mess of this. But then, how often was it someone she knew on the receiving end of such dramatic events?

'I know what you mean,' Vicky told her, letting her off the hook. 'Hope I didn't cause too much of a problem, with your work or . . .'

'I'm owed some time off,' Robyn reassured her. 'From both my jobs actually.' Gordon had been more than happy for her to take some time away visiting family, and she'd already had so much time off from uni because of what had happened that they told her it was better if the students finish the year with the substitute lecturer.

Vicky nodded. 'I'm just so pleased to see you, Robs, you have no idea.'

'Same goes,' she replied. 'How . . . how're you—'

'It's like a nightmare,' Vicky broke in before she could even finish the sentence. 'Honestly, I keep waiting to wake up from it. You know what I mean?'

Robyn nodded. Sadly, she knew all too well – and a picture of being hauled around that lock-up flashed into her mind. She'd woken from the darkness, only to find more waiting for her . . . even when the lights had been turned on. And there hadn't been one moment in that place of mirrors Robyn hadn't prayed it was all some kind of dream, that she'd wake up properly in her own bed in her own flat. It didn't happen, though, because she'd been awake already. Unfortunately for Vicky so was she.

'I can't even begin to get my head around—'

It was then that a noise – a bumping and thumping noise – cut through the conversation. Robyn looked up and over to see a small figure scrambling down the stairs, holding on to the rail so far and then just giving up and sliding the last few steps on her bottom. Then that same little missile came hurtling towards her, pigtails flapping from side to side, hugging her just like her mother had, except this time it was around the legs and knees.

'*Aunty Robyn!*' shouted the girl. Robyn looked down and when the little girl cocked her head back to meet her gaze, she was shocked not only by how much she resembled Vicky at that age, but also how much she'd grown in the time since she'd last seen her. She'd been what, three then? And, thinking that, Robyn was suddenly incredibly impressed that the girl – who was wearing a T-shirt and a miniature set of dungarees – even remembered her at all.

'Wow!' Robyn said, reaching down to pat her on the back, not having the faintest idea how to respond.

'Mia! Put your Aunty Robyn down now, let her get into the house properly.'

'It's okay,' Robyn said with a faint smile, and actually it was. She found she was getting used to having those arms around her knees and thighs. 'Really. I can't get over how you've . . .' Robyn broke eye contact to glance over at Vicky again. 'She's how old? Six now?'

'Nearly seven!' Mia announced and when Robyn looked back again she saw her pouting. Realised she should have been talking to Mia anyway, addressing the question about her age to the child herself. Rookie mistake.

'You're a big girl now,' she stated and the pout quickly transformed into a smile.

'Come on, young lady,' said Vicky, holding out her hand and having to practically prise Mia away from Robyn, 'let's all go into the living room. Tracy's making some tea.' Mia pulled a face at that. 'I'm sure if you asked her nicely, she could fix you a juice instead.'

With that, Mia went racing off towards the kitchen to put in her drinks request.

Vicky wrenched her neck to the side, and Robyn followed as she made her way through into the lounge. 'I can't believe she remembers me,' said Robyn as they went, putting into words what she'd been thinking. 'It was what, four years ago . . .'

'Your mum's funeral,' Vicky said sombrely. 'I brought her to the city for the day.'

'That's right,' Robyn replied, feeling embarrassed that she'd forgotten the exact nature of their last meeting – but then there'd been a lot to organise. Distant relatives flying in to pay their respects, friends from the home and their carers. She vaguely remembered saying hello to Vicky and Mia, but not really spending a vast amount of time with them. Certainly not enough to catch up. Then the evening had become a haze of alcohol and condolences.

Vicky and Mia, but no Simon. The reason Robyn was here today.

She was about to ask again about exactly what had happened, when suddenly the little girl was back with them again, having put in her order for juice. Tracy wasn't long after that with the tea, carrying it in on a tray – if she was a FLO worth her salt she was probably used to making it every hour or so anyway. They all sat down, Mia flocking to Robyn again who was taking off her jacket; she cuddled up to her aunty on the sofa. Nobody really spoke except the little girl for a while or so, telling the newcomer about this and that, her friends and getting into trouble for talking to her bestie Jay in class the last time she'd been in school.

'I haven't been there for a while, though,' Mia concluded with. 'Maybe it's because I was talking?'

Robyn glanced over at Vicky sitting in a chair, who answered. 'It's . . . it's not because you were talking, sweetheart. You're not in trouble. You just finished school a bit early this year, is all.'

'But how come I'm not allowed to play outside?'

'We talked about this, Mia. It's just for a little bit longer, till the rest of your friends break up. You can play with Tracy upstairs if you like? You'd like that.'

'Can I play with Aunty Robyn?' asked the child hopefully, which drew a bit of a strange look from Tracy.

'Aunty Robyn . . . I need to have a chat with her myself first, if that's all right?'

The girl pouted again. 'But I haven't seen her in sooooo long. Not since I was really, really little.'

Robyn's turn to save her cousin now, let her off the hook. 'There'll be plenty of time for us to play, Mia,' she promised. 'I'm not going anywhere anytime soon.' Robyn couldn't help noticing the expression of relief on Vicky's face at that. Tracy appeared less impressed.

Mia seemed to accept this, hopping down off the couch, holding out her hand and saying to Tracy, 'Come on then.' Before she left the room completely, however, she turned and asked Robyn: 'Why haven't you ever been here before? Why did it take you so long to come?' Thankfully, she didn't draw out the 'so' this time, but it still left Robyn lost for words.

'Your aunty's a very busy lady, Mia,' Vicky chipped in. 'A very important lady.' And was there a hint of resentment there, or was it just Robyn's imagination? Then the moment was gone and Vicky was attempting a smile.

Mia simply shrugged and went off up the stairs with Tracy to play with whatever toys she had up there. Finally able to, Robyn reached forward to the coffee table, took hold of her cup and had a sip of tea, her mouth suddenly incredibly dry. Seconds later, Vicky was up and walking across, taking Mia's place next to her on the sofa.

'She doesn't know yet?' asked Robyn.

Vicky shook her head, eyes tearing up again. 'I wasn't sure what to say to her.'

'No,' agreed Robyn. 'She's bright though. She remembered me.'

'Sharp as a tack, that one,' Vicky told her, with no small amount of pride. 'Like you were back then, Robs. Must be from your branch of the family.'

'Like her mother, too,' Robyn said to her. Vicky was definitely no idiot; might not have been academically minded (or perhaps just never had the chance?) but she was far from stupid. Robyn wouldn't have got on with her so well if she had been. 'Who does she think Tracy is?'

'Just a new friend of Mummy's, and a sort of nanny I guess.' Vicky shook her head. 'Oh, I don't know. It's all such a mess.'

Robyn wondered what the little girl thought about the crowds that had probably been outside until today, what she thought about Tracy answering the door and telling people to get lost, like she'd almost done with her.

Wondered where she thought her father was.

Now she couldn't help it; Robyn was scanning the room, taking in the photos hanging on the walls and those standing on the small wooden mantelpiece. Snapshots of a life she'd had nothing whatsoever to do with. Simon – tall, broad, short dark hair, stubbled chin and a warm, charming smile – with his arm around Vicky in most. Then ones with Mia over the years. A couple with the proud grandparents, Robyn's Aunty Sue – her mother's sister – and Uncle Trev, though Mia had only been a baby when they were still alive. Finally a wedding photo – Simon and Vicky being sprayed with confetti . . .

Robyn had missed that bit of the day, only managing to get to the evening reception – at a cheaper venue outside town, rather than The Majestic – and then only for a couple of hours before heading off to the motel she was staying in. Her thoughts, her memories, were interrupted by Vicky putting her head on Robyn's shoulder like she'd done so many times when they were younger if she was upset about something. Her summer 'sister', a little younger than herself, who she'd spent so much time with when Robyn's mother used to offload her here for the holidays. Robyn responded by doing now what she'd done on all those occasions in the past – she put her arm around Vicky, comforted her.

'She hasn't asked where Simon is?' said Robyn, bringing it back to the conversation about Mia.

'He . . . he very often stays out for a few days at a time,' Vicky told her, half mumbling into her shoulder. 'It's why I wasn't particularly worried when he didn't . . .' *Really?* thought Robyn, *I would have been*. Most folk would have been, wouldn't they? But if that was their routine . . . And Robyn knew absolutely nothing about their private life; wasn't sure she wanted to. 'Wasn't worried. Not until . . . Simon works . . . *worked* a few different jobs, you see. Had to since I lost my job at the newsagent's, and that was only part-time anyway. It's not easy finding employment around here, Robs. A lot of it's seasonal. If . . . if he was working at the local Spa shop, he might stay over – particularly if they were busy, like they are at the moment.'

'Spa?' asked Robyn. Like the pound shops, this was obviously a new-ish thing in Golden Sands. They definitely hadn't had one when she'd been visiting this place.

'Er . . . yeah, started up a good few years ago,' Vicky said, voice wavering. Might just have been her getting upset again, or . . . 'It's at the old castle,' she then said suddenly. The one neither of them really had any interest in when they were young. Who needed history?

'Okay . . . Listen, Vicky, I know you told me a little on the phone and this must be so hard for you, but . . . well, could you tell me a bit more about what happened?'

Her cousin shifted about uncomfortably, pulling herself up off Robyn and drying her eyes with the backs of her sleeves. Robyn opened her handbag and pulled out a pack of tissues, passing one to her. 'Thanks. I'm not sure what else to tell you, Robs. They . . . Someone found him. Simon. Not long after that big storm we had.' Vicky said this as if Robyn had been around. 'He'd been . . . He was on the beach. Someone came to tell me, from the police, that he'd been found. I think . . . T-There was some talk that he might have drowned or something? That's another thing, he helps out on the boats occasionally. Fishing, you know.'

'Though surely it would have been reported if he'd fallen overboard?' Robyn offered.

Vicky shrugged, then shook her head as if she couldn't decide. 'Not necessarily.' And she got what her cousin meant then, that not all of his work was legit. 'But, anyway . . . that's not . . .' Vicky began to cry again and Robyn reached for her cousin's tea, handing it to her.

'Take it slowly,' she told her. 'There's no rush.'

Vicky nodded. 'You should have seen him, Robs. There on that metal. In the morgue. I-I had to—'

Robyn was aware of someone lurking in the doorway then. Tracy – she hadn't even noticed she'd come back down again. Had she been listening? Seeing she'd been spotted, Tracy entered and picked something up off the sideboard; Robyn didn't even see what it was. 'Sorry, I just forgot . . .' Didn't really help in identifying the object, either – and then Tracy was gone again.

'Is she . . .' Robyn said, frowning.

'Tracy? Oh, she's okay,' replied Vicky, who apparently saw nothing odd in the woman's behaviour. 'Been a big help, actually.'

Robyn was still frowning, but told her cousin to continue. 'You were saying you had to . . .'

'Right, yeah. It was horrible. I had to identify Simon, you see. Next of kin.' Sadly, that wasn't an uncommon thing for Robyn, seeing dead bodies – in the morgue or at crime scenes – but she said nothing. 'He didn't have anyone else since his folks passed, same as me.' She caught Robyn's eye and apologised. 'Not that . . . I mean you're—'

She held up a hand. Vicky had every right – she hadn't been around for a long time. They hadn't been close for a good while. 'It's okay, really.'

'That's why I called. You're still family, Robs. I still think of you as . . .' She shook her head again and sipped more tea, then put down the cup. 'There were these marks, you see. Around his throat. They said it was consistent with . . . with strangulation.'

'He'd been choked?' asked Robyn, and immediately her mind flashed back to Sykes. What he'd done to those fathers, how he'd ruined so many lives. She was beginning to get a very uneasy feeling.

No. A coincidence. Just a coincidence.

Another nod from Vicky. 'They asked me if I could think of anyone who might want to do him harm, but for the life of me I . . . You know what I'm like, I'm quite a private person anyway, don't really like talking about that kind of stuff with anyone who's not . . . And Simon, he was so lovely, he didn't have any enemies; he'd make friends with anyone, you know? Would help anyone out. But I can't really find out anything more about . . . I get the feeling I'm being fobbed off, Robs. I mean Tracy's really nice and everything, but she doesn't seem to know a great deal.' *Or won't tell you*, thought Robyn. 'And I can't . . .'

Robyn sat back on the couch. 'That's why you got in touch with me,' she stated, without trying to make it sound like an accusation.

'Not . . . not the *only* reason, Robs. I needed . . . *need* you. To be honest, there have been times over the last few years that . . .' The tears were coming once more, and she dabbed at her eyes with the tissue. 'I picked up the phone so many times. I mean I had your numbers . . . Just didn't think you'd come.'

'I . . .' Robyn began, then opened her arms wide and beckoned Vicky to hug her once more, barely feeling the pain from those wounds this time. 'I'm sorry,' she said.

'Why . . . why *didn't* you ever visit?' Vicky asked, twisting on the sofa and speaking into her neck this time. Echoing her daughter's question.

'I . . .' There was a noise from the stairs, Mia barrelling down them this time, making up for Tracy's stealth. Vicky pulled away from Robyn, straightening herself, drying her eyes – though it was plainly obvious she'd been crying. Trying to protect her kid, though how much longer she could do that for was anyone's guess; if Robyn had learned one thing from those psychology lectures and seminars at uni, it was that kids pick up on things. All kinds of things.

Case in point: 'What's . . . what's the matter, Mum?' asked Mia, as soon as she was close enough to see her obvious distress. Tracy was making her way back down the stairs again, saying she was sorry, that Mia got away from her.

'Nothing. Nothing sweetheart.' She mirrored Robyn then, opening her arms wide so that the little girl could run into them for a hug. Which Mia did, but kept glancing sideways at Robyn – who reached out and rubbed the kid's arm.

And there they sat, the three of them huddled up together on the sofa.

Sat there for what felt like an eternity.

Chapter 4

Robyn stood back and looked at all the papers, the pictures that were covering the bed.

This was how she always did it, stepping back and looking at the big picture, though ideally on an evidence wall or board. Maybe walking to clear her head and making use of the 'dead time', if you'd pardon the expression: when you switched your mind off and your subconscious was doing the work for you. She knew of people who could ask themselves questions just before going to sleep, only to wake up the next morning with solutions. It wasn't quite as easy as that for her, but she did dream about the cases she'd worked on. Dreamt – when she could sleep that was – of her time in the lock-up in the dark, then surrounded by reflective glass throwing back images of her own face.

She gazed at the photos of Simon's wounds, copies taken out of Manila files and laid on the bed. Robyn was glad this room, the spare room of the house, had a lock on it from the inside because there was no danger of Mia barging in and seeing all this. Vicky was putting her to bed anyway.

The files, the photos and paperwork done so far hadn't been easy to get hold of either. But she'd promised Vicky she would look into things, so that's what she intended to do. Robyn had left the house that afternoon, after Tracy had fixed people sandwiches and she'd asked the FLO for directions to the police station. There had been another one of those flickers then, those looks of wariness, and she thought the woman might not tell her or might ask why she wanted to know, but in the end she just told Robyn how to get there. As with the castle, the station was one of those places she'd never really had cause to frequent – though she could think of at least one occasion when she probably should have.

Like everything else, it was within walking distance – but Robyn took the car anyway, as she figured it would be quicker. Though not before Vicky had shown her where to put her case – the spare room Robyn was presently standing in and remembering her day . . .

Robyn had found the place she was looking for without much difficulty this time, a squat but long two-storey brick building with a grey entrance lumped on the side. A faded yellow handrail guided the way to the door, covered by one solitary CCTV camera, and when she entered Robyn found it pretty quiet inside the waiting room. Only two people sat in there, one guy with his head in his heads for some reason. The desk sergeant on duty, leaning on the wooden desk in question, was talking to a thin man with a backpack. There was no glass – safety or otherwise – separating them and she thought to herself what a far cry from Gateside all this was.

Not safe, not secure.

Posters covered the walls in that room, some dating back to the years of 'Watch Out! There's a Thief About!' – the helpful illustration of a silhouetted man stealing a letter getting the message across for the hard of understanding. She pretended to read some of them while the sergeant and thin man conducted their business, but couldn't help overhearing the tail end of the conversation.

'Well, could you just let them know that Jeremy Platt was in again. And if there's anything else I can do to help . . .'

The sergeant, whose comb-over wasn't fooling anyone and who

looked about one pork pie away from going the way of late Uncle Trevor – a heart attack in his fifties – nodded. 'Yes, I'll tell them, Jeremy.' The use of the man's first name and the conversational manner implied that they knew each other. 'Just like I told them yesterday and the day before. They have your statement.'

'Yes. Yes, I know. I just thought maybe we might have missed something about that morning. I was the person who found him, you know.'

The desk sergeant sighed. 'I know you were. We all do. But I'm sure Inspector O'Brien and DS Watts didn't miss anything. *They* know what they're doing.' He emphasised 'they' to drive home the fact that this man was not actually part of whatever inquiry was happening, regardless of what he thought. 'Look, shouldn't you be somewhere else. Your dad?'

The man hung his head, and sighed himself. 'Yes, right. Okay. But if you need me, Bob, you know how to get hold of me. I'll be at the hospital, Chester Ward. But I'll have my mobile on me. The number's—'

'Yes, yes. We have your numbers, Jeremy – mobile, and landline. Thank you!' For a second or two, Robyn thought the sergeant was going to come round and start chasing the man away with a broom. She watched as he slunk off without any further provocation however, wondering if what she'd heard related to Simon's case at all. If it didn't, then given his talk of finding someone, Golden Sands was rapidly become a crime capital. Then again, how did she know the man was talking about a person? 'Him' might have been a pet dog for all Robyn knew, though somehow she doubted it.

Facing front, now the way was clear, she'd stepped up to the desk, ignoring the way the policeman there was looking her up and down. Robyn couldn't tell if he was being lecherous or just didn't like strangers in his nick. Possibly both, she decided. Another 'warm' welcome. 'Yes, miss,' he said at last. 'What can I do for you?'

'I'd like to speak with the people in charge of the Carter case, please.'

The comb-over man's left eyebrow – which, as if to mock the top of his head, was thick and bushy – had shot up. 'I see. And who might you be?'

'I might be the cousin of the victim's spouse,' she informed him, her back up.

His right eyebrow rose now to match the other one. 'Right. I see . . . Very well, I'll go and see if they're around.'

He disappeared momentarily, leaving her to stare at the posters once again. When he returned, the sergeant told her that there was nobody around who could see her right at that moment and perhaps she could come back another time.

It was Robyn's turn to sigh. 'Look, Bob,' she said, watching as the thick eyebrows that had just about settled down again both rose in response. 'Why don't you tell . . .' She went for broke. 'Either Inspector O'Brien and/or DS Watts that *Dr* Robyn Adams would like to see them.'

'Now look here—' said the man, finger up and wagging in her direction.

She'd had enough of his 'run along, dear' bullshit and needed to front it out. 'No. *You* look. I'm well within my rights to ask to see them; I'm more than versed in police procedure. So why don't you go back there and talk to them again . . . *please.*' She added the last word to be nice, but she was fast running out of patience. Throwing her weight around didn't come naturally to Robyn, especially at the moment, but the situation demanded it.

The sergeant opened his mouth and looked like he was going to say something else, but then straightened out the rest of his fingers and flapped his hand. It just wasn't worth the hassle of causing a scene; there were people above his pay grade who should be handling this. Vanishing again behind the scenes, Sergeant Bob returned a few minutes later with a woman in her early to mid-forties wearing a trouser suit not dissimilar to Robyn's, but with a navy blouse instead of a cream one. Her nut-brown hair had been layered to give it volume, and fell almost across one eye in a way that would have driven Robyn crackers if it had belonged to her. The woman's face was pretty, features delicate, but she was giving Tracy's stern look a run for its money. If Robyn was feeling pissed off, then this woman's face embodied it.

'Thanks Bob,' she told the uniformed man, who took up his place again leaning on the desk. Then she motioned for Robyn to step to the far side, away from the people in the waiting area. 'Dr Adams?' she asked, making sure she used the full title that had been passed along with the sergeant.

'Please, call me Robyn,' she said with a weak smile. Now she'd got past Bob, who had definitely needed a firmer hand, she was trying to be tactful. After all, she wanted information from these people and was so far off her own patch it was ridiculous. Off her patch and vulnerable.

'I'm Inspector O'Brien, SIO on the Simon Carter case. That means—'

'Senior Investigating Officer, yes I know,' said Robyn, without thinking. But, in her defence, it had been the second time someone had tried to explain these terms to her today; even if she didn't work with the police herself, they were fairly common weren't they, from the amount of cop shows on TV?

O'Brien nodded, perhaps thinking this was the case rather than Robyn having first-hand experience. 'All I can really disclose at this time is that we're following up every lead we can.' It was the standard line she'd probably been feeding to the press since this whole thing began. 'So, unless there's—'

'I-I was just wondering if forensics had turned anything up,' said Robyn.

'Forensics . . .' The inspector frowned, definitely thinking now that this woman fitted into the category of 'watched too many episodes of *Luther*' or simply fancied herself as an armchair detective, like the guy Bob had sent off with a flea in his ear.

43

But then the frown turned to one of puzzlement, like she was trying to work something out. 'Dr Adams . . . Where do I know that name from?'

Robyn was about to answer, when a figure appeared from behind the DI. This man was a good ten years younger than O'Brien, with hair that was shaved at the sides and swept over the top of his head so that it resembled one of those waves out there on the ocean. He was smartly dressed, his suit cut well and his tie pulled so tight it looked like it was threatening to cut off his oxygen (like Simon, Robyn couldn't help thinking . . . then shoved the comparison aside). 'You *should* know it, guv,' he said, causing the woman – his superior – to turn around. The inspector still looked puzzled. 'The Spider, the Postcode Killer . . . Oedipus.'

The last one caused Robyn to wince, an involuntary action but the man couldn't help spotting it. O'Brien turned back around, a look of slow, dawning realisation washing over her face. It appeared that her 'exploits' had not only reached cousin Vicky, but the local plod at Golden Sands. They didn't know the half of it though, no matter how much they'd read or seen; none of them did. 'Right,' said the woman.

There was an awkward silence then, not dissimilar to the one that had passed between her and Vicky when she first arrived. In the end, Robyn broke it, saying: 'I thought I'd come along and see if—'

'And you're the cousin of the victim's wife, is that right?' O'Brien asked, knowing full well that she was.

Robyn nodded. 'That is true, but—'

'With all due respect, Dr Adams . . .' Still not Robyn. 'We have enough on here trying to investigate this without relatives or any other do-gooders getting under our feet.' It was the young man's turn to frown now, staring at the back of O'Brien's head as if something was crawling out of it. 'Christ, the guy who found Mr Carter keeps coming in and offering to help as well. This is a police investigation. I don't want it turning into some kind of bloody circus.'

'I just want to help.' *A fresh pair of eyes* . . . 'I-I might be able to offer some—'

'And I suppose it's your relative who's asked you to look into all this?' O'Brien wasn't budging an inch, that much was clear.

'Guv, maybe we should—' began the man behind her, and she gave him a withering glare.

'Maybe you should return to your duties, DS Watts.' *So, he was the other detective assigned to the case,* thought Robyn. *Good to put a face to the name.* 'As for you, Dr Adams, I think the best thing you can do is go back and comfort your cousin. She's been through a lot.'

O'Brien turned that withering gaze on Robyn, but she tried to hold it. A respect thing, if nothing else. In the end it was the DI who looked away first, but only because she was walking away, taking her DS with her, who looked over his shoulder apologetically at Robyn. She didn't know what she'd been expecting, definitely not to be welcomed with open arms – the same way Vicky had done – but not that kind of rudeness, either. Cav's team had been wary at first, until she'd proven herself – and perhaps she thought that might earn her a shortcut here. Might buy her the chance to look over the case at least, and if it had been up to Watts that definitely would have happened. But O'Brien . . . No, she was a different kettle of fish altogether. Sure, the woman had a right to be worried because Robyn was related to the dead man's wife, to the man himself – conflict of interest and all that – but she hadn't even bothered to find out their connection. That she wasn't . . . that she and Vicky hadn't been close for years; that they hadn't even seen each other since her mum's . . . That Robyn could remain detached. Probably. Definitely.

But if it was a pissing contest she wanted, psychology 101, then Robyn seemingly had no choice. She took out her mobile and sighed again when she saw there was no signal, before drifting over to the payphone near the entrance.

Fifteen minutes after placing her call, and sitting down in the waiting area – putting some distance between herself and the guy with his head in his hands, who'd since begun moaning softly too; it was actually quite unsettling – DI O'Brien appeared again behind that desk. She pulled a face when she saw Robyn there, then pointed at her. If it had been a gun, the psychologist would have been filled with lead in no time. 'You. Dr Adams.' The rigid finger crooked then. 'Follow me.'

Robyn got up and went to the desk, waiting for Sergeant Bob to let her through. O'Brien, however, didn't wait – had already rounded the corner into the station proper by the time Robyn was allowed past the barrier. She caught the woman up, turning the corner as well and catching the door that was being held open for her after the DI had carded herself back in. *At least they have* some *kind of security here,* thought Robyn, *not just old Bob and his desk, sitting there like a guard at a set of medieval gates.*

The room she found herself in was small compared to the station back home, maybe a dozen desks or less – and only a few of those were occupied at present. O'Brien strode up to the closest, where DS Watts was sitting with his back to them, his jacket off and slung over his seat. She tapped him on the shoulder and he shifted around in the chair, which didn't even look like it was a swivel one. Without looking at Robyn, O'Brien said, 'DS Watts here will assist you with whatever you need to see . . . Within reason.'

Then she strode off again away from the desk, away from the pair of them as if washing her hands of the whole thing. Once she'd gone, the DS grinned up at Robyn. 'Friends in high places, eh? That'll put a few noses out of joint.'

Robyn flashed an awkward smile, reminding herself of the promise that she would spring for dinner and a pair of tickets the next time The Boss was over in this country; it seemed appropriate given they'd just shown O'Brien who was the real person in charge. 'Friends of friends, I think. Really shouldn't have come to that, though,' she told him.

'Aww, don't mind Grace. She's okay once you get to know her,' said Watts. 'Just doesn't like being told what to do, being pushed around. Most of the time this is like her little private kingdom.'

Robyn nodded. 'I can see that.'

The man rose, holding out his hand. 'DS Watts. Ashley Watts . . . Ash.'

Robyn took the hand and shook it. 'Pleased to meet you DS Watts, Ashley Watts, Ash.'

He gave her another grin. 'Likewise.'

'I'm Robyn, as I tried to tell your DI.'

She wasn't sure whether he'd heard her or not; he was busy gaping at her like he had done with the back of O'Brien's head. Then suddenly he said, 'You're a bit of a legend around here.' Watts looked about him, where nobody else was taking any notice whatsoever. 'I mean . . . that is, as far as I'm concerned.'

'Well, that's very . . .' She looked down at her hand, which Watts was still holding even though he'd stopped shaking it. He followed her gaze and let go of it like it was a live electrical cable with a bare end.

'Those cases, I mean . . . God, where do you start?'

'Where indeed,' replied Robyn, hoping he wouldn't.

'The guy with the foetuses, you know?'

Robyn thought about correcting him, telling him there had actually been no foetuses involved in 'The Baby' case, but remained quiet. Up to now, Watts was the only ally she had in this province. So she nodded once more and said, 'Uh-huh.'

'I'd love to work on something high-profile like that. It would . . .' Watts stopped, aware that he was going on a bit. 'I'm sorry, I'm just—'

'Excited?' she ventured.

His cheeks flushed red, though he didn't say anything back. Instead he segued into: 'But you're not here for . . . You want to know what happened to your cousin's husband, right?'

'Yes,' she confirmed, then added, 'So anything you can give

me – scene of crime reports, autopsy records, forensics – would be really helpful . . . Ash.'

He'd smiled a final time at that, then gone off to round up what he could about the case, promising to give her copies of anything that was relevant – though not before arranging for someone to get her a coffee while she waited.

When he returned, handing her what he'd gathered as she sat at his desk, Robyn had got up and thanked him, shaking his hand again. He made a deliberate effort this time not to hold on for too long, but had broken off the shake with, 'Maybe . . . well, feel free to give me a call or drop me an email or whatever if you need anything else, Dr Adams . . . Robyn.' Then he handed her his card.

She held it up as she said, 'I'm sure I'll be in touch.'

Leaving with the files and case notes, relieved to note the moaning man had disappeared from the waiting room, she'd almost opened them up on the way to the car; Robyn had never been the most patient of people. Instead, she looked around her, did a quick check of the back seat, got in, then started reading inside. Eyes scanning the information, she took in how Jeremy the 'do-gooder' had found Simon – buried on the beach – while he was searching for treasure with his metal detector. How SOCOs had carefully dug him up to take him away, as if he was some kind of artefact from centuries ago that had been preserved. How the sand, water from the rain and the tide, had all obliterated any evidence of real value.

Then the pictures of his wounds, indentations at the neck showing that it had been strangulation, rather than a garrotte or anything else, used to end his life. That took more effort than people realised, a powerful grip – especially given Simon's physical fitness and build. She scanned more and more of the pages and pictures, losing track of time cocooned in her car, and when Robyn finally sat up, sat back again with her head against the rest, she caught a glimpse of herself in the rear-view mirror. Another reflection.

It was then that she realised she was crying. Twin tears tracking down her cheeks, which she brushed away, just as Vicky had done, with the backs of her sleeves. Vicky . . . poor, poor Vicky. And Mia. Jesus. Having to grow up like those kids who'd had their fathers snatched away – literally – by Sykes.

Exciting? Hardly.

There was a sudden bang on the top of her car that made her start. Robyn twisted around, trying to see who it was . . . only for the seagull that had landed on there to hop onto the bonnet from the roof. It glared at her through the windscreen, reminding her of the way Tracy, Sergeant Bob and O'Brien had regarded her.

Catching her breath, she took out a couple of her pills and washed them down with the water from the glove compartment, then started the engine and pulled away, forcing the seagull to take off. By the time she arrived back, Tracy had left for the day, having helped Vicky with the evening's dinner: pasta and sauce, something simple. Vicky had asked Robyn if she wanted any, shoving the food around on her own plate like she was trying to create abstract art, but she'd said no – didn't have the stomach for it at the moment. Would head up and get straightened out if that was all right, unpacked or whatever. Mia had been getting up from the table to go to her, but Vicky made her stay where she was and finish.

Once up there, however, Robyn had totally ignored the case of clothes, instead sitting down with those files again on the bed. Though not before making sure the bolt was on . . . It felt almost like she was locking herself away in one of the cells at Gateside.

She was aware that time had passed again, Vicky coming up and knocking on the door to see if she was all right a couple of times – which again made her jump – then informing her eventually she was putting Mia to bed, and asking if she wanted to say goodnight. Robyn *had* slipped out then, closing the door quickly behind her, to give Mia a kiss and a hug, then returned to her room saying she'd be down shortly.

That had been . . . she glanced at her watch as she stood looking at the bed . . . bloody hell, two hours or more ago! The action of looking broke the spell, and she gathered up all the case files again, placing them on the top of the wardrobe.

It was time to head down, face Vicky. Talk to her. But before that, she needed to wipe away the tears that had come again.

Tears she'd had trouble getting under control this time.

Chapter 5

Finally, the tears had stopped.

Vicky sat in the living room on the sofa, staring at the TV but not really watching it. She'd switched over from the news a while ago to some gardening programme, but while she hadn't been concentrating that had morphed into an old black and white movie about a guy who was trying to kill some woman's husband at her behest. That was the last thing she wanted to watch or think about. Husband killing.

'And when did you last see your husband, Mrs Carter? Can you account for your whereabouts in the couple of days after that?'

Vicky switched over again, only to find an American sitcom with a laughter track that sounded so fake it hurt, the image pixilating like a son of a bitch and making the actors look like Transformers. She pressed another button, which gave her a wild-life documentary. That would do, and she zoned out again, having another drink of the wine she was clutching.

No more tears. Not now . . . Maybe they'd dried up completely? But then she'd thought that before Robyn arrived, and yet there they'd been again, her blubbing and holding on for dear life. Whatever must she have thought? Getting all worked up like that, when Robyn was so used to dealing with death.

51

Getting all worked up because it was Simon. *Because Simon is gone,* she reminded herself and felt that familiar pricking at the corners of her eyes. Because she'd never see him again, would she?

When was the last time she'd seen him? On a slab in the morgue, his skin blue-white, those marks around his neck. And before that, a flying visit, barely enough time to say hello and goodbye he was so busy – bringing in money to make sure they were all right (she couldn't help wondering how they would cope now . . . don't think about that).

But the last time, the real last time she'd seen him, when they'd spent time together . . . That Saturday night, when Mia was at a sleepover with some of her mates. Vicky had been drinking that night as well; they both had. An evening of drink and chat and watching that live band massacre Bon Jovi numbers at the pub that had once been called The Barnacle. Then, rolling home after last orders, practically falling in through the door. Kissing in the hallway, then upstairs, knowing they had the place to themselves and could be as loud as they liked. Pulling each other's clothes off and tumbling into bed, acting like they had when they first met, when they were so young and everything had been brand new.

Simon was right – it had done them good. After months of barely even bothering, and, when they did, it being over in minutes; hardly even worth getting worked up. Yes, there was Mia to consider, but even so . . . Vicky was beginning to think he'd gone off her. When was the last time they'd done that, just let themselves go? It wouldn't happen again now. Would never happen again . . .

Because he was dead. The man she loved, the man she'd married – who worked so hard for them – was gone. Murdered and buried, covered up like some dirty secret. And as she thought back to the day she was told, those police officers at the door delivering the message, she realised she'd drained the wine in her glass and reached out for the bottle that was already well over half empty. The one she'd started in on after she'd finally got Mia

52

to bed, after telling her again and again to just go to sleep and stop asking questions about what was wrong. After looking in her daughter's eyes and understanding that she knew something pretty serious had happened.

'She doesn't know yet?'

'I wasn't sure what to say to her.'

'What's . . . what's the matter, Mum?'

'Nothing. Nothing sweetheart.'

After days of trying to keep the truth from her, protecting her the best way she knew how. Of lying about why Tracy was there, why she was answering the door and fielding phone calls . . . And shouldn't she have answered some of those? Vicky had friends . . . kind of. The school mums, Jay's mother especially. If anyone knew how she felt then it was that woman, just in a different way. But she hadn't felt like talking to anyone. Just wanted her own mum back; fucking cancer! Her mum and dad. Needed her family. Needed—

Robyn. The sister she'd never had. The one person she'd always been able to turn to, rely on . . . until she couldn't. Until that connection had been severed somehow, two people drifting apart who had nothing in common anymore. But still family.

That was when she'd dug out the numbers and made the call, not even knowing if it was still current or not. Getting the answerphone on the landline, finally getting her on her mobile. Realising something was 'off' about Robyn herself. Like she was also upset; like she'd caught her at a bad moment or something.

Vicky would have laughed at that if she'd had it in her. Bad moment? What could possibly be worse than all this mess?

You know what helps with that? More alcohol.

Vicky took a gulp of the wine she'd just poured.

She'd left it as long as she could before ringing her, had been surprised really when she agreed to come – so much for being busy. In fact, hadn't she sounded like she wanted to get away from there, for whatever reason? Didn't matter, she reminded herself, because Robyn was here now; had been owed some time off. She was helping her. Although she hadn't seen her most of the day, all evening. Had left Vicky alone with the TV, with the wine. Grappling with those tears again she thought she was done with, letting David Attenborough's lecture about the lifespan of a turtle wash over her.

She started, suddenly aware of someone in the doorway – almost spilling the wine on herself. Classy. How long had she been there, Robyn, watching her? Hadn't been around all this time and then appeared as if by magic, or like that blue guy from the *X-Men* movies Mia used to watch with Daddy. Wouldn't ever watch again, because—

'Sorry,' said Robyn, rushing into the room and pausing again, like she'd lost signal as well, had pixilated and been forced to freeze. 'I didn't mean to . . .'

'It's . . . it's okay,' Vicky told her, grabbing the remote and turning the sound down. 'Are you . . . is everything . . .'

'May I?' asked Robyn, nodding at one of the empty chairs. Since when had they become so polite with each other, so . . . ill at ease? Even that afternoon, the crying, the hugging – it hadn't felt the most natural thing. They used to talk, share everything, be so close. When exactly had they become like this? Like strangers?

''Course,' said Vicky. 'Our home's your home, Robyn . . . Robs.' Even that shortening of her name, which used to trip off the tongue, sounded so odd. Didn't fit with the person taking her seat, with the person Vicky knew her to be now – not that she really knew her at all, or anything much about her world. Didn't even know if she was seeing anyone, living with anyone. If so, how did they feel about her just taking off like this to help her cousin? 'Would you like a . . .' Vicky held up the glass of pinot she'd almost ended up wearing. 'It's only cheap stuff, nothing fancy.'

Robyn shook her head. 'I shouldn't.'

'I guess, as a doctor, you'd tell me not to either.'

'I'm not that kind of doctor, Vicky.' There was another pause.

54

'But if I was, I'd probably say, "Fuck it, pour yourself a large one".
After what you've been through . . .'

'Have one too,' Vicky said. '*Please.*' Her cousin nodded and
Vicky made to get up and fetch her a glass.

'You stay where you are, I'll get it,' Robyn told her. 'Where . . .?'

'Top cupboard just as you walk in,' Vicky informed her. 'There's
another bottle in there as well.'

Moments later, Robyn returned with the wine and a glass for
herself. She opened the fresh bottle, as Vicky was in the process
of polishing off the first one, and poured herself a small measure.
Took an equally small sip. 'It's nice,' she said.

'Probably not what you're used to.'

Robyn shook her head. 'To be honest, I'm more of a vodka
girl these days.'

Vicky gave a single nod, impressed. 'I'll have to get some in.'

'Please, not on my account.'

'Maybe I'll get some for me,' Vicky told her. 'If . . . if it helps.'

'I . . . I'm really not sure it will,' Robyn informed her, sadly.
Vicky reached down the side of the sofa and took out the pack
of cigarettes that were there, opened it up. Robyn's face soured.
'Now those, they certainly won't help.'

Vicky let out a big sigh. 'I quit you know. Used to use those
vape things for a while, chew gum. But what with everything that's
. . .' She put the pack down again. 'You're right, though. Horrible
habit – you always used to say that didn't you.'

'I still do. Not good for Mia, either.'

She knew Robyn was absolutely right, but something about
that last statement made her angry.

'*She doesn't know yet?*'

Robyn wasn't a mother, didn't know what it was like to have
kids. Wasn't a wife either, as far as Vicky knew. Didn't understand
what it was like to suddenly not be one anymore, because—

'Look,' said Robyn, as if reading her mind; as if they weren't
really strangers after all. 'I can only imagine what you're going

55

through. All I can say is that I'm very sorry this happened and I'll do all I can to help. In whatever way.'

'I *will* tell her, you know,' Vicky blurted out. 'It's just . . . I haven't found the right moment. I need more time to—'

'Is there ever going to *be* a right moment to tell a child something like that?' asked Robyn and Vicky bristled again.

'Probably not,' she replied with an edge to her voice.

Robyn nodded slowly. 'If it helps, they're more resilient than you think. And she definitely knows something's happening.' Before Vicky could answer that, her cousin continued: 'I used to know with Mum at that age, her . . . problems. Kids pick up on things. It affects them. Hiding stuff is the worst thing you can possibly do.'

'I know,' snapped Vicky. Then, more softly, 'I know. Sorry. You're only trying to . . . And I'm sorry about your mum, I never said that to you. I know it was rough.'

Robyn took a much larger sip of her wine this time. 'All . . . It's water under the bridge.'

Vicky doubted it was. 'How did you . . . I didn't want to talk about it while Mia was still up, but did you—'

'How did I get on with the police?' Robyn smiled weakly. 'They teach us well at psychology school. I . . .' She shook her head. 'You really want to talk about this tonight? Maybe it's not the right—'

'Is there ever going to *be* a right moment?' said Vicky, throwing Robyn's words back at her.

'Touché. All right then. Well, I dealt with a rather charming officer called O'Brien who you've probably come across yourself.'

Vicky nodded. She'd been the one who asked her the questions about Simon.

'Makes Attila the Hun look like Mickey Mouse, right?' Vicky wouldn't have put it quite that way, but the woman *was* intimidating it had to be said. Not that Robyn had let it put her off, apparently. Strong Robyn, always knew what she was doing; always so together. 'Fortunately I'm owed a few favours and her DS, Ashley Watts, was very helpful.'

'First-name basis already; you do work quick.' Vicky hadn't meant it to come out that way – the wine talking – but Robyn didn't take anything from it. Or if she did, she didn't show it.

'You probably guessed I've been going through everything, piecing it all together.' Her cousin drank more wine. 'And the good news—'

'There's *good* news?'

Robyn continued, in spite of the interruption. 'The good news is that the police haven't been stonewalling you, Vicky. They haven't told you anything because they don't really know that much yet. Where the body was . . . where *Simon* was found . . .' Robyn sucked a breath, let it out again. 'It didn't really help matters in terms of gathering evidence, and there was the storm you told me about . . . All they really know for sure is what you do: that he was killed by asphyxiation. He died from lack of oxygen. There were no ligature marks, but there were indentations consistent with strangulation – not a hope in hell of getting any fingerprints, regrettably – although they did also find salt water in his lungs.'

'What . . . what does that mean? He was drowned *and* strangled?' Those tears were threatening to come.

Robyn held up her hand flat out horizontally, then tilted it left and right to show it was unclear. 'The water got in his lungs when he was still alive, but . . . Well, I'd say it was probably the strangulation that killed him.'

'Oh Jesus,' said Vicky, images of her husband gasping for air flitting through her mind. Clutching at the hands that were taking his life away from him. Taking him away from her. Those tears finally broke free, and Robyn came over to sit with her, putting an arm around her again.

'I'm so sorry,' she whispered.

'You . . . you deal with this kind of thing all the time, don't you?' Vicky said, between sobs.

'Not exactly this,' Robyn told her. 'But I see a lot of death, yeah.'

'How . . . how can someone do something like that?'

Robyn took another deep breath, something Simon had been unable to do at the end, Vicky thought bitterly. 'In the kind of cases I deal with, it's complicated. It usually goes back to childhood, to teenage years, that kind of thing. And they're repeat offenders. I don't think that's what happened here, with Simon.'

Vicky lifted her head to look at Robyn. 'What do you mean?'

'I think there was a reason he was killed. I don't know what it is yet, but . . .'

'But you're going to find out, aren't you? I mean, that's what you do.'

'Working with the police usually, Vicky. I-I'm not sure how much they even want me here. O'Brien certainly doesn't.'

'*I* want you here,' she said then. 'Mia definitely wants you here. You're all we've got. We're family; we should stick together.'

Robyn opened her mouth, then closed it again and gave a nod.

'And I want you to know . . .' Vicky shook her head. 'Talk to me, Robs. You asked me if I was okay, but are *you*?' Not that much of a stranger, she could see it in her eyes. They never had been very good at hiding things from each other, at keeping secrets. Robyn had been the first person she'd told when she got her period, when she first slept with a guy – and vice versa. They'd talked constantly back then; *shared* those secrets. 'Has something happened, you know, in your world?'

Robyn drained the last of her wine. 'Not enough of this stuff in the world, Vicky.'

'Did someone . . . Has someone hurt you?'

She looked down then, avoiding Robyn's eyes. 'Please. Not now, not tonight. I can't.'

'Okay, okay. But, I want you to know, I'm always . . . I know I'm a bit of a mess at the moment . . .'

'With good reason,' said Robyn.

This time she made a concerted effort to finish what she'd been trying to say. 'But I'm always here for you, Robs. I always was.'

'I know,' came the reply.

'So why . . .'

'*Why haven't you ever been here before? Why did it take you so long to come?*'

'Have some more wine,' said Robyn, shuffling forwards and reaching for the bottle to pour herself a glass as well, twice the amount as last time.

'Yeah, thanks.' A distraction and Vicky knew it; Robyn wasn't the only one who understood how people ticked. 'We used to be so close, Robs. What happened?'

Robyn shook her head.

'I know we kinda went our different ways, but I always thought we'd stay . . . We were so, so close,' Vicky repeated. 'I've missed you.'

'I've missed you too.'

'So what happened?'

'We've seen each other over the years,' argued Robyn, but there was no weight to it. It sounded apologetic more than anything. 'When Mum passed, your wedding . . .'

'I hardly even got to spend time with you then, to speak to you at those. But I guess it wasn't really the right . . .' Vicky's sentence tailed off. 'You spent most of your time at our reception with one of Simon's mates from back then. What was his name now . . .'

'Ben,' said Robyn and sounded even more apologetic.

'Went off with him at the end of the night, if I remember rightly. Which is fine, that's okay, don't get me wrong. Glad you had a good time and everything.'

'Wasn't that great a time,' Robyn assured her. 'With him, I mean.'

'Okay,' Vicky said. 'That's not what I was trying to say. I would have liked to have chatted more, just—'

'It's . . . Look, Vicky, it's complicated.'

'Like your criminals,' she ventured.

'Not really. It's just . . . It's the same with my old home; I never really had a lot to do with Mum after I went to uni. That place where she lived, it had mostly bad memories. Golden Sands . . .'

'I thought you liked it here,' Vicky chipped in. 'That's what you told me. You couldn't wait to get here, hated going back.'

'There are lots of good memories, definitely. I was thinking about some of them on the drive over.' Robyn looked sad again, as if she wanted to be back there. If she was being honest with herself, at that precise moment, so did Vicky.

'We had some great times, didn't we?' she said then, thinking back herself. Remembering days on the beach, evening barbecues in the garden, fishing for crabs.

Robyn leaned back into the couch again, relaxing. 'Yeah. Yeah we did.'

'Do you remember . . .' Vicky started chuckling, couldn't help herself because the memory was so funny. 'Do you remember, we used to wait till Dad was asleep in his deckchair and then we'd do a pincer movement with the water pistols.'

Robyn laughed too, though whether it was the wine or the shared memory was unclear – perhaps both. 'Then we'd spring up and shoot him, wet him through.'

'And run off in opposite directions so he didn't know which one of us to chase after.' She thought Robyn was going to spit out the wine she had in her mouth. 'Mum would pretend to be mad, but really she'd be pissing herself. Covering her mouth up so Dad didn't see it.'

'Good times,' Robyn said with another chuckle and Vicky agreed.

'Then everything changed. We graduated from school, you went off to university and—'

'You could have gone too, Vicky. You're clever enough.'

Vicky touched her chest. 'Me? Naw. Plus which, I'm nowhere near as confident as you were . . . are . . .'

'I'm not that confident,' Robyn protested. 'Really. Just good at pretending. A bit more savvy now maybe, I'll give you that. In my old age.'

Vicky laughed at that one. 'You're not old.'

'Perhaps I just feel it,' said her cousin, knocking back the wine she had left.

Silence for a moment or two, then Vicky broke it with, 'I was so jealous of you, you know. Back then.'

Robyn gaped at her, brow furrowing. '*Jealous?* Of me? Why?'

'You were going off on your adventures. Studying, having fun. Meeting people.' Meeting guys, she meant, but didn't say it. Robyn had always been more confident in that way as well in the end. There certainly seemed to be a different bloke every other month, according to her letters. Going by her stories when she summered with them.

'I probably made it sound better than it was. Uni was a *lot* of hard work, basically.'

'Even so . . . It was worth it, look at you now!'

Robyn levered herself up off the cushions and poured herself more wine. For someone who shouldn't, she'd definitely decided to. 'You want to know something now?'

Vicky pushed herself up on her elbow, almost spilt her drink again. Maybe this was it, maybe she was about to find out the thing that had been nagging Robyn, that had kept them apart all these years. That was still on her mind. 'Sure,' she told her.

'I was jealous of you, too.'

She hadn't been expecting that. 'You were . . . *Why?* I just stayed where I was, too scared to go anywhere, do anything with my life.'

'You *built* a life. Here, with your family, in the place you love. The place you call home.'

Vicky blinked once, twice. Robyn sounded genuinely envious; she'd had no idea. But at the same time, that line about family and home made her think about what she'd lost this past week, and how easily everything had fallen apart. She began to cry again. 'I *had* a life. A home. Now . . . Oh, Robs, I'm just not sure how I'm going to cope.'

'You'll be all right,' said her cousin, facing her, in a way that almost made her believe it. 'You're stronger than you realise. So's Mia.'

'But . . . *God*,' she said, suddenly realising something. 'I don't even know how I'm going to pay for the funeral, let alone . . .' She waved her free hand around to indicate the home Robyn had been talking about. They'd been struggling before, especially since Vicky had been let go from the newsagent's; hence all the jobs Simon had to work. She shouldn't even be thinking about that, but now he was gone . . .

'That's another thing I can help with,' Robyn told her.

'I can't let you—'

She smiled warmly. 'It's not even up for discussion.' Then Vicky looked down, because Robyn had taken her free hand in her own. 'You said it yourself, we're family. We're all we've got, right? We need to stick together.'

Vicky smiled back. 'And that means . . . You'll find the person who did this? Who did this to my . . . our family?'

'I can't make any cast-iron promises, but I . . . I'll do my best.'

'Robs,' said Vicky, putting down her glass and motioning for her cousin to do the same. 'That's good enough for me.'

They hugged then, like they had earlier on with Mia in tow. On the couch, Vicky not wanting to let go. But when they did, she found that she wasn't crying.

That, finally, the tears had stopped.

Chapter 6

They're crying with laughter.

Tears rolling down their faces as they share a joke, probably fuelled by the alcohol they're drinking: blue and pink liquid in bottles, that aren't very strong but if you drink enough of them . . . Music is playing, some kind of dance remix of an old number – well, a few years old anyway – and they're swaying, half-dancing to the beat as they stand near to the bar. It's one of those places that fancies itself as some kind of half-arsed nightclub come nine o'clock, but really all they do is turn the ordinary lights down low, switch the multi-coloured ones on and let the mirror ball on the ceiling do its thing.

One of the girls, dressed in a short satin skirt and boob tube, plastered in make-up, knocks the other one's shoulder when she tells her something. The first, in a low-cut black dress that stops just below her waist, with tights to match, puts on a mock 'what?' look, then starts laughing again. They both have hair that's back-combed and sprayed to within an inch of its life, whoofed up and home-styled because neither of them have that much money and what they do have they save for nights out like this one.

They're looking over to a group of guys in the corner, a couple of them they recognise as being those hunks that go out with the lifeboat when seafaring vessels get into trouble. The men – boys really, not that much older than them – are all holding pints, wearing tight-fitting jeans and shirts that are open at the top, some of them almost to the stomach like that parody their mums and dads used to watch; all that's missing are the medallions.

A guy in his mid-forties, or maybe even older, who's had far too much to drink, takes to what they laughably call the dance floor here, which basically means they've moved a few of the tables and chairs to the sides of the room. He's really giving it some – gyrating, throwing out his considerable paunch – and in danger of throwing out his back at the same time, whilst still holding his own pint, which is only half-full but slopping over the sides.

The girls, distracted by this – who in the entire place isn't? – start to point and laugh at him instead. Hanging on to his youth for grim death, but not doing a very good job. He's known for it. For some reason he seems to think it will attract a mate, because his eyes keep sweeping left and right, flitting from female to female – doesn't matter what age, including them – like he's a monkey in a jungle or something. Looks a bit like one, as well.

This time when he looks over at the two young girls and points back – perhaps thinking this is part of the mating ritual, not that they're making fun of him – the one in the boob tube whispers something along the lines of, 'Imagine doing it with him!'

The second, the one in the black dress, just pulls a face and shouts this time: 'Urgh!'

Maybe he sees the face, maybe he hears what she says, but the middle-aged man suddenly spins around in search of more amenable fare – good luck! Except he spins a bit too quickly and ends up toppling over, the pint going flying and smashing on the ground. The barman is there in seconds, helping him up again and walking him to an empty booth where he can get his bearings again. The barman wags a finger at hi, though, a warning probably that he should stay off the 'dance floor' or perhaps that he's not getting another drink, seeing as one of the barmaids is now having to mop and sweep up the one he dropped because of his acrobatics.

Both the girls are wetting themselves now, hands over their mouths. And it's only as the excitement dies down again that they remember the guys over in that corner, the ones they've been looking at all night and who have been looking over at them. One of the girls, the one wearing the satin skirt, catches the eye of a muscular lad in a T-shirt. He smiles; she smiles back. The girl in the black dress nudges her friend, dragging her attention back – because she's just got another round in. Cocktails this time, or this place's version of them at any rate – like something Del Boy might drink in Only Fools and Horses *because he wants to look cultured. Pink and blue drinks again, only this time they're served in glasses with tall stems and what look like upside down triangles on top; miniature umbrellas and bits of fruit that have no right to be anywhere near an alcoholic beverage complete the look.*

It's only a matter of time before one of the guys in the corner comes over and tries his luck – with black dress or boob tube, or maybe both – then the floodgates will have broken, leaving the way clear for any of them to have a crack. More mating rituals, no less ridiculous than the older generation's. Nobody really knows what they're doing, boy or girl. They just pretend they do – give off an air of confidence . . . or at least some of them do. That's probably why alcohol was invented in the first place, to make all this easier. To grease the wheels.

And all the time, this whole time, they're being watched. They're being observed, just like an animal on a wildlife programme might be.

The man watches the guys in the corner, watches the two girls, safe in the knowledge he hasn't been spotted.

Watches, and waits to see what transpires.

Chapter 7

The first thing she'd done that morning was pop a couple of her painkillers.

Wasn't just for her back, they were a cure-all for the hangover she was nursing as well. Robyn had stayed up with Vicky much later than they probably should have, but they'd drunk more wine, done more reminiscing – steering clear of any of the trickier subjects – and in the end both passed out on the couch. It had probably done them good, regardless of the way she felt: her mouth as dry as a desert, limbs like lead. Regardless of the restless sleep she'd had, which was nothing new of course. At least she hadn't dreamed about Sykes.

It was the banging around upstairs that had woken her, really – the TV having turned itself off at some point, probably because it was sick of being ignored. The sound of little feet getting out of bed greeted Robyn instead, then more banging: those same feet rushing to the toilet upstairs, followed by a slamming of the door. Robyn had left Vicky – who'd had a lot more of the wine than she had – asleep on the couch and wandered into the kitchen for some water to take those pills with. She was probably still over the limit, but took them anyway; it wouldn't be the first time.

Robyn filled her glass again and gulped down the water

greedily, trying to rehydrate herself more than anything, though if it also got rid of that taste . . . It was only now that she looked at her watch and saw it was quarter to seven. They'd been asleep just a few short hours, and though she didn't have access to a mirror she was willing to bet that she looked like Freddy Krueger on a bad day.

Another bang – not from upstairs this time, but from the front door – drew her attention. Puzzled, Robyn headed towards it, hearing another couple of raps – wanting to get there before it woke Vicky.

Then suddenly everything was quiet. She undid the locks, pulled the door open, but there was nobody there. Just the media vans from when she arrived, but no one had got out. Robyn looked left and right; she had a strange feeling she was being watched – but couldn't see anyone at all.

It was then that she looked down, spotted a folded piece of paper on the mat inside; something that had been shoved under the door. Closing it to, she stooped and picked it up – thinking maybe it was a note for Vicky from one of those well-wishers Tracy had mentioned.

Only it had *her* name on the front of it – Robyn Adams – scrawled in handwriting.

Frowning, she opened it up, only realising at the last minute she shouldn't be handling this, was contaminating what could be evidence, but needing to see what it said.

Two words, plain and simple: 'GO HOME!'

'Aunty Robyn?' came a voice from behind her, making her jump for the second time that morning. She hadn't even heard Mia come downstairs. She shoved the note in her pocket as she turned towards the kid at the bottom of the stairs. 'Are you all right?'

'I . . .' she began, then asked, 'Did you just hear that? Someone at the door?'

Mia shook her head emphatically.

Robyn looked back at the door, then at Mia again. 'Only, I . . .'

'I'm hungry,' stated Mia and grabbed hold of her hand, tugging her back towards the kitchen.

'You're up and about early,' was all Robyn could think to say as they entered.

'Am I?' said the girl, looking around mystified. 'I thought I was late.' Probably was for her. Robyn had no idea what time kids of her age were up and about. She figured it was probably early, but her idea of that and a six-year-old's (sorry, nearly seven) were probably wildly different. 'Did Mummy sleep in the living room again? She's been doing that a lot. Is there something wrong with her bed?' asked her niece.

'I . . . er . . .' There was. Somebody was missing from it, thought Robyn, though according to her cousin that wasn't an unusual thing. 'No, we both fell asleep down here last night. We were catching up. A lot to talk about.'

'You'll be able to do that with Daddy too when he gets back,' stated Mia, and Robyn felt a sudden twinge in her heart. 'You do know him, don't you?'

'I . . . yes. Yes, I know your dad. Listen, what do you normally have for breakfast?' she asked, changing the subject. 'I'll sort it out and we can let Mummy sleep, eh?'

Mia thought about this for a moment, fingers pinching her lips. 'I want Sugar-Hoops,' she said adamantly, pointing to a box up on the counter. Robyn picked it up and regarded the colourful cartoons on the front, designed to catch a kid's eye. Didn't look the healthiest of options, but she shrugged. Who was she to argue, especially when the cereal was in the house and she didn't know what Vicky usually made for Mia.

'Now then . . . bowls,' she said out loud, but the girl had beaten her to it, fishing one out of a lower cupboard and putting it on the kitchen table – the one they'd been eating at the previous night. It was only as she filled that bowl and fetched milk from the fridge to pour on top, that Robyn realised how hungry she was herself, in spite of everything. She'd barely eaten yesterday, shouldn't have been drinking on that empty stomach (*or* mixing it with her meds), and now she had a peculiar hollow feeling inside.

Maybe some toast or something, she thought to herself, looking around for bread and failing to find any. She did spot coffee though, and desperately needed one of those – filling up the kettle and putting that on while she continued her hunt for food.

'Can I have some juice please, Aunty Robyn?' asked Mia. That was definitely her drink of choice, going by yesterday.

'Sure,' Robyn replied and returned to the fridge.

Juice poured and accepted gratefully with a 'thank you!' – at least Mia had manners – she managed to find a blueberry breakfast bar and figured that would be better than nothing. Better than Sugar-Hoops at any rate. Robyn poured her coffee, taking it black that morning, and brought the drink and bar over to the table, sitting next to the little girl. Mia was still wolfing down those sugary wheat-hoops, not caring in the slightest what kind of chemicals had turned them blue, or crimson or green.

Once she'd finished, she threw Robyn by asking: 'Do you know when Daddy's coming back?'

Robyn stopped chewing. She wasn't quite sure what to say. It wasn't her place to tell Mia about Simon – even though she'd offered to help broach it. 'I-I'm not entirely sure, sweetheart,' was the only thing she could think of. That wasn't strictly true: what was going round in her head was 'never, he's never coming back, you're never going to see him again', and that made her heart ache for the second time that morning.

There was a yawn from the doorway and they both turned to see Vicky standing there, still wearing the hoodie and trackies from the day before, face as white as the dregs of milk still left in Mia's bowl, eyes as red as one of the Sugar-Hoops left drowning in there. She raised a hand in greeting, yawning again, and nodded when Robyn offered her a coffee. As she got up to make it, Vicky came over and kissed Mia on the top of the head.

It wasn't long after that the door went again and Robyn shot up, insisted on answering it . . . just in case. When she did, it was a reversal of the previous day and she saw Tracy standing there on the doorstep.

'Dr Adams,' said the woman warily. Clearly undecided as to whether she was friend or foe, regardless of her status as a relative.

'You didn't . . .' Robyn started to ask.

'What?'

'You haven't knocked before, have you?'

Tracy's brow furrowed. 'Knocked before?'

'Yeah, someone . . .' Robyn paused then, looking left and right.

'Someone what?'

She thought about telling the FLO, especially about the note. But what if it had been something to do with her? No, surely not. Her paranoia working overtime, and yet . . .

'Are you going to let me in?' asked the woman, brusquely.

'What?' Robyn refocused on the person in front of her. 'Oh . . . yeah, sure.'

As Tracy stepped inside she asked, 'How did your visit to the station go?' in a way that told her she knew exactly how it had gone. Which also meant she knew why Robyn was here.

'Like I said to your colleagues, I'm just here to help if I can.'

A stiff nod, but she could tell Tracy didn't believe a word of it. Had O'Brien in her ear probably, going on about how she'd be trouble.

Robyn was still thinking about what she'd said to Vicky last night (or this morning – depending on what time it had been), that she'd do her best to find out what happened. *You know what*, she thought, now that she'd got the bit between her teeth, *I just might be . . .*

I just might.

Word hadn't just spread through Golden Sands constabulary, however.

By the time Robyn was ready to leave, a little after ten – once

70

she'd had a shower, changed her clothes and was feeling more or less human again – she discovered there were a handful more vans waiting on the street, and a lot more reporters flitting about than there had been earlier on. Interest was building again in the case, and that was probably down to the arrival of this newcomer to the Carter household.

She got to her car quickly, before any of them had time to run up and bother her, checking the back seat – once again, force of habit – and climbing in, slamming the door behind her. Robyn started the engine and drove off, waiting until she'd passed them before stopping again and consulting the map to see where she should be going: the best route to her destination.

As Vicky had told her, Simon was holding down a few jobs to keep things afloat – which included odds and ends down at the fairground – and according to the reports, PCs and DCs had been sent out to ask around at all of his places of work. Nothing had been flagged though, which rang warning bells with Robyn. Either it had been sloppy investigating, or they hadn't really been trying to find out anything. Nothing like a scandal to put people off coming to a seaside resort, particularly with the peak holiday period fast approaching.

She'd told Vicky she didn't think this was one of *those* cases, the ones she was used to consulting on. But what if it was? What if this was just the start of something like Sykes? Would more dead fathers be found, strangled to death and buried in the sand on the beach? She shook her head, was fairly certain this would all turn out to be a one-off, as devastating as that was for the Carters. This place was just too damned small for a serial killer to operate in.

But what if this was just the start of it, a practice gig before taking his – or her – show on the road? Her . . . because although it would have taken quite a bit of strength to kill Simon, there were women more than capable of doing such a thing. Female serial killers, though rare, did exist. Female killers in general.

Vicky had asked her where she was going today, what her plans were, but she was wary of saying anything indoors in case Tracy was listening again; tab-hanging at doorways. Robyn had pretty much decided where she would be going, however, when she told her cousin 'just doing a bit of noseying around'. She didn't need to know any more than that, was probably better off that way. Mia had asked if she could go with her, of course, but Robyn had told her she'd be back later on and they could do something together then. The little girl had pouted, folded her arms across her chest, but had perked up when her aunty promised to bring her something back from her travels.

'We'll talk about the best way to approach . . . you know what,' she'd said then to Vicky, who'd given a resigned nod.

This time, she'd got a hug and a kiss not just from Mia, but her mother as well – and this time she'd returned it. Last night had done them both good in that respect too, building a few burnt bridges and reminding them that family was indeed everything.

Who do you have? Nobody you can turn to . . . nobody who'll ever really need you.

'Fuck you, Sykes,' she said out loud now. 'Fuck you!'

Her route more or less memorised, Robyn set off again and drove through the streets of upper Golden Sands, the roads twisting and turning like some kind of serpent dancing to a snake charmer's flute. There was no way of getting lost today, though, because the building she was looking for was far bigger than Vicky's three-bedroom house.

Robyn could see it from a distance, actually; planted there looking down on the cliffs, but not close enough to be worried about erosion – just yet. Looking down on everything, essentially, which she figured was the point of it: royalty having been in residence there at one time or another.

She suddenly realised that she knew next to nothing about the history of that place; it just hadn't crossed her mind when she was younger. History wasn't one of her interests anyway; it just hadn't grabbed her in the way other subjects had. But even just looking at it from here, as she found the gates – which were wide open, no intercom cameras or anything; security quite lax – and coaxed the car up the long driveway towards it, you could *see* its history. It wore its past like a badge of honour.

Robyn remembered the toy town thing she'd thought about on approaching Golden Sands, and if you were to apply it again here, this was like a child had thrown several sets of building bricks together that really shouldn't fit. Parts of it were definitely castle-like, with turrets and battlements, but a lot of it wasn't. It more closely resembled a stately home, if anything, though the architecture was all wrong. The colours, too, were browns and greys, which didn't really go together, square windows competing with curves here and there – and one huge arched entrance. All surrounded by the lush green of the gardens, hedges and trees, which cut it off from the rest of the world, making it feel like she was suddenly in another reality.

There were a number of cars already parked up in the square of concrete designed for that purpose, so she joined them – but at the same time parked well enough away from the rest so as to not be lumped in with the others. Somehow that made her feel better about her mission: the fact that she had no intentions of coming here but needed the staff to believe she was thinking about it. Besides, she'd never really been one of society's sheep. Never just followed anything blindly like the herd. Always made her own decisions, her own mistakes.

After climbing out, Robyn walked over towards that impressive entrance, finding one of the huge wooden doors open as if she'd been expected. More likely, it was just so people could come and go as they pleased. One of the pluses of being surrounded by such wide-open spaces must surely be that people could walk around them at their leisure.

She was aware of her shoes clacking on the floor, though the noise was nowhere near as off-putting as it was in Gateside. The foyer area looked like it could double as the overspill for the car park because it was massive, with a decorative fountain in the middle that looked as if it had been carved out of ivory, but was almost definitely fake: all classical figures pouring from jugs and cherubs spitting. If you stood there long enough and listened to the water, it would make you want to rush off and find a loo.

Robyn eventually spotted the reception desk, made out of that same fake ivory, though there was nobody manning it. There was a button to press instead, so she did that – and while she waited she looked up and took in more of the vastness of the building, above and around her. While she stood there, a couple in their late twenties appeared, causing her to tense. But they wandered by, both wearing white towelling robes; both sporting equally impressive smiles like they were having the most relaxing time of their lives . . . and probably were. Robyn doubted this place was cheap, so they'd certainly be paying enough for it. They looked at her, puzzled, perhaps wondering why she was wearing clothes, but then nodded in greeting. Robyn tentatively nodded back and they carried on smiling, carried on walking to their destination . . . wherever that was.

'Hello?' came a voice from over her shoulder, and Robyn whirled around now. She didn't like people creeping up on her; people even *being* behind her. When she saw the girl there, also dressed in white – a dress that hung off her like curtains, giving the whole thing a toga-like appearance – Robyn realised how she'd managed to be so quiet, glancing down at her white pump-like slippers. Her braided hair did nothing to detract from the impression that Robyn had somehow wandered onto the Olympus set of *Clash of the Titans*.

'Oh . . . er, hi,' she said, regaining her composure. Not the best of starts for a place that was supposed to calm you right down. 'I'm . . . That is, I'm thinking of booking in here and was wondering if you might be able to—'

'Give you a tour of the place?' the young woman finished for her.

'Ah . . . yes, if that's possible.'

'Have you arranged an appointment?' the girl – who was no more than nineteen, if she was a day – enquired.

'No, I didn't. I was just in the area and . . . Is that going to be a problem?'

Robyn couldn't tell from her face whether it would be or not. Perhaps they taught them here to keep their expressions neutral, all part of trying to maintain a sense of peace and tranquillity. Or maybe she was just bored? 'I'm sure it'll be fine, let me just see if I can find someone . . .' She skirted around Robyn, then skirted around the desk, picking up the phone and punching in a number before explaining what was needed. 'There'll be someone here shortly to escort you and answer any questions,' the girl told her. 'I've been Cathy, I hope I've been able to help you today.'

'Er . . . yes. Thanks,' said Robyn. 'That's great.'

Cathy nodded and wandered off again, presumably to continue doing whatever it was she'd been doing. Fluffing clouds or something. But it wasn't long before Robyn was joined by a man in his thirties, dressed in a white T-shirt and shorts. He looked for all the world like he'd just won the men's final at Wimbledon, like he was fit enough to do so as well.

'Hi there!' he said, bounding up to her and holding out a hand. If Cathy was lacking in emotion and enthusiasm, then this guy had an overabundance of it. 'My name's Brad,' he told her. 'I'm one of the instructors here. You're thinking of coming for a break?'

'I . . . yes, that's right.' Robyn shook his outstretched hand, which pumped hers a couple of times before letting go; the opposite of Watts' technique.

'Any particular reason, or just wanting to relieve the pressure of modern life?' he asked. 'Only we cater for all your tastes here, whether you're into more physical pursuits – we have a full gym, an indoor swimming pool and tennis courts out the back . . .' So he might well have just come from a match, figured Robyn. 'Or if you simply want to unwind a bit, we can cater to that as well.'

'Things . . . things *have* been a bit . . . tense at work lately,' said Robyn, which wasn't really a lie.

'Okay, yes. I can see that.' *He could?* she thought. 'Then you've come to the right place . . .' Brad waited for a name and Robyn didn't see any point in lying about that either, so she told him.

'All right, Robyn, let me take you around and you can get a sense of the place.'

Brad led the way down a corridor off to their right, which took them past a large room containing chairs and sofas that he called the 'rec area', where people could just chill out and mingle with other guests, forget about their worries and perhaps even make new friends. Then they reached the saunas and hot tubs section. 'This is probably where you'll spend most of your time if you're here to relax,' he informed her. 'We utilise the healing properties of Golden Sands' own salt water, for a more thorough overall cleansing.' The people she saw in the tubs clearly looked like they were enjoying it, heads back and eyes closed, beaming from ear to ear.

'Ah, now in this section you can get a massage of your choice – you just need to book it in with one of our skilled professionals. Whether you require a massage just for pleasure, or something deeper to get rid of those annoying aches and pains . . . we can cater to all your needs.' They really did like that phrase here. 'We also offer reiki, aromatherapy, mud treatments, herbal healing, full body wraps and even *ganban-yoku*, which is hot stone treatment.'

In this section, Robyn saw people flitting about wearing mock scrubs and tunics, again all white, probably to give the impression that a lot of these treatments were based on more scientific methods than they were.

'Whatever you need, you'll find it here at The Castle Spa!' said the man, cheerfully. 'And if beauty treatments are what you're looking for – I can't imagine that would apply to yourself obviously . . .' He offered her a smirk then, used to the practised flannel working a treat on potential and existing clients alike.

'Well, we offer waxing, manicures, pedicures, hair care and the removal of such with electrolysis . . . The works!'

'It's all very impressive,' Robyn admitted, because it was.

'Ah, now here we have something very special. You've heard of isolation tanks, right?'

Robyn nodded. It was basically where they put you inside a 'coffin' and you floated in water. It had obvious psychological benefits, so she'd been told – took you back to being in the womb apparently – but wasn't her cup of tea.

'Okay, so in here . . .' He opened up a room on their left, which was empty at the moment. 'Here we practise what's known as Dark Therapy, a relatively new treatment whereby clients are kept in complete darkness for periods of time. I don't normally work down here, so forgive me if some of this is a bit fuzzy, but it apparently blocks the blue wavelength lights – I think that's right – which stops the breakdown of the melatonin hormone. It can be used to help with all kinds of problems. Things like headaches, chronic fatigue syndrome and insomnia.'

Again, Robyn was sure it did in some cases – and hadn't she even heard that this kind of treatment could help with bipolar disorders? It just wasn't something she'd ever consider, or advise people to try – especially now. Even standing here thinking about it brought back memories of that lock-up and waiting for Sykes to return. The banging. Not knowing if she'd live or . . .

Robyn swallowed dryly and Brad noticed her discomfort. 'Not for everyone, I grant you. But, well, this *is* the full tour, right?'

She nodded and he moved things quickly along. Taking her to their pool, or rather to the observation area just above it so she could see the people jumping in and splashing about. This was more her kind of thing; brought back pleasant memories of larking around in the ocean not far from here with Vicky and her folks.

Brad ended with a full tour of the gym facilities, which had everything from cross-trainers, running or rowing machines and bikes, to weights and pull-down machines. 'All supervised by our experienced trainers,' Brad assured her, 'who can even come up with fitness regimes for you, if you so wish. Or dietary plans, based on your particular needs. And we do have a full kitchen and restaurant area, plus twenty-four-hour room service delivery, of course.'

Robyn had been wondering what Simon might have been doing up here until then. He was a fit bloke, but no expert as far as she knew – or Vicky had informed her. But then there were dozens of activities he might be involved in as a member of staff here, from delivering that all-day, and night, room service to just keeping an eye on people in the pool area. One thing she did know was he could swim – which made sense if he also worked on the boats as well. And if he was working a few jobs, this place clearly didn't pay their staff very well – unless you *were* one of those aforementioned experts, naturally. It was how they made their money, kept costs down; they were probably paying the general staff peanuts.

'We also have excellent Wi-Fi signal here, which is more than you can say for a lot of Golden Sands,' said Brad with a chuckle. 'Apart from the beach itself, bizarrely.'

Robyn had to wait until they were outside and he was showing her the tennis and volleyball courts, which complimented the squash courts inside, to start asking a few questions herself. She'd had to wait for Brad to shut up, for starters. 'This all must have cost . . . I can't even imagine. And it's fairly new, is that right? It's definitely happened since I used to come here when I was younger.'

'Mr Boyd turned things around, basically. Oh, Sebastian Boyd that is – our boss. He actually lives on the outskirts of the grounds,' Brad said waving his hand in the vague direction of where that might be. 'A lot of the building was in disrepair until he inherited it. He brought in investors and thankfully had the business sense needed to set this whole thing up.'

'Mr Boyd . . .' Robyn repeated. Now that was a name she had

heard of around here; the Boyd family had been associated with Golden Sands for a long time. Had once been the royalty she'd thought about as she drove to the spa. 'But surely . . . I mean, those renovations . . . Wasn't the place listed or whatever? How could he—'

'Listen, I'm just glad that he did,' said Brad with another smile. 'Or I wouldn't have a job, and I wouldn't be showing you around today.'

'Right, of course.' She paused before the next bit. 'While I'm here, Brad, can I just ask you—'

'Anything, sure. That's what I'm here for. We cater to all—'

'I was wondering if you . . . Did you know someone who worked here called Simon Carter?'

The smile quickly faded from his lips; mask slipping, doing a Tracy. 'Why . . . How do you . . .' He looked around furtively, as if someone might be watching him. 'What's this about?'

'Nothing, I was just . . . He was the man who died, wasn't he?'

Brad's eyes narrowed, suspiciously. 'Who are you?'

'Nobody. I was just wondering if—'

'I thought there was something off about . . . If you're another reporter, I'll—'

'I'm not a reporter,' she told him, and that was the truth as well. 'I promise you.'

'Then what . . . Did you know Simon?'

Robyn nodded. 'A long time ago. But yes.'

'Look,' he said eventually, 'the police have already been here and asked their questions. There was nothing . . .' His eyebrows knitted together. 'And, another thing, I'm a busy person. I've got things I should be doing, not showing people around here who've got no intentions of . . . In fact, I should probably call the police myself.'

'And say what?' she asked him.

'Have you done for wasting my time. Impersonating—'

'I wasn't impersonating anyone!' Now Robyn was getting angry

79

again herself, regardless of the fact she probably *had* been wasting Brad's time; it hadn't been a waste of hers, though. 'I just said I was thinking of coming here, which for all you know I might be. I was *offered* the tour.'

'I think you ought to leave now,' the man told her. For a second she thought he was going to take hold of her arm – was she trespassing? It was a grey area – but instead he pointed the way to the car park. There was no reason to stay here anyway now, Brad wasn't going to answer any of her questions and the rest of the staff would be told likewise. Word would soon spread here.

Robyn nodded reluctantly, then walked off in the direction he was indicating. When she got some distance away, she looked back again to see Brad still watching her leave – wasn't *that* busy then – hands balled into fists, knuckling into his waist like some kind of tennis-playing Superman.

Sighing, she made her way back to the car park. It was funny, but for a place that was meant to make you feel relaxed, she'd never felt so ill at ease. She also hadn't been able to shake the feeling of being watched, and not just by Brad or the residents. It was a feeling she was starting to get used to here in Golden Sands.

Taking out her mobile, she checked on that excellent signal Brad had told her about. Nothing. Probably had a blocker or you needed a password for it or something.

By the time she'd got back into her car, with a quick check behind her, she'd already decided to do more digging. And if she couldn't rely on modern technology, she'd have to go old-school, just like she very often did when she was studying back in uni. Robyn started the engine, put the car in gear, and drove off.

Leaving the castle, the stately home, the spa, behind her in the rear view.

Chapter 8

Some things were not so easy to leave behind, no matter where you were.

Robyn found the more time she spent here, the more things were surfacing that she really wasn't prepared for. Her drive back through town – grabbing a burger and some fries from a fast food place on the way, because she was still hungry – brought more memories. Of playing on street corners, of Mr Whippy ice creams and a lost childhood she could never get back again however hard she tried. Of lost innocence, growing older and older with each summer that passed. Every year bringing her closer to her future career, not just as a tutor but as a consultant.

Closer and closer to Sykes.

The work, ironically, would take her mind off such things waiting at home *and* in this place on the coast where she'd once again found herself. Studying always did – it was something she could throw herself into. Though she couldn't say she was particularly looking forward to dry historical research. She knew lecturers and professors, who lived and breathed this day in, day out, and loved it; she took her hat off to them. For her, history – in particular ancient history – was never going to be as interesting as the present.

Although, as her profession often taught her, in some instances you had to look back to learn. To spot the patterns. History repeating itself.

Her first port of call, therefore, had been Golden Sands' tiny library, located – so the map told her – a few streets north of The Majestic Hotel. Like the castle, she'd never really had much reason to visit before; she was always on her summer holidays when she was here, didn't want to be reminded of musty class-rooms and exams. Whichever way you looked at it, libraries did that – being cousins to schools, reminders of them because most schools even had their own. Robyn had only really learned to love these when she'd started university, because there they could be your best friend: a place to help you with that last-minute essay, a quote that you might not be able to find anywhere else; a place of quiet if uni life was getting too much and you were peopled out; a place to hide if you needed it, from those who might be looking for you, or simply hiding away from the world in general.

She was amazed, frankly, what with all the budgetary cuts, that Golden Sands still had one, even if it was meant for Borrowers and Hobbits apparently; but was just glad they did. Polishing off what she had left of the burger in the attached car park that was about a tenth the size of the one at The Castle Spa, she wiped her hands on the napkins she'd grabbed with the 'meal', swigged back a couple more pills with the remnants of her Coke, and clambered out of the Citroën. Then she made her way to the building and stepped inside, her entry accompanied by the tinkling of a bell above the door, which set her teeth on edge.

It was quite dim, but she could just about make out half a dozen rows of bookcases ahead of her, spaced a few feet apart, the ends facing Robyn like sentries or soldiers on parade. Every single wall was covered as well, with shelves that were heaving with books. There didn't appear to be any kind of information desk at all, which made her wonder how you could actually take the books out. But when she took a few more steps she heard a cough and saw that it was tucked away in an alcove on her right. The lady behind the counter there looked trapped, with no possible way in or out from behind her desk other than leaping over – which Robyn wouldn't have advised because the woman made Miss Havisham look like a young spring chicken. At least she'd announced the fact she was behind her, unlike 'I've been Cathy' who'd snuck up on her like a ninja.

'Oh . . . er . . . hello,' said Robyn.

The old lady put a finger to her lips, then pointed to a sign that read 'For the convenience of all library users, please keep your voice down'. Robyn looked around, couldn't see another soul in the building, but whispered the next bit anyway. 'I'm looking for the local history section.' Section? She'd be lucky.

Miss Havisham's older sister said nothing in reply, just pointed to the far corner of the library. Robyn nodded her thanks, then went off to have a look. *Of course, it would help if there were labels telling you where things were*, she thought. Instead, the books were arranged like it was a bring and buy sale, shoved in any which way – presumably because the librarian hadn't been let out to rearrange them since 1923.

Eventually, and after turning on her mobile's torch, she found some books about the area and in lieu of any tables for her to take them to, Robyn sat on the floor with her back propped up against the shelving, careful not to lean too hard in case anything fell off and gave her a concussion.

One of the books she'd found told her that Golden Sands' castle was originally a medieval fortress, built on the grounds of an Iron Age settlement and a Roman signal station. For centuries it belonged to and was maintained by the earl of the region, the duty being passed down through generations of the Boyd family line. Various battles – in particular the sieges of the English Civil War – and a couple of fires meant that over time it had been transformed into the building she'd seen today, which explained its odd appearance. One particular major renovation took place during the nineteenth century and was funded by the then countess, who liked to throw weekend parties and invite the likes of the Prince of Wales and the Duke of Devonshire.

The countess's husband, Robyn read, moving the torch over the pages, *was scarcely around at that time, due to his hobby of exploring, something of a craze during the Victorian era. Franklyn Boyd was a noted traveller, having visited the four corners of the earth, bringing back with him tales of his expeditions and often strange foreign plants, which his staff would be encouraged to maintain in the giant greenhouses that were once in the grounds.*

He had a singular love of desert regions, and it is said that one such little-known Arabian tribe of nomads took him in and made him an honorary member. Rumour even has it that he married one of their women, accepting all of their traditions and practices, religious or otherwise. This was something that almost saw him ostracised from British society upon his return in 1885.

Robyn put the book down and rubbed her chin. All their practices . . . Didn't some of those nomadic tribes out there in the desert bury their dead in the dunes? She'd need to do some research into that, and it was a tenuous link at best, but some of her cases had been cracked with less.

In another book, she read that the castle had proved of strategic importance during the Second World War, as part of an early warning system in case of possible aerial attacks on this island. Again, it had sustained damage during one such incident where a bomb had been dropped in the grounds – destroying all of the late Franklyn's precious greenhouses in the process. The last remaining living member of the Boyd family died not long after the war, and the building was claimed by the state who – much to the chagrin of the population of Golden Sands – turned it into a hospital for people suffering from various mental conditions. That had definitely piqued Robyn's interest.

In short, for some years the castle had served as an asylum.

She flicked through pages of pictures from that time, showing patients in straitjackets, kept in cell-like padded rooms (this . . . now this was the real Arkham, if ever there was one). And she balked at some of the treatments the book described, such as experimental electroconvulsive shock treatment, lobotomisation and various medicinal concoctions.

Records were obviously not as thorough back then as they tended to be later on, and it was thought that many people died unnecessarily during this time – the forgotten victims of Golden Sands castle. Some claim that their ghosts walk the corridors even to this day.

Robyn didn't believe in ghosts herself, but if she did it would have gone some way to explaining why she'd felt so uncomfortable there – and she could certainly understand why they might want to come back and have their 'revenge' for all those years of torment. Absently, she wondered if the people who visited the spa, lying back and enjoying their own much more pleasant treatments, were aware of its dark history.

All that came to an end in the 1970s, however, when the government shut the institution down. There was a half-hearted attempt to turn the castle into a tourist attraction next – but people were much more interested in places like Whitby Abbey, because of its connection to Dracula. Golden Sands was 'famous' really for its beaches, not its castle, and so that idea soon crashed and burned. For many years it stood unwanted and unloved, falling into disrepair – which is how Robyn remembered it, she had to say. A pit-stop on tours of the region, but not safe to venture inside.

It took another book – more of a self-published pamphlet actually – to fill in the gaps leading up to the present. One of those kinds of publications clearly written by a resident with a proud interest in it all, another guy called Platt . . . and Robyn thought then that it must almost certainly be a relation of Jeremy's from back at the police station. The book was mostly concerned with trade in the area over the years, a good chunk solely devoted to the smuggling that had gone on – something Golden Sands was notorious for.

But, bringing everything up to date (or as up to date as she could find, this was still published a good while ago) it also detailed the coming of one Sebastian Boyd: the long-lost heir to the Boyd family estate. An illegitimate distant relation, an orphan who was already a noted businessman in his own right, this man had traced his roots back and subsequently claimed ownership of both the name of Boyd and the castle, not to mention the land that came with it. Wasn't as if anyone else wanted it anyway by the sounds of things, thought Robyn. Platt didn't come down on one side or the other, just delivered the facts, but there was no denying Boyd had been a breath of fresh air for the region – turning the castle into a destination spa, and bringing much-needed investment into the area.

There was a banging off to her right and Robyn shifted the torch from the page to flash it in that direction, which just lengthened the shadows – although one did look like a figure. 'Hello?' she called. 'Is . . . is someone there?'

Nothing, except another bang.

'Done wonders for Golden Sands, he has, bless 'im,' said a hushed voice on the other side of her, not far away from her ear. Robyn leapt, scrambling sideways and abandoning the book. The old librarian, who she'd assumed was still mummified behind her desk, was somehow out and about and had been leaning over to see what Robyn was reading. Now she pointed at the picture of Sebastian Boyd in the open publication on the floor.

'God! You scared the . . .' The old lady put her finger to her lips and shushed Robyn.

Robyn took a few deep breaths, regained her composure, telling herself to get it together. She moved back towards the interloper, training the torch on the book again: on the picture of Boyd with his trimmed moustache and sunglasses, wearing a . . . white suit. His favourite colour, it seemed, judging from his staff.

'Done wonders,' the old lady repeated.

'So . . . so I gather. Do you know him, then?'

The woman shook her head, and for a moment Robyn thought dust and cobwebs were going to shake free. 'I wish,' she told her sadly.

Robyn wasn't sure what wonders Boyd had done for the library, as such, but this lady seemed to be one of his biggest fans. Not so much the coming of Boyd, but the Second Coming it appeared.

'What . . . what was that banging?' she suddenly asked of the old lady.

'Banging?'

'Yes. Before . . . Didn't you hear the . . .?'

The librarian shook her head. *Probably stone deaf*, thought Robyn. 'Might have been the pipes I suppose,' she offered.

Robyn nodded, if they were as old as her then . . . Suddenly she spotted the time on her phone, the lateness of the hour. 'I think I'll take all these out,' she told the ancient keeper of the books, so she could look at them at her leisure – and without anyone commenting on the contents.

The woman looked horrified, as if nobody had ever asked to take anything out of her library ever before; as if it would destabilise the place, upset the delicate equilibrium. 'Do you live locally?' she asked.

'I'm . . .' Robyn almost said no, then realised she wouldn't get the books at all if she did that, so instead told her: 'Yes. Yes, I do.' At least for the moment. 'But I'm afraid I don't have a library card.'

The woman let out a weary sigh, then beckoned Robyn to follow her with the books. Although she was moving incredibly slowly, by the time Robyn had gathered up her things, the librarian was already behind her desk again – so she still had no idea how she'd got in or out. Robyn gave her Vicky's name and address, gambling on the fact that her cousin probably didn't have a card either. *Now* she did anyway, and Robyn watched as the lady took the tickets out of the books and stamped them (when had she last seen that kind of system?) which somehow didn't surpise Robyn. This library seemed to exist outside of the usual procedures . . . outside of time, even; sucking it up as well, making hours feel like minutes.

It was only now that she remembered! It was too late to grab something for Mia from a shop, especially around here, so she asked the old woman to wait while she scoured the shelves for a book she thought a six . . . sorry *almost* seven-year-old might like. Finally plumping for a tale about a runaway elephant, she brought it back to the counter to go through the motions again.

'Thanks,' said Robyn when she was done, not realising her voice had gone up again.

The old woman said nothing this time, so Robyn left her alone to go back into hibernation.

She spotted them almost as soon as she left the library.

How long they'd been waiting there was anyone's guess; as was why they hadn't come inside to find her. Or had they? Had the shadow been one of them? In any event here they were, Watts sitting in the driver's seat of a silver saloon – door open with his legs swung out – and O'Brien leaning against the bonnet with her arms folded over her chest, face the very definition of a bulldog chomping down on the business end of a wasp.

It was the only other car on that patch of concrete the size of a handkerchief, and the pair of vehicles looked uncomfortably close to each other – but like they couldn't stand one another either. Robyn raised a free hand, almost dropping her cache of books in the process. She thought she saw Watts rising to come and help her, but O'Brien pushed herself off the car and he remained in place.

'Inspector,' said Robyn with a nod when she was close enough.

'*Dr* Adams,' answered the woman, who still had her arms folded. Still not Robyn, she noted, and it still sounded like she respected the swastika more than her credentials. 'You've had a busy day.'

Robyn glanced down at the books she was still attempting to hold on to. 'Just a little light reading.'

'I would have thought you'd have enough to be going on with now you have our files,' O'Brien mused. Again, she had this way of making everything sound like an accusation, like Robyn had stolen the folders from their station. O'Brien craned her neck, peering at the top book. '*The Missing Elephant* . . . Hmm, sounds like a case for you, Watts.' She looked back at the DS, half inside and half out of the car, then grinned.

'Very funny, Boss,' said Watts. His expression said it was anything but.

'Is that all you've got there, Dr Adams?' the policewoman asked her, still trying to see what she was carrying.

'I-Is there something I can help you with, Inspector?' asked Robyn, struggling to keep the irritation out of her voice.

'Help me with?' said the detective, as if she hadn't quite understood the question. 'I wish there was.'

'I'm sorry, I don't . . . Isn't there . . . I mean, don't you have more important things you should be doing than hanging around in library car parks?'

O'Brien frowned. 'Well, you'd think, wouldn't you? But we've received a complaint.'

'I see,' said Robyn. She knew exactly where this was heading.

'Seems you gained access to The Castle Spa under false pretences.'

'I did nothing of the kind!' Robyn protested, shifting the books to her other arm and feeling a bit like a contestant in some kind of game show trying to keep her prizes.

'Then proceeded to ask awkward questions,' O'Brien continued as if she hadn't even said anything, 'and generally stick your nose in where it wasn't wanted.'

'Wanted?' Robyn asked. 'That's an interesting choice of words.'

She thought she heard O'Brien mumble something about 'bloody headshrinkers' then the woman said: 'Needed then. Care to tell us what you were doing up there, Dr Adams?'

'Like I said to them, I was thinking about visiting while I'm here.'

'I suppose the fact that your cousin's spouse, our victim, worked there occasionally had nothing to do with it. Or why you were asking about him.'

Robyn didn't reply. How could she, when that was exactly the reason why she went up there? Instead she attempted to change the subject. 'It's . . . Wait a minute, how exactly did you find me this afternoon, Inspector? Are you keeping tabs on me? Having me followed?'

O'Brien laughed and it surprised Robyn, deep-throated and coarse like that bloke from the *Carry On* movies. 'Followed? This isn't *The* bloody *X-Files*, Doctor. Don't flatter yourself. It's just a small place, that's all.'

And you probably have your spies everywhere, thought Robyn, then chastised herself for thinking along those lines again – like she was in the middle of a conspiracy. Maybe not spies then, but busybodies. People who owed the police a favour or several; neighbourhood-watch folk who had nothing better to do than report to O'Brien. No wonder she felt like she was being observed everywhere she went. Vicky's mum always used to say that you could sneeze at one end of Golden Sands and someone at the other would know about it, be there moments later with a tissue. Sometimes it worked out for the best, community spirit and all that. But sometimes . . .

'It's also a free country, last time I checked,' was Robyn's reply.

O'Brien let out a slow breath. 'You have the statements we took at the spa. We *let you* have them, out of professional courtesy.'

After you were strong-armed into it. 'They make for very interesting reading,' Robyn replied. 'The handful that there are.' She got it, they weren't exactly overstaffed at Golden Sands station, but not carrying out thorough interviews was one way to completely muck up a case.

O'Brien stepped closer, bringing her face within inches of Robyn's. 'Just don't forget who's actually investigating this crime, Doctor.'

'That would be you, would it?' she asked, trying to keep her voice level; not show that this woman was actually scaring her a little.

O'Brien missed the inference completely, that Robyn wasn't entirely sure *anyone* was investigating it. 'That would be me. Yes,' she told her. 'Listen, why don't you just do everyone a favour, Dr Adams, and just go home.'

GO HOME!

'What did you just say?' asked Robyn, mouth open, flashing back to that note.

But O'Brien was already gone, heading to the passenger side of the car. Watts hopped out, rounded the car and opened the door for his superior, slamming it again once she was inside – a little too forcefully. On his way back round to the driver's side, he paused and spoke to Robyn, keeping his voice low. 'Those friends you have in high places? Well, Sebastian Boyd has them too. Just be careful.'

Robyn shook herself, still stunned by what she'd heard. But told him that his concern was noted, that she'd bear it in mind.

'Oh, and while I've got you here . . . I was just wondering if you might . . .' He rubbed the back of his neck, eyes looking anywhere but at her. 'Whether, y'know, you might like to go for a drink sometime? Not tonight, obviously. Not unless you're at loose end or anything. But maybe, y'know, sometime?'

Robyn couldn't believe this. First his boss was giving her a hard time, alluding to that threatening message – no point telling the police about it then – and now she was being asked out on a date! And a relative of the victim at that!

'I mean, that is if you—'

The sound of a horn blasted through what he was saying and Watts turned to see O'Brien leaning across, leaning on the steering wheel. His summons, his signal to go. Watts shrugged. 'You've got my number anyway, so . . .' The DS trotted off back to the open driver's door and climbed in.

Then he manoeuvred the saloon out of the parking spot, Robyn stepping out of the way in case O'Brien decided to lean over again and tug on that wheel – run over her foot or something.

She watched them drive off, shaking her head, before slinging the books on the back seat of her own car and getting in herself. Driving off.

Leaving the library, the bizarre confrontation, and everything else behind her.

Chapter 9

She's been left behind.

The girl in the black dress, left behind by her friend – the one in the satin skirt and boob tube, wearing far too much make-up. One of the guys from the group in the corner approached them – the muscular guy in the too-tight T-shirt that showed off his obvious hours in the gym – offered to buy them both drinks, but definitely had his eye on the girl wearing the least; the one he'd already exchanged smiles with. Not hard to figure out why.

They'd chatted, or at least that pair had for a while, but it soon became obvious the girl in black was the third wheel of the bicycle, or fifth on a car . . . or is that the steering wheel? Doesn't matter . . . what did matter was the unspoken look they shared eventually, those two girls. Not really asking permission, but seeing if the first girl would be okay to go off and pursue this avenue.

It's the unspoken rule, a deal you make whenever you go out just in a pair: if one of you pulls, and especially if that person really likes the looks of the puller, if they click, they have the other half's blessing to actively see where it leads. That's what happened here, in not so many words . . . or even no words at all. A slight nod from the girl in black and away the first girl went, peeling off and wandering off with too-tight-tee.

Leaving her all alone. Not that she will be for long, that's for sure. Pretty girl like her, she'll be pounced on within minutes now she's on her own. Doesn't mean to say she'll like the people doing the pouncing, might even head off home early in fact; it's why they usually went out with more than one mate, in case something like this happened.

Fortunately for her, there's a spiky-haired youth from the group in the corner. He's already been making eye contact. And she's been making eye contact back. He gives it a reasonable amount of time, before making to walk over . . .

Too late – she's already been approached by someone from the other side of the bar area. This guy thinks he's Elvis or something, all quiff and leathers. He manoeuvres himself around her, putting himself between her and any potential admirers. Blocking off their line of sight; blocking them off completely. The spiky-haired lad stops dead in his tracks, looking crestfallen. He's deflating like someone has just let all the air out of him.

Elvis is already giving it all the chat, had been even before he propped himself up on the bar with one elbow, signalling to the barmaid like some kind of twat. Like he deserves special treatment. Which is one of the reasons the barmaid's completely ignoring him, that and she can see the look on the girl in black's face – she's giving her a chance to get rid of this creep before he can buy her another cocktail when she's finished her own.

Blah, blah, blah, blah, blah . . . He's talking, but she's not even leaning in – won't be able to hear a bloody thing over the booming sounds of the music blaring in this pseudo-club. Then she's shaking her head: not interested. She wasn't interested before he even walked up, before he entered the pub, before he was even born! Learn to read the signals, mate!

But he's still not getting it, reaching out and actually grabbing her elbow like she's his property. The girl in black yanks away her arm, shakes her head again and shouts something that can't really be misinterpreted in any way and ends in 'off'.

Elvis is still talking, but she's saying nothing, just standing there. In the end, he gets fed up and slopes off. It's only now we get to see that famous curled lip of his. Seconds later, he's found some other woman in the pub to harangue who looks equally unimpressed. Still, it's not the girl in black's problem now, is it.

She's peering over, looking around to see if there's any sign of her friend. Maybe it didn't work out – just as suddenly as it was on, it can be off again. She knows that; she's been there. But she can't see her anywhere. It's probably because she's gone out with lover boy to the beer garden, so they can hear themselves think . . . or one or both of them smoke, not that those laws have come into effect here yet where you have to go outside.

Or maybe they're doing something else . . .

That doesn't matter either; she's gone. The girl in black is on her own again, thankfully she probably thinks. Better than listening to tales of Blue Suede Shoes and Jailhouse Rock. And that's when they lock eyes again, now that the coast is clear. The spiky-haired lad who'd looked so disappointed because The King had interrupted.

A glance, holding that gaze. Now a smile. He's smiling and it lights up his face; he has a kind face. She must think that because she smiles back. It's all the encouragement he needs to head on over himself, breaking away from the group in the corner and rounding the bar. He doesn't strut, doesn't do a stupid mini-dance as he comes over. Just walks normally, comes and stands with her.

They talk, and this time she does lean in so she can hear what he's saying. He has that whole 'not-too-confident-actually-quite-shy-and-a-bit-vulnerable' thing going on, which she's responding to. He must have offered to buy her a drink, because she nods and then he's trying to attract the barmaid's attention but waiting for his turn like a good boy. All the while leaning in to chat to the girl in black, her leaning in so she can hear more. Smiling, then she's laughing at something he says. Bats his arm playfully and he beams again – that winning smile. This could be good. They might be clicking; are they clicking? It's as close as dammit for two people who've only just met and started talking.

Time passes. More chat, a few more drinks. They're even closer by this time, whispering in each other's ears. You can tell they're really into each other, hardly even notice the time passing. Then he leans in one last time, whispering something and nodding at the door. Asking if she wants to leave with him, perhaps do the same thing as the other pair and just go outside so they can hear each other properly.

Or something else.

She nods anyway, seems happy. She's having a nice time with him, so why not? Anyway, they leave together and he even takes her hand, which she looks down at and smiles again. Blokes don't usually do that kind of thing, like holding the door – as he's doing for her now. The old ways are dying out; the gentlemen are few and far between.

Now they're gone, so she doesn't see what happens next.

Doesn't know that this whole time someone's been watching them, waiting to see what transpired.

Doesn't know that he's about to follow them outside.

Part Two

One of the things Golden Sands is particularly proud of, is its seafront.

Providing access to the wonderful beach via a variety of steps and also ramps (which are totally accessible), you can just stroll along it and watch holidaymakers making use of the idyllic surroundings, whether it be playing on those sands or swimming in the clear blue waters.

A little further down you'll find the harbour, which is flanked by lots of places to eat and drink – many of which are family friendly – so you can watch the boats coming in and going out again. One of Golden Sands' main sources of income is fishing, so you'll be able to see the people who do this for a living at work if you catch them at the right time.

Not far from here are plenty of amusements, shops and, of course, the pier. This is home to a wonderful funfair that's operational throughout the summer months. Experience the thrill of the rides, try your hand in the shooting gallery or test your weight. Or go up on the big wheel, which offers a magnificent 360-degree view of the whole of Golden Sands.

Chapter 10

She woke up wishing the last couple of days had been a dream.

Why stop there, why not the last few months? Robyn rubbed the gunk out of her tired eyes; she still wasn't getting much rest, in spite of the fact she'd taken sleeping tablets the previous evening . . . probably shouldn't have because she'd been drinking earlier, though not that much. Not really. Not as much as the two evenings before that.

Memories were coming back to her, more recent than the ones that had been bombarding her since she hit the motorway. Since she came off the exit and hit the coast. And they weren't pleasant memories, either – beginning with her run-in with O'Brien outside the library.

When she returned home – to Vicky's home at any rate – there had been more surprises waiting. The crowd of reporters had grown in her absence, or returned, because according to Vicky it had been like this when news first broke about Simon. This time it was almost definitely all about her, though. Dr Robyn Adams, fresh from the city, fresh from her high-profile cases, which included catching the Oedipus Killer – though none of them knew the full story about that one, what she'd been through. The fact that she was related to the victim in this case, to his wife, made it all the more juicy as far as they were concerned.

Which was why they'd formed a barrier at the head of the street, forcing her to drive through slowly because she didn't want to knock anyone over – and they were banking on that. They piled in on all sides, shouting questions through the windows and windscreen.

'Dr Adams, does your presence mean there might be a serial element to this or—'

'Are you just here for your cousin, how—'

'Is everyone coping? How are *you*? Are you—'

'Working with the police with regards to this particular case?'

The questions all overlapped, but were the same ones pretty much – just broached in a different way. Robyn finally made it to the house and parked up, grabbing her book haul from the back and then practically having to force open the door to get out. She alternately held the publications clutched to her like a baby, and used them as a shield against the reporters. Someone stuck a camera in her face and she flinched, instinctively turning away to avoid being snapped, almost dropping everything.

'You! Hey you lot, back off!'

Robyn attempted to look up, but wasn't able to – simply couldn't see. But she recognised that voice. She never thought she'd say it, but Robyn had never been happier to see . . . *hear* anyone in her life. Then, before she knew what was happening, Tracy was wading into the crowd, holding her warrant card aloft and barking at people to back off, to give Robyn some room to get through. Finally, they took notice, creating a narrow trough for Tracy to escort her through to the front door, which was hanging open.

Robyn almost fell into the hallway, but righted herself at the last moment – flinching again when the bang came of Tracy slamming the door in those people's faces. She brushed her hands together as if she'd just tidied up a mess, which Robyn supposed she had in a way.

'Thanks,' she said to the FLO.

'No problem,' said Tracy, the smirk telling Robyn that actually she'd quite enjoyed putting them in their place.

'Just a thought, but you might want to have a word about getting a uniform or two posted out there again.'

The woman said nothing in return, pushing her glasses back up her nose. It was obvious she didn't care for people telling her how to do her job.

'Robs!' Vicky called out, rushing from the kitchen. 'Are you all right?'

'I am now,' she told her. 'That was worse than some of the scrums back home.' Though of course there she'd have folk like Cav and his team helping her get through those. 'It was bound to happen eventually, though I had hoped for a couple more days.'

'I'm . . . I'm really sorry.' Vicky's hands were holding her cheeks. 'I didn't think that . . . I'm really sorry.'

'No need. Honestly. It's—' There was a scream and suddenly Mia was in the hall as well, having pushed past her mum, and was now grabbing Robyn's legs again – her signature move.

'Aunty Robs!' she shouted, picking up on the abbreviation Vicky always used and running with it. 'What did you bring me?' It was clear where *her* priorities lay.

'Let your aunty get in through the door first, Mia!'

'It's okay. I . . . Here,' said Robyn, giving her the book she'd grabbed from the library. 'It's only on loan, but if you like it I'll get it for you.'

Mia took the book, delighted. Then her face dropped when she saw what it was. She looked up at Robyn like her aunty was mad. '*The Missing Elephant*,' she said, almost with contempt.

'Is that not . . .'

'You don't have kids, do you?' said Tracy on her way past, shaking her head.

Vicky stared down at the book. 'She's . . . she's kind of grown out of this stuff. Clever girl, remember?'

'Didn't they have any David Walliams?' asked Mia.

'The guy from the talent show?' said Robyn.

'He writes as well,' Vicky informed her. 'He's her favourite . . . But it's the thought that counts. Say thank you, Mia.'

'Thank you,' repeated the little girl, who, to her credit, made it sound like Robyn had just given her the best present in the world. Didn't matter that it was wrong, and it wasn't really Robyn's to give.

'Come on, we're just about to eat.'

As a change of pace, they were having pizzas that evening, three of which were already in the oven cooking. Vicky offered to make Robyn a tea, but she asked for coffee instead, which she blew on and – when she thought nobody was looking – took a couple more of her painkillers with.

'What are those?' asked Mia, popping up at the side of her like a whack-a-mole. 'Sweets?'

'Not quite,' answered Robyn.

'Robs?' asked Vicky, who placed a pizza down in front of her. She was frowning, knew exactly what her cousin was doing – thanks to Mia flagging it – and Tracy was once again clocking everything.

'It's nothing, really. Just an old injury flaring up again.' Vicky's frown remained. She knew it was bullshit, but thankfully didn't push it at dinnertime when everyone was sitting down to dig into meat feasts and Hawaiian.

Once Tracy was gone, they put Mia to bed – Robyn actually saying goodnight to her properly this time, and even reading to her at the girl's request from *The Ice Monster*, which Robyn found herself getting into as well. 'See?' said Mia, stifling a yawn. Once the girl had finally dropped off, Robyn went into the bedroom to get the note from that morning out of her pocket. However, her clothes – which she'd left in the bedroom – were now gone.

Robyn headed downstairs, where Vicky had already made a decent start demolishing another bottle of wine on the couch.

'Vicky, my clothes from my room . . .' she began, thumbing back towards the stairs.

Her cousin looked at her blankly, then realised what she was asking. 'Oh, right. Tracy put those through the wash earlier. Figured they were for the laundry, I guess.'

'Tracy . . .?' Two questions came then: what the hell had Tracy been doing in her room? And what had happened to that note? 'Vicky, there was something in my trouser pocket. Do you know what . . .?'

'I think Tracy emptied the pockets. You get used to doing that when you have kids, you know – they're always leaving shit in there, tissues or—'

'Vicky, this is important. Do you know what she did with it all?'

Her cousin simply shrugged. 'Binned it? I dunno . . . Couldn't have been anything that important or she'd have put it on the worktop.'

Or would she? thought Robyn. Maybe O'Brien had put her up to leaving the thing in the first place? Robyn made a mental note to check the bin in the kitchen, but doubted she'd find anything. She was about to say something else when she saw Vicky pouring herself another large glass of the wine.

'Aren't you hitting that a bit hard?' she said to her.

'Am I?'

Robyn held up her hands. 'I'm just looking out for you, cuz.'

'Want one?' was the answer she got to that. 'Or maybe you can't on your meds?'

Robyn pursed her lips, took the bottle and poured herself a generous amount. Saving Vicky from herself, she thought, which of course was more bullshit. It had just been another long day.

'So?' asked Vicky.

'So . . .?'

'You going to tell me about it?'

'What?' she asked, thinking it might be about the missing note.

'Whatever you're taking these for?' Vicky held up the pills she'd fished out of Robyn's handbag while she'd been upstairs.

'What the actual fuck, Vicky?' She went over and snatched them from her. Was there no such thing as privacy in this house?

'Pretty strong, aren't they?'

103

Robyn shrugged and took a seat opposite her.

'What happened?' asked Vicky.

So – seeing little choice – she told her, or the bare bones of it. Hunting down Sykes, getting kidnapped, being held in the lock-up. Being attacked and Cav arriving at the last minute – warning her that none of this was public knowledge. By the time she was finished, Vicky's jaw was hanging. 'Bloody hell,' she said. 'And you still came here to help me.'

'I'd just got out from seeing Sykes again in jail.'

'Bloody hell,' Vicky said again, swigging back more wine. 'Why?'

'Research,' Robyn replied flatly. She wasn't about to go into the complex reasoning behind why she visited those she'd helped to put away. She wasn't even sure she fully understood it herself.

'And this guy, this copper Cav. The one who saved you.'

'He didn't really . . . His whole team, they—'

'Are you two close?'

Robyn understood what she was asking, what her cousin still thought of her.

You do work quick . . .

'He's just a mate,' she told Vicky.

'More than that, I reckon.'

'It's . . . Me and him, it's . . . He's married.' She looked at Vicky, waiting for her to say, 'Since when did that ever stop you?', daring her to even, but she said nothing. It seemed a good time to steer the conversation towards what she'd been doing that day and in what way she was trying to help Vicky.

'Tracy saw your books, you know. The ones about the history of the town, about the castle.'

'Her friends know I was there anyway. I was warned off.'

'What?'

'Twice, in fact. Treading on too many toes. Specifically that guy Sebastian Boyd's, I think.'

'You don't think he has anything to do with . . .' Vicky let the sentence trail off.

'I don't know what to think yet, I really don't.' And as they drank more – Vicky had stocks of white wine in various cupboards in the kitchen – Robyn finally got her to open up more about Simon's other jobs.

'Just helping out, as and when.'

'With the fishing. With the funfair.'

'Right. He always liked to keep himself busy.'

Robyn had nodded. 'I can relate to that . . .'

She'd already decided by the time Vicky turned in – slightly earlier and making it to her own bed that time . . . though not before making sure Robyn had a spare key – she would sleep downstairs herself and be out of the house first thing to beat those reporters.

She'd woken when it was still dark outside, though – thinking she could hear that knocking again. Even getting up when she saw another shadowy figure in the living room doorway. 'W-Who's there?' she asked again, just like in the library – then felt foolish when she rounded the corner to find it was nobody. Just a trick of the lamplights outside; a quick check through the peephole in the still-locked front door told her there was nobody outside either.

Nevertheless, it took her a while to get back to sleep again.

And Robyn had felt like death once more when the alarm went on her phone at stupid o'clock, but had forced herself to get up and leave the house, leaving a note on the nearby pad to tell Vicky she'd gone. Only a couple of reporters had camped out overnight, as she'd seen earlier on – some almost definitely from the local paper, *The Torch* – but they weren't nearly quick enough to catch her as she drove her car off down the street and then off the estate. She found a place that did breakfasts and ate more stodge, figuring it would not only sober her up but also keep her going for the day. The coffee refills were particularly welcome, the first of which she used to take more pills with.

From there, she'd parked up near the front and visited the places Vicky had told her about: beginning with the harbour, where she watched the colourful boats coming and going – whites, yellows, blues – taking photos on her camera, especially of the vessels that Simon would probably have been working on. As pretty as it all was, Robyn still couldn't shake that feeling of being watched even here. Something that followed her as she wandered further along the seafront, by which time everything was in full flow. Robyn didn't need to rely on memory, because it was all happening around her: families re-creating her formative summers; children in and out of the amusements there, pestering parents for candy floss or coins for the machines. Easy to hide in plain sight here, if you were spying on someone.

She'd been able to see the wheel from there, towering above everything and the closer she came to it the more of the funfair she saw and heard, the sound of screams and laughter especially. Robyn paused at the red tollbooth, then pushed on and paid for one ticket. Looking left and right, cautiously walking past booths and those mini-rides she remembered from before. Everything looked smaller now, less wondrous somehow and more . . . run-down was the only word she could think of that fitted. More threatening. The paint was peeling everywhere she went and Robyn had to wonder when health and safety had last visited to check the rides, especially the big wheel that was at the heart of this place.

Robyn had a mental image then of it coming off its hinges and rolling out to sea, like a set piece in some kind of disaster movie. As it was, hardly anyone was braving the thing today, so they were all right . . . unless it just fell sideways of course, like the flat tyre of a car that was being changed. Then it would just squash everyone and everything around it.

Shaking the stupid thoughts away, Robyn carried on taking photos all around her. Of the Ghost Train, which adults were struggling to climb inside with their kids – knees up around their chins almost. A supposedly spooky 'oohhh' sound followed the shunted carriages of the train into the tunnel. The hole was a skeleton's mouth, the rest of which had been painted around

106

it. Here it didn't matter if the white was chipped, it just added to the gothic feel.

The requisite Hall of Mirrors, which was closed for repairs due to vandalism at the moment, Coconut Shy and Hook a Duck were all here, not to mention a fortune teller's hut – the woman painted on the side staring into a crystal ball with hypnotic yellow eyes. Robyn took photos and moved on. As with the fishing boats, she didn't ask any questions here – not yet – mainly because everyone seemed so busy and she didn't want to get in the way, but also because this was really just a recce. Getting the lie of the land.

There was also a very good chance she might get another tug from the boys – plus one girl especially – in blue. Interfering with the merry-go-round or something . . . Could they charge someone with that? It was ridiculous – the *whole thing* was ridiculous. O'Brien had spoken with Gordon, and Robyn was pretty sure he would have sung her praises – regardless of the fact he'd thought she was coming here to take a break, not look into a murder. Even if he hadn't, her track record spoke for itself – they should have been welcoming the assistance! It wasn't as if they were actually getting anywhere with the case, was it?

Or maybe that was intentional. Had they been warned off themselves, told to leave it alone? If so, by who? This Boyd character? Based purely on what she'd found out herself, she was intending on doing some more digging into him. Unless she ended up in the cells at Golden Sands nick. Then again, maybe she *was* being paranoid. Maybe the answer was much simpler than that. Perhaps it was staring her in the face and she didn't even know it.

As she was thinking all this, dawdling by a carousel ride that looked to be switched off and out of commission, she heard that noise again. A banging . . . Then a couple of swift, sudden bangs. When the ride started up again with a jerk, the music blaring and the horses going round, it gave her another fright. Stepping back, she felt her heart racing – and turned around quickly, certain there was someone there. Somebody still following her.

Robyn ran back out of the fair, and thought she saw someone trying to get away. Thought to herself that he looked an awful lot like Watts. Had he been ordered to keep an eye on her, she wondered? How had he known where she'd be? Followed her from the house?

But then the man in question caught up with his girlfriend, slinging an arm around her and kissing her – and Robyn realised how stupid she'd been. How paranoid again. She cast a look back over her shoulder at the fair, having had no fun whatsoever inside. *Maybe I should ask for my money back,* she thought. But she hadn't been there to have a good time, had she? Had entered knowing that was hardly a possibility.

The next bit of her journey wasn't exactly a laugh riot either, heading down to the beach to visit the place where Simon's body had been found – or as near as she could figure it. At least she'd be fairly alone there, could see if anyone was tailing her. She'd spent the last couple of days absorbing what his life was like, the places he'd worked, and now Robyn was about to see where he'd met his end. Where someone had placed their hands around his throat and squeezed until there was no air left in his lungs, even drowning him to help the process along.

Once again she found herself there, standing on the beach staring – and crying. What the hell was wrong with her? She'd only stopped when she heard people in the distance, walking along the beach with their kids. Robyn had wiped her eyes, taken more photos and left that place of death . . . not that those folk had any idea, by the looks of it. For that family, life went on. For Vicky and Mia, not so much.

She got back late afternoon, this time bracing herself to run the gamut of reporters – ready to wade her way through them if necessary. But it actually wasn't as bad as she'd feared, mainly because a couple of uniforms were on duty now to maintain order; Tracy had taken her advice after all. Head down, she'd soon found herself on the doorstep of Vicky's house.

However, standing there in the hallway again after letting herself in, she soon realised she might be better off going back outside and braving the sharks. Both Tracy and Vicky had come through from the living room when they heard the door, the former with an extremely concerned look on her face – an emotion she'd yet to see the FLO display – while the latter had a face like thunder, arms folded. For just a second she reminded Robyn of Inspector O'Brien.

'What's . . .' she began, wondering if she really wanted to know.

'Mia found your files,' Vicky told her. 'The ones on top of your wardrobe.'

'Shit,' said Robyn. 'How?'

'She got a chair,' Tracy explained. 'Climbed up.'

'But I didn't—'

'Kids are curious, Robyn.' Not Robs now, because she was angry. 'They get into all sorts.'

No such thing as privacy . . .

'Where was I supposed to—'

'I don't know,' replied Vicky. 'Anywhere else. Somewhere she wouldn't be looking.'

'Why was she even in my room?' Robyn shook her head, looking at Tracy as well when she said this.

'Because she looks up to you. Because she wants to know what you're all about.' Vicky sighed.

And what had been Tracy's excuse?

Robyn bit her lip. 'How is she?'

Vicky was still glaring at her. 'How do you think? I'm . . . I didn't know what to say to her about . . . I mean, *Christ!* Those pictures in there. Of her dad. Of Simon with his . . .' Tears broke free from the corners of her eyes then, tracking down her face like they knew exactly where to go; using the same routes as before.

Robyn flashed back to going through the pictures, imagining Mia's reaction when she saw them. Imagining Vicky's when she found her. 'I'm really sorry. Maybe I could talk to her or—'

'I think you've done enough!' snapped Vicky. 'We've only just managed to calm her down.'

'Hey!' said Robyn, touching her chest, suddenly annoyed. 'I came here to help you, *because* you asked. I'm looking into all this, *because* you asked. That's what the files are doing here in the first place!' She could see Tracy backing away, heading towards the kitchen. If there was about to be a row she wanted no part of it, didn't want to get dragged into the argument.

'This isn't the way I wanted her to find out,' Vicky stated.

'No,' Robyn agreed. 'It's not ideal, I'll grant you. But maybe if she'd known . . .'

'What? It wouldn't have been so much of a shock?' Vicky threw her hands up into the air now. 'You're kidding me.'

'Look, like I said before, kids are strong. They're resilient.' At the same time she was thinking: things like this can really fuck a child up. Can turn them into the kind of person she – or someone like her – might be hunting in years to come. And that would be on her. Robyn took a step towards Vicky, hand out. 'I can—'

'You? You don't even know what books to get her. You don't know *her*, because you haven't been around. Been too busy with your psychos.' Oh, it was all coming out now. All the resentment because she'd stayed away, not been in touch, not really been in Vicky or Mia's life. It was fair comment: she hadn't.

'I've tried to explain that. I—'

'You haven't explained a bloody thing!' Vicky barked. 'What did we do? What did *I* do?'

'Nothing,' Robyn whispered. 'You didn't do anything.'

But Vicky was already taking herself off to the living room and when Robyn followed she saw her curled up on the sofa in almost a foetal position. Like those people Dennis Wilde had killed, placed like that because he thought he was sending them back to the womb; because he thought no one should ever have left it. Robyn was beginning to see his point.

110

She considered just leaving then, getting in her car and driving back home.

GO HOME!

But that would have been the easy way out, wouldn't it. Would have been like letting them win, the people who wanted her out of the way. Robyn was invested in this now, wanted, no *needed* to see it through no matter what. It was how this always got her. So she spent an uncomfortable couple of hours in the house, most of the time upstairs locked inside the spare room. Hadn't gone anywhere near Mia's room, with its door shut: she'd probably cried herself into oblivion. Even though everything was screaming at her that she should, that she had to make this right again if she could. But Vicky was right: she'd done enough damage for one day.

It was as she'd sat with her knees pulled up on the bed that she'd heard someone knocking on her bedroom door. 'Yes?' Robyn had answered, but got no reply. She'd gone to see who it was, unlocking the door and peering out – thinking maybe someone had come to see if she wanted something to eat (yeah, right!). But there'd been no one out there on the landing. Robyn had even gone downstairs, asked if anyone had knocked on her door – but Vicky had ignored her and Tracy had just given a small shrug. Had that woman been messing with her? Robyn felt like asking her about the note then, but realised there was no point; Tracy would only deny having seen anything.

In the end, desperate, she'd tried to find a mobile signal to ring the outside world and – failing – resorted to going outside to the back garden where she found she could get a couple of bars in the very far corner. Wasn't a bad thing, because she didn't want anyone overhearing her conversation – Tracy especially, who even as she dialled was scrutinising her through the kitchen window.

It rang out a few times before it was picked up. 'Y'ello,' said the voice.

'Er . . . Watts? DS Watts . . . Ash?'

'Robyn?' She could imagine his surprise, thought she might

111

even hear the phone drop as he let go of it in shock. In all honesty, she was just as surprised as he was that she'd called him. But she needed to get out of here, needed someone close enough to see in person, rather than just hear a voice. And didn't part of her feel like she owed him something for thinking he was following her? 'Hi . . . What's . . .'

'Y-You know that drink you were talking about,' she said, tentatively.

'Yeah.'

'Is the offer still open?'

'*Of course!*' His reply almost deafened her.

'Right. Okay then . . . To discuss the case,' Robyn added.

'Yes. Yes, of course.'

So they'd arranged a time and place, the only pub she really knew in town – or had known – eight p.m.

'See you there,' she told him before he got any ideas about picking her up or anything.

You do work quick . . .

'Gotcha,' replied Watts. 'See you later.'

Then she went back inside to get ready, ignoring the looks from Tracy; booking a taxi and leaving without saying anything to anyone.

She thought it would probably be better for everyone that way.

Chapter 11

Robyn had got there a good half hour early.

She wasn't sure why, maybe to get the lie of the land again. It wasn't so she could chat to anyone – she didn't speak to a soul there, didn't know anybody – but in the end someone found her.

She'd just ordered a double vodka on the rocks from the barman, a fellow in his fifties with a rosy complexion – like he was used to sampling what he served – who was also glaring at her for some unspecified reason. What was it, national pick on Robyn day or something?

She'd been in the process of working her way quickly through her drink; still a little in shock of how much The Barnacle (as she'd known it back in the day) had changed now it was part of that chain. Everything had so much less character now. Instead of timber beams, which you could pretend were parts of a ship, there was white plaster and blue walls. It still had wooden furniture, but again that wood was too . . . clean. As if it had been bought wholesale from somewhere, which it probably had. Light brown instead of dark, and varnished to within an inch of its life.

There were still photos dotted about on the walls, but instead of the sepia-toned pictures of Golden Sands throughout the years, now they were more tasteful and colourful shots of seagulls and crabs, a bucket and spade, a windbreak, a deckchair or two. Still a seaside theme, but more modern. More generic. It was the only thing differentiating this place from a million other chains she'd been in over the years. Whenever they were taken over, pubs tended to lose their personality and that had definitely happened here.

Leaning on the bar, she'd looked around at the punters inside as well. Only a smattering of people really, some coupled up, but it was still early. Unlike the bars down on the front, this place was still mainly for adults it seemed – there were no families present. And those adults, especially what looked like the locals, were either ignoring her, or doing the same as the barman — regarding her with downright hostility.

Robyn turned back to her drink. She'd chosen to wear something a bit more casual that night, dark jeans and blue top with her short jacket. She didn't want anything to scream 'date night' to Watts, but didn't want to feel too uptight either.

Was it a date night? she thought to herself then. Of course not. As she'd told him, there were a few things she wanted to talk about regarding the case and seeing as she wasn't really welcome at the station right now . . . Wasn't welcome at Vicky's either, which – let's face it – was the biggest reason for getting out of there. Watts was the only ostensibly friendly person she knew in the area, even if he was a Golden Sands copper. The only person who'd offered her a drink – and boy did she need a drink at that moment in time.

Hadn't been the only person to offer her a drink, as it turned out. She'd been there what, five, ten minutes or so when she was joined by a tanned guy who came over and leaned on the bar next to her; she'd been aware of someone even as they'd approached and wasn't about to get caught out this time. Robyn shifted sideways and took him in. Handsome, in a kind of rugged way, but not chiselled or manufactured like so many guys were today. Didn't look like he took ages in the bathroom before heading out, styling his hair, trimming his stubble to get it just the right length. There was something . . . real about him, like he didn't have to bother that much in order to look good.

Dark-haired, with sideburns that were a little too long, he also had a gap in one of his eyebrows – though she could tell this wasn't just for effect, it was an actual scar where something had happened to him in the past. The deep brown eyes they were shielding also had what her mum used to call 'a certain sparkle', which in her case meant that they could make her melt if someone looked at her the right way. He was wearing the more usual colour of jeans – worn, but again not in a designer way – and a grey shirt that hadn't been ironed. His sleeves were rolled up just far enough for her to see the bottoms of his biceps, and open at the front far enough for her to see a shadow of hair leading down to his broad chest. He was nursing a pint of some nondescript lager, his hands rough – used to hard work – and he placed the glass on the counter beside him.

'Hi there,' he said. At least it wasn't, 'How're *you* doin'?'

'All right,' replied Robyn by way of a greeting, mustering up that fake confidence again.

'I am,' he said, though she hadn't really been enquiring as to his wellbeing. He stared at her, eyes narrowing. 'I feel like I know you from somewhere,' were his next words.

Not very original. Robyn shrugged. 'Maybe. I do have one of those faces.'

He nodded at the sage words. 'Can I . . .' The man nodded at her glass now instead.

She thought about it for a second or two, then nodded herself. Why not? She had a bit of time to kill.

'I'm John,' he informed her, holding out his hand. She was having trouble placing his accent; definitely not local, but there were hints of all kinds of places.

'I'm . . . Nice to meet you, John,' she said, shaking it. His grip was firm, but didn't outstay it's welcome. More like Brad's than

Watts's. He grinned at her remark, then asked the barman for two refills.

'You here on holiday?' he said.

'Kind of.' Robyn thanked the barman – who ignored her – and then John when another vodka was set down on a coaster in front of her. The tanned man held his pint glass up for her to chink it.

'Cheers. Well, you've picked a nice part of the country for a break.' He paused, smiled again. 'Have to say, you don't look very happy for someone on their holidays.'

She gave him a weak smile. 'I'm . . . I sort of made a bit of a mess of things. Not intentionally, but . . . You know, back at . . . at home.'

'Oh. Okay.' John didn't pry, for which she was grateful. 'Actually, I'm glad you came in.'

'Oh?' said Robyn.

'Thought I'd be celebrating on my own.'

'Celebrating?' Was this another line? she wondered.

A single nod. 'Had a stroke of luck. A windfall you might say. Bit of a gamble came right.' He didn't go any further into it, but from the way he was still smiling Robyn thought it must be true. Horses more than likely, or cards. 'Not massive, you understand. Enough to see me right for a bit, though. Enough to buy a lady drinks.' Another smile.

'That's . . .' Robyn held up her glass and chinked his again. 'Congratulations John.'

'Ta,' he said, then faced front, leaning more heavily on the bar with his elbows and taking a sip of the lager. He looked sideways at her. 'You know, I think I might have seen you . . . Maybe just wandering around or something.'

'Maybe,' said Robyn.

'It's a small place.'

'So I'm told.' This time she offered him a smile; couldn't help it, she was starting to quite enjoy his company. No history, no hassle. Just easy-going.

116

'Do you want to grab a seat or something?' asked John.

Quick worker . . .

Robyn looked at her watch. 'Oh, no. That's okay. I'm actually waiting for someone.'

If John was surprised, he didn't show it. A slight twitch of the scarred eyebrow. 'Of course you are. Of course. I should have . . .'

'It's not . . .' Robyn shook her head. She didn't know why she felt she had to quantify it, or even justify it to this stranger. But anyway, she said: 'A colleague.'

'Ah,' said John. 'Maybe another time then?' There was a hopeful tone to his voice and Robyn wasn't sure whether or not to dash that or encourage it. Did she really want those kinds of complications while she was here?

Before she could say anything though, she heard the door to the bar open and was aware of someone else coming up behind her; it sent an involuntary shiver up her spine, but she knew who it would be before she even turned around.

'Robyn?' said Ashley Watts, looking a bit like a schoolboy who'd just caught his best mate hanging around with another lad. It didn't help that he was still wearing his suit and tie, which even resembled a secondary school uniform.

'Oh, hiya,' she said by way of a greeting.

Robyn could see Watts looking the other man up and down, now he'd pushed himself off the bar. 'Who's this? Is he bothering you?'

She shook her head. 'This is—'

'It's okay. I was just leaving,' John told Watts, though he was looking at Robyn when he said it.

'Because if he is . . .'

'He's not,' Robyn insisted, but Watts wasn't even listening – to her, or John apparently.

'I was just buying the lady a vodka, mate,' said John. 'No biggie.'

'Well, she's got company tonight,' spat Watts, squaring up to the larger man. 'So piss off!'

'Watts!' gasped Robyn, a little taken aback by his tone. He'd been hanging around with O'Brien too long, clearly. John looked from Robyn to Watts, and back again. 'I'm so sor—'

She hadn't even got the apology out before Watts was getting in John's face. 'What are you waiting for, a written invitation, *mate*?'

John looked off to the side, trying to calm his breathing. Then he faced front again and shoved Watts.

'No, wait . . . stop!' Robyn was saying, attempting to get in the middle of them without much success. Watts shoved John back and before she knew it, they'd grabbed hold of each other and were wrestling, each one trying to drag the other to the ground. A schoolyard scuffle. 'What are you doing? *Stop!*' shouted Robyn.

Seconds later the gruff barman was there, pulling them apart. 'If you're going to start that kind of thing,' he told them, 'you can *all* piss off!'

Watts, straightening his tie and smoothing down his suit, pulled out his warrant card. 'Police, hands off.'

'I know who you are right enough, Ashley Watts. Put that thing away. I know yer mother as well, and from where I was standing, you bloody well started this. She'd be ashamed of you.' The mention of his mum seemed to scare Watts more than anything else that had happened, certainly the prospect of being filled in by John.

'*He* shoved *me*!' Watts pointed out.

'And you weren't provoking him in the slightest,' said the barman, words dripping with sarcasm.

Robyn had been watching all this, fascinated, and when she looked around again she saw that John had gone. Made himself scarce, and she couldn't really blame him. How embarrassing.

She wasn't far behind him, either. In fact, was she outside looking for him? To finish saying that sorry she wasn't able to? But he was nowhere in sight and, she reminded herself, he *had* shoved the DS . . . even though he'd been asking for it.

'Robyn?' She jumped, hadn't heard Watts come up behind her this time.

'Would you stop doing that!' Robyn said, spinning around with her finger up.

'What?'

But of course he didn't know her history, what had happened in that car with Sykes. She'd probably never tell him now; it had even been a mistake to tell Vicky. Instead she jabbed an accusing finger and said: 'What the fuck was all that about?'

'What?' he repeated.

More jabbing, getting closer to actually touching him she was so mad. 'That macho bullshit in there!'

'He looked like he was hassling you.'

'He bought me a drink, Watts. Big deal.' Two jabs, right in the chest to drive home the words. 'He was going anyway when you showed up.'

'I just thought . . .' Watts closed his mouth, then opened it again; he looked like a guppy fish.

'You were coming across as more than a bit . . .' She sighed, shook her head. 'Look, I haven't had the best of luck with guys. Or relationships. But the one thing I really cannot stand is . . .' Robyn trained her finger on the pub now and jabbed at that. 'It's just so . . .' She struggled to find the right word: territorial; stalkery . . .

Frightening.

'Look, I'm sorry,' said Watts. 'I just didn't want you to—'

'Believe it or not, I *can* look after myself.'

'That wasn't what . . . You said you wanted that drink,' he offered, turning the phone call back on her.

'And I did. I still do. Just not with you anymore, Ashley.' He looked like a puppy that'd just been told off for being on the couch. 'Goodnight.'

Robyn thought about going back inside the pub, then remembered what the barman had said; he hadn't exactly been well disposed to her in the first place. Instead, she headed off down the road in the direction of The Majestic. There was no way she was going back to Vicky's just yet, but she certainly didn't want to spend any more time here with Watts. Robyn looked over her shoulder just once more, to see he was watching her walk away, and almost felt sorry for him.

Then she'd turned the corner and was at the hotel.

Robyn had never really spent much time in here, because when you were younger you just didn't – those prices, the notion that somehow it was too upper class – but unlike The Barnacle, there was nothing she found inside to indicate it might have changed in any way since she'd been in Golden Sands last. The outside certainly hadn't, as she'd already noted, but if anyone had touched the inside then she'd be amazed. Faded grandeur, wasn't that what they called it? All gold and maroons, but décor that had definitely seen better days.

The bar was open, and that was all she cared about – though there were less people in there than at the pub. Probably because they were charging about three times more for their drinks, as she soon discovered.

Robyn drifted around a bit, taking in the place – the staircase, the function rooms downstairs, the ballroom, which was showing a movie to about three people who looked asleep. She glanced at posters for future events, craft fairs and such, coach trips, a medium who was doing a show there every Thursday.

Then she found a quiet corner and nursed her drink. Had a couple more after that, just to pass the time . . . there was no signal in the hotel either, at least not for visitors, so she couldn't even ring Cav (not that it was a good idea when she'd been drinking) or check her mails. But, when she figured it was late enough, she headed to reception so they could arrange a taxi.

'Thanks,' she told the stocky woman wearing an ill-fitting waistcoat and sporting a bow tie. 'Oh, just one more thing. Do you have any rooms available at all?'

'We're full at the moment,' the lady told her; Robyn found that hard to believe. 'But there are some singles opening up next week.'

She told her she'd bear it in mind. It was definitely an option in the short term.

Then she'd got in the taxi when it arrived, had gone back to Vicky's, and headed off to bed without speaking to anyone. Vicky was passed out on the sofa anyway.

Taking a couple of sleeping pills, she'd knocked herself out till the morning. She didn't want to hear any more knocking. See any more shadows.

Then she'd woken up, remembered what had happened.

And prayed that it had all just been a bad dream.

Chapter 12

She would have prayed, if she thought it'd do any good.

But, unlike her mum, Vicky had never really been very religious – not that it had done that woman any favours in the end. Vicky hadn't set foot inside the chapel at Golden Sands since her Sunday school days, and even then she hadn't really taken much notice of what they'd been trying to teach her.

Perhaps if she had, if she'd believed, then none of this would have happened to her. To her family. Was God taking it out on her because she'd never actually thought he was real? Did she think he was real now? A vengeful deity who'd smitten her because of her misdeeds? Was that better than nothing? Than randomness?

If there really was a God, she thought to herself, then surely he wouldn't have let this happen in the first place; not just to her, she was nobody special, but to Mia. To take away that little girl's daddy, who she thought the world of . . . well, that just made him a special kind of bastard, didn't it?

Vicky didn't really believe in all that, angels and harps and whatnot, but she wanted to believe in *something* after you were gone. That it wasn't just blackness and misery forever. She knew what Jay's mum, Julie, believed – she'd talked about it often enough at the school gates, Vicky dismissing it as nonsense. Yet it gave the woman comfort, gave her the peace she'd been severely lacking. But you had to be really desperate to try something like that, didn't you?

You mean really desperate like you are right now? she reminded herself. Her husband gone, no one to turn to. And the one person she *had* turned to, the person who'd become a stranger, had upset her child so much.

Mia. In floods of tears, looking at those photos of her dad in the morgue. It had been bad enough for Vicky to see them, a reminder of the live version. But for a kid that young . . . Robyn's fault, all Robyn's.

Except it wasn't, and she knew it wasn't. Her cousin had come all this way to help her, dropping everything when she'd just gone through a trauma of her own. Vicky couldn't begin to imagine what she'd been through in the lock-up. It was terrifying. It was what she'd always worried would happen with her cousin, the way she was with guys. One of these days, she'd warned her, you'll get a wrong 'un. Except Sykes hadn't been some fella she'd gone off with for a one-night stand in uni, he'd been somebody her cousin had been hunting. Her other profession, putting herself in harm's way like that. Did she have a death wish or something? Couldn't think much of herself.

But she remembered then about her being jealous of Vicky's life. A life that had escaped her. After everything she'd told Vicky the other night, it was no longer mutual. Vicky didn't crave the excitement that came with Robyn's world anymore, that had come with uni and then . . . whatever job you'd call this. Consultant, wasn't it?

The files had been part of that, part of the process of trying to help her – Vicky understood that now she'd had time to calm down. Would have known it back when they were arguing if she'd been thinking clearly, if she ever believed she'd think clearly again.

You know what helps with that?

She did. More alcohol . . . Except it didn't, it only made things worse. Rather than making things clearer it made you not care they were so messed up. Smoking, then, which she'd taken to doing out the back when Mia wasn't around. Fuck it, there were worse things than dying from fags.

Only she should be thinking about her daughter, about how she was the one person she'd got left. No, she had Robyn. Robs . . . Now that she was back. If she really *was* back. She'd already been talking about moving out to The Majestic, though Vicky could hardly say she blamed her after the way she'd carried on. If only her cousin had put the files somewhere safer.

But you know how Mia gets into everything. Nothing's safe around here.

Bloody hell. Bollocks. What she needed was her mum and dad, needed to talk to them more than anything. Needed Simon. Needed to know what happened, if he was okay.

Okay? What the fuck are you talking about, girl. He's dead! Dead and gone!

But Jay's mum . . . Julie said—

Don't. Just don't even go there.

All of this shit going round and round in her brain, it was no wonder she couldn't think. Conversations with herself, arguing with – Robs – herself.

Better than conversations with the dead.

Depended very much on what you believed. If you believed in something. *Do you? Do you believe, Vicky?*

She should talk to Robyn, apologise. Let her talk to Mia, perhaps? Might even do some good. Couldn't make things any worse, could it? Was better than this plan of action, surely? Where she'd wait for Tracy to be upstairs playing with Mia, wait for Robyn to be out – like she was again today, God knows where – and then ring . . .

Ring up Julie.

Like she was doing now. Desperate, see? Needed that peace. Needed to talk to—

'Hello,' said the voice down the line.

Vicky took the cordless into the living room and kept her voice down when she answered: 'Hello . . . Hi, Julie?'

'Vicky? Vicky is that you? Oh, I've been so worried about you. I tired ringing a few times, but got a woman who told me you couldn't come to the phone.'

'That was Tracy, the FLO,' Vicky told her.

'Oh, yeah. Right.' Julie said it like she was talking from experience, and she probably was. She never went into much detail about what had happened in her past, but Vicky knew it was bad. She knew the woman had lost a lot: a whole life, not just a daughter.

'She was just being protective of me.'

'Quite so,' said Julie. 'Are you all right? No, scratch that. Of course you're not.'

'No, I don't think I am at all.'

'I'm so, so sorry, Vicky,' the woman told her. 'If there's anything I can do . . .'

'Well,' said Vicky, looking over her shoulder, then around her. 'There is actually. That woman you see, the one who helped you. Bella, isn't it?'

There was a pause, then: 'Yes.'

'Julie, I think I need to see her too.'

'Are . . . are you sure about this. I didn't think . . . You didn't strike me as someone who'd want to—'

'Were *you*?' Vicky broke in. 'Before what happened, happened I mean?'

Another pause. 'There's a session a bit later on. It's Kim's day off, so she's picking Jay up from school and babysitting for a while.' Kim was Julie's next-door neighbour. Nice girl, studying to be a nurse so she welcomed any extra cash she could get. 'Is there someone . . . Is Mia . . .?'

'She'll be fine with Tracy for a while. To be honest, she's not come out of her room much in the last day or so. There was a bit of an upset.'

'To do with her dad?'

'To do with her dad,' Vicky confirmed, biting back the tears. 'Look, Julie. I-I'm just feeling a bit lost right now, can you understand that?'

A final hesitation, before the woman said: 'Yes. Yes, I can. Don't worry, all right? I'll have a word and see if you can join us. I'm sure it'll be fine. She doesn't turn people away who are in need.'

'Thanks,' said Vicky, slumping down on the sofa before she collapsed. 'Thank you, Julie. I really appreciate it.' Then she looked around for the pad and the pen she always used for her shopping lists, the one Robyn had used last, scribbling down an address.

'Do you want me to swing by for you?' Julie asked.

'No, no. I'll meet you there,' she told her, before saying her goodbyes. Vicky pressed the button to hang up and then clutched the phone to her chest. She didn't know why, but she felt like a weight had been lifted suddenly. Excited, hopeful, for the first time in days.

Hopeful, but more than a little scared as well.

Chapter 13

She'd had to return eventually.

Figured that morning it was best to get out of the way again, avoid her cousin as much as possible – the only conversation between them being a quick word about Robyn possibly moving out to the hotel. Vicky had looked stunned by that, but hadn't said anything; what had Robyn expected, begging? Avoiding Mia hadn't been a problem, because she was still in her room, had locked out the world. Just like she did in hers when things got too much. The only people who'd seen her had been Tracy and her mum, and apparently 'Aunty Robs' had gone from flavour of the month to public enemy number one in a very short space of time.

Robyn had planned on taking a drive up to see Sebastian Boyd, those warnings from O'Brien just making her want to stick her oar in all the more. But on the way, she couldn't stop thinking about the shitty last couple of days. All she'd wanted last night was a bit of time away from things, to have a drink and maybe talk a bit of shop with Watts (Had it been a date? A drink? Had he *thought* it was a date? She'd probably given him that impression; she was good at that). But no, that wasn't allowed apparently . . .

And John, she'd been thinking about John too. He would have ended up being just another memory in the end, even if something had happened with him. But you never knew. You just never knew – and now she never would. Because of Watts. Watts who was clearly interested in her: hero worship tipping over into . . . Watts, who had that whole toy boy thing going for him, and yet—

Bloody hell, Robyn, what's wrong with you? Just what the fuck is wrong with you?

How long have you got? she answered.

Distracted, she decided it probably wasn't the best of times to be going up to see Boyd. She wouldn't be on form; that was for sure. Anyway, she seemed to be driving away from Golden Sands. Driving . . . Just driving.

GO HOME!

No, not yet. Just escaping from a place that no longer made her feel welcome. Driving to somewhere a little further down the coast, apparently, parking up and walking again. Grabbing a pub lunch in a nice little place she'd spotted which, if she'd caught it in winter, would have had a roaring fire going. The perfect spot to sip a fine brandy and watch the waves crash onto the shore. Now, that place *did* have personality. Bags of it.

She'd called up Cav then, because, unlike some areas she could mention, the signal here was strong.

'Oh, hi Robyn.'

'I-I didn't catch you at a bad time, did I?'

'You know how it is, when is there ever a good time?' he'd replied, but then laughed to show it was all right. 'How're things?'

'They're . . .' She'd almost burst into tears, but didn't want to do that on the phone with him. He'd have come to the coast to see her if she had. But she really needed someone to talk to, needed to feel as if the whole world wasn't against her. Robyn gave him the broad strokes of what had happened since she got there – leaving out the bit about the previous night with Watts and John.

'Fuck,' he breathed when she was done. 'Sounds like a total

128

shitstorm. But listen, Robyn, you didn't do anything wrong. Kids do get into everything.' *You should know, right?* 'You left those files out of reach. How were you to know she'd get to them? It's not like you left them just lying around. Sounds like your cousin's pretty messed up, wanting to blame someone for something.'

'That's just it, I know exactly what's happening. And I should be able to . . . I don't know. I don't blame *her* for it.'

'I hate to say it, Robyn, but maybe you should just come back. I'm not even sure you should have gone in the first place, I thought you were . . . We all miss you here.'

We . . . Do you? she thought and then hated herself for it.

He's just a mate.

It was tempting to return, in spite of all the bad memories she'd run away from there. And if this was one of those crime shows on TV, she and Cav might have had a 'will they, won't they?' plotline that would have been stretched to breaking point over about eight seasons, ending happily ever after. But this was real life, and in real life he had Liz at home, his wife. He had those two kids who got into everything. Robyn wouldn't have wanted to get in the middle of that. She realised she'd zoned out and started listening once more.

'. . . doing any good there. Unless you think this is the kind of case you're used to dealing with? And even then . . .'

Robyn transferred the phone to her other ear. 'No. No, nothing to suggest that.'

'Then perhaps you should let this O'Brien person handle it.'

That was just it: did Robyn *trust* her to handle it? To get to the bottom of it? But why did that matter? Why was she doing this again? For Vicky? For Mia?

For herself?

'I . . .' She could hear someone in the background; they were calling to Cav and asking him something. 'I'd better let you get back to it. You sound busy.'

'It's nothing that . . . Ring me later if you want.'

'Yeah, I just might,' she told him. 'Thanks for listening, Cav.'

'Anytime, you know that.'

Then he was gone. Just like all the men in her life. Like Luke Thomas who she'd lost her virginity to. Like John, like . . .

It was no good, she had to make a decision. Go home, or go back to Golden Sands. She couldn't hide away forever in this oasis. So Robyn had walked back to her car, driven back to Vicky's – where the reporters were beginning to thin out once more – and let herself in. Worst-case scenario, she grabbed her stuff and slept in her Citroën till The Majestic had a room available. But it hadn't worked out like that at all. The TV was on when she let herself in, and Robyn popped her head around the corner to catch Tracy attempting to watch some late-afternoon soap. Robyn had no idea why, not when they were all apparently living in one.

'*Sharon, your husband's been found dead and buried on the beach. Strangled . . . oh, and a plane's just crashed into the corner shop!*'

The picture kept pixilating, giving the whole thing a weird surrealistic quality that was mesmerising Tracy. Eventually she realised she wasn't alone. 'Oh. It's you.'

'Hi,' said Robyn. 'Where's Vicky?'

'She went out. A while ago.'

'Okay.' And that was the end of that. Robyn decided it was probably for the best her cousin wasn't here – that way she could just pack up and get out quietly without Vicky even knowing what had happened.

As she headed to the stairs, though, she saw a figure at the top of them. A little girl who'd run and hugged her when she first arrived, almost knocking her off her feet. All that excitement was gone now, and she stood there in her pyjamas, bottom lip out, staring down at her. It was like Mia's batteries had run down and nobody had bothered to recharge her. Robyn thought about calling for Tracy, as Mia still seemed to be okay with her, but then the girl beckoned her with a cupped hand.

Swallowing dryly, Robyn put one foot on the bottom step, then another. Yesterday, she'd been suggesting this: a talk with Mia, trying to straighten things out. Now it was the last thing in the world she wanted – frightened she'd just muck things up even more – and her slowness reflected that.

By the time she'd got to the top, Mia had already returned to her room. Robyn followed her, saw that she'd climbed back into bed where she was surrounded now by cuddly toys – including one bear that looked like he'd been in a warzone (an ear missing, arm hanging off); obviously her oldest one, the toy that gave her the most comfort.

'Where have you been?' asked Mia softly as Robyn sat on the edge of the bed, keeping quite a bit of distance between them.

Did she mean since yesterday, last night, today? 'Just been driving, walking. Trying to clear my head. Get some things straight in my mind.' She didn't know whether Mia could understand that at all, but her niece gave a little nod. 'I know what happened.'

'Mummy shouted at you because of it. I heard her.'

'She was probably right to,' said Robyn. 'I should never have brought all that into the house.'

Mia looked close to tears, her eyes still red-raw from the last deluge. 'I shouldn't have gone in your room. Shouldn't have . . . I just wanted to see your stuff.'

'I know,' Robyn replied. 'Did your mum tell you what I do?'

The girl thought about this for a moment. 'A little, I guess. You teach people, like my teachers at school.'

'That's one of my jobs, yes. But older kids.' They'd call themselves adults, but in Robyn's experience they really weren't. Some of them acted younger than Mia. 'I teach them about . . .' She tapped her head to illustrate.

'What's in their brains.'

Robyn couldn't help laughing a little at that. 'Yeah, kind of.'

'And you're . . . Mum said you were kontifried to do that.'

It took a minute – quantified? – but then she laughed again. 'Qualified? It means I know all about it.'

'Yeah, that you're kwol . . . kwolifried. Are you?'

She thought about it for a moment, thought about all the troubles she was having herself at the moment. The way she wasn't really dealing with it all that well. 'I hope so,' she said to the girl. 'I really do.'

'And you're a police person too,' Mia said.

'Not quite, but I do work with them. I help the police catch people who are doing bad things.'

'Like Batman does.'

'Erm . . . Not quite.' She couldn't help thinking about Gordon then – about Gateside and what people called it. About how useless she'd been in Sykes' lock-up, so far from that comic book hero it was laughable. 'I just . . . well, I help them work out how those kinds of people think.'

'Oh.'

There was silence again for a few moments, so Robyn inched closer and continued: 'How did you feel after you saw those pictures?'

Mia gave a tiny shrug. 'Sad,' she said finally.

'Because you know what's happened to your daddy now?'

'A bad thing,' Mia said quietly. 'Like Cinnamon.'

Robyn frowned. 'Cinnamon?'

'The cat we had for a while. Somebody ran her over.' Mia then looked very serious and said, 'She died.'

'Then yes, that's right. Just like Cinnamon.'

'Nobody . . . I don't think the person went to prison for killing Cinnamon,' Mia went on.

'It . . . That was probably just an accident, sweetie.'

'Was what happened to Daddy an accident too?'

Robyn hesitated before answering that one, but knew she had to practise what she preached. What she'd said to Vicky about being open and honest with Mia. 'No,' she said finally.

'So . . . so you're going to help the police to catch who did the bad thing?'

It was a question that demanded an answer. A promise to a little girl, not just her mother who understood how the world worked. She could have said she'd try, or do her best like she'd said before. But Mia needed more than that. Needed to know someone was going to pay for this. 'Yes,' said Robyn. 'I will.'

Mia was quiet, hugged her bear harder than ever, before asking: 'Did . . . did something bad happen to you, Aunty Robyn?'

'I . . . Yes,' she said again.

'Is that why you haven't visited for so long?'

Robyn's answer had been about Sykes, about what had happened just before coming to Golden Sands and this line once again threw her completely; Mia had a habit of doing that. She opened her mouth to answer, but found she couldn't speak.

So her niece spoke again, saying quietly and sincerely: 'I'm sorry. I'm really sorry it happened to you.'

Robyn looked at her, and Mia looked back. Then suddenly she was reaching out for the girl, and Mia in turn was letting go of her bear and reaching out for Robyn. They fell into each other's arms, squeezing tight, neither wanting to let go. Robyn was aware that the girl was crying into her chest, but what surprised her was the fact she was crying as well. Crying in sympathy or . . .

As quickly as it had happened, Mia pulled away, breaking off the hug. 'You're not going away again, are you?' she asked.

'I-It depends on what your mum wants, really.'

'Because you argued?'

'Yeah,' said Robyn with a sigh, though she felt what had happened here this afternoon would go a long way to fixing that particular problem – once Vicky could see Mia wasn't a complete basket case or anything (not that Robyn had ever assumed she would be).

'I don't want you to go,' said Mia.

Robyn smiled. 'That will help, definitely.'

Mia smiled back, the first time since she'd seen her again. Immediately she frowned again, something obviously striking her. 'Where do you think Daddy is now? Is he with Cinnamon?'

Thrown again. Christ. Was Mia seriously asking her to answer one of the greatest mysteries of all time? Something people had debated and argued about for centuries? 'I-I don't know, love. I wish I did. I'd like to think so.' But did she really? Was that what she thought, what she believed in?

'Mummy's gone to talk to him,' Mia stated suddenly. 'She told me before she said goodbye. So maybe she'll ask.'

'Talk to who?' Robyn was thrown for the third time in as many minutes.

'Daddy.'

Now it was her turn to frown. What was Mia talking about? How could Vicky . . . *Jesus*, thought Robyn, *she's not going to do something stupid, is she?* The woman was lost, but she still had her daughter.

'Before she said goodbye.'

She still had . . . she still had her cousin.

Robyn got up, apologising and racing to the door. 'Where are you going?'

'I just need to . . . to check on something,' she told Mia. It wasn't a lie. 'You stay here, sweetie, okay?'

Mia nodded reluctantly, but Robyn wasn't convinced she wouldn't follow. God, what was Vicky playing at? What was she planning on doing, chucking herself off a cliff or something? Or under a bus? Or just wading out into the sea, leaving her clothes on the beach? How would they find her? Maybe Tracy knew where she was heading, perhaps she'd told her something?

Robyn almost tripped, rushing down the stairs to get to the bottom, skidding around the corner and into the living room. 'What?' asked Tracy, tearing herself away from the soap and rising. 'What's happened? Is it Mia?'

A little out of breath (*you need to renew that gym membership, Robyn*), the psychologist shook her head. 'V-Vicky.'

'What?' Tracy asked a second time.

'Where is she?'

The woman stayed silent. 'I'm not sure I should—'

'Tracy!' snapped Robyn. 'Where the hell is my cousin? Mia says she's gone to talk to Simon.'

A look of dawning realisation passed across the FLO's face. 'Ah, well, as it happens, actually I think I do know what that's about,' she said.

'Tell me,' Robyn demanded.

Chapter 14

She'd waited at the entrance to the place, after the cab had dropped her off.

Anything else would have felt like she was intruding. It felt that way anyway, truthfully. Like she shouldn't really be here. Like all of this had been a really big mistake. What had she been thinking?

Vicky had almost turned around and headed away again, at least twice, but something kept her rooted to the spot. Something had wanted her to come here, wanted her to stay. So she'd waited, even when three or four other people had turned up – walking past her and knocking on the door, being let inside. Still she'd waited for Julie, who'd shown up just as she'd decided again she was going to back out.

'I'm sorry. Really sorry,' said her friend, rushing over. 'Kim was running late, so I had to pick up Jay and wait for her to come round.' She opened her arms and gave Vicky a hug.

'People have been going in,' said Vicky nervously.

'Don't worry, it won't have started yet. They'll be having a chat, a cup of tea or whatever. That's what usually happens first. Bella likes to put people at their ease.'

'I-I have to say, it's not what I imagined,' Vicky admitted, pointing back over to the place they were going. The place full of lots of other structures like it.

Julie let out a small chuckle. 'No. Me either when I first started. But it's not . . . Well, I'll let Bella explain to you when we get in there. She likes going through it all with new folk.'

And, with that, Julie took her arm, hooking hers through Vicky's. 'You ready?'

'I'll say yes,' Vicky replied, which meant she was anything but. She was trying very hard to stop trembling.

'Come on, don't be scared,' encouraged Julie and began walking so that Vicky didn't really have a choice but to move forwards. Through the gates of the caravan park, and towards the fifth van on the right – the place Julie had told her they'd be going. Bella's static caravan, permanently mounted on metal 'legs', a slab of concrete beneath it to keep it off the ground. There was a new style VW Beetle parked next to it, lime green in colour, which made it look more like a grasshopper than the insect it was named after. And shoved up against the door were some metal steps, four to be precise, which Julie climbed up first – rapping on the door when she reached the top.

There was another wait of about a minute or so and the door suddenly opened. Standing there holding it was a plump woman in her sixties, with a severe perm, wearing the most hideous flowery dress Vicky had ever seen. She thought to herself, *yes, that's exactly how I pictured Bella. Talk about a cliché* . . . To her surprise, though, Julie said:

'Miranda, how are you?'

The woman pulled a bit of a face, but said, 'I'm all right, I suppose. It's coming up to that time of year again.'

'I know, I'm sorry.' Julie seemed to remember that she had company and tilted herself sideways so that this Miranda person could see Vicky. 'Oh, where are my manners. Miranda, this is Vicky. She's new.'

Vicky held up a hand to say hello.

'How do you do, Vicky,' said the larger lady.

'Miranda's husband passed a couple of years ago on . . .'

'Next Friday,' Miranda clarified, sadly. 'Forty years we were together. Inseparable. I still miss him every single day.'

'Vicky's husband is the one—'

'Yes, yes. I read about that in *The Torch*. So sorry, love. Oh, look at me, blocking the way. Come on inside, the pair of you.'

Miranda moved and Julie was able to step through finally, leaving Vicky to climb the steps and do the same. She had to say, when she entered, the size of the place took her by surprise. The caravan was like a TARDIS, way bigger on the inside than it looked from out there. To her left there was the kitchen bit, complete with oven and sink for washing up. On her right there was a booth-like table, with seating that was fixed to the walls – but she was willing to bet could be made up into a spare bed. Behind her, a small door was closed – the toilet perhaps – but the one next to that was open and she could see a glimpse into a room with a double bed inside it. Next to that was another closed door, which was probably where the fridge and food shelves were.

Everyone was down the far end of the caravan, where the bay window was. Hugging this was padded seating, which ran round in a semi-circle, and that's where the rest of the people she'd seen entering were. Miranda joined them once more, the willowy woman at the side of her passing back the cup of tea she'd been holding while Miranda answered the door.

Vicky followed Julie up through the caravan until the woman stopped, turning to introduce her to the others. 'Everyone, this is Vicky.' Now she looked back at her friend, to present her to the strangers sitting and watching. 'Vicky, this is Andrew.' She pointed to a man in his late forties, whose hair was jet-black apart from a couple of patches of grey at his temples that made him look like Reed Richards. He smiled a greeting. 'That's Keith.' Julie indicated the man sitting next to Andrew, who was in contrast totally bald – and seemed to be making up for the fact by having a faint beard. Keith gave a small wave. 'Miranda you know . . .'

'Hello again, dear,' said the woman.

'And next to her is Fiona.' Who was of course the very thin lady to Miranda's left who'd been nursing the tea for her. 'Then there's—'

'I'm Bella,' came a voice from beside Vicky, a woman who'd been tucked away around the corner, at such an acute angle she hadn't really noticed her. Now she was standing, rising and holding out her hand – Bella didn't have a drink apparently, the only one not to – the first thing that struck Vicky was how young she was. Younger than her by a good few years, and pretty, with a short pixie cut that made her look almost elfin. Her intense grey-blue eyes were framed by dark lashes and thin eyebrows, the dark shade of lipstick she'd chosen completing the look. 'Bella Prescott,' the woman finished.

'P-Pleased to meet you,' said Vicky, shaking Bella's hand. The woman closed her eyes and then slowly opened them again, in a way that unnerved Vicky a little.

'And I you,' said Bella. Her voice was soft and soothing, with a musical lilt to it.

'Thanks for . . . I know this is short notice, but . . .'

Bella released Vicky's hand and waved hers. 'Don't mention it. Any friend of Julie's . . .'

Julie smiled at this, as if she hadn't realised she was classified as a friend yet. 'Bella's helped me so much, Vicky.'

'It wasn't really me who helped you,' Bella cut in. 'I was just the messenger. Your daughter was the one who wanted to tell you what happened wasn't your fault. The same as Andrew's wife and her accident.' Vicky saw the man tip his head, hiding his face so they couldn't see his sadness. 'Same as Keith's dad wanted him to know he was happy with his mum now, not in pain and never would be again.'

'And my Geoff, he just wanted to make sure I was all right,' Miranda chipped in. 'That I was coping, y'know? Typical Geoff, that is.'

'I'm . . . I'm not sure *I* am,' said Vicky.

''Course not. No one expects you to be,' Miranda told her. 'Not right now.'

Nothing was said about Fiona, and Vicky didn't ask – figured it was something private, that she might get a sense of it if she attended these meetings for long enough.

'Doesn't always work,' Bella warned her. 'And very rarely the first time. But you never know . . . Anyway, have some tea, Vicky, and sit yourself down where you can find room.'

'Oh, I'm okay, really,' she protested, but Julie furnished her with a cup anyway and they both sat down at the table. Absently, she wondered whether this was where the session would take place; if so, it really didn't look big enough for them all to fit around.

As if reading her thoughts, Bella – who was still standing – walked over and said: 'You were probably expecting something a bit more . . . All lace and candles, darkened rooms and lightning.' She gave a small laugh. 'The spirits of our lost loved ones are all around us, all the time. They're as likely to speak to us in the daylight as they are at night.'

There was a bit of chat after that, people nattering to each other over the tea – which was when Julie told her Bella also did an evening at The Majestic, for a much larger crowd. 'That's where I first saw her actually,' Julie clarified. 'She then suggested coming to this more . . . intimate gathering. She's a mental medium, Vicky, rather than a physical one. She *hears* the messages, like a kind of radio receiver – that's the way it was explained to me. A physical medium is the other kind. The kind that can be taken over, and that can actually be quite dangerous.' Julie sounded like she was repeating passages from a book, or from a pamphlet she'd been given about mediumship. 'Gifts like hers run in the family, apparently, and she's chosen to help folk with their troubles. Bella does a few of these kinds of afternoons a week; I can't speak for anyone else, but there aren't the words to express what a difference they've made to my life. I was in a very bad place when I found her.'

'And you think that . . .' Vicky shook her head, wasn't even sure what she was doing here in the first place. This had been a bad idea, a very bad idea indeed.

But it was also too late, because Bella was on her feet again and starting – already had a message coming in. 'Keith. It's your dad again, Keith.'

The bald man looked up at the roof of the caravan, as though he might see his late father's ghost floating around there. 'What is it, Pop?' asked Keith, as laid-back as if he was talking to the man on the phone. Vicky guessed he must have done this any number of times.

'He says you need to keep an eye on young Anthony. He's getting mixed up with a bad lot. That's how he puts it, a bad lot.' Vicky expected Bella to start talking in a deeper voice any minute, channelling Keith's father, but then she remembered what Julie had said about radios and physical mediums; Bella wasn't that kind . . . if you believed in any of this stuff, that was.

'At school?' asked Keith.

'No, these are older youths. He hangs around with them some-times at the park. You need to keep an eye on him or he's going to come to harm.'

Keith nodded, the information understood. 'Cheers, Dad, I will.'

'Now . . . who is . . .?' Bella let the sentence trail off. 'Fiona,' she said and the thin woman looked up, anxiously. 'Jodie knows about Linda. She says . . . she says it's okay. She just wants you to be happy, for things to work out. You have to let her go, move on.' Reading between the lines, Vicky could see that Fiona must have begun a relationship with someone else, that this Jodie person had been her partner and she'd lost her. That she was looking for . . . what, some kind of understanding? Permission to go ahead? Let her go, even if it meant not coming back here anymore, thought Vicky. Those weren't the words of someone who was trying to get one over on someone, just someone trying to help. So maybe Bella might be able to—

'I . . . I don't want to,' Fiona said then, eyes glistening.

'She still loves you, Fee.' That name clearly had some resonance for Fiona, because she cried freely at that point. Perhaps a pet name Jodie used to call her. 'She'll always love you. But this will be good for you, she promises.'

Fiona didn't look convinced, but managed a weak nod.

'All right, all right . . . My, you *are* talkative today, you guys, aren't you? Probably showing off for our newcomer.' Bella smiled.

The spirits showing off, or Bella in an effort to impress Vicky? The woman placed her fingers to her temple, and again Vicky was reminded of those movies Mia used to watch with Simon; the professor who was as bald as Keith, moving things with his mind, poking around inside *other people's* minds. 'Julie,' she said then and the woman Vicky had rung, come inside with, sat upright opposite her across the table. 'Julie, I'm getting Jordan again.'

'Jordan? Jordan sweetheart? I'm here.' The look of hope on Julie's face was incredible, the love coming off her in waves. Unlike the others though, Julie was looking from side to side her rather than upwards – taking what Bella had said about the spirits being around them to heart.

'She knows. Again, she wants you to let go of the guilt about what happened. You couldn't have known,' Bella informed the grieving woman. 'But there's something else today, something she hasn't said before but needs you to know. Something long overdue. She says . . .'

'Yes?' asked Julie, leaning forwards, desperate to hear the message.

'She says you need to let *him* know about Jay. Does that make sense?'

'Jay?' Julie shook her head, had obviously understood what was being said; she just didn't want to hear it.

'It's time, she says. Time for him to get to know his father. For his father to *know* about him.'

Julie put her hand to her mouth. 'I-I can't. He'll never forgive me. Neither of them will.'

142

'She says it'll be okay,' Bella passed on. 'In the end it'll all be okay. You have to trust in that.'

There was no nod this time, however. Julie was having some trouble processing things, apparently. She'd never really spoken much about Jay's dad, and Vicky didn't like to pry. From what she gathered from Mia – who hung about with the lad a lot – he didn't know who his father was. If Julie followed her late daughter's advice, though, he'd soon be finding out.

The medium received a couple more messages that afternoon, one for Miranda and one for Andrew, but nothing for Vicky. 'I'm sorry,' she told her. 'Sometimes it just goes that way. The departed . . .' She used that word when talking about them, never dead, just departed like they'd gone on a journey somewhere. Vicky supposed in some ways they had. 'Sometimes they can be a little confused when they first . . .'

That was fair enough if you were talking about Simon, but her mum? Her dad? If this was all real – and Vicky was still on the fence, no matter how desperate events had made her – then surely one of them could have told her *something*. 'It's . . . it's all right,' she told the medium. 'I wasn't really expecting—'

'Wait. Hold on a second,' interrupted Bella, face contorting as if whatever was happening was hurting her. 'It's faint but . . . Yes, I can hear something. Someone's coming through, calling your name.'

A shiver went up Vicky's spine, tears pricking her eyes.

Bella leaned against the side of the caravan, like she was a character in a Shakespeare play clutching at the scenery. 'Oh, wow . . . They're coming through loud and clear now. I think they were worried you'd . . . we'd given up on them.'

Vicky was rising herself now, standing on legs she wasn't quite sure would hold her. 'W-Who . . . who is it?' she asked, voice low and reedy.

Bella turned and looked at her seriously. 'It's your husband, Vicky. It's Simon.'

Chapter 15

Of all the bloody stupid things to . . .

Robyn changed down gears, negotiating a corner and almost not making it. Not concentrating properly on what she was doing, head buzzing with thoughts about what she'd just found out. As if Vicky wasn't messed up enough, she'd gone to visit one of *those* people. The kinds of people who made money out of others' misery, who gave them false hope when they were at their most vulnerable. If only she'd been there, at home with her when—

But you weren't, were you? You were miles away, on the phone to Cav, remember? Needed someone to talk to yourself, a friendly voice, someone to lean on. That's all Vicky needed as well, and she turned to—

Robyn had recognised the name as soon as she'd heard it, as soon as Tracy told her she'd overheard the conversation on the phone between Vicky and someone called Julie; surprise, surprise, Tracy listening in again. 'She's rung a few times, asking if Mrs Carter was all right. Seems nice enough.' But then the mention of that other name, Bella – someone who'd helped Julie in the past. And that poster from The Majestic had come back to Robyn immediately.

'A psychic,' she said to Tracy.

'Yeah. I think that's probably where she's gone.'

'Why didn't you try to stop her?'

'I don't get involved in stuff like that,' Tracy informed her tersely. 'It's really none of my business!'

Robyn nodded, conceding her point. 'Right, okay. Fair enough. Do you at least know where this woman lives?'

Tracy had just shaken her head. And then some proper Nancy Drew stuff, spotting the notepad again and seeing that it had been used – the indentations there on the top sheet. Asking Tracy for a pencil and rubbing that piece of paper furiously with it to reveal the address, like a magician waving a wand. Simple, basic detective stuff from too many cop shows to count, yet there was a reason it kept being used: because it worked. As she was ripping it off, she was asking if Tracy was okay to watch Mia – because they could both hear her stirring upstairs.

'Look, maybe you should just leave her to it? My nan went to see one years ago, said it really helped.'

'The only people they're interested in helping is themselves,' Robyn retorted. 'I'm not having Vicky fall for any of that rubbish!' Tracy looked at her, was about to say something, then realised today really wasn't the day. And suddenly Robyn was off, out through the front door and into the car – the uniforms still doing their job of keeping what press were still present off their backs.

She consulted the map again, picking out the fastest route down to the caravan park. Which was where she was on her way to now, before it was too late. Before Vicky got suckered into anything. It wasn't as if she had money to spare at the moment. Just the other night, she'd been so worried about finances that Robyn herself had offered to pay for the funeral when they eventually released Simon's body – and now this! But anyone could see that Vicky wasn't in her right mind (*like you can talk!*). What was next, joining a bloody cult or something?

People were aware of what had happened, as well, so this Bella character was bound to know – just enough to convince Vicky she was on the level. That's all they needed, that's all it took. But Robyn was here to make sure she wasn't taken for a ride.

Assuming you get there without killing yourself, that is, she thought, stamping on the brake pedal, easing up slightly on the speed after accelerating out of the turn. It didn't take too long to arrive at the park, which had a lovely view of the sea. In addition to being rented out to holidaymakers, these static caravans were also home to some of Golden Sands' permanent residents, including the medium she was looking for.

Parking up with a screech of tyres, Robyn was out of the car in seconds and racing towards the number of the caravan she had on the graphite-coated paper in her hand. Seconds after that, she was pounding on the door, only for it to be opened up by a woman whose hair looked like it had once been a fiery shade of red, but had faded over time. What hadn't faded was her temper, which was on display when Robyn demanded entrance.

'You can't just barge in here, this is private property!' growled the woman.

'Robs?' came a voice from just behind her, from a figure also standing. 'It's okay, Julie, this is my cousin.'

'It's *not* okay,' Robyn threw back. 'What's going on here?'

'I think you know already,' said another woman who was standing, this time with short dark hair. 'Or you wouldn't be here.'

'Vicky, come on,' said Robyn holding out her hand. 'Let's go.'

'Robs. Robs, you don't understand. Simon was here. I . . . I talked to him.' This was what she'd been afraid of.

'No. No, he wasn't, Vicky. Simon's gone. He's dead.'

'Yes, I *know!*' Now it was Vicky who was snapping, her own temper on display. 'I know he's . . .' There was a hitch in her voice, a catch there as her cousin thought about the words she was saying. 'But still, he was here, Robyn. He was talking to me.'

Robyn was simply gaping at her, not really understanding. The next thing Vicky said though totally knocked her for six.

'He was talking to me and . . . I know now.'

'Know what?' asked Robyn.

'I know who killed him,' came the solemn reply.

Chapter 16

Robyn stared at the man from behind the glass.

The two-way mirror, to be precise. She couldn't believe what had happened since she'd practically had to drag Vicky away from that séance, from Bella Prescott and her followers. Believers, those who *wanted* to believe. A group that now included Vicky, sadly: the conviction on her face when she stated that she'd been talking to her deceased husband was undeniable. She totally and wholeheartedly believed it, and wouldn't listen to a word Robyn had to say on the subject; had only come with her in the first place so that she didn't cause a scene. *Even more* of a scene.

'You're being played,' Robyn told her, told all of the people in that caravan. 'Can't you see that? She's taking advantage of your grief.'

'She's doing nothing of the kind!' the lady called Julie insisted.

'Nobody's got a gun to our heads!' said another one, with a few more miles on the clock and a few more pounds as well. 'We're all here of our own free will.'

'Free will?' Robyn had harrumphed at that point. Did they even have any free will anymore, now that this Bella person had poisoned their minds? She directed her next barrage at the medium. 'You should be ashamed of yourself. You belong down there on the pier with the other fortune tellers staring into their crystal balls!'

'Please. Please everyone,' said the 'psychic' in question. 'Let her go. And, Vicky, you know where I am if you need me.'

Vicky had given a nod that said she'd be back. Not if Robyn had anything to bloody well do with it, she wouldn't – and to her knowledge she hadn't returned since. Robyn hoped that was the case anyway.

'But before you leave,' said Bella. 'Your mum has something she wants to say to you.'

They'd both turned, Robyn expecting this charlatan to impart something from Aunty Sue, general words of wisdom she could have dredged up from anywhere, but instead she said: 'She says you don't have to be like her, Robyn. That there's time to change.'

'What did you just say?' That was it – Robyn practically lunged at the woman, and if Vicky hadn't held her back, pulled her away, she didn't know what she would have done. Pretending to be *her* mother! Jesus Christ! She knew nothing about her or her family!

'And she says to be careful,' Prescott called out after them as they exited, almost tripping down those metal steps.

'God, Vicky,' she'd said to her cousin when they were inside her car – the people from the caravan having gathered outside it to watch them leave. 'What's got into you? There was no need for . . . For this! You have people who care about you, who . . . who *love* you.'

'Like you, you mean?'

'*Of course* me!' Robyn said, gunning the engine, wanting to put as much distance between them and this place – that woman – as possible. 'And Mia.'

'Leave Mia out of this,' said Vicky.

'How can I, when you told her you were going off to have a talk with her dad?' Robyn filled her in about the conversation they'd had that afternoon, how there was no need for her to be mad anymore because the pair of them had smoothed things over. That

149

she was making progress getting the little girl to understand about her father, maybe even come to terms with what had happened. 'Then . . . this. How am I supposed to . . . How can you possibly explain to your daughter what you've been doing, Vicky?'

Her cousin was silent.

'Do you know, she made me promise to find out who did this. Who killed Simon.'

'I *know* who killed him, didn't you hear me back there?' Vicky exclaimed.

'Okay, all right,' said Robyn as she drove them back towards town. 'Let's have it then. Who killed him?' This was all she needed, crime solving from beyond the grave . . . Now they really were in the middle of an episode of *The X-Files*.

Vicky was sobbing, gurgling it through a mouth filled with phlegm. 'I-I didn't want to believe it, but . . . well, now he's told me. Apologised for it.'

'For what?'

'He cheated on me, Robs. Simon admitted it.'

Robyn nearly drove the car off the road and onto the pavement. 'I . . . Vicky, it was just that woman, Prescott. Just her talking, not—'

Vicky shook her head, a violent shake. 'No. No, you didn't hear it. I could tell they were his words. The way he spoke, it was—'

'It *wasn't* him, Vicky! Just a trick – all of that kind of stuff is. Haven't you ever seen Derren Brown? Those people who debunk it on TV?'

'She hears the voices, Robs!'

'So do the people *I* deal with, and look what happens to them!'

'I know it. I feel it in here,' Vicky maintained, slamming her fist into her chest. 'I didn't want to believe the rumours, but . . . There's this woman called Lisa Newton. She's always had a thing for Simon, because he's kind. Because he's nice. Her husband works with him on the fishing boats.'

'And this is what that Prescott person told you?'

Vicky looked across at her. 'Not in so many words. She said Simon was sorry. That he hadn't meant to hurt me, that there had been someone else and it was just the once, but . . .' Vicky was shaking her head again, more slowly this time, resigned to the fact. 'It all makes sense, don't you see?'

Robyn couldn't say that she did, and told her so.

'Graham, her husband. It *has* to be him. He's a violent man. If he found out about Simon—'

'You don't even know there was anything to find out *about*!' argued Robyn. 'Just what that faker told you.'

'She's not . . . I was sceptical at first but—'

'Ouija boards, knock once for yes and twice for no . . .'. *The knocking, that knock* . . . 'Give me a fucking break,' Robyn spat. 'They find out about you, use it to convince you. Wouldn't even have been that hard for her – you've been in the news, Vicky! So has what's happened.' In the time since, she'd also found out Julie had been too, back in the day; Bella must have found out about that as well. As for the rest of them, the cosy little welcoming tea sessions, listening to the chat in those. It wasn't hard to see where she got her material from. All one big scam, and Robyn hated her for what she was doing.

'Julie believes in it.'

'She's as crackers as the rest of them, if she does,' said Robyn.

'Then I suppose I'm crazy too?'

Robyn had sighed. 'Look, you can't go hurling accusations around based on . . . On what? On something some Madame Rose-type character said?'

'It's something. It's more than we've got at the moment,' Vicky said. 'More than you've been able to find out.'

Good grief, she'd only been trying for a few days! Didn't Vicky know how long these types of investigations could last? Then again, how would she? Her cousin wasn't a part of that world; sometimes Robyn wished she wasn't herself.

But she'd steer her right, try and find healthier ways for her to process her emotions than trips to see Bella fucking Prescott. She'd already done enough damage, leading Vicky to think her husband had been playing away. That kind of thing affected how you handled your grief, and she could see the more Vicky thought about it the angrier she got. 'So how much did she charge for this information?' Robyn had asked at the time.

'Nothing. She doesn't ask for money, only donations. What you think it's worth,' said Vicky, sniffing back the last of her tears – her stubbornness drying them up.

'She charges for the stage show, though, right? I've seen the posters up in the hotel.'

Vicky remained silent. Either she didn't know, or knew that nothing she could say would ever convince Robyn. And about that she was correct: nothing would. It was all a far cry from behavioural sciences. Deductive reasoning. Just a way of hanging everything on the dead, letting the living off the hook.

None of this had stopped Vicky from reporting it to the police, though she hadn't said anything about where it had come from. Only that she had reason to believe her husband had been cheating on her, that she thought it might be significant. The cops had, quite rightly, wanted to know why it had taken her so long to report it. Why she hadn't said anything the first time they'd questioned her, asking whether Simon had any enemies or not. Vicky's stance had been that she didn't want to admit to her husband's infidelity, but certain information had come to light that made it hard to ignore. What that information was, she'd rather not say.

Which was why O'Brien and Watts had called around at Lisa Newton's place. (In spite of how they'd left things, Ashley Watts had texted Robyn to let her know . . . probably looking for a way back into her good books.) Newton denied having a thing with Simon, naturally; she would have done that whether it had been true or not.

'She'd looked guilty, though,' Watts had told Robyn when she finally agreed to have coffee with him, the only way she could get that information first-hand. 'When we pushed her, she finally admitted that her and Simon had been good friends. *Very* good. That he was a shoulder to cry on when things were going wrong with Graham . . . but that's all. So she maintains.'

Simon, he was so lovely, he didn't have any enemies; he'd make friends with anyone, you know? Would help anyone out.

'Going wrong?'

Watts nodded. 'She had bruises, old ones but . . . you could see them on her . . .' The DS had touched his own shoulder and neck. 'Nothing unusual there, mind. Her husband's been done for GBH in the past; it's common knowledge Graham Newton likes to knock her about. He's someone we've had our eye on for some time. Even suspect him of being involved in the drugs scene here at Golden Sands.'

'There's a drugs scene at Golden Sands?' spluttered Robyn. It was news to her. But then most places had their problems with drugs these days, didn't they? Nowhere was immune, especially in a time where drug-related deaths were at their highest since records began in this country. She thought back to whether there'd been anything like that when she was younger, and drew a blank. Perhaps she just hadn't hung about with the right . . . the wrong people.

'Yeah,' Watts had said, unable to look at her. It made her wonder whether he'd been part of that 'scene' when he was younger, maybe even used? Or was it just because he felt bad about his behaviour when he'd been with her before? Something he brought up towards the end of the meeting. 'Listen, about the other night. I'm . . . It's not like me, really it's not. I'm not one of *those* kinds of guys.'

'You were doing a very good impression of one,' Robyn informed him.

'Yeah,' he repeated. 'I'm sorry. It was just . . . I saw that guy with you and he looked like he was bothering you and . . . and I suppose I was a bit—'

153

'We were just talking, Ashley. Y'know, like grown-ups do.' That was unfair of her, but she hadn't been able to resist it. Luckily, he didn't seem to take offence. Watts nodded, but he was frowning like he still couldn't understand why she'd been talking to the guy. If she was honest with herself, did she either?

Fast worker . . .

She says you don't have to be like her, Robyn.

'I guess I thought . . .' Watts began.

'You thought you were on a promise, that it?'

'No . . . *No*, I didn't . . . I just figured we could maybe get to know each other a bit better.'

'Ashley, I do like you, but . . .' Robyn didn't know what else to say, so she told him they should just forget the incident. Move on. 'Okay, what's the next step?' she asked, and there was a brief flash where he was confused again – did she mean him and her? – so she quickly cleared that up: 'In the case. What's happening now?'

'Oh,' said Watts. 'We're bringing Graham in to have a little chat. Uniform have been sent out to nab him.'

She thought about it for a moment, then said, 'I don't suppose there's any chance I could be around for that, is there? The chat I mean?'

His reaction had been one of complete and utter terror. If O'Brien even knew he was talking to her about Lisa Newton behind her back, she'd go mental – which was why she appreciated it. But, he said he would ask on her behalf. 'You never know, I might catch her at a good time.'

Robyn wondered if there were ever any good times in O'Brien's life, but again that was unfair; she knew nothing about that woman either, little more than she did about Watts. Maybe the good times in the inspector's life coincided with when Robyn buggered off and left her alone to do her job. When she'd bugger off completely.

GO HOME!

She'd waited next for Watts to get back to her, contemplating calling Gordon up again to ask yet another favour of him, when the DS had rung and told her that – miracle of miracles – O'Brien had agreed. 'You can come in and watch while we question him,' Watts said, sounding as shocked as she was. He must have caught her at the *very best* of times.

But then, as she realised when she got to the station and saw the glee on O'Brien's face at the prospect of getting Graham Newton in an interview room, there was no reason not to have Robyn around. Might even help, in fact – now that attention had been diverted from The Castle Spa and Sebastian Boyd's business dealings (the DI didn't know yet that Robyn still fully intended on chasing up that particular lead).

The perfect scapegoat.

'Nasty piece of work, this one, Doctor,' O'Brien had warned her. 'Gave uniform a bit of a . . . hard time when they found him. But anyway, he's here. Any excuse to get him off the streets.'

Though of course it would just be for a little while unless something else cropped up. Newton was only doing the routine 'helping the police with their inquiries' thing at the moment. He wasn't under arrest; for one thing, there was no evidence to charge him with anything. Robyn couldn't help agreeing with the inspector when she saw him sitting there in the interview room, however. A nasty piece of work pretty much summed the guy up, in her professional opinion.

She stared at him through the glass, studying that scowling face. He was the living personification of hatred, like it was oozing from his pores. If it weren't for the fact his features were a little . . . off (too squashed up in the centre of his face) and of course for the fact that his expression said he loathed everybody and everything – he might have been handsome. His hair was more matted than tousled, and the vest he was wearing not only showed off his considerable mass (not fat exactly, though not toned either – just bulk), but also the more imaginative examples of his tattoos, which wasn't saying much.

It wasn't that Robyn had anything against those – it was a way of expressing yourself, and some she'd seen were like works of art. Graham Newton's, however, were more like the work of an epileptic blind person. Amateur was being generous, and she had to wonder how many of them had been done while he'd been inside. Something resembling a skull competed for space on his arm with a winged creature that had horns. And across his chest, running up onto the other shoulder, was the delightful phrase 'Fuck This Shit!' If it hadn't been old and faded, it might well have been a statement about where he'd found himself that day.

The uniformed officer who was standing by the door – and looked about nine stone soaking wet, his clothes hanging from him – kept glancing over at the detainee nervously, and Robyn couldn't say that she blamed him. Had he been one of the coppers who'd 'escorted' Newton in? He'd had backup if that was the case. If he was of a mind to, Newton could have picked him up and broken him like kindling over his knee.

How long he'd been waiting was anyone's guess, though there was an empty cup next to him on the table – so at least the length of time it took to drink a tea or coffee. She wasn't sure who was the most relieved when O'Brien and Watts entered the room, the PC or Newton, for entirely different reasons: the former because he wasn't alone anymore with this person; the latter because he just wanted to get on with this, say his piece and hopefully get let out so he could pummel his wife again.

Robyn found herself thinking about that, about how someone like Lisa could end up with Graham. She didn't know the woman, only from Watts' description, but she seemed like a nice person.

Nice, like Simon. Wanted to be treated better? No, they didn't even know that was real. That they'd even been together.

Had Graham Newton always been like this, or had he acted nicer to get that woman in the first place? It happened. But why did she stay with him? That, unfortunately, was also something she was all too familiar with from her time working with the

156

police: brainwashing, gaslighting, whatever you wanted to call it. Or just plain scared to leave. That happened too, though Robyn wished to God it didn't. One day he'd do more than just beat her up, and – like O'Brien – now Robyn herself wanted to put this scum inside where he couldn't hurt anyone except people like him.

'About fucking time!' were his first words to the detectives. 'What's all this about?'

O'Brien took a seat opposite Newton and Watts nestled in beside her. 'Good afternoon to you too, Mr Newton,' the inspector said, giving him a run for his money in the scowling stakes.

'I should fucking sue you,' growled the man, folding his arms. 'Get you charged with something.'

'On what grounds?' she enquired, hardly able to keep the disbelief from her voice.

'Harassment.'

'*Have* you been harassed?' O'Brien looked around her. 'Are we harassing you now? DS Watts, would you say we were harassing this gentleman?'

Watts shook his head.

'Fucking yes,' Newton countered.

'By asking you to come in for a talk? Giving you a nice cuppa?'

'Your lot, you've always had it in for the likes of me.'

'And who might the likes of you be, exactly?'

Newton thought about it, then said nothing in case he might incriminate himself. 'What's this about? Shouldn't I have a lawyer present?' said Newton.

'Do you think you need one?' asked O'Brien. 'You're not under arrest, Mr Newton. That's been explained to you.'

'Then I can go, right?'

'Be my guest. Or don't, as the case may be.' O'Brien held out her hand, waved it at the door. Newton half-rose, then stopped when she continued: 'But be advised that your lack of co-operation here might not look good. Might look a tad . . . suspicious. We may also want to take another look at your lack of co-operation when our lads picked you up.' O'Brien left another deliberate pause. 'If you want to talk about who's been harassing who, or who should really be charged.'

He sat back down again.

'Better,' said O'Brien. 'So, shall we get started?'

'What's all this about?' Newton asked for a third time.

The DI switched on the recorder that was also on the table, stating for the record who was in the room and what time the interview was commencing. Newton shifted about in his seat. Robyn leaned in, staring at the man again, watching for any tiny reaction.

'Mr Newton.' Now it was Watts' turn to speak up, the suddenness of it and the shift in direction actually causing Newton to flinch. 'Tell us . . .

'How well did you know Simon Carter?'

Chapter 17

The girl in the black dress has followed the guy outside.

There are a few streetlamps dotted about, the moon up there in the sky – it's a clear night, hardly any clouds – and when she catches her reflection in the windows of the pub, she looks like a disembodied head and arms. It makes her laugh, and it's a nice laugh.

A pretty laugh, just like she's pretty.

The guy, the nice guy who wasn't Elvis – the guy who she'd listened to, as he'd talked and talked, as she'd talked back to him, and they'd had more drinks – suggests something to her. Not going back to her place (she can't anyway) or even his. But . . .

He points. There's a side street not that far away. It's much darker in there. Private, quiet. The perfect place for more talk and perhaps a kiss and a cuddle if they feel like it, but only *if she feels like it. He's not one of* those *guys. He promises her that, and she believes him. He doesn't come across that way at all. Not like some of the other fellas she's encountered on nights like these and wouldn't have gone near with a bargepole.*

Still, there's a moment or two's hesitation, but then she figures: what the hell? There are so few private places around here, and she really likes him. Could be one of those 'you might regret it if you don't' moments. You always regret the things you haven't done, right? Especially when you're young.

So she nods, and they go – hand-in-hand – chatting, laughing. It's all so easy, like they've known each other longer than they have. When they get to the alleyway, he asks her if it's all right for him to kiss her. That's nice, asking permission.

She nods.

And he plants his mouth on hers, soft, tender. None of this trying to jam your tongue down someone's throat. It's just . . . nice. Like he is. A nice guy, friendly.

He's cupping her face now as he kisses her, lips moving sideways to her cheek and then down her neck, making her feel all tingly. Those familiar sensations, that warm feeling spreading throughout her. She shifts slightly, so he can kiss her lips again. So she can kiss him. More passionate, both of them getting lost in the moment.

His hands exploring, both of them on her waist – then suddenly one of them moving upwards, searching out and cupping a breast through the thin material of her dress, fingers finding a nipple and rubbing that. She gives a little moan, those sensations building.

But no, they can't go any further. Not here. Not in some alleyway. He's grinding against her and she can feel him, but . . . Not here. They can't. So she pulls away, breathless. They should cool it a little, not get carried away. Some heavy petting, snogging, sure. But not . . . Not that, not here.

'What's . . . what's the matter?' he asks, confused.

'Can we just . . . I just want to take it a little slower. Is that okay?'

'Of course. Whatever you want.'

His hand falls away from her breast and she misses the contact. Is she making a terrible mistake? Will he go off her if she doesn't . . . She kisses him again, rubbing the back of his neck, his hair. But it's him that pulls away this time.

She's definitely put him off. Didn't mean to do that, but at the same time wasn't ready for—

'I . . . Look, there's something I need to tell you. I-I haven't . . .'

A virgin? Wow! And he's what, twenty, twenty-one? Maybe even older. She laughs. Doesn't mean it to come out like that – she just thinks it's sweet. But he bristles, thinks she's making fun of him. 'I didn't . . . Listen, it's okay, really. It's fine.' She kisses him, hoping it'll reassure him, that he might relax a bit, especially now she knows and there's no pressure. Perhaps they can arrange to see each other again, take it from there. This is just a kiss and a cuddle. Just a kiss and a—

'Hey! Hey, you two. Leave some for the rest of us!'

She breaks off the kiss, and now she's the one bristling. The voice is rough, and there's a hardness to it. She hadn't realised it, hadn't noticed, but they've been followed. Out here. Out to this side street where it's dark (so far away from everyone back at the pub) and it's quiet and private and—

The only thing she can see is a shape. A large figure. A man standing there. And when he suddenly rushes towards them . . .

All she wants to do is scream.

Chapter 18

'Mr Boyd? Mr Sebastian Boyd?'

The man getting out of the car, out of the very expensive gold-coloured Jag by the way – door being held open by his huge chauffeur – looked like someone out of *Brideshead Revisited*. Dressed all in cottons and silks, creams and whites, matching the angelic members of his staff back there at The Castle Spa, his exit from the vehicle was no less cool.

She'd decided it was time for a visit.

Graham Newton was back on those streets they'd kept him off for a brief while, though O'Brien had the sense to post a couple of uniforms at least on Lisa Newton's street. They couldn't prevent what happened when – or if – he returned home, couldn't stop things happening behind closed doors (never had been able to, sadly), but a visible police presence might make him think twice about doing something drastic to her.

Christ, Robyn hoped so.

Because now he thought she'd been playing away, heaven help her. Robyn had watched that interview, seen the dawning realisation of what they were saying to him sink in – O'Brien and Watts actually bouncing off each other quite well . . . she'd been impressed – and come to conclusion that if he had killed Simon,

162

then his wife playing away and him finding out about it probably hadn't been the motive.

'He . . . They wouldn't have dared!' Newton growled.

It was something she'd argued about with O'Brien afterwards. 'Look, you could just tell, Inspector. That man knew nothing about any affair. If, indeed, there had ever been one.'

'They were *close*, Lisa Newton admitted as much,' argued O'Brien. 'Even if there'd been nothing going on between her and Simon Carter, it could have been *mistaken* for something. Graham might have mistaken it for something. After all, your cousin obviously did.'

Only after that bloody medium put the idea in her head, thought Robyn.

O'Brien was just looking for a way to make it fit. And the fact Newton might also be involved in the distribution of narcotics in the area meant that they could kill two birds with one stone. Indeed, after a while the line of questioning focused more on that than Simon's murder. Possible smuggling using the fishing boats, where it was coming from and who was in charge – like he was going to roll over about any of that!

When Robyn asked her about it, the DI began to speculate that maybe there had been a connection between Simon's death and drugs; after all, he had worked with Newton. A connection between the whole sordid business with Newton's wife and the dealing. It wasn't too much of a stretch. 'How do we know Carter wasn't up to his neck in all that?' O'Brien had suggested, then went back over her words – realising what she'd said, how it related to the way Simon had been found.

Buried.

None of it tracked and Robyn said as much. She wasn't used to meeting with this much resistance to her opinions, however. And when the inspector asked Watts to give them a minute, she'd changed tack once more, starting in on Robyn and her DS's relationship.

'W-We don't *have* a relationship!' Robyn assured her.

'I've got eyes; I can see what's going on in front of me. How you're using him.' It was exactly what she'd accused Prescott of doing with the people in her group and it touched a nerve; she was nothing like that con artist! Now there was someone else the police ought to be looking into. Then again Robyn *had* asked Watts to get her in there to observe the interview, *had* relied on his account of the Lisa Newton interview, which he'd told her over coffee. *Was* she using him? Using his crush on her?

'I'm . . . It's not . . .' was all she could muster.

'He's a good kid, and – just don't tell him I said so – he has the makings of a decent detective. Inspector someday in the not too distant. The last thing he needs is you coming along with your big serial killer cases, turning his head and cocking it up for him.'

Before she could say anything in response to that, O'Brien had stormed off; gone to impart a few words of warning to Graham Newton before he departed, no doubt.

When Watts returned, Robyn had thanked him for his help but declined his offer of a spot of dinner that night, saying she was pretty tired. Outside, she'd popped a couple more of her painkillers. The irony that they'd been leaning on a guy known to be involved in the drugs game didn't escape her.

It was as she'd neared her car that she spotted it, mistook it for a parking ticket to begin with actually – if it had been, she'd have been back inside the nick taking it up with someone. But no, there under her wiper was a folded newspaper cutting – as she opened it, Robyn recognised the photo that accompanied it immediately. A black and white picture of Sykes, looming towards the camera. A recent piece from *The Torch* about her, cobbled together from previous things that had appeared online or wherever, only vaguely accurate. She looked around, and quickly realised that whoever had left this would probably be long gone.

She thought about going back inside anyway, but that probably wasn't a great idea given the way she'd left things. Besides, she couldn't rule out the possibility that it had been left by a copper messing with her, some kind of practical joke. Wasn't exactly the most threatening of things – more unnerving. And the chances of getting any fingerprints off it – even if they bothered – given the number of people who might have handled the original paper, and now her as well, were slim too, especially if whoever had left it had worn gloves. She'd also ascertained that the only camera around here was focused solely on the entrance of the nick, so no chance of it catching the culprit on video. In the end Robyn had put the thing in her pocket, same as last time – remembering though to take it out when she returned home, to put it inside her case for safe keeping.

Robyn had dinner with the clan then, rather than Watts – Tracy having to bow out early, for which she was grateful. It was still rather awkward between them all, but Mia was returning to her old self slowly and surely. Had even run up to Robyn and given her one of those famous leg hugs when she got back, and insisted on her aunty reading some more to her at bedtime that night.

'If . . . if it's okay with your mum?' Robyn had said.

'Yes. Yes, of course,' had been Vicky's reply – there'd even been a little smile hidden in there somewhere.

When she headed back downstairs, Robyn couldn't help seeing through the gap in the door, that Vicky's room – the room that she'd shared with Simon – was full of cardboard boxes, some on the floor, some on the bed itself.

'You're not thinking of moving, are you?' she asked her cousin, who was in the living room with some wine on the go and was halfway down the cigarette she was smoking; Robyn was long past lecturing her about that, even though she was doing it in the house now.

Vicky blew a stream of smoke out of the corner of her mouth, shook her head. 'No, why?'

'The boxes. Your bedroom door was open,' she added quickly before Vicky thought she'd been creeping around, spying. Robyn would have definitely understood if she was thinking of getting away from this place, but it very rarely helped. It was more likely to destabilise Mia, and you always took the baggage with you no matter where you went.

'Doing what you told me to. It'll help with the processing, right? Going through his stuff, getting rid of what we don't need anymore. Hey, like you said in no uncertain terms: he's dead. He's not coming back again.'

'That's not quite what I—'

'Even if he did, he'd probably want Lisa Newton wouldn't he?'

'I don't think . . . Vicky, listen, there's no proof that . . . Lisa says nothing happened. That he was just a good listener.'

Vicky laughed bitterly. 'Yeah, he was that. Good at lots of things.'

'Don't do this, Vicky. Please don't let what that woman said sour your memory of Simon.'

'What else . . .?'

Robyn took a seat, puzzled. 'What else what?'

'Did Lisa say? I thought about going to see her myself, you know.' Another huge drag on the cigarette, then she washed that down with another glug of wine.

'I'm not sure that's a good idea.' Even though she probably shouldn't have been doing it, Robyn filled her in on the Graham situation. How the woman's life was clearly a misery, how she would now be living in fear of whether her husband did some-thing serious to her – *even more* serious.

'Serves her right, for knocking off another woman's bloke.' Robyn ignored the comment, thought it best not to go over the same ground again about there being nothing concrete. 'Serves *him* right, as well!' Vicky held her glass aloft, as if toasting Simon wherever he was. That medium had certainly done a number on her.

'Oh, Vicky. Please don't.'

'What? I mean, Mia's dealing, isn't she? 'Bout time I did too.'

This didn't look like dealing to Robyn.

'Mind you, she knows her clever Aunty Robyn's going to crack the case, doesn't she. You promised her, right?'

'I . . .' Robyn closed her mouth again. There was just no point.

'You promised her and you promised me,' Vicky told her, winking, though she'd said no such thing to her cousin. Just that she'd do her very best . . . to help.

'I think you should probably have an early night, cuz.'

'Naw,' Vicky replied.

'Come on. What if Mia wakes up and comes down, sees you like this?'

Vicky flicked the end of her fag over the ashtray on the coffee table, before using it as a kind of pointer in whatever lecture *she* was readying to give. 'Then,' Vicky said at last, 'it'll teach her a valuable lesson about what life can do to you if you're not careful. About how it can fuck you up. Might as well learn it now.'

Robyn got up at that point, said goodnight. Headed up the stairs thinking: *I came here to help, but that woman is more lost than ever.* Thinking: *I've just made things worse; I always do.*

Thinking that if she owed her, and Mia, nothing else, it was to find out the truth about what had happened to Simon. And that her first port of call should be what it would have been before Bella Prescott, before Lisa and Graham Newton.

She determined right there and then, that she should go and see Sebastian Boyd.

Which was how she'd ended up in his driveway, had arrived just as the X-Type was returning from somewhere and she'd nipped in through the gates behind it. Robyn didn't think she'd have been let in otherwise. That probably explained the look of confusion on both their faces when she got out and called across to them.

The large chauffeur was setting off towards her, the intention being either to ask or force Robyn to leave, but the fellow dressed in creams and whites with the moustache said something Robyn didn't quite catch. The chauffeur stopped dead, turned around again.

167

'Mr Sebastian Boyd?' Robyn asked once more, sheepishly approaching the pair and the expensive car. She'd assumed the person dressed in grey, the chauffeur – who looked like they doubled as a bodyguard or something – was a man. But the closer Robyn drew, the more she could see that it was a woman. A very tall, broad woman, who looked like she'd be the one snapping Graham Newton in two if he gave her any trouble. If Boyd was *Brideshead*, she was Brienne from *Game of Thrones*.

'Yes,' replied her boss, though Robyn had known it was Boyd from the pictures she'd seen. 'I am he.'

She held up a hand in greeting, and to show she had no weapons. She didn't want to be cut down by a massive sword the chauffer might have been hiding behind her back. 'I'm Robyn Adams.'

'Ah, Dr Adams!' Boyd said, beaming. 'I'm surprised it's taken you this long to call upon me.'

'I see I was expected,' she replied, close enough now to hold out that hand for him to shake. Instead, he took it, bent, and kissed her knuckles. He didn't break eye contact once.

'You were indeed,' Boyd said as he straightened again and let go, though his focus never left her face. 'But pleasantly so. I've heard a lot about you, and not just from the local constabulary . . . or the media.'

'My reputation precedes me, it seems.'

'Quite,' said Boyd. She couldn't tell whether he was putting on the gentlemanly act or genuinely thought he was from a bygone age of chivalry – a specific kind of delusion. 'And what brings you here today? The same thing that brought you to my spa the other day?'

'The murder of Simon Carter, one of your staff working there.'

Boyd sucked in a breath and tutted. 'Yes, I heard about that. Awful business. Truly awful.'

'I know you're a busy man, but I was wondering if I might have a moment of your time, Mr Boyd?'

'Certainly, certainly. For a pretty lady such as yourself, you can have an hour if you want it.' There was a certain something in this guy's eye as well, with the patter to match; his words could charm the birds from the trees, thought Robyn. But he was blatantly full of shit. 'Indeed, you catch me on one of my rare days of leisure. I've just been at the golf course. That reminds me, Anderson . . .' He looked over at the chauffeur.

'Yes, sir?' The accent was foreign, possibly Swedish, which would fit with the hair colour. Might even be an extra 's' in that surname?

'Would you do me a favour and get the clubs from the boot.' A nod from the big woman and she went around the back of the car. 'I don't know what I'd do without her,' said Boyd, leaning in conspiratorially, as if sharing some big secret. 'She's been with me more years than I care to remember. Has pulled my fat out of the fire so many times.'

I can imagine, thought Robyn.

While Andersson hefted the clubs out of the boot, something that would have had Robyn on the floor – though to that woman it was no more than picking up a bag of shopping – Boyd led the way to the house.

It was like a miniature version of the spa really, or parts of it, but had ivy climbing up the sides. 'This used to be the servants' quarters at one time,' Boyd explained as they neared the door. 'But it's big enough for my needs.'

Big enough? You could have fitted Robyn's city flat in there several times over, and still have room for one of Vicky's new builds. As Boyd opened the door, a beeping sound went off and he stepped inside for a moment to key the alarm code into a box on the left. Then he came back again, leaving the door ajar, and held a hand out for Robyn to go first.

'Come into my lair, said the spider to the fly,' he said, smiling again.

Was that just an expression, or was he referencing the kind

169

of people she'd helped hunt down in the past, helped to catch? The *real* spiders.

I've heard a lot about you, and not just from the local constabulary . . . or the media.

Those friends in high places . . . Not that her cases weren't public record, of course. But why bother to really dig down into them unless – unless you wanted to find out just who you were facing?

Whether they were capable of catching you, too.

He'd obviously spotted the expression on her face, the hesitation she was feeling palpable. 'Just my little joke,' Boyd said, though the smile didn't go away. 'You'll be made most welcome here, Doctor. Most welcome indeed.'

For some reason Robyn believed him, but that didn't put her at her ease any.

If anything, it made her even more wary.

Chapter 19

Vicky had been hesitant, wary.

Had to work herself up to this task. But here she was, starting it anyway. *Thinking* about starting it. Staring at the boxes she'd had delivered, at any rate. That was a start, wasn't it?

'You're not thinking of moving, are you?'

Robyn's words to Vicky the previous night, not that she could remember much of that conversation. Much of anything these days.

You know what helps with that?

She recalled saying that Lisa Newton deserved whatever was coming to her, for doing whatever she did with Simon. What, talking? Confiding in him, when that bastard of a husband flung her around? Or more than that?

Remembered saying that Simon had deserved his fate too, but she hadn't really meant any of it. What had she been talking about, what had she been thinking? No one deserved what had happened to her Simon (if he still was hers . . . *No, he's dead, remember? he's not anyone's*). And Robyn seemed so certain, based on what Lisa had said to the police – but then she would deny it, wouldn't she?

Oh God, she was so confused.

Her cousin was sure that Bella had been a fraud, as well, but she hadn't been there and seen what Vicky had seen. Heard the words, being channelled through from the other side.

'I'm so sorry. Sweetheart, it was only the once . . .'

Confused, just like she was now. In the moment. The thought of them together, of Simon on top of Lisa, of her on top of him – it was too much to bear.

'Don't let what that woman said sour your memory of Simon.'

That was the easy way out of it: think the way Robyn thought. That it had all been bollocks. Vicky'd gone there for some kind of comfort, hadn't she? A sign that he was okay . . . or as okay as someone could be who had been throttled and drowned and left buried in sand on a beach for fuck's sake!

No, be honest with yourself Vicky, you went there for answers. You got them as well. Nobody said they'd be easy to hear, no one said you would like what you found out. Wasn't that partly the reason she hadn't gone back again, because she was scared of what else she'd find out? Scared that it might all be real, that she'd begun to trust it . . . then wasn't sure at all. Robyn had got her so turned around on the whole thing.

Yet, hadn't there been a message for her cousin too? Something from her mother about not going down the same road as her. Wasn't hard to figure out what that meant, the number of guys Robyn's mum had torn through, the addictions. That was mainly the reason she used to leave Robyn here every summer, so she could get on with all that.

Oh, right? And who exactly's the one thinking about wine right now, just a glass or couple in the middle of the day? A smoke or several? Vicky had no high ground. But she'd had enough to make her, hadn't she. Been through more in the last week or so than most people do in a lifetime (apart from Julie . . . poor Julie). Than most people should do.

It was all so . . . so fucked up.

'It'll teach her a valuable lesson about what life can do to you . . . how it can fuck you up. Might as well learn it now.'

172

No. She didn't want Mia to learn that at her age – there was time enough when she was older for that. Or, y'know, she might be happy, have a good life. Not off to a great start though, was it? Dad killed that way, possibly by the husband of the woman he was sleeping with. Not to mention those pictures she'd seen, all because Robyn had them in her bedroom.

All because you *asked her to help, Vicky.*

Was she regretting that now? Picking up the phone and calling her cousin? Mia wouldn't have seen anything at all then. But Vicky still would have; she'd carry those memories of Simon in the morgue to her own grave. They'd haunt her more effectively than any ghost Bella Prescott could conjure, that was for damned sure. And Robyn was out there right now, trying to fulfil her promise. To find out what really happened to Simon, if it wasn't down to Graham Newton. Trying to offer them some sort of peace.

Tracy rattling the pots downstairs – the exact opposite of peace – snapped her out of her thoughts. Tracy, doing the dishes from yesterday, who'd been so brilliant while all this was going on. Who shouldn't be doing any of that, because it was *Vicky's* job. Tracy was a policewoman not a housemaid, not a babysitter; she had a family of her own to take care of. She'd shown Vicky the photos on her phone just the other day. One of each, thirteen and fifteen (the terrible teens, Tracy had joked). She'd put the phone away again though when she got to the pictures of her husband, and apologised. 'Insensitive', the older woman had said under her breath, but what was she actually apologising for? Still having a partner who was alive, for being luckier than Vicky?

She needed to pull herself together, get on with the day-to-day. Needed to put what had happened behind her, put the pictures away (later, she couldn't face that just yet). Put all of his clothes and belongings somewhere.

Put them in these boxes. Like she'd put him in as well at some point.

Vicky opened the wardrobe door, peered into his side at the

clothes hanging there. His good suit – he very rarely wore one – a few shirts, T-shirts, pairs of jeans, his uniforms from The Castle Spa, so crisp and white. She reached for one of the shelves there on the right, pulled out a jumper. He'd worn this the last time they'd all gone walking along the cliffs, an autumn day, the warm weather giving way to much cooler breezes especially up there. Vicky scrunched up the top, fingers brushing the roughness of the wool, and she hugged it to her chest.

Backing up, she felt her legs going. Wondered if she could make it to the edge of the bed, which she just about managed before collapsing onto it – but then slid off and onto the floor with a bump. Vicky began crying into the jumper, burying her head, not caring whether she could breathe or not. Simulating what Simon must have felt when he took his last few gasps.

'Mum . . .' The voice was little more than a whisper – and the fact that her ears were covered hadn't helped – but still she heard it. Something, some motherly super-sense telling her Mia was in the room and speaking to her. 'Mum, are you all right?'

Vicky was reluctant to take the jumper away from her face, because then her little girl would see just how *not* all right she was, especially compared to her.

'*What? I mean, Mia's dealing, isn't she? 'Bout time I did too.*'

Wasn't going off to consult with mediums, talking to her dead dad. Robyn had been right: how on earth was she supposed to square that away with a six-year-old? Luckily, she hadn't asked about that again . . . yet.

'Mum?' Mia repeated, so concerned it made her heart ache.

Vicky took the jumper away, looked at her child. 'Sweetheart, I . . .'

'What are you doing?'

'I-I'm . . .' Trying to wipe out all the traces of your father from this house. No, she wasn't . . . She *shouldn't* be doing that. But what if he had been unfaithful with Lisa? What then? 'I'm just going through some of Daddy's things.'

'Why?' she asked, no mention of the tears rolling down Vicky's face. Perhaps she was used to seeing her like that now? Instead, Mia was looking around at all the boxes.

'Because some of them, they might be of use to people—' She was going to say less fortunate than them, because Vicky fully intended to donate the stuff to charity when she was done . . . whenever that was. She'd made a start though, hadn't she? That was the main thing. Had done more than just think about it.

'Like the jumble sales at school?' Mia chipped in, saving her from embarrassing herself any more than was necessary.

Vicky nodded. 'Yeah. Like that.'

'Can I help?'

Vicky bit her lip, not knowing how to reply. It felt like something she should tackle on her own, felt personal. But then, Simon was Mia's dad – she had just as much right to do this as her. It might even help, if Robyn was correct. With all those diplomas, she should be, right? 'Ye . . . yes sweetheart, you can help. But first, come here for a minute.'

The little girl stepped forward, stopped, before rushing all the way into her mother's arms. Not for the first time recently, they hugged each other tightly. Vicky stroked the back of her head, more for her own sake than for Mia's. Made a silent promise to herself to try and be better – for her. To try and get it together, before she – before everything – fell apart.

'It'll be okay, Mum,' said the girl from out of her armpit, and it was all Vicky could do to hold it together even for a few minutes.

For now, all the hesitation, all the wariness and worry, was gone, even if it only lasted a little while. All the thoughts and thinking about starting – about starting *again* – went away.

It was just them, mother and daughter. Whatever happened next, good or bad, they'd look out for each other.

They'd be there for one another.

Chapter 20

What happened next, she hadn't been able to believe.

Boyd had really turned on the jets, trying to impress her. The veritable charm offensive. No spiders, no flies, nothing like that. At times it was hard for Robyn to even imagine this was the same person who'd pulled those strings, who'd complained about her 'snooping' around up at the spa. Indeed, if you listened to Sebastian, the pressure hadn't come from him at all, but from those who held shares in the company; an attempt to protect their business interests in the area.

'We all have to answer to someone, Doctor. My investors are more than a little concerned about the link that's currently being drawn between the deceased Mr Carter and that particular property, simply because he happened to work there. Bad publicity, you understand.'

It was a fair enough line. Something like this could drive a place like The Castle Spa out of business, making a lot of locals unemployed in the process. All the more reason – she pointed out – to clear things up as quickly as possible.

'We have people looking into the situation ourselves, investigators who will get to the bottom of what really happened – you mark my words. And *if* anyone at the spa is found to be at fault . . .' He put it exactly like that, as if the whole thing might have been some kind of accident, as if it had just been a misplaced piece of gym equipment. 'Then they will be brought to justice, and we can all get on with our lives.'

'Which is more than can be said for Si . . . for Mr Carter,' Robyn reminded him. Or his family, she thought to herself. Investigators? Was he really trying to put her mind at rest by promising that his own people would look into the crime? PIs on his payroll, professionals who wouldn't bat an eyelid at covering something up? Absently she wondered how O'Brien and, yes, how Watts would feel about that? Or were they being told not to feel anything at all?

'I know. Very sad. We are more than willing to make a donation on his behalf somewhere, or offer a payment to his widow with our condolences – your cousin, I believe? – in return for his sterling service.'

Hush money, if it was discovered that something *had* been going on that brought his company into disrepute? Or a genuine offer of help? The more he talked, the more – even with her training – she couldn't tell if he was on the level or not.

When they'd first entered, he'd taken her through the hallway, which was adjacent to an ornate flight of steps. The corridor had paintings and photographs relating to the Boyd family the length of its walls and Sebastian spoke proudly of their accomplishments over the centuries: which included a lot of work for charities, in particular children's homes. Robyn had recognised one member of the Boyd family straight away and pointed him out.

'Ah, good old great, great, great . . . Is that enough, too many?' He laughed. 'Grandfather Franklyn. The adventurer, the explorer! Now, there again was a man who gave as much back as he possibly could. Did you know some of the herbal remedies he returned with from overseas are still being used up there at The Castle Spa? We have glowing testimonies reflecting their benefits. Proof, if it were needed, that they've helped tremendously with all kinds of malaises.'

'He spent a lot of time living with certain nomadic Arabic tribes, isn't that right?'

Sebastian grinned, turning from the old sepia-coloured likeness of Franklyn to regard her. 'I'm not the only one who's done their homework, am I? You're quite right.'

'It was rumoured that he even took a wife out there, wasn't it?'

A laugh emerged at that remark. 'Rumoured, never established.'

'You're not worried there might be another pretender to the throne somewhere?'

A slight twitch of the cheek was the response to that question. 'If I have more family somewhere, Doctor, then I welcome them to get in touch. As far as I'm aware, however, I am the only remaining Boyd left.'

'If you don't mind me asking, how *did* you come to realise you were a Boyd?'

'I don't mind in the slightest.' Sebastian had held out his hand for them to proceed into the living room, which was no less ornate than the stairs or the hallway. This time bookcases covered the walls, apart from where the massive fireplace was – which had an equally massive mirror above it – and a grand piano resided in the far corner. Bay windows not only let in plenty of light, they also provided a fantastic view of the acres of green surrounding the house and, in the distance, The Castle Spa; right where the Lord of the Manor could keep an eye on it. He offered her a seat on a chair that looked like it had cost more than her entire school's budget at the university that year and she perched on the edge of it. 'But first, Andersson . . .' he said to the chauffeur who had somehow, regardless of her size, appeared behind them, minus the golf clubs. 'Would you do me a favour and make us a pot of tea? Perhaps a few cucumber sandwiches?'

'Oh, none for me,' Robyn said, but Sebastian flapped his hands in protest.

'Nonsense. Andersson here makes the most mouth-watering sandwiches you'll ever taste in your life. Don't you, Andersson.'

'If you say so, sir,' she replied with a curt nod.

'It'll be like you've died and gone to heaven, believe me.' Andersson withdrew, Robyn assumed to the kitchen. 'There used to be more staff here, but nowadays I find it beneficial to keep the numbers down to just the cleaners and Andersson. People I can trust, you see.'

'You have trust issues?'

Boyd cocked his head. 'I entertain a lot of businesspeople within these walls, Doctor. I'd rather the ears those walls might have were loyal. There's a lot of competition out there – I learnt that even before I discovered I was a Boyd. And competition breeds conflict.'

'An interesting way of phrasing it,' Robyn pointed out.

He laughed again. 'I forgot whose company I was in. I shall have to mind my p's and q's. Can't have you analysing me now, can we?'

Robyn simply smiled back. She'd been doing that since outside, but was having real trouble with him. Yes, he was hiding things – but he was quite open about the fact, and he did operate in a cutthroat world where secrets were currency. Had been a part of that world for a long, long time. But there was also an air of someone quite lost, somebody who'd never really known who they were until they'd had this history behind them. She was keen to uncover more about that, then she might finally be able to get a handle on the man. 'You were saying, about finding out you were a Boyd?' Robyn prompted.

'Ah yes, of course! Well, I assume you know about my background.'

'A little,' she told him.

'My parents . . . They died in a car crash when I was very small. I only really have vague memories of them. I know they loved me, though. I remember the smell of a certain perfume my mother used to wear, my father lifting me up on his shoulders. Very little else, I'm afraid.' Boyd stared at a spot on the carpet.

Here was the vulnerability and sadness that had been lacking before – but also a resentment at life itself – all masked by an insecurity that forced him to play a certain part. 'They . . . I had no other family, Doctor, so I was placed into care. Those were . . . hard years for me.' That explained why he was so proud that the Boyds had given a lot to those children's charities. 'I suppose I can't really complain. These are the kinds of things that forge us, are they not? You, more than anyone else, would know that.' She flinched at the remark, again wondering just how much he knew about her own past, then he clarified with: 'In your line of work, I mean. Cause and effect, yes?'

'There are definitely links between your . . . *a person's* formative years and what they become in adulthood. I don't think you need to be in my line of work to understand that, Mr Boyd.'

'Sebastian, as I said.' He regarded her again, his eyes moist. 'Anyway, it did with me. I made my first deals in those children's homes, learnt how to negotiate my way out of trouble – I've never been much of a fighter, not in the physical sense at any rate. That place taught me how to use this.' Boyd tapped the side of his head. 'It also taught me the value of real family, Doctor. So, when I was old enough – and by this time I'd made a bit of a name for myself out there doing deals in the real world – I wanted to know more about where I'd come from. Turned out I'd been adopted, something nobody had ever told me. Can you imagine!'

'You must have been angry about that?'

'Not really. I mean, possibly that the authorities never said anything to me. But I was never mad at my parents. They chose to bring me up, chose to give me a family, a home. It wasn't their fault they died before they could deliver their end of that particular bargain.'

Again with the business speak; Sebastian Boyd had been living and breathing that for so long everything came down to deals with him.

'I suppose I could have gone off in search of my real family

180

sooner, but – wouldn't you know it – they were all dead as well! Everyone thought that was it for the Boyd line. But they were wrong, as you can see.' He opened his hands wide to illustrate that the line was very much going strong now the prodigal son had returned. 'Turns out one of my ancestors like to put it about a bit, as it were. That resulted in my grandmother, which resulted in my mother – my real mother – which finally, low and behold, resulted in me. Dear old Mum was a chip off the old block, you see. Wasn't too fussy. I do so hate that, don't you?'

Once again, he said it like he knew more about her than he should. Like maybe he knew more about her own mother than he should.

'You can only push your luck so far, and Mum went and got herself pregnant at quite an early age. She had me, then gave me up for adoption. Sort of explains why nobody would adopt me again, doesn't it? Sloppy seconds. Couldn't even get any takers on the fostering front. Ah well, their loss in the end.'

Robyn leaned back slightly in the chair, engrossed in the tale. If there was one thing she hadn't been expecting today it was for Boyd to be opening up so easily about his origins. And was it her imagination or was he becoming more relaxed as he went on, almost like he was seeing this as some form of therapy? Perhaps he hadn't spoken much about this to anyone before. 'You never thought about seeking her out?' asked Robyn in the obvious gap.

'Oh, yes. I mean, I tried but—' It was at that point Andersson returned with a tray of containing a tea pot, cups and saucers, and sandwiches made from white bread with the crusts cut off (Robyn had to admit they did look quite appetising, but it was difficult to equate such delicate work with the chauffeur). The china rattled as the giant of a woman placed the tray down on the table between them. 'Ah, thank you so much, Andersson,' said Boyd. 'That all looks rather wonderful, wouldn't you agree, Doctor?'

'Yes, indeed.'

If Andersson was happy about the praise, she didn't really show it, but gave a small nod and then left the room again – though didn't go far probably. Robyn got the feeling that the woman never really wandered far away from her employer. Boyd poured the tea into two cups then asked if she wanted milk and sugar, which was also on the tray. 'Just milk please.'

Boyd placed a couple of the sandwiches on a plate and encouraged her to do the same. 'Your taste buds will thank you, trust me.' Her stomach actually agreed with him, letting out a faint moan and she thought: *traitor*. So she leaned forward and popped one on a plate, then picked the sandwich up and nibbled at the bread. Before she knew it, she'd eaten three-quarters of the thing and was contemplating another.

Boyd was grinning again, swallowing down his mouthful before saying: 'See? I told you so.' Satisfied, he leaned back in the chair again and finished off the rest of what was on his plate.

'You were talking about finding your mother . . .?' Robyn prodded for the second time in this particular conversation, as much because she was genuinely interested as anything. She sat back again herself, readying to listen.

'That's right. I did try to find her, but sadly – I say sadly because I never really got the chance to meet her or get to know her; she could have been horrible for all I know – and not to be the voice of doom and gloom again, she was dead as well. One of her suitors got a bit too handy with her. Fractured skull, brain damage. So I never got the chance to ask her why exactly she gave me away, although I can guess of course.'

'Must have been hard to come to terms with,' offered Robyn.

Boyd shook his head slowly. 'By that time, I had all of the history out there to catch up on. A family who, although I would never really know them in person, I could get to know through my research. A family whose legacy I could get behind.'

'A legacy that included these properties at Golden Sands,' Robyn reminded him.

'You make it sound like all this made my fortune, Doctor. Quite the reverse. When I came along, the castle was so run-down nobody wanted anything to do with it. The place wasn't even being used as a tourist attraction. I turned things around, found those investors I was talking about earlier, ploughed a significant amount of money into the project and hopefully wiped out any of memories of what it was used for once it was out of the hands of the Boyds.'

'The asylum,' stated Robyn.

Boyd pulled a face. 'The asylum. But, well, it's all good now. The Castle Spa is thriving, we're helping the economy here at Golden Sands: rich people using those facilities also visit the town, purchase from the shops and spread the word amongst their own employees, who in turn book their holidays here.' Robyn's mind flashed back to Miss Havisham the librarian, how she'd been singing Boyd's praises. 'And it enables me to give generously to various good causes myself, including continuing the tradition of working with children's charities.' Boyd beamed at this, something that was clearly close to his heart – and Robyn didn't get a sense that he was being anything but sincere. Wasn't doing it for tax breaks or to pull a fast one, but genuinely wanted to help those kids; ones like him who'd been having a hard time of it. 'So, there you have it, Doctor, in a nutshell. What's the diagnosis?'

She gave a thin smile. 'I think I've probably taken up enough of your time.' Robyn looked at her watch. 'I should be thinking about heading back anyway.'

Boyd did the same. 'My, wherever do the days go? But do feel free to drop back in anytime you like; my door is always open. That is, just press the buzzer at the gate and if we're around one of us will let you through. There's no need to sneak about, trailing us inside.' He chuckled. 'You're more than welcome in my home.'

She had to say this much for him, she had been made to feel very welcome regardless of her initial reservations. And, as she got up to leave and was shown to the door – Boyd telling her that the gate opened automatically from this side – she really didn't know what to think. Moreover, she still wasn't sure whether anyone at the spa had anything to do with Simon's death. Including Sebastian Boyd.

Through her rear-view, she'd watched them as she drove off: Boyd and Andersson now, joining him, standing next to – and towering over – her boss. Watched them even as she reached for her bottle of water and swigged back a couple of her pills.

It was a meeting she hadn't expected to go like that, and one she couldn't really believe. But as strange as she'd found all this, she'd be able to believe what happened next even less.

Chapter 21

As he watched Dr Robyn Adams' car head off down the driveway towards the gate, clouds of dust in her wake, Sebastian Boyd smiled again.

He really had enjoyed talking to her, talking things *through* with her. Giving the doctor a little guided tour of the family on his walls, then hosting her with the tea and cucumber sandwiches; Andersson's speciality, they were hard to resist. Cautious to begin with, as he was sure she was as well – Sebastian had been told time and again he was incredibly hard to read – he'd grown to enjoy Dr Adams' company more and more as the afternoon wore on. So much so that he really had been sad when she said she had to go.

For someone in his position, opportunities for social interactions were few and far between. He couldn't remember when he'd last had a conversation with someone that hadn't involved percentages and stock growth. Especially face-to-face – all that was usually done via Skype or what have you, the signal being particularly good up here and at the spa. If you had the proper codes, naturally.

It was probably because of her training, though he prayed it wasn't *just* that, but he felt like he could really talk to her, tell her anything – be himself – and that as much as she was quizzing him, he'd also gained a lot from their . . . what would you call it, session? Lord, that made it sound like something from the place he ran, when it had been infinitely more pleasant than that. He'd done his best to put her at her ease and hopefully now that would be the end of her inquiries. There were professionals at work, both the ones they'd hired and also Golden Sands' finest police. With a bit of luck, Dr Adams would see that; leave them to their own devices. It would be such a shame if she got hurt doing her Agatha Raisin thing.

He sighed. Deep down Sebastian knew she wouldn't be able to let it go. That she'd keep digging. It was, after all, why he'd been expecting her in the first place. It was also why he said the next thing he did to his personal bodyguard and chauffeur, turning and craning his neck so he could look at her properly – you could get such a crick doing that!

'Do me another favour, would you, Andersson?'

'Sir,' she replied. Andersson was a woman of few words, but then that was one of the many things he liked about her.

'Keep an eye on our friend there.' Then, because he wasn't sure whether he'd conveyed everything he needed to, whether Andersson might have thought she was supposed to protect Dr Adams, he added: 'The last thing we need is that bitch fucking up everything we've been working so hard on here all this time.'

Then he turned around and headed back into his home.

Chapter 22

In his defence, the young guy she's with – the virgin – does try and stop what's happening.

He's shouting out to the shape that's just spoken, getting in the way, but in the scramble he gets shoved aside and actually into the opposite wall in that alley. Then the figure is on her, hand over her mouth before she can actually get that scream out, arm across her and pressing so that she can't raise her own arms or hands.

The young guy's still saying something, but his voice is getting weaker by the second. Fucking virgin! He sounds pathetic. If this is his idea of watching out for her, protecting her, then it's rubbish! The figure – the man – with his hand over her mouth is breathing hard into her face and she can smell the booze on him. Someone from the pub then? Someone who'd been watching them, who'd followed them outside when she'd nodded and said to the virgin: 'Yes of course I'll go out there with you to a dark side street where absolutely anything *could happen . . .'*

And is right now.

Stupid, how fucking stupid!

She mumbles, moans – trying to urge the guy she'd been with to do something. To be a man. Moments beforehand she'd loved the fact that he wasn't like that, a blokey bloke. Now she'd give anything for him to prise this newcomer off her, because he's just too strong for her to do it alone. This guy who's pawing at her, still keeping her pinned with that arm, but the hand attached to it is reaching up to squeeze a breast hard through that thin material of her black dress. It's painful and she winces, tries to cry out through the fingers muffling her – which she suspects he's taking as some kind of passion thing, like she's enjoying this.

Far from it.

But still he's squeezing and then tugging at the dress, ripping it. She can hear the tearing, even though she can't see it because he's preventing her from tilting her head down . . . and anyway it's still quite dark, even though her eyes are adjusting. The breast's exposed to the air now, her nipple hard because of the cold rather than any attention the virgin was giving it before.

Then the hand over her mouth is removed, and she sucks in a breath greedily, but it's soon replaced by his mouth, rough and forceful like the rest of him. His stubble burns.

She can feel this guy. He's excited as well – just like the virgin was. His hardness is jabbing at her through his jeans. 'You know you want it,' he says pulling his mouth away for a second. 'And he can't give it you. Stop struggling.'

Suddenly a knee is up, an involuntary action – a knee-jerk reaction, if you like – up and into that hardness he's so proud of, right between his legs. He lets out a cry of his own now, because that would have hurt. Really hurt. And he's letting go, falling backwards, away from her. She has another stab at screaming, calling out for help, but where her body was just helping her – the knee thing – it's working against her this time and she can't find her voice.

She should just run. Actually, she turns and makes to do that. Spring up to the opposite end of the alley and escape. But there's a hand around her wrist, pulling her back. The man's recovered enough to do that, knows he can't let her get away no matter how much pain he's in. She notices the virgin now, and he's just watching all

188

this happen. Just staring . . . Why is he just gaping like that, why isn't he running off to fetch help?

Okay, so he's in shock. Frozen like that, but come on! Snap out of it!

That's not the only reason he's not getting help, though. She looks at him then back at the other bloke, making things out, the shape no longer just a shadow but a face. And she recognises it. Realises what's going on, that they know each other. That she can't expect any help at all from the virgin, because these two are friends.

Absently she wonders whether this was the plan all along. Whether he was the good cop. The bait she fell for. Thought he was nice and that something might come of it all. Not this, never this.

Then another thought strikes her, as the man tugging on her wrist drags her back into his clutches. A terrifying thought, one that makes her want to scream again, but she can't because even though she's finding her voice again, the man who has hold of her is giving her a backhander. 'Fucking bitch!' he says with a snarl.

Reeling slightly, she doesn't know where she is for a moment. Can't quite work out where the pain is coming from, why the side of her mouth is wet, why it tastes coppery. Why her breast is out, flapping around. She can't remember what she was thinking about a second ago, until it hits her harder than his hand did.

The thought, the utterly terrifying thought she's thinking, is this:

She's wondering where the rest of them are. But she knows now, because she can see them.

The others have joined their two friends in the darkened alley.

That's when she understands, if she hadn't before . . . That's when she knows for sure.

She's in really big trouble.

Chapter 23

The message came, not through Robyn's phone – though apparently Watts had been trying to get hold of her that way; she'd not done her morning trip up to the end of the garden to check her messages – but via Tracy when she arrived after breakfast.

Tracy had just assumed she already knew, that she'd been told the news about the beach. But when Robyn's brow had furrowed, totally confused, she'd hesitated. Robyn had gestured for them to go into the living room so they could talk in private.

'Tell me,' Robyn said.

'You really don't know . . .'

Robyn shook her head.

'That they've found something there? Under the pier?'

'Something . . .? What do you mean, *something*?'

Tracy checked that they were out of Vicky and Mia's earshot, which was ironic given her own tendencies. Probably not a bad thing, though. The pair had, Robyn discovered when she returned home the previous day, made a start on filling those boxes with Simon's belongings. So the last thing they needed was to hear about this. 'Another body,' she whispered finally.

'*What?*' replied Robyn, a little too loudly – and guaranteed to draw attention.

Tracy just nodded as if to say, 'That's right.' It was the kind of information the woman definitely wouldn't have passed on when they first met, but after the incident with the medium . . . Plus word had spread about her being invited to watch the Graham Newton interview, which she guessed made her okay in Tracy's eyes. Enough to assume she'd know about all this already. But in spite of everything, Robyn still felt like she was on the outside looking in. If Tracy had any more information, like who the body might belong to, she didn't get a chance to tell her. Mia appeared in the doorway, asking what they were talking about.

'Oh, nothing, sweetie. I've just got to pop out,' said Robyn. Tracy shot her a look, but she ignored it.

'You're *always* going out!' whined the child.

Robyn went over to her and kneeled down. 'I'm just making good on my promise to you. Okay?'

Mia thought about it for a moment, then nodded. 'Yeah.' She held her arms open wide and Robyn pulled her in. Hadn't realised how much she'd got used to these kinds of hugs, how much she'd come to rely on them. 'Will you play with me when you get back?' she asked, head resting on Robyn's shoulder.

'You bet! Try and stop me, kiddo!'

She'd said goodbye to the little girl, then to Vicky – telling her something had come up. 'Connected to Simon?' asked her cousin.

Robyn shrugged. 'I don't know yet. Maybe.' She gave Vicky a kiss on the cheek, another routine action whenever they parted these days and it suddenly struck her just how – without even realising it – they'd slipped back into those old routines from when they were younger.

'You be careful,' Vicky said to her.

'Always,' Robyn replied, then left the house to drive down to the pier.

* * *

191

That feeling of being on the outside only got worse when she arrived at her destination.

There was no mistaking the bottom end of Golden Sands as anything other than a crime scene. There were police cars – and uniformed officers – everywhere, more than she would have imagined being stationed at Golden Sands (which meant they'd probably been drafted in from nearby authorities), white vans that Robyn recognised as belonging to forensics personnel, blue and white tape . . . *Good luck trying to keep all this on the down low*, Robyn thought as she parked her car and made her way through the crowds of tourists that were gathering to see what the hell was going on. Sometimes she wondered if that tape had a kind of magnetic effect, drawing rubber-neckers like flies around a sugar bowl.

It took her a while, but she finally got to the front, elbowing her way through like someone trying to swim in a sea of people. The only difference between this and when she'd tried to get to Vicky's house through a similar crowd was that nobody seemed to realise who she was here. And that was part of the problem, especially when she reached the tape and was told to stand well back by one of the PCs there. A face she'd never seen before; maybe one of those who'd come to bolster the ranks.

'But, officer, I—'

'I said get back, ma'am. Do as you're told.' A couple of onlookers got in front of her then, cutting her off from the PC and the tape. Robyn glanced sideways and saw surfers out on the ocean still going about their business, trying and failing to ride the waves. One even looked like he was drowning, but then got back on his board again and began paddling it. She guessed Golden Sands didn't have an aquatic division that could keep them at bay, and thought about just donning a wetsuit to try and reach the crime scene that way.

No. She wasn't about to be put off by a few thoughtless and pushy members of the public, who were just looking for a good

192

story to tell people down the boozer when they got back home from their holidays. Inspired by those surfers, Robyn waded in again and barged folk out of the way. 'Officer,' she called out, getting his attention once more. 'Officer, could you tell DI O'Brien I'm here? Or DS Watts? They know who I am and—'

'I'm sure they do,' snapped the policeman, sounding like he didn't believe a word of it.

'I'm Dr Adams, I've been working with them.' She realised as soon as she'd shouted it out that this was a mistake. Heads turned in her direction, not just members of the public but a few with cameras and Dictaphones; some she even recognised from back at Vicky's, who she hadn't spotted until now, and they obviously hadn't clocked her either.

Journalists.

The PC saw their reaction as well. Saw the frenzy that was about to happen and spoke quickly into his shoulder radio. As the journos got closer, more police arrived and Robyn saw the unmistakably 'happy' face of O'Brien behind them. 'Get her inside the cordon!' she heard the DI order, 'before we have another crime scene on our hands!' Suddenly the tape was being yanked up so she could limbo underneath. One man tried his luck and attempted to do what she had back at Sebastian Boyd's, sneaking in behind her, but a copper placed a hand on his shoulder and gently shoved him back again. When it looked like he was going to give it another whirl, the PC stopped him with a 'just try it' glare and he saw sense, backing off.

'Shit,' said O'Brien to Robyn, even more bad-tempered than usual. 'You're *all* I need.'

'Inspector.' Robyn gave a tip of the head.

'Dr Adams.'

The PC who'd summoned his colleagues made himself scarce, face redder than a pillar-box when he realised that, yes, actually they did know each other – although they apparently weren't on the best of terms.

'I heard about the body.'

'You and every other fucker in Golden Sands,' sniped the inspector. 'Watts tipped you off, I'm assuming?' Robyn shook her head, but then looked at her phone and found that he had made an attempt to and it had only appeared on there as she'd travelled through a much better reception area somewhere. She stuck with the 'no', however, because she didn't want him getting into trouble. 'Then I'm guessing you must be psychic.'

Robyn's lip curled at that. 'Hardly.'

There was an awkward moment of silence, which neither of them broke, then O'Brien said: 'I suppose you want to see the crime scene, then.'

'Want is probably not the word I'd use, but . . . I wouldn't mind,' Robyn told her. 'Now I'm here.'

'And if I say no to that, I suppose you'll ring up your friends in high places again.'

Robyn said nothing; she didn't have to.

'All right, all right.' O'Brien wrenched her neck sideways for Robyn to follow her over to the steps. They were wooden and ran parallel to the pier itself; they were also covered in sand and very steep, so Robyn had to watch how she went down them. She was guessing they wouldn't bring the body up this way when it was time; it would probably be by one of the accessible ramps on the other side instead.

'Speaking of powerful people, you were pestering Mr Boyd yesterday, weren't you.'

'Did he make a complaint?' asked Robyn. After the way they'd left it, she wouldn't have thought so, but at the same time she wouldn't have been surprised. That was the nature of the man: you didn't know which way to take him.

'No,' O'Brien admitted. 'But you *were* there, weren't you?'

She wondered how the inspector had known if Boyd hadn't contacted her, but then remembered the network of spies again – the feeling of being watched wherever she went – assumed she'd been spotted heading off in that direction or something. Hell of an assumption that she'd been going there, though. 'I had a chat with him, yes.'

O'Brien stopped abruptly on the steps and Robyn almost fell into her. 'Thought I told you to leave well enough alone.'

'He didn't seem to mind. I think he quite enjoyed himself, as it happens.'

It was O'Brien's turn to curl her lip. 'If you know what's good for you, you'll keep this out.' She pressed the end of her nose, which presumably had been bent out of shape again.

'Above the law, is he?'

'Two things,' said O'Brien. 'One: you're not the law, you're just a pain in the arse. And two: nobody's above the law.'

Robyn could think of a few people who thought they were, but let it go. Waited for O'Brien to continue on down the steps leading to the beach, which she did eventually.

The closer to the sands she drew, the more Robyn saw – the angle so acute, and the cordon so far back up there that none of this had been visible from above. Not that the body itself was on display, because the police had erected a white tent around it – but those journalists would have had a field day taking snapshots of the general buzz around the area just beneath the pier. The tide was out at the moment, but the sand was still wet when she reached the bottom – which meant it hadn't been for that long.

'This way,' O'Brien practically grunted, pointing, as if Robyn hadn't already seen where they were heading. 'A fisherman, one of the really early morning brigade who like to sit on the pier up there, discovered it. Thought he'd got a tug, caught something big.' O'Brien gave a small gravelly laugh. 'He was right, just not in the way he would have liked. When he looked over the side, flashed his light into the water, he saw he'd hooked the leg of someone's jeans. That's when he called it in.'

'Any CCTV coverage around here?' Robyn asked, looking about her.

'Not so's you'd notice,' came the predictable reply. 'Not this far down the pier. Definitely not on the beach itself.'

O'Brien strode into the tent first, making no attempt whatsoever to hold the flap open for Robyn. When she pulled this back, she saw men and women in white suits – though they were pretty much indistinguishable – and she saw Watts, eyes cast downwards at what was in front of him. Photographers of the more official kind were skirting around the discovery, snapping off shot after shot with huge cameras. One of the suited figures was crouching off to the side and examining something; they looked like one of those crown green bowlers following the trajectory of a roll. Robyn's eyes followed their own trajectory, down to the body half-covered in that wet sand. The jeans leg was sticking up and out, pulled free by the fisherman's hook presumably, and the foot was covered in a sock – though there was no sign of any footwear.

Parts of the corpse were buried and others exposed: the flash of a bare arm; what looked like material from a T-shirt; an ear and jaw. You couldn't see the face yet, however, and for that small mercy Robyn was grateful. It wasn't that she hadn't been to crime scenes before, or seen dead bodies in a much worse state than this, it was just if she couldn't see the face yet then it wasn't really a person. It was a puzzle to be worked out, and she knew a lot of forensics people felt the same way.

What made it a person, of course – someone who'd lived and breathed, had a life until it had been snatched away from them – wasn't just seeing a face. It was a name, it was connecting that name to loved ones and seeing their reactions, too.

Loved ones like Vicky and Mia.

But *they'd* already lost the one person in the world they cared about the most; they couldn't lose him again. No matter the similarities between this death and Simon's, it wasn't him. It couldn't possibly be him.

A horrible thought struck her then. What if this had been done to get at her? *There you go, that ego again!* But she *had* helped

196

to put a lot of people away; people with friends, family. What if all this was some kind of revenge thing? Was she responsible for Simon's death somehow? Had the killer done it just because Vicky was related to her? That worked if you thought about the first murder in those terms, but not this one. She didn't even know this person . . . did she? Was it some kind of message, someone messing with her? Maybe the killer was around, watching her even now?

It was only now that Watts looked up and saw Robyn; that he noticed she was even in the tent. He skirted around the body and joined her. 'Robyn? Robyn, you okay? You look a little . . .'

'Hmm? Oh, yes. Just thinking.'

'You got my message then?' he said, and O'Brien whipped her head around.

'I thought you said—'

'No, I didn't,' Robyn cut in quickly. 'Signal's so bad at Vicky's place.' It sounded like a lame excuse even though people here seemed to know all about its patchy technical problems – nevertheless, it was the truth. But at the same time she didn't see the point of getting Tracy in hot water either, so she just kept her mouth shut.

'Watts?' said O'Brien, (as a kind of blanket 'let's have an explanation, shall we?')

'Oh, well, I just thought . . . This is more Robyn's . . . Dr Adams' thing, isn't it?'

'Her *thing*?'

Watts frowned, perhaps wondering why he had to give any more justification. 'Yeah, y'know, serial killings.'

O'Brien looked like this was the first time she'd ever heard this term. 'And is that what this is then, Watts?'

'I . . . er, well . . . The burial on the beach stuff. Isn't that a, what you call it, MO?'

Robyn winced slightly at the clumsy analysis, but then again Watts wasn't wrong. Both this body and Simon's had been found on the beach, and they'd been buried. That is, there had been some attempt to bury the pair. And perhaps bury a few secrets with them? Perhaps it was just a coincidence about her connection to Simon; maybe they *were* simply dealing with the start of something bigger? She really hoped not. 'There have only been two murders, Sergeant.' He winced now at her use of his formal title. 'Not enough to qualify as serial killings.'

'Yet,' was his reply.

'So, you're hoping there'll be more?' O'Brien said to him.

'That's not what . . . I didn't mean it to sound like—'

'Perhaps you won't be happy until the whole bloody beach is littered with bodies, is that it?' O'Brien's nostrils were flaring at the thought of such a thing, and the knock-on effect it would have to this community. But Robyn had to also wonder whether this was in part due to her DS going behind her back again and contacting her . . . regardless of whether she'd received the tip-off or not. Either way, there *had* been a kind of glee in Watts' voice; excitement that he might finally get to work on one of those cases he'd so admired from Robyn's past.

He hung his head, suitably chastised, and probably knowing there was no point arguing the toss with O'Brien when she was in this frame of mind. The DI sighed loudly, turned to her instead. 'Doctor, and I can't believe I'm asking this, in your professional opinion then . . .' Was there a tremble in her voice at the very thought of what she was going to say next? 'Could that be what we're facing in the future?'

'It's very hard to tell. And would depend on a lot of factors.' Factors she'd already been thinking about before the inspector even broached the question. O'Brien was scrutinising her, though, waiting for something substantial; this was obviously way out of her own personal comfort zone. 'I'm not going to lie to you: it's a possibility, yes.'

O'Brien's hand went to her forehead and began rubbing; so hard that Robyn fully expected smoke to appear.

'But I'll need more to go on. The reports, anything from the autopsy – in fact, if I may, I'd like to attend.' The people in white had stopped what they were doing and were looking over at her, almost as one. Probably shocked she was making such demands. 'Anything you can give me, basically. It'll all help.'

The DI nodded sombrely, realising she had very little choice if this was the beginning of a spate of similar murders. If they had any chance of catching whoever was doing this.

'And . . . well, frankly I really need you to start cutting all the crap,' Robyn said to her. 'We follow this, no matter where it leads. Right?'

O'Brien gaped at her, but there was no nod this time. Instead, she just told her: 'You'll get what you need, Doctor. I'll make sure of that.'

It should have reassured her: finally she was getting some cooperation from these people. Finally they might start to get somewhere with cracking not just this crime, but Simon's death as well. Only then would Vicky and Mia be in a position to move on with their lives. Lives that Robyn hoped she might be more a part of from now on. Words, a promise of assistance. It should have reassured her.

So why did it sound so very much like a threat?

Chapter 24

She'd been here before.

The next day or two felt very familiar to her. A different team, a much smaller team, but going through the same motions after a murder – especially one that had more than a few parallels to another killing. Once forensics were finished with the scene, and the body removed from the wet sand, it had been taken to the local morgue: the same place Victoria Carter had identified her husband not that long ago.

The same place the parents of Kieran Thackery made the formal identification of their son (after his plastic driver's licence had been discovered in the front pocket of his jeans; a good job, as his mobile phone was ruined). Robyn had been present when it happened, had watched as Mrs Thackery – a woman in her late forties, who had insisted on being there – fell into the arms of her husband once the sheet had been pulled back. Mr Thackery, whose hair was as white as one of Boyd's golf balls, had fought back his own tears and said mournfully: 'Aye, that's my lad.'

He was definitely a person now, he had a face now – and he was so, so young.

Sitting with them in the relatives' room, Watts had gleaned more information from the pair while O'Brien looked on. Robyn had been impressed again at the way he handled that, showing more sensitivity than she thought him capable of. Or perhaps he just seemed sensitive compared to O'Brien's 'sledgehammer to crack a nut' form of policing.

'Take your time, it's all right,' Ashley Watts had said.

Mrs Thackery had detached from her husband long enough to say, between sobs: 'I just . . . don't understand . . . who'd want . . . to do . . . something like this . . .?'

'That's what we're going to find out,' the DS told her. One of O'Brien's eyebrows rose at the word 'going to' – because he should have said 'hoping to'. It was never wise to make promises like that to grieving relatives – but it only reflected his determination to get to the core of all this. And Robyn found herself admiring that a little, too. She hoped to God he was right, that they'd figure this one out, because she'd made a promise herself hadn't she . . . to a very special little girl.

They'd informed them that he worked nearby, at the funfair on the pier – which had raised the question of whether he had simply fallen over the railings onto the sand below, and sunk in. That notion only lasted a brief time because even if it was wet, or the body landed while the tide was in, it wouldn't have been buried in the way that it was. That had been deliberate, as it had been with Simon Carter. There was also the small matter of the cause of death: strangulation once again, the marks there on the neck; there'd been no need to wait for an autopsy to confirm that. Once again, the combination of sand, salt and water had destroyed all foreign DNA or anything even approaching evidence. Lastly, Mr and Mrs Thackery had told them that Kieran was seeing someone.

'A nice local girl called Cathy,' the father informed them. 'She's been round to ours for Sunday dinner quite a few times.'

'Excuse me,' Robyn chipped in. 'But she doesn't happen to work at The Castle Spa, does she?'

'That's right, aye. Do you know her?'

Both Watts and O'Brien had turned to look in her direction,

puzzled. How did Robyn know her when they didn't? 'We've met, yes. When I called in up there.' Robyn might not have known Kieran, but here was a link – however tenuous – to her.

A connection also to both the funfair and the spa, the choking as a means of death and the burial . . . It wouldn't take the deductive powers of Poirot to see a pattern forming. As the hours passed, it was looking more and more like the same killer. A killer who might only just be getting warmed up.

A killer, they were told in no uncertain terms – because he'd gone off in a huff on a fishing vessel that had been away for the last few days – who couldn't possibly be Graham Newton. Good news for his wife that he was gone, bad news for them.

Back at the station and in the makeshift incident room, which was actually the small canteen that they'd taken over for the time being, Robyn studied the photos that had been stuck to what was usually the menu board.

Had been studying them so closely, and especially the ones of Simon – though she'd seen those so many times by now – that she started as O'Brien and Watts came up behind her. When were people around here going to get that she didn't like anyone sneaking up on her? Not that they thought they *were* sneaking; it was just—

Robyn had also been getting more flashbacks to Sykes, the last serial case she'd tackled. Earlier on she'd almost had a panic attack thinking about it all, the thoughts going round and round in her head, and she'd ended up in the ladies popping a couple more of her pills – panicking even more when she realised how low she was on stocks of them. But Kieran wasn't a father, that they knew of . . . so it *wasn't* another Sykes, all this. Not really. An admirer then? Not *The Silence of the Lambs*, but *Red Dragon* – a fan of sorts? Someone picking up where he left off but in a different way, sending her a message? The same person who'd left the clipping on her windscreen, whoever that was? Baiting her? But if that was the case, why tell her to leave when she first got here? It made no sense.

'We didn't mean to . . .' Watts told her, when he saw how jittery they'd made her.

'It's . . .' Robyn shook her head. 'Don't worry about it.'

'So, come on then, Doctor. Give. What are you thinking? Why the beaches? Traumatic incident with a sandcastle when this creep was a kid or what?' O'Brien's facetiousness aside, she had no idea how close to the mark she was about people's backgrounds and childhoods leading to behaviour such as this. To staging like this.

'You're not going to like it,' she told the DI.

'Oh?'

'At the moment I'm thinking Franklyn Boyd used to spend a lot of time with nomadic desert tribes.' Another theory she'd been pondering.

Watts appeared confused. 'Who's Franklyn Boyd?' He was obviously as fond of history lessons as Robyn.

'You're not seriously suggesting we're looking for a man who's been dead over a century?' O'Brien gave another one of her deep-seated chuckles.

'Who's Franklyn Boyd?' Watts repeated. 'And why has he been dead so long?'

'Because that's when he was born, Einstein,' said O'Brien. 'He's one of Sebastian's ancestors.'

'We were talking about him when I visited his house,' Robyn said and watched O'Brien's lip twitch once more – possibly because *she'd* never had the invite there. 'He was telling me about the herbal remedies the man brought back with him, some of which they're employing up at that spa. The one Simon worked for part-time and where Kieran Thackery's girlfriend still works.'

'So?' asked O'Brien.

'So, I'm saying what if those weren't the only practices that made it back over here which are still in use? Those sorts of tribes used to bury their dead out in the dunes, you know.'

O'Brien's eyes narrowed to slits. 'Seriously?'

Robyn shrugged. 'You asked me what I thought.'

'I'm beginning to wish I hadn't. I'm beginning to wish I hadn't brought you into this at all frankly.' Robyn thought about reminding her that she hadn't had a choice in the end, but bit her tongue. Now wasn't the time to antagonise the inspector – but funny how it was the mention of Boyd that set her off again.

Nobody's above the law!

'I think maybe we should be having a talk with Cathy Rogers from the spa, seeing if she knows anything,' suggested Robyn.

'You want to put that poor girl through a grilling, all because of some long-dead explorer?' snapped O'Brien.

'No. Because it's good police work, Inspector.'

'Police work?' O'Brien spluttered. 'You're not even a police *officer*.'

'I'm an official consultant,' Robyn protested. It had been a long time since she'd had to win a pissing contest or justify her place on an investigative team, particularly to a person who'd asked her to help in the first place – albeit grudgingly. Just what the fuck was O'Brien's problem? It would probably take a dozen people more highly trained than Robyn to unravel that one. What she had done was successfully divert things away from Boyd and Cathy Rogers, then 'won' the argument by flapping a hand and heading back out again.

Watts apologised on her behalf, making sure his voice was low enough so she wouldn't hear, then trailed after her like a puppy following its owner.

She'd mentioned all this on the phone to Cav in the station later, desperate to hear the voice of someone who actually appreciated what she did – even if it was just in a professional capacity. 'The bloody idiot!' he'd grumbled. 'Doesn't she know what a resource she has with you? She's lucky to even have you there offering your help! I . . . We *definitely* know how lucky we are. Look, should I have a word with a few people at this end. Maybe Gordon could—'

'Naw, leave it. It's not worth it, Cav. But I really appreciate the kind words, thanks. I'm beginning to feel like I'm in a western and they want to drive me out of town.'

He'd ended the conversation, after listening to her moaning for ages when he should have been working, by saying: 'How are you, Robyn?'

'I'm . . . I'm okay, I suppose.'

'You don't sound very sure.'

'I . . . It's just . . .' Don't cry in the police station, she told herself. Pull yourself together, for fuck's sake! 'I'm okay,' she repeated, trying to sound more convincing.

'And your family?'

'They're . . .' Robyn stopped and realised that she didn't have to pretend for the next bit. 'We're all right; we're coping.'

'That's good,' Cav said to her. 'Well, even though they don't know me from Adam, give them my love won't you?'

Robyn promised that she would. Was even looking forward to doing that when she got in the house, perhaps having a glass of wine with Vicky that evening – who'd actually begun to cut back a bit on her alcohol consumption. For one thing it was costing a fortune!

When she got back though, expecting the usual dinner prep to be in full swing – Vicky now helping Tracy, with Mia pitching in too – she'd found the house eerily silent. 'Hello!' she'd called out after letting herself in through the door. 'Anyone hom—' It was only as she turned the corner, looking into the living room, that she saw Vicky sitting in her usual position on the couch, only this time she had her arms folded. No TV, no cigarettes, no wine. It was like she'd been sitting there waiting for her. 'Oh hey, where is everyone?'

'Mia's at Julie and Jay's. I sent Tracy away.'

'Okay . . .' said Robyn. There was something in Vicky's tone, a hardness she hadn't heard since they were kids and used to fall out over something or nothing. It was toneless, emotionless. Chilling. 'Is everything all right?' she asked, knowing full well that it wasn't.

Vicky stood up, unfolding her arms. In one of her hands she had a piece of yellowed paper. 'Mia found this in Simon's belongings, with his swimming certificates and all of that stuff. Things he kept because they meant a lot to him. Thankfully I got it off her before she had a chance to read it but . . .' Tears were straining at the corners of Vicky's eyes, but she wasn't letting them break free. Holding it all back, holding herself in check. Not even letting her obvious anger out, although that came across when she walked over and slammed the thing into Robyn's chest – hard enough to push her back a step. 'What the fu . . .' she began, then looked down at the letter and understood exactly what had happened. Understood precisely what this was, and it sent a shiver through her. 'Oh shit,' she breathed.

'Oh shit's right,' said Vicky. 'I know what you did, Robyn. I know exactly what you did. Now . . . get the fuck out of my house!'

Part Three

One of the jewels in Golden Sands' crown is The Majestic Hotel. Built in the mid-1800s for a cost of around half a million pounds (and substantially renovated in the 1960s and early 2000s), it was often called one of the most impressive structures in the region. A temporary home to visiting royalty and dignitaries in its heyday – though thankfully more accessible these days – the building has always had a unique atmosphere all of its own. Even today, it is *the* place to stay if you want to see in-house entertainment, which includes screenings in its very own cinema, cabaret and bingo. A popular wedding venue, The Majestic also hosts various fairs – ranging from craft and pottery to memorabilia of all kinds. In addition, there is a regular psychic evening that's proved extremely popular, in which a local medium communes with those who have passed over to the other side.

Chapter 25

She knocked back her third double vodka of the evening, straight no tonic, which burned all the way down. Then burned her stomach.

Robyn had asked for the most expensive brand they had there every time, which apparently wasn't saying much in this place. The Majestic! She snorted; what a fucking joke. Why had they ever thought it was so posh? Yet it had been her temporary home for the last couple of nights, the change in her circumstances enough to make her head spin . . . and the drinks weren't really helping in that respect.

Tipping her glass for another, the bartender there – who looked like he'd barely evolved from caveman days, complete with low forehead and unibrow – reached for the bottle, tipped the clear liquid into a silver tube to measure it, before transferring it into a fresh glass. 'Thanks!' she said when he handed it to her. 'Put it on my room again, would you?'

'Very well,' said the man in an accent that was completely at odds with his features; almost as if an Oxford don's brain had been transplanted into a gorilla. Then he got her to sign a slip, pulling a face at the squiggle she'd managed.

Carrying it back to her table this time, she slid onto her seat and reached for her pills. Slipping one into her mouth when she thought nobody was looking, Robyn sipped the alcohol and swallowed, before repeating the action. Take two and call me in the morning . . . Ha ha!

She took in the room again and saw a few of the same faces from last night, from last week actually: those who were probably having a two-week holiday. Nobody was paying any attention to her, thankfully. She was safe enough here, with all the people around. Then she took out her phone, examined the thread of messages – at least this place had decent Wi-Fi, once you were a resident – which had initiated this meeting.

Where have you been?
Not been feeling great to be honest . . .
Oh no, are you okay now?
Feeling a bit sick, but I'm all right.

Yeah, sick all right. Sick to her stomach – which was still burning. In fairness when she'd sent that she *had* been feeling sick, from the sheer amount she'd been drinking the previous night. She'd camped out in bed, rushing to the loo every now and again until it was all out of her system and the most she could manage was dry-heaving. Cat-napping, with the 'DO NOT DISTURB' sign planted firmly on the handle outside – which hadn't stopped a couple of random knocks on the door, that she totally ignored – waiting until it was time to do the whole thing again.

Waiting for company this time, though.

Do you fancy meeting up? Filling me in?
Sure. Absolutely. Where?
The Majestic?

Written like she wasn't living there, like she'd just suggested it off the cuff as a place to grab a drink. It was where she'd been heading the night they'd first tried this, after all. After he'd ballsed it up with all of his nonsense.

You were talking to another guy, Robyn. Just chatting, but you knew Watts liked you.

A fucking mess. It was her speciality, wasn't it? Messes. Whether it was creating them or wading into other people's and trying to untangle them. Trying to prevent future ones. How many kids would still have their fathers in the future because they'd nailed Sykes?

Let's face it, Cav nailed him. You were playing the helpless damsel in distress. Again, your speciality, a little voice said.

Go fuck yourself, she told it.

Robyn drank some more, waited for him to come through the door. DS Ashley Watts. With his schoolboy looks, and schoolboy mentality to match – or was it? The way he'd handled the Newton interview, the grieving parents of Kieran Thackery. Strong, but caring as well. Easy to misread . . .

'He's a good kid, and – just don't tell him I said so – he has the makings of a decent detective. Inspector someday in the not too distant. The last thing he needs is you coming along . . . turning his head and cocking it up for him.'

Was that what she was doing? Making another mess?

'I've got eyes; I can see what's going on in front of me. How you're using him.'

'You do work quick.'

Click her fingers and he'd come running like a puppy dog, though O'Brien could talk – she might as well have him on a lead. Robyn let out a slow breath; she *was* using him, it had to be said. Had used him before for information, like finding out what had happened when they'd talked with Lisa Newton, but would have used him to lean on (maybe for more) when she'd had that first row with Vicky.

Looking back, that was more like a friendly disagreement compared with the last time they'd spoken. If you could call that speaking.

'Get the fuck out of my house!'

211

Robyn closed her eyes, drank more of the oily liquid. When she opened them again, Watts was in front of her, standing by the table. He raised a hand. 'Hey.'

'Oh, hey.' Robyn was surprised herself at exactly how happy she was to see him.

I've got eyes.

So happy she gave him a big smile – something she hadn't done since packing her things and heading to this hotel. It grew wider when he smiled back. 'Do you want another?' Watts pointed at the glass, which was now virtually empty.

'Oh, I should be the one to—'

He batted that suggestion away with the same hand, then went over to the bar. She watched him gesturing back towards her table, clearly asking what she was on. He returned with another double and a pint of generic lager for himself. 'Here you go,' Watts told her, sitting down opposite. 'You look like you need it.'

'That bad, eh?'

'I wouldn't go that far. You look pretty good to me.' He grinned and took a gulp of his pint.

'Flatterer.'

'Always.' Watts frowned suddenly, realising he probably shouldn't be going down this road given all that had happened, and she felt a little crestfallen at that. 'So, you've been sick?' he said then, changing tack.

Robyn nodded. 'Not been great, no.'

'Not unusual. Different town, different bugs. No immunity. Happens most holidays when folks get back home.'

She agreed, but of course her particular bug had been self-inflicted . . . in more ways than one. 'I miss anything?'

'Not a lot. To be honest the station feels really weird now without you there,' Watts admitted, swigging more of the lager.

'I bet O'Brien doesn't see it that way,' she said, starting in on her own fresh drink.

212

Watts shrugged. 'Her bark's worse than her bite, I promise.' More dog analogies.

'Good job, because I'd hate to be on the receiving end of one of those bites.' Robyn laughed, the alcohol providing cartoon images of O'Brien as a rottweiler opening up her huge maw; then Watts sitting beside her as a puppy wagging his tail. She shook the latter away.

'What?' he asked.

'Nothing,' she assured him. 'You guys spoken to Cathy from the spa yet?' Her turn to change the subject.

'Not brought her in or anything. O'Brien went and had a poke around at the funfair, though, where Kieran worked.'

'And . . .?'

He shrugged again. 'Nothing really to report.'

Robyn took another drink, a larger one than she'd intended, and Watts raised an eyebrow. 'She'll keep dancing around this until you all wake up. There's a connection at that spa, and possibly even with Sebastian Boyd.'

'Like I said, friends in high places,' was his response. 'Piling on the pressure.'

'Friends who might be willing to kill?' she asked him seriously. 'He talked about his investors getting antsy.'

'When you went to see him?'

'When I went to see him,' Robyn verified, and she had to admit she liked the hint of jealousy in his voice. 'He was quite charming actually,' she continued, then waited, watching for the reaction.

There. A twitch of the cheek. 'I'm sure he was.'

'Not my type though,' she reassured the DS and thought she noticed him let out a small sigh of relief. 'Listen,' she said, 'everything at the moment is pointing there. If I was back home, Cav would be—'

'Cav?' She could have sworn she'd mentioned the officer she worked with most closely before, but maybe that had been to Vicky?

He's just a mate.

More than that, I reckon.

Me and him, it's . . . He's married.

Since when did that stop you?

'DI Cavendish, he's . . . Well, he's not O'Brien that's for damned sure.' Another laugh, bitter this time. 'We work well together. *All* the team works well together,' she added, just to show it wasn't only her and Cav cosying up in some office somewhere.

She's lucky to even have you there offering your help! I . . . We definitely *know how lucky we are.*

'Right,' said Watts sadly, possibly wishing she'd been given a better reception when she arrived. Wishing they were giving her one now. Probably thought that was the reason she'd cried off work the last couple of days. It couldn't be further from the truth.

'Hey,' said Robyn, reaching out a hand and grasping his. Squeezing. He looked down, then up into her face, then down again – as if he was witnessing the Big Bang happening right in front of his eyes. 'I know it's not you. All you've done since I got here is be nice to me, try to look out for me.' There was a moment then, but it scared her so much she let go of his hand again quickly. It looked for all the world like Watts was going to cry, he missed that touch so much – but he took another big gulp of his pint instead.

Robyn called over to the barman, pointed at the two of them for him to bring the same again. For a second it appeared as if he was going to refuse, knowing the amount she'd already put away, but then he set to work with the vodka bottle and pulled back on one of the taps to pour Watts his accompanying lager. To be honest it looked so weak Robyn felt sure they were diluting it with lemonade. Could you get shandy on tap?

Silence had descended, maybe due to shock – at least on Watts's part – and she was grateful when the monkey-man with the posh accent brought the drinks over on a silver tray. Another cartoon image flashed into her mind and she almost burst out laughing when he set down the glasses.

'Just put it—'

'On your room again? Of course. Madame, sir,' said the man, grabbing another half-hearted signature, before walking off with a bewildered look on his face.

Watts was still working on his first shandy, but took a second to ask: 'Your room? You're staying here now?'

'I am,' Robyn confirmed, raising her glass for him to chink. He opened and closed his mouth, then lifted his own glass to tap hers.

'What happened? I mean, if you don't mind me—'

'You want to take these through to the entertainment bit?' she asked suddenly, aware that she was slurring her words – which didn't stop her having another swig of the large vodka.

'The entertainment?' If he'd been confused before, then he was totally lost now.

'Yeah!' she told him. 'Might be some music on or something. Last night they had these singers . . .' Robyn laughed, and it came out much louder than she'd planned, drawing some stares from the other punters. She put a finger to her lips and shushed herself. 'Yeah,' she whispered this time. 'Last night there were these singers on dressed like ABBA or something, except they were singing . . . wait for it: "We don't have to take our clothes off to have a good time."'

Watts looked at her sideways. 'Right,' he said slowly, drawing out the word.

'But . . . but wait for it, here's the punchline. The average age of the audience was about ninety, I swear!' She guffawed at this. Had been dying to tell someone about it since last night. '*Ripley's Believe It or Not!* eh?'

'Robyn?' he asked softly. 'Robyn, are you okay?'

'*I'm . . . I'm okay, I suppose.*'

'*You don't sound very sure.*'

'*I . . . It's just . . .*'

'*And your family?*'

'*They're . . .*'

215

She shoved her chair back, so hard the legs made scraping noises on the floor. 'Come on! Who knows what hilarity we might be missing!' Robyn grabbed Watts' hand and pulled him to his feet, not even giving him time to bring his pint along. Ignoring the protests of the bartender who was shouting something about not being able to take her vodka, Robyn dragged Watts out through the door and across, past the area with seating and the foyer, over towards where the largest of the rooms in the whole hotel was located. The place where they did bingo, where they put on the cabaret.

Only there wasn't any music coming from there tonight. Just a voice, a very familiar voice, speaking into a microphone. Robyn slowed down to a crawl when she heard it, allowing Watts to catch up. She downed the rest of her drink, then realised she was still holding Watts' hand and shoved the empty glass into it, before moving forwards once more. Speeding up the closer she came to the large, open doorway, and beyond it the seating that was arranged theatre style – for the shows, films or whatever. Beyond that was the stage and there was a lone figure on it. A figure she recognised even from this distance. A person she'd last seen in a caravan spouting her poison.

'. . . coming through now. Was your sister's name Joan at all?' she was asking someone in the audience, an elderly lady who was standing and nodding. 'She wants you to know that she's surrounded by all the family who have passed over and are on the other side.'

Before she even realised she was doing it, Robyn had stormed into the room and was shouting: '*Fraud!* Don't listen to her! She's a fucking liar!'

Robyn felt hands on her, pulling her back. Watts, who'd obviously put the glass down somewhere. 'What are you *doing?*'

'Con artist! Swindler!' Robyn was calling out. Everyone in the seating area was turning around to look towards the back, and the woman on the stage – Bella Prescott, with her short pixie haircut – was shielding her eyes to try and see who was causing all the ruckus.

'Robyn? Robyn that's enough now,' Watts was saying to her, still trying to tear her away.

'Enough? I don't fucking think so!'

Bella had stepped down from the stage, leaving the mike behind her on the wood. She was walking along the middle aisle towards Robyn, closing the distance between them. 'Robyn? It is Robyn, isn't it?'

'It's all your fault!' she screamed at the medium. 'If she hadn't gone to see you, she wouldn't have—'

'You need to calm down, Robyn. Please,' Bella was asking in a polite enough tone, but for some reason it just wound Robyn up even more. 'None of this is—'

That was it: Robyn shrugged off Watts and lunged at the woman. Her balance wasn't great, probably because of the vodka and pills, but she still managed to swing her fist and catch the other woman with a glancing blow on the side of the head. Bella stumbled sideways, grabbed a chair, or she would have fallen to the floor.

'*Jesus!*' exclaimed Watts.

Robyn laughed. 'Ha, some psychic! You didn't see that coming, did you?'

Staff from The Majestic had finally woken up to what was occurring, two guys and a woman grabbing Robyn and pulling her away, while Watts had rushed over to Bella and was helping her straighten up again. 'Are you . . . God, I'm so sorry,' Robyn heard him say and wanted to shout out not to apologise on her behalf, but she was having her own problems struggling with the staff. 'I don't know what's come over . . . She's been drinking and—'

'It's all right, it's all right.' Bella was telling him. 'She's just lost, Ashley. *So* lost.'

'How do you . . .' But then the barman back at the pub had known him, why not Bella Prescott as well?

217

'You need to . . . She's in so much danger and she doesn't even realise it.' Bella touched her forehead, winced, then patted him on the shoulder. 'Go. Help her.'

Reluctantly, he left the medium and returned to Robyn and the staff members. 'Wait, where are you—'

'We're chucking her out,' said one of the men.

'No . . . No, you can't,' moaned Robyn. 'It's not safe.'

'Listen,' Watts said to the man who'd spoken, 'she's had a skinful. The lady back there's okay; they know each other. Let me see this one back to her room where she can't cause any more trouble.'

'I don't know about that, we—' began the female staff member, then saw Watts' warrant card that he'd pulled out.

'Leave her to me.' The three members of staff looked at each other, then looked over at Bella, who nodded. They let Robyn go, let Watts take her by the arm. 'Cheers,' he told them.

As he led Robyn off, they both heard an announcement come over the speaker system back in the entertainment section: 'There will be a short intermission. Bella Prescott will be back on stage shortly.'

Robyn giggled. 'I gave her what for, didn't I?'

'Yeah,' Watts replied.

'I'm *not* a damsel in distress,' she told him.

'Well, *I* wouldn't like to get on the wrong side of you, that's for bloody sure. Come on, let's get you back to the room.'

As they waited at the lifts, Robyn suddenly turned and kissed him. If the hand-holding had been like a minor miracle, then heaven knows what he thought of this. It had just felt like the right thing to do in the moment, and as a thank you.

Still slurring her words she said: 'I'm in room 203.'

Chapter 26

When they entered the room, Watts having to keep Robyn steady or she'd have toppled over, she kissed him again.

Regardless of her state, it was one of the best kisses he'd ever experienced. It might have been because he wasn't massively experienced in that department, though nobody at the station realised – they'd go to town on him if they knew that! – but also because of how he was starting to feel about this woman.

He should just keep his mouth shut, let events take their course – he'd regret it forever if he didn't, he knew that too – but he just couldn't help himself. 'Robyn. Robyn are you sure about this?'

She nodded, but he could see the effect of the drink in her movements, her eyes. What if they . . . and then she regretted it in the morning? What if it was just the booze fuelling this? She hadn't exactly been keen before, especially after the pub that night – had seemed more interested in the other bloke, that tanned guy. And he hadn't been able to help himself then, either. Stepping in, assuming the man was bothering her when he should have just scoped it all out first. Idiot!

But the more important question was: why had she been drinking that heavily in the first place? Something to do with her family, her cousin? And that medium downstairs, what the fuck had been going on there? Good job O'Brien hadn't been around, she'd have thrown Robyn in jail and not thought twice about it – just to teach her a lesson. Tough love, the woman called it. He had to admit she'd taught him a lot, *but* when it came to that particular practice, he guessed they would never really see eye-to-eye.

That had always been his dad's line. Tough love, arguments, hitting him if it got that far. A hard upbringing.

'I know yer mother as well . . . She'd be ashamed of you!'

Not as ashamed as his father always was. Sometimes, just sometimes – especially after those beatings – he wished someone had shown some real love at home. Wished someone had said they were proud of him, just once.

Real love. Like the kind he was starting to feel for Robyn. He didn't want to fuck that up with a one-night stand. The state she was in, he doubted she'd even remember it. She *wasn't* sure, no matter what she said. 'Robyn, it's probably not a good idea.'

Wrong. So wrong . . . Wrong thing to say on so many levels. Those half-closed eyes were suddenly wide open, filled with hurt. Rejection. He knew that look; he'd seen it in the mirror so many times after—

Then, just as suddenly as she'd been all over him, she was shrugging him off again. Stepping backwards into the room, legs catching the edge of the bed – and he thought he'd have to rush forwards and catch her again, but she managed to remain upright, a determined expression on her face. 'Why don't you just go,' she said to him.

No. That wasn't what he'd been . . . He was just trying to do the right thing. 'I didn't mean . . . Please, Robyn.'

She looked down then, sadly. 'I don't blame you for not wanting me. I'm fucked up, Ashley. I'm worthless. I hate myself.'

'No, you're not. You—'

'You don't *know* me!' she shouted. 'I'm a horrible person.

Everything I touch turns to shit!' Another small laugh. 'It's like the Midas touch in reverse.'

He moved across to join her, so she tried to back away – and this time did end up sitting on the bed. Watts stood above her, but kept his distance. 'I'm . . . I'm sure that's not—'

'You don't want to get involved with me. I don't really want to get . . . I always choose the wrong guys.'

'I'm . . . I don't—'

'Guys who aren't good for me. Or if they are, they're . . . I fuck their lives up too. I do it on purpose, you see.' Robyn laughed again, but this time it sounded more like a mewl. 'Can't switch that training off, even when I look at myself.' She was rambling now, more mumbles and mutters than anything. 'I've hurt someone, two people . . . I think, I don't know if she knows yet about . . . I've hurt someone I love. It's why I never came back, you see?'

Watts got down on his haunches, knees cracking in spite of his youth. 'Robyn, I don't understand.'

'They found the letter. Vicky knows.'

All he could do was shake his head. He knew this was the thing, the big thing he'd been puzzling over. The thing that had seen her move out into The Majestic. 'What letter?'

Robyn looked about her, finally spotting something on the bedside table where she'd placed it – obviously after reading it again and again, many times – before rolling over and reaching out to snatch it. She tried to sit up again, but needed his help to do so. Robyn passed him the piece of paper she'd been holding. The letter. A letter that was in her handwriting; he recognised it from things she'd written down at the station. A bit different, less smooth here, but basically the same.

'That's . . . that's who I am, Ashley,' she told him, then fell back onto the bed.

His eyes scanned the words and he rose at the same time. When he'd finished, he read it a second time and looked up to ask something of Robyn. Unfortunately her eyes were closed and she was snoring softly, fast asleep.

Watts read the letter one final time then said to himself, 'Holy crap . . .'

'Holy. Fucking. Crap.'

Chapter 27

They're fighting over her like she's a piece of meat.

Like a pack of hyenas. Like she is nothing. Less than nothing. A receptacle to be used, abused, in any way they see fit. They tear at her clothes, tear into each other, one pulling the other off her. She is still dazed from the backhander she received, but aware enough to know what is happening. What will happen in a few moments, when they get their act together. When they've decided on a pecking order, who'll go first, go second . . . Just how many of them are there?

Too many. It won't just be her clothes that they'll tear, or into each other. These bastards will tear her apart – literally. She'll be lucky if they don't kill her. Lucky to walk away from this one, or walk properly ever again.

Fight. She should try and fight them. But there are simply too many.

In the end maybe it would be better to just give up and let them get on with things. It's how she'd been conceived after all. A mistake – that's what she'd called her once in a fit of rage, in the middle of an argument – a mistake, a product of rape. Hardly surprising, considering the type of men her mother gave the come on to.

That's how this had all started, with an attack – a violation. Made sense for it to end that way, didn't it?

Didn't it?

But that isn't how this is going to pan out. Fate is about to step in, though in years to come she might wish that it hadn't. That things had just played out the way she thought they were going to. That would have been the end of it, then.

'Hey! Hey, you lot!' comes the voice. Strong and sure, but also with a streak of kindness running through it. A streak of decency.

The sort of man who had spotted what was happening, figured out what was about to happen. Followed these guys outside here and was about to get in the middle of something he really shouldn't.

'Who's that?' asks one of the beasts.

'Fuck knows!' answers another.

'Piss off, mate, can't you see we're busy here?' says the first one, the one whose breath she'd smelt up close and personal. The one she'd kneed in the privates, who'd drawn first blood from her.

'I don't think so,' the voice comes back. 'I've already called the police. They're on their way.'

'The fuck he has!' says another.

Somebody is already running off, running past the newcomer who appeared in the mouth of the alley. The virgin, the bait, getting out of there while the getting's good.

'They're on their way, and if you don't stop I'm going to kick the living shit out of the lot of you.'

'Like to see you try!' snarls one, then immediately regrets it when the interloper rushes towards him and punches him squarely in the face. There's a crunching sound, a gurgling scream.

'By dose!' cries out the beast who pushed his own luck. 'Be's boken by dose!'

'Won't be the only thing I break if you don't fuck off out of it!' promises the figure, kicking out at another one of them and knocking him to the ground.

There's a different kind of scrabbling around then, a shared sense of self-preservation. Even if he hadn't called the cops, this guy could probably take them on his own. Cowards, the lot of them! Big men when they're forcing themselves on a woman – so many she couldn't possibly fight them off – but pit them against a real opponent . . .

Then they're scarpering, following the virgin. Getting out of there before they either get their arses handed to them or get arrested.

Leaving the man with the voice behind. The person who'd saved her. 'Are you okay?' he asks.

'I . . .' She doesn't even know how to answer that, so just says, 'Could've been worse.'

'Yeah,' he replies.

'Are the police really on their way?' She's worrying about what they'll say, how all this will look – when she should probably be reporting it anyway. Definitely should.

'Didn't have time to call them. I saw you heading out with . . . Then those other guys, his mates. Shall we call the coppers now?'

'No . . . No, please.'

'All right, whatever you want. Come on. Let's get you away from here.'

He holds out his hand to help her up, and she takes it. It's strong, like he is. And it's only when they step out into the light, the better light, that she recognises him really; probably still shaken from the blow to the face. 'S-Simon . . . Is that you?'

Simon. Vicky's Simon. Vicky's fiancé.

'Yeah,' he says again. 'Come on, let's get you home.'

'No . . . no, I can't. My aunty, she'd . . .'

'Understood. Okay, let's get you back to my flat then. Get you cleaned up a bit.' He drapes his jacket around her, covers up her nakedness. 'There are some of Vic's clothes there.'

She stops then, forces him to stop too. 'S-Simon. Promise me. Promise you won't tell her. Vicky I mean, when she gets back.'

He shakes his head. ''Course not. Not if you don't want me to, Robyn.'

And as they head off up the road, he places a gentle arm and hand around her shoulders.

Chapter 28

She awoke in darkness.

For a second or two Robyn panicked. She was back in that lock-up, not knowing what was going to happen to her – but at the back of her mind having a sneaking suspicion – waiting for Sykes to return. Wondering how long she'd got to live, when exactly she was going to die. Hearing a banging sound, a knocking. But that had been complete and utter blackness, whereas she saw now there was a streak of light where the sun was making its way in through the closed curtains; creating shadows.

It brought to mind another time in her life when that happened, when she'd been waiting in the dark about to be attacked. Thinking about it all, about the dream she'd just had – the dreams she'd been having since she returned, the drive to Golden Sands dredging up more than just the happy memories – she began to cry. Long, hard sobs. Tears she hadn't allowed herself all the time she'd been staying with her cousin, but had come out when she least expected it. Tears for a life not lived, a direction it could have taken but didn't because neither of them could let it.

Tears for Simon.

The Simon that was, the Simon from the past. The one who'd saved her (not a damsel in distress – remember that knee in the groin? – but there was no way she could have got out of that mess herself). The one who'd reached out his hand and pulled her up off the ground. They were different people now; she was different and he was—

Dead. Gone. She'd never see him again. Not that she ever really wanted to. It had been easier for her *not* to see him. That's why she'd only dropped in to the evening do on their wedding day; that's why she'd gone off with that other guy. To try and block out the pain, the hurt. The longing. It's what she'd used sex for most of her life, if she was being absolutely honest with herself – turning that laser vision on herself. Analysing herself again. Blocked things out to such an extent that she'd hardly thought about them over the years, though couldn't return to Golden Sands and watch the life Vicky was building with him. The child they'd had. The child that, but for a twist of fate, might have been theirs.

Except the past has a way of catching up with you, always. Buried secrets don't stay buried forever. And the letter brought everything rushing back in a surge: the letter Mia had found; the one Vicky must have read with shock and horror. The letter she'd thought he'd destroyed, but had kept for some reason – maybe because he still felt that way about her? No, that wasn't it; the incriminating piece of paper in question had been tucked away, buried with all the other things from his past. Not meant to be found, apart from, of course, when you were dead and your wife and kid were sorting out your stuff. Nobody ever thinks of that, we all think we're immortal.

Perhaps he kept it thinking he'd look back at it when he was an old man and remember the short time they'd had together? Or had he just simply forgotten it was there? Either way, it had been a ticking bomb at the heart of that family waiting to go off someday. Waiting to devastate the one person they both loved more than anything, the person they'd been trying to protect.

The person who now hated her.

Something or nothing . . . Definitely something.

Hiding stuff is the worst thing you can possibly do.

Robyn lay there and pictured Vicky's face, so cold and emotionless as she'd slammed that letter into her chest, as she'd told her to get out. Not even listening when she'd tried to explain – although the letter pretty much said it all.

We can't do this to Vicky. It would break her heart.

But they'd already done it by then, hadn't they? The act that would break her heart if she ever found out about it. Going away wouldn't do a damned thing about that, wouldn't change it. Wouldn't change what would happen if Vicky ever found out the truth.

'It was such a long time ago. And it was just the once, Vic.' The first time she'd used the shortened version of her name since she returned, and now wished Vicky would call her Robs again to match. 'Simon . . . He helped me. There were these guys, who were—'

'I don't want to know the fucking details, Robyn!'

She'd carried on anyway, trying to explain. 'We'd had a few drinks and . . . It was when you were away for the week doing that course.' A course in something or other. Robyn couldn't even remember – doubted Vicky could either – she was always doing them, weekend things, week things. Chopping and changing, not knowing what she wanted to do with her life. Probably brought on by Robyn's talk about uni life. That's how she'd ended up going out with their mutual friend Brenda (whatever happened to her?); the one who liked to plaster that make-up on. It always worked when it was the three of them, but Brenda had sodded off with a fella and left her alone, and then that one guy – who'd seemed so nice – had approached her. Gullible idiot that she was, Robyn had followed him outside and the rest . . . the rest was history.

Luckily Simon had been in The Barnacle that evening, though she hadn't spotted him – had been tucked away in one of the booths, he told her afterwards, filling in the gaps of the story. Simon had spotted the lads who'd followed them outside. Knew

228

what was about to happen and had trailed them too. Looking out for Vicky's cousin.

Afterwards he'd been so kind, had taken her back to his bedsit and let her use the shower. The marks on her face hadn't been too bad once the blood had been cleaned up, nothing she couldn't explain away or cover with concealer for a few days. She should have gone to the police, reported them – would have done these days – but was scared to back then. After all, *she'd* gone outside voluntarily with the virgin. But Simon said that he knew some of their faces, would put the word out with a few of his mates who'd put the fear of God into them. They'd never do it again, would know they were being watched now. And off she'd gone back to Aunty Sue's and Uncle Trev's, letting herself in late when they were in bed. They hadn't been expecting her to be that early anyway, not from a nice night out.

Nothing had happened until she'd called round with the wine a couple of days later, as a thank you. Had she been hoping something would? Had she felt that spark? Had Simon? Whatever, they'd ended up chatting and drinking and one thing had led to another – even though he'd been engaged to Vicky.

She'd known it was wrong, but as Vicky said: 'You just couldn't help yourself, could you? Selfish cow! The one guy you hadn't had. *My* guy. What the hell is wrong with you, Robyn?'

She felt like saying: takes two to tango, or some bullshit like that. It wouldn't have helped. So she'd just shaken her head, crying. Should just leave, get out of there – run away.

GO HOME!

Isn't that what she always did with her problems, try and escape them? Not face them, just like she hadn't faced this family in all those years? What had happened, happened towards the end of the summer, and she'd headed back to uni early making some excuse about parties and such, when the real reason had been she just couldn't be here anymore. Couldn't look at Vicky, but also couldn't stand to watch her and Simon together.

Once she'd packed again, this time in the present – she hadn't unpacked that much anyway, to be fair – Robyn had slunk down the stairs again, only to find Vicky waiting for her with her hand out.

'Key,' she said. If looks could kill, right at that moment she'd be joining Simon and Kieran Thackery in the morgue. Robyn had rummaged around in her handbag and given the key back to her.

As she was opening the front door, Robyn heard from behind, practically a whisper: 'Did you love him? Do you *still* love him?'

Biting her lip, Robyn continued out through that door and headed for her car, really hoping she wouldn't get any shit from the hard-core journos still there . . . which she didn't; they probably saw her 'don't fuck with me' face. Not today. How could she answer that question, look her in the eyes and tell her: 'No. Absolutely not. It was just a bit of fun.' When that would have been a lie, a blatant lie. Vicky'd read the letter, the connotations of it.

You know how I feel. And I think you feel the same way . . .

He'd never said it, never said as much but . . . Not something his wife, sorry his widow, wanted – needed – to hear. She'd been through so much recently, and all Robyn had done was make things harder. Upset her even more.

If it hadn't been for the bloody psychic! Stirring things up, causing Vicky to think Simon had had a fling with Lisa Newton. When the truth was, Simon had been apologising for—

No. It hadn't been him; that was all nonsense. All cooked up by that—

'*Fraud . . . fucking liar!*'

Oh no.

'*Con artist! Swindler!*'

Recollections now, not of Kevin Sykes, not of Simon and what they'd done, nor the night Vicky had thrown her out, but of the previous night. All that drink, the pills.

Watts.

Robyn looked around, as if expecting to see him hiding behind

230

the wardrobe – a figure in her room – or might hear the flush and see him emerge from the bathroom, naked and grinning. 'What a night! You're an animal!'

But of course he'd turned her down, hadn't he. Not surprising given the state she'd been in, a complete and utter wreck, going around punching people. Regardless of what she thought of Prescott, there was no need for that; it just wasn't like her. Robyn wouldn't blame the woman if she decided to press charges. She'd have every right to. Watts had been there, though, to smooth everything over, just like he'd done with the hotel staff. Persuading them to let him take her back to the room. And she'd kissed him – an impulse thing, hadn't been intending to, but he'd been so, so sweet.

Then, back in the room, the rejection, the confession. The letter, which was now all the way over on the dresser again. Where Watts must have put it before leaving. No chance of seeing him anywhere naked, because he'd simply left. Put her to bed (fully clothed, she realised when she lifted the covers), pulled the curtains and then done a 'Robyn'. Nicked off out of it. She'd probably never hear from him again, and for someone she'd kept at arm's length why did that thought make her so miserable? When she was done here, she'd go back home to Hannerton, he'd stay in Golden Sands – and that would be that. Simon all over again.

Hardly.

Robyn pushed herself up off the pillow, her eyes still wet with tears. Her head was banging, same as it had been the previous morning . . . afternoon.

That banging, the knocking.

And the first thing she did when she managed to get herself up was head to the bathroom, fill a glass with water and take a couple more of her painkillers, vaguely aware that there was no pain anymore in her back. That she was taking these because she was on the verge of being, if not addicted already, then certainly dependent on them to function.

231

As fuzzy as her head was, as much as it hurt – the pills yet to take effect – she shook it. Ran some more water and splashed it on her face. Then she made the mistake of looking up and seeing her reflection in the mirror. It was not a pretty sight. All the more reason for Watts to leave her alone.

She stared at it until she couldn't look anymore, until she felt the hatred welling inside her as well, the same as it must have done with Vicky.

'I'm worthless. I hate myself . . . You don't know me! I'm a horrible person.'

Horrible and ugly, just like Sykes really – and she wondered then if that's what he'd seen in all those mirrors, when he was young *and* in the lock-up. Wondered if it might help to—

Before she knew it, she was doing it. Knuckles still tender from the previous night, but worse when she punched that mirror and splintered it. There was a moment or so of calm, but she didn't feel any pain – which meant those lovely pills were kicking in. Then she looked at the mirror, her reflection fractured and even uglier than before. Cracked. As if looking at herself through a spider's web.

'Come into my lair . . .'

But she knew at least what she had to do next. There was one thing she could do before leaving. One thing that might help.

She would finish the job, fulfil a promise. Catch Simon's killer, with or without the police's help. Not just for Mia, though. Or for Vicky. But for him. And for herself.

For the people they had once been.

Chapter 29

She hadn't just done it for Mia, she'd done it for herself.

When all she'd felt like doing was drowning herself in wine, smoking like a chimney after she'd found that letter. Read that letter. It'd actually had the opposite effect, putting Vicky off both those habits. She hadn't touched a drop or lit up since she'd confronted her cousin, if you could call it that. Vicky hadn't even been able to get mad: she was beyond anger, beyond disappointment. Truthfully, she was still trying to get her head around it. She felt like she was in one of those sci-fi shows where the timeline was somehow altered and reality had changed around her. Everything she knew to be true, everything she thought she could believe in, was gone. All these years and they'd both kept it from her – something so massive she would have thought twice about marrying Simon in the first place if she'd known.

'It was such a long time ago,' Robyn had said, like that made it fine. But all it did was make her question the years of being with someone like Simon. Somebody who could go behind her back and do that. 'It was just the once, Vic.' That was the other thing she'd been at pains to get across. Whether it had been or not, now she didn't know what to believe. It begged the question had Simon cheated on her again? She'd been so quick to believe he had with Lisa Newton, perhaps knowing somewhere at the back of her mind that he was capable of it (well, she'd been right). Without going back to Bella – and she was definitely thinking about doing that – how would she know? Simon was saying sorry for being unfaithful, but was he talking about Robyn? About Lisa? Or was it just a blanket apology for all those nights he said he had to work, but might have been . . .

Sorry for basically being a shit?

There was a twinge of guilt then, again. Because Simon had been killed, murdered. Strangled. Even if he was an adulterer, choking to death was not a fit punishment. Castration, possibly. Fuck, what had happened to them? To their lives? She felt like she didn't know the one person she'd pledged herself to for all eternity.

Robyn, she didn't know anyway. The Robyn who'd shown up at her door because she'd asked her to (Vicky had bloody asked her! *Imagine that!* It would be funny if it wasn't so tragic). There had been a gulf between them from the start; they were so different now it was untrue. You only had to look at what had happened with Bella to see that, the widely different viewpoints. But she'd – perhaps naively – thought they were making headway. Getting back to the old Robs and Vic, who'd been closer than any sisters could ever be.

Wrong. Sisters didn't keep secrets like that from each other, at least none that remained friends. It wasn't unheard of that some relatives went off with partners of siblings or whatever, but they were the territory of TV talk shows and dramas. She never thought anything like that would ever happen to her. The betrayal of it! From people she loved, who she thought loved *her*. When, if you got right down to it (like they had), they'd only loved each other.

No. That wasn't right. Robyn had kept away all these years, had left so that she could have some kind of life with Simon. But had he wanted her to? He'd kept the letter when all was said and done. Did he look at it sometimes and wish that he was with her instead of Vicky? Had he wanted a life with Robyn instead, thought of her every time they made love? She had no real way of knowing – except possibly through Bella.

All these thoughts and more had been rattling round in her head since the shitstorm had hit. And getting back Simon's watch – the gold-plated one that had belonged to his dad which he never took off – not to mention his wedding ring, now they'd been released, hadn't really helped with all that. Had made things so much worse. The anger had finally surfaced, just not in the way she'd expected or wanted it to. When Mia got back from staying at Julie's for example, and wanted to know where Aunty Rob-Rob was: the pet name she'd eventually given her during Robyn's time at their house. At first, Vicky had managed to fob her off– Christ knows her cousin was always flitting off somewhere (investigating Simon's death, but who exactly was she doing that for again?).

Mia had carried on and on though, asking when she was coming back – Robyn had been right about that, about kids picking up on stuff – until Vicky had snapped: 'Aunty Robyn's moved out, Mia. She's gone! Okay?'

The little girl's bottom lip had trembled, which usually meant tears weren't far away. 'But why?'

Vicky had closed her eyes, opened them again. Not knowing quite what to say. How do you explain to a six-year-old that her aunty slept with her father before she was even born, and that it made a difference? She was too young to know about all that stuff yet – at least Vicky hoped so – but she knew about love.

You know how I feel. And I think you feel the same way . . .

'Did you love him? Do you *still love him?*'

Just not about the different kinds of love, that yes absolutely Aunty fucking Rob-Rob *should* have loved Daddy, because they were family. It was just that . . . well, two people can't love the same person in *that* way, or they can't stay together. Bloody hell, that didn't even sound right in her own head let alone if she had to explain it.

Can. Worms. Consider yourself open.

The next thing Mia had said, just before the floodgates opened – and she hadn't seen them do that in the same way since she'd found those pictures of Simon that Robyn had left lying around (hardly fair, Mia had climbed up to get them; and Robyn had been the one to make her feel a bit better about it all) – floored Vicky completely. 'Was it because of me? Is that why she stayed away all this time?'

Vicky shook her head. 'No. 'Course not. Why would you even think that?' But then children didn't think like adults. They made connections that weren't really there. Blamed themselves for things that weren't their fault, although sadly they didn't have a monopoly on that.

With no other explanation given, Mia had rushed up to her bedroom bawling her eyes out. Tracy had looked at her then accusingly. Had no idea what this was about, or she shouldn't do, but still said: 'I know it's none of my affair, but—'

'You're right, it's not!' That anger coming again, being directed at someone else who didn't deserve her wrath. Who'd only done her best to try and help. Her use of the word 'affair' hadn't helped, it had to be said.

Tracy had recoiled like she'd been slapped. 'All right. Maybe *I* should go, then?'

But Vicky had caught her arm as she turned to leave. 'I'm sorry, Tracy. I'm really sorry. You're the one person . . . You're the only person I have left here, in this house. Please don't go.'

The policewoman had searched her face for answers, those glasses she wore magnifying her pupils. 'What's happened? You guys had a row?'

'It's . . . complicated. Family stuff,' she'd told her.

'That's why I called. You're still family, Robs.'

'We're family; we should stick together.'

'Okay, right,' said the Family Liaison Officer, but that didn't entitle her to know all the ins and outs of that family – just act as a conduit between them and the police, though heaven

236

knows Tracy had been much more than that, yet still respected the boundaries . . . mostly. 'But whatever it is, I've learned from experience with my lot that you shouldn't take it out on your kids. Shouldn't take it out on your friends, either.' She'd said this with a warm smile and patted Vicky's hand at the same time.

'You're right – thanks, Tracy.'

'But if you do need to talk . . .'

She'd nodded. Knew she could rely on her, knew she had her best interests at heart. Tracy had been the one to tell her about the new line of inquiry, for example. The other dead body that had been found in a similar state to Simon. What it all meant, she had no idea. Had Simon's death just been an arbitrary thing, killed by some nutter who simply liked to strangle and bury his victims on a beach for some reason? Or was something else going on none of them were aware of?

Only time would tell, she guessed. Time revealed everything. All the secrets that were hidden, everything that was buried.

Whether you wanted it to or not.

Chapter 30

The car was hers, wasn't hard to recognise.

A Citroën, that was it. That's what she'd been driving around in, and what was parked just off the kerb. Tucked away, but not really camouflaged as such. Parked a good way from the entrance to the place. Not as good a snoop as she was a psychologist, not really army material or whatever. *SAS: Who Dares Wins* and all that, sneaking in under the cover of darkness – which was what she'd done. Waited till dark, it looked like, then returned to this location for whatever reason . . .

No, not for whatever reason. It was pretty bloody obvious what her reasons were, what her intentions were. She thought there was some link between this place and the murders, between here and Simon Carter, and now the latest kill, Kieran Thackery.

Blundering around, poking at wasp's nests with a stick. Well, you know what? You keep on doing that for long enough, you get stung. Maybe you get stung lots of times? Maybe you even get yourself killed.

The instinct was to follow, right now. But that wasn't possible. Had to wait, it was the only way. Rather than going tearing off, blundering around like she was doing. It was the right way to do things . . .

The only way.

Chapter 31

She hadn't been able to think of any other way.

Yes, it was stupid. Yes, it was breaking the law even. The law she'd been on the right side of since she began working with Cav and his team, since Gordon had brought her on board. Always sticking to the letter of it, because sloppy work got arrests quashed, got convictions overturned. You really didn't want to play that game when you were dealing with the most dangerous kinds of criminals on the planet. Didn't want them flying the coop.

But that was usually when Robyn had the backing of people behind her, people who actually *had* her back. She missed that, missed it *a lot*. If Cav had been here he would have told her this was crazy, told her to stay where she was at the hotel. He would also have sent people into that building to take detailed statements, would have been talking to Cathy who worked there and who just happened to have been going out with the last victim. Cav didn't believe in coincidences, and neither did she. She believed in connections, in drawing comparisons and working with the data at hand to form hypotheses. And those hypotheses usually ended up with them catching the culprits.

Or her getting kidnapped by them . . .

No, that was just the once. That was different, this time *she* had the element of surprise. She was only going to take a look anyway, see what was what. The gates were still open. She'd seen that on the drive past – probably to allow the guests passage in and out – so it wasn't like she had to actually break in. She'd just walk in, sneak in. Trespass. Leave the car a good distance down the road and creep across the grounds; there hadn't been any cameras that she'd noticed when she came up here the first time, recalled thinking to herself the security was pretty lax.

At The Castle Spa, the building linked – however indirectly – to both of the murders. It couldn't be a coincidence, regardless of what Sebastian Boyd – and his investors – would have people believe. There was something here, she just knew it . . . had known it right from the get-go. As Robyn made her way across those grounds though, the only light coming from the half-moon above, she saw that there were actually people patrolling the area. Not security guards as such, but members of staff – you couldn't really miss them because they were also wearing those white 'uniforms' that were so prevalent inside. They were in pairs, taking turns to do wide arcs of the building.

In contrast, Robyn had donned her darkest black jeans, a navy T-shirt and black leather jacket – fortunately she favoured those kinds of colours over lighter, brighter ones anyway. What did that say about her? So, she hunkered down, waited for the 'guards' to pass each other, waiting for her opportunity to slip between them, and sprinted headlong towards the castle itself. She had to wonder if this was what Simon did here at night sometimes, the walking, patrolling. He was in the right kind of shape for it. Had been.

As she ran, her hand, wrapped in a bandage she'd bought earlier on, throbbed in time to her heartbeat. She'd left the 'DO NOT DISTURB' on the hotel room door so chances were they hadn't even seen the damage she'd done yet, but she was more than willing to pay for it. Explaining it, now that would be another matter entirely. How else would that have occurred, but someone punching it? Breaking it intentionally (hey, just ask

Kevin Sykes). At the end of the day it wasn't their business, and it wasn't as if she was throwing TVs out of windows or whatever. Just going around hitting mediums and mirrors. Fuck's sake, what was happening to her?

What exactly are you doing now? she asked herself. Nothing she found tonight would be admissible, she understood that. Robyn just had to know, for her own benefit. Might even be able to convince the local coppers to come and raid the place. Yeah, right, dream on.

Still she ran, still she made her way towards that castle. The gates might be open, but those big wooden front doors were closed; she could see that from here. Not so welcoming tonight. But then she wasn't intending on entering the property itself, because there was much more chance of getting caught doing that. No, she was intending on . . . what, doing her best Peeping Tom impression? If that's what it took, yes. Spying, just like she'd been spied on since she got here.

The whole of the inside was lit up, so she made her way around, checking in through windows, none of which were obscured by curtains (why would they bother, all the way out here? – upstairs in the bedrooms, possibly) and finding nothing. A few more members of staff wandering around, going about their business.

Nothing at all happening; nothing suspicious. She didn't know quite what she was expecting to see, crates filled with straw being unpacked, machine guns and explosives being placed on desks while the staff let out belly laughs and talked of bringing the government down? It was just a business, a spa where people – loaded people – went to wind down. She'd been taken around it, *shown* around it. There were no hidden rooms or hidden agendas. She was wasting her time; it would take an entire undercover operation to sniff out anything amiss here.

Or would it? When she rounded the corner, she came upon the window connected to what Brad had called the 'rec area'. That place he said people could just chill out and mingle with other guests, forget about their worries and perhaps even make new friends. Well, she supposed, that was one way of putting it.

Robyn's mouth fell open at the scene in front of her, as she gaped in disbelief. There were bodies everywhere. At first she thought they were dead, like this was some kind of storage room for the people they'd killed and they were taking them down to the beach one by one over time to bury them.

But no.

These bodies were very much alive, and most of them were very naked. Everywhere her eyes settled, she saw some new debauchery. She was by no means a prude, but this was another level entirely. Different combinations of men and women, different sexes, the same sex, which in itself wasn't that shocking. The fact they kept flitting between partners, taking on multiple partners at once . . . So many and in every conceivable position that they blurred into one. Glimpses of arms, legs, breasts, buttocks. People in masks, people with equipment that made the gym look understocked. Plus, here and there, faces she thought she recognised. There was the couple she'd seen wandering through the castle in their robes, pleasuring not only each other but also the other pair they were with, heads back in the throes of ecstasy. Brad too was present, servicing a woman who looked to be in her mid-sixties wearing leathers. Of Cathy there was no sign, and part of her was quite relieved about that – though technically it didn't mean a thing. Might be her day – her night – off? She might have taken some time after Kieran died? Might even have left if she suspected there was some link between the two? If she truly loved him.

A woman at the far end was getting up and leaving, having a chat with one of the members of staff at the doorway – fully dressed and watching the activities with wry amusement. As she put on her robe, they handed her some money. So, this wasn't just consenting adults stuff, there was cash changing hands – which made it illegal.

But that wasn't all. Here and there she spotted people reclining on sofas or chairs now, passing around bongs, sniffing up white power on plates using tiny metal straws, and even injecting.

Drugs.

Most places had their problems with drugs these days . . .

That was the connection to the boats, to Graham Newton and what the police suspected him to be tied up in. He – or whomever he worked for – had to be the suppliers here. Had Simon seen something he shouldn't have done?

How could he have failed *to see all this?* thought Robyn. Bit hard to keep it quiet, although it was possible she supposed. She liked to think the best of him, that he wouldn't have been involved in all this . . . Though he never did say who the friends of his were that would make sure those guys never attacked another woman, the way they had her. It'd be known they were being watched . . .

If she had ended up with Simon, would she have been dragged into all this too? Yet Vicky didn't seem to know anything about it, did she? Would she even admit it? Definitely wouldn't have put Mia in such danger . . . would she?

Robyn wanted to tear her eyes away – tear them out actually – but there was a strange fascination to it all. And that was when she saw it, the final piece of the puzzle. Brad had moved on from the older woman, to divide his time between two younger ones. Again, hadn't Robyn spotted those on her tour? They certainly looked familiar . . . That was it, they'd been in the hot tubs! But it was what he was doing with them that was the important thing. As he thrust inside one, then switched to the other, he would hold them by the neck with both hands. Then he would squeeze, cutting off their air supply.

Autoerotic asphyxiation. It was becoming more and more popular in the bedroom, so Robyn had read – though she'd never been interested in it herself. The lack of oxygen heightening the pleasure sensations in both men and women, and the spa clearly had people who were trained in such techniques. It was only a hop, skip and a jump from massages to this after all. Would only

243

take a little more pressure to strangle the life out of someone; the MO that had killed both Simon and Kieran. An accident, or something else? Getting rid of witnesses?

All these thoughts and more were racing through her brain, so much data now that it was impossible not to draw conclusions. Everything was laid out on a plate for her, just like the narcotics on offer in the rec room of the spa.

Chill out and mingle . . . and perhaps even make new friends.

Just another service this place offered, a secret one that guests paid through the nose for. Money was certainly being pumped into local businesses: the kind that could land you in prison for a long, long time. No wonder the investors didn't want any undue attention. Didn't want the police sticking their oars in too much.

Robyn shook herself. She should be taking photos on her phone. They might not be admissible in court or anything, but the police – Watts especially – wouldn't be able to ignore the evidence of their own eyes, surely? Making sure the flash was off, because she didn't need it and a sudden spark of light would only give her away, she held up the oblong and readied herself to snap off a few shots of what was going on. All her photos would be automatically uploaded to the cloud when she got to somewhere with signal, so even if the phone got damaged or was taken off her the 'evidence' should still be accessible.

Pinching the screen to zoom in, she looked up and just about had time to see the reflection of someone standing behind her. One of the staff, the 'guards', or someone else? Someone who'd been following her, at a distance but still there – the time she'd spent gawking at the orgy had allowed them to catch up.

She had no more time to speculate because they were raising something that looked like a metal bar. Something they were bringing down on the back of her head. There wasn't time to cry out, or even register any pain.

All Robyn knew then was blackness.

Total and absolute.

Chapter 32

That was all she knew for a long time.

At least it felt like a long time, she had no way of knowing. No way of telling whether she was awake or still out cold. Because even though she was sure she'd opened her eyes, lids fluttering and snapping back in the way they always did when she neared the surface of consciousness, all Robyn could see was nothingness.

There was pain as well, this time a throbbing at the back of her head rather than in her hand. But it was a dull ache, muted, as if she'd been given something similar to her painkillers. And she couldn't move. Her arms, her legs. Nothing.

You're on the floor of the lock-up again, she thought to herself. *You're lying there waiting for Sykes.*

But you're awake . . . aren't you? Not dreaming.

She still wasn't certain. Was this the nightmare from her past, the one where he'd open the door and flip on the lights and she was in a room filled with broken mirrors? Ones like she'd left back in the hotel bathroom. Perhaps she had more in common with that man than she cared to admit?

There was a knocking sound, then she could see shadows – darkness upon darkness. A figure standing there in front of her, a fist rapping on nothingness but still making the knocking

– banging – sound. A fist, then the rest of him. Looming over her with the knife, not saying a word. Sykes, standing there, but framed by the darkness rather than the light. Suddenly, so suddenly it made her start, he said: 'Hello, Dr Adams. I wondered when I'd see you again.' His smile was the same chilling one he'd given her back at Gateside, before she'd left home and driven here. Going back in time . . .

'How are the scars, Doctor?'

The ones on her back, healing. The mental ones . . . Not so much. All this did was prove it. 'You're not real,' she spat. 'You're not really here.'

'Aren't I? Feels like I'm here.' He touched himself then to illustrate it, making sure he was solid. 'I'll *always* be here.'

'No,' she managed. '*No!*'

The scene changed then, subtly at first, revealing an elbow here, an ear there – uncovering bodies on a beach. But it was more like a spotlight being trained on them, picking them out in the blackness, ready for their performance. The writhing bodies, the images she'd witnessed in the rec area. Scenes that wouldn't have looked out of place in Sodom and Gomorrah, except they were being driven by chemicals in the system: smoked; sniffed; injected. Causing people to strive for more, to *feel* more. A select clientele.

Only they weren't simply having sex, abusing each other now. They were killing in various ways: one stabbing, raising and plunging a blade again and again, blood spurting from the numerous wounds; one being chopped up by an axe, into tiny pieces (reducing the form to manageable chunks of memory, revenge for slights that had been committed so long ago); another feasting on the flesh of the woman beneath him, chomping down on body parts, ripping away skin and tendons, seeing it simply as raw meat; machines being used for torture, looking like something out of the Spanish Inquisition; bodies in the foetal position, placed like that after being killed; others being strangled – hands around the throat until the life was choked out of them.

All of this happening, on and on until Robyn thought she was going mad. Not even closing her eyes – if indeed they were even open – helped. The images were still there, plaguing her. Driving her to the point of insanity, until all she could do was scream and scream and—

Until it changed, quickly, focusing on a specific image: a specific set of bodies. All the rest faded out, distortions of the recent past (or at least she thought it was recent; again, she had no idea how long she'd been here, wherever *here* was). Leaving just that one scene, the collection of bodies. Male bodies, half-naked, bottom halves anyway – their trousers pulled down, fighting over something. Fighting over whatever was on the ground, like it was just another piece of meat.

Fighting over the girl, in her twenties, wearing the black dress, the black tights – who'd gone outside with a guy she thought was nice. Who was being attacked, being violated. Yet there was no sign of Simon this time; where was he? Wasn't it about time he stepped in, saying the police were on their way, laying into the lads and chasing them off? Somehow she knew he wasn't going to appear, that this would play out in the way she thought it would all along.

'What's the matter?' asked Sykes. She'd forgotten he was still around, this warped version of the Ghost of Christmas Past, showing her the edited highlights of her life. Was this a highlight then? Weren't there any better memories than this? Probably none as important right now. It was one of the things that had stayed with her, albeit under the surface; one of the deepest scars long before Sykes had created any more. 'This is what you wanted, isn't it? This is what you think you deserved?'

Robyn couldn't deny it. She nodded, hoping Sykes would see her in the gloom. He could. 'Even after Simon saved you, it didn't work out, did it? He didn't want you either.'

'No! He had Vicky. We both loved . . . *love* Vicky; we didn't want to hurt her.'

'Are you sure?' Sykes grinned that disquieting grin of his. 'Are you *quite* sure, that you didn't jump before you were pushed? That you got out before he could reject you? Isn't that why you wrote the letter? Why you ran?'

'No, I—'

'Why you continued to throw yourself at all those guys?'

'Fuck off!' she shouted.

'Or maybe we need to go back a bit further than that?' The image in front of her shifted again, changed. Morphed into a different one. Now she saw a room, a small flat. The place she'd been brought up in. Her mother, drunk, with another one of her boyfriends, staggering off to the bedroom.

'No . . . No, please.' It came out as a little moan, but begging didn't seem to help in the slightest. The show had started and wouldn't stop until it was done, going back to that night – was it just the one night? – when she was little. Not that much older than Mia, hearing the grunting and banging through the walls. Then later, her mum's boyfriend toppling out and seeing her there in the living room, playing with the handful of toys she had. Seeing her and walking towards her.

'Hey there. Aren't you a pretty little thing, sweetie?'

'*No!*' screamed Robyn. She didn't want to see this, nor did she want to see the things that followed – like her mother telling her what a waste of space she was, how she'd been conceived . . . Which brought more images flooding into the space in front of her, things she couldn't have possibly witnessed: her mother being pushed up against the side of a toilet cubicle. The details of this had been furnished by her mother at some point, and her mind was just filling in the gaps, as they often did. As they had with Simon's tale of the night he saved her.

If anyone knew how the human mind worked, it was Robyn. And history always repeated itself.

'No wonder you're so fucked up,' said Sykes.

'You . . . You're not real!' Robyn shouted.

'As real as all those times you thought you were being watched, but weren't. As real as that note you thought had been sent to you.'

'No . . . That *was* real,' she protested.

'Was it, though? Too many pills, too much booze. Think about it . . . "Go home?" That was a message to yourself, nothing else. To spare you all this pain.'

'No.' The word was little more than a breath this time. Not real. But she'd held it in her hands, hadn't she? Heard the . . . the knocking, the banging. No one outside the door. Banging inside her own head? Christ . . . What was going on? What . . .

So what's happening now? What's happening here? Where. Are. You?

'It's quite simple,' Sykes replied, as if she'd asked the question out loud. 'You're in hell.'

'No,' Robyn said a final time. She didn't believe in hell. Or heaven. Didn't believe people could talk to you from beyond the grave, like Vicky did when she visited that Prescott bitch. When you were gone, you were gone. Returned to the universe or something, your energy being absorbed and put to other uses. Which meant that if this was a hell, as the figure of Sykes was insisting, just like everything else it was one of her own making.

One of her own in a place that had looked like a heaven, and was anything but. People dressed in white, in creams. A man dressed in cream, with a chauffeur who'd been taking golf clubs out of the back of the car – clubs that looked a lot like the thing in the reflection behind her when she'd been spying on the orgy.

Robyn laughed, quietly at first then building into a guffaw. 'I-I know where I am!' she shouted between those laughs. 'I know what this place is!' Somewhere that was very real indeed, something to grasp hold of in this place of shadows and illusion.

She'd been shown it, after all. Been introduced to it.

Blocks the blue wavelength lights . . . Can help with all kinds of problems.

Not hers.

As soon as she'd thought it, the lights came on – probably more of a response to that maniacal laughter than anything. Sykes was replaced by the figure she'd been thinking about, accompanied by his bodyguard, the huge lady with the blonde hair and Swedish accent. The door was open to that room, the lightproof room that she'd been told was used for Dark Therapy. That she'd been thrown in after she'd been whacked on the head by Andersson, more than likely with one of those golf clubs.

Sebastian Boyd was bending to stare at her as he approached and Robyn worked out she was sitting on something. Some kind of chair she was fastened to, strapped at the ankles, wrists and . . . yes, at the neck. Robyn tried to move her head and felt it there, holding her, choking her. If someone tightened that, then maybe it would be enough to—

'What's so funny, Doctor?' Boyd was asking her and Robyn realised she was still laughing, couldn't stop. She sounded like the Joker on nitrous oxide. Boyd was grinning. 'No, seriously. We could use a laugh or two right now, couldn't we, Andersson. What's the big joke?'

'You . . . you are,' she managed.

His face scrunched up. 'There's no need to be like that. I was just curious. I'm a curious sort of fellow – you probably noticed that. It was how I found out about my history in the first place, my birth-right. But then, you're a curious sort of woman, Doctor, aren't you?'

She didn't even bother to reply this time, but at least her laughter was dying down. It wasn't funny, this situation she'd found herself in. Not funny at all.

'People have reported all sorts of things when they come out of here, haven't they, Andersson?' He turned to the tall woman behind him.

'Yes, sir.'

'I mean some really weird shit. Hallucinations, all sorts.'

Ha! thought Robyn. *Apparently I was having those before I even came in!*

'Nobody's turned into a monster, though, thankfully,' Boyd continued, then waited a moment or two, perhaps for another laugh at the joke or even to see if she'd got the reference. Then just to make sure, he added: '*Altered States*? No?'

She'd got it, just didn't want to give him the satisfaction. Although it did remind her that they'd done something to her before sticking her in here. 'W-What did you give me?' she asked.

'Drugs?' Boyd said innocently, like they hadn't pumped her full of something. As if that hadn't been – in part – responsible for what she'd been witnessing in the Dark Room. 'Oh, nothing much,' he finally admitted. 'Just something to help you along, to relax you . . . though apparently it worked a little too well. I assure you, nothing as bad as what you've been taking yourself. The stuff we found on you. Wow, those are some strong meds, Doctor.' He drew a little closer. 'You should have come to us, come here. Like I said, you're more than welcome in my . . . home. We'd have sorted it all out, one way or another. You wouldn't have needed those.'

'I-I've seen the kind of . . . I've seen what you give the people here,' she managed.

'Give? Oh, we don't *give* them anything. We charge them an arm and a leg!' Now it was Boyd laughing, but she didn't join him. So he looked back at Andersson, who gave the thinnest smile imaginable.

'Very good, sir.'

'*I* thought so.' Boyd returned his gaze to Robyn. 'No, but really, they take what we give them willingly. Some of it we owe to dear old great, great, great . . . whatever grandfather Franklyn. Keeping it in the family, I like the idea of that. Family's so important, don't you think?'

Robyn remained silent.

'I mean, that's coming from someone obviously who's never really had one. Only a dead family. But if I did, if they were still

251

alive . . . I probably wouldn't have crapped all over them the same way you did, Doctor.'

'I-I don't know what—'

Boyd shushed her. 'Oh come now, we all have our little secrets. But you know what, they tend to get uncovered eventually.'

Robyn's mind was racing. How could he possibly know about what had happened, about her secret? The only other person who knew was . . . Jesus, not Watts. Please no.

'Even all this . . .' He waved a hand around him. 'I knew it couldn't carry on forever, but make hay while the sun shines, yes? The bills won't pay themselves and you'd be surprised how lucrative all this can be. Our investors are more than happy at the moment. That is, they were until very recently.'

Until Simon, she thought to herself. Until he'd found something out and they'd had to get rid of him, not to mention Kieran Thackery who'd probably discovered something through Cathy. Enough to bring the whole house of cards down around their ears, perhaps.

'Steps had to be taken, more care taken with the arrangements. But we couldn't stop. Just couldn't afford to. And now there's you, Doctor. What are we going to do about you?' He looked genuinely upset. 'It's why we put you in here for now, so we could decide. So I could talk to a few people and ask their advice. The truth is, I really like you. I don't want to . . . But you're not going to keep quiet about all this, are you? Not like you kept quiet about other things. I would say you're too moral, but then we both know that's a sliding scale where you're concerned, isn't it.' He let out a weary sigh, then suddenly he was right next to her, patting the chair she was in. 'A relic, from when this place was an asylum. They used this when they were administering electro-shock treatment. The barbarians. You'd be amazed what we found scattered about the place when we renovated, turned it into the spa. Handy piece of furniture, mind, on occasions like these.'

To kill people, choke them to death and dump the bodies

on the beach? Make it look like some kind of random thing, or even a serial killer? Was that what they had in mind for her now that she knew?

'And equally handy items of clothing . . . isn't that right Andersson?' He beckoned the big woman to come forward now and, with a nod from Boyd, she brought out what she was holding behind her back: an old-fashioned straitjacket. 'We're going to get you to slip this on in a moment,' Boyd informed her. 'Andersson will help you, adjust it to your size or whatnot. I've said this before, haven't I, but I really don't know what I'd do without her.'

Robyn started to struggle, but that just cut her air off quicker. Part of her had to wonder then if that's what had happened to the other two victims, Simon and Kieran. No, there had been indentations. More likely Andersson had done it with those strong hands of hers. Carried the bodies as easily as those clubs.

'It'll be like you've died and gone to heaven, believe me.'

Not heaven: hell, she reminded herself. And in front of her were a couple of demons . . . No, Boyd was the architect of all this. The Devil himself, if you wanted to resort to such descriptions.

'My reputation precedes me.'

Yet he'd said himself, hadn't he: 'We all have to answer to someone, Doctor.' Had talked about asking people what to do with her . . . This didn't end with Sebastian Boyd; the buck didn't stop with him.

But she had more immediate concerns at the moment. 'Please don't resist – you'll only make all this harder for yourself.' Boyd nodded again for Andersson to get on with the task in hand, to get Robyn out of the chair and into that straitjacket – something that took remarkably little effort in the end, even though Robyn put up a struggle. 'Now, there. Don't you look a picture,' Boyd told her. 'All right, Andersson – if you would be so good as to escort our visitor out.'

Those same hands that had shoved her into the straitjacket now grabbed the back of it, half dragging and half carrying her towards the door.

'Oh, and the back way if you don't mind. There might still be some of our guests around, though what state they'll be in is anyone's guess.'

'Yes, sir,' replied Andersson – which seemed to be one of the only things she ever said – and then carried on dragging Robyn to that door and through it. Out into the corridor. Out to face whatever they had in mind for her.

And she couldn't help thinking to herself then, if she hadn't before:

I'm in really big trouble.

Chapter 33

It looked so different now compared to before.

Darker, not just because she knew about what went on here now, but because the lights had been dimmed in this section, casting everything in yet more shadows. Robyn had a vague idea where they were going, heading towards the swimming pool area – where the back entrance Boyd had talked about must be – so she didn't bother asking about that. Instead she said: 'What are you going to do with me?'

As if the huge Swede would tell her, and not just look down on her with utter contempt. Maybe they were heading for the pool so she could drown her first, throw her in and watch her sink to the bottom wearing this bloody contraption. Simon had been half-drowned as well, although there'd been no chlorine found in his lungs, just salt water. It was more likely that Andersson would just throw her in the back of the car – where those golf clubs had come from – and take her down to the beach to do the deed there, get rid of their 'visitor' as Boyd had called her back in the Dark Room. Bury her like dear old great, great, great . . . however many . . . grandfather Franklyn had learned to do living with those desert tribes.

There were just the two of them now, which in Boyd's head

probably gave him plausible deniability. If Andersson was caught, she'd go down and, judging from the loyalty she'd displayed already, would be happy to do so. Like she'd been happy to murder the others and would take the fall for those, if necessary. Robyn shook her head, trying to clear her mind. That wasn't easy; whatever they'd given her was still in her system. The further down that hall they went, the more shadows appeared. Coming alive in her imagination.

Robyn twitched, squirmed, thought she saw figures there.

'Stop that!' Andersson warned her.

But she couldn't. Those shadows were leaping out at her now, all around her. Something had lodged in her memory from her research, about this place being haunted. About ghosts . . .

You don't believe in those, she reminded herself. *It's just more hallucinations.*

Didn't alter what she was seeing. Those shadowy figures – a carry-over from the Dark Room, probably. 'Can't . . . don't you see them?' she replied. 'They're everywhere.'

'Shut up!' Andersson barked, hauling her to the feet she'd been dragging along – being carried like a dead weight (poor choice of words).

'But they're—' Robyn paused, stopped talking altogether. Because one of the shadows was detaching itself, forming into a person. Hadn't been there during this scene back in the Dark Room, where those men from the side street had been pawing her, but he was certainly here now. Standing in front of them, blocking their path – which, if he'd been solid, would have been incredibly helpful.

As it was, he just spoke: 'You don't deserve this, Robyn,' he said softly. 'You didn't deserve it back then, you haven't since. You don't deserve to be treated so badly when you were only trying to help. You have to live, because this isn't over yet.'

Part of her knew they were her own words echoing back, what she'd thought about Boyd – that there was more to it than this.

At the very least, *he'd* go unpunished if she let them kill her. Him and those in charge of him, his investors?

'You *have* to live,' Simon said again, looking as he had done on that day when he'd come to her rescue. Young, handsome – and very, very taken.

'I-I have to live,' she repeated, mumbling the words.

'What?' Andersson said.

'There! Can't you see him?' screamed Robyn, which actually did make the chauffer-bodyguard look, making her think perhaps someone had seen what she was doing. Someone else she'd have to deal with. Andersson peered into the gloom ahead, clearly seeing nothing.

But it was enough of a distraction for Robyn to act. On her feet again, raising one and then bringing down the heel on the foot – on the toes – of the Swede, grinding hard and causing maximum pain. Andersson let out a howl, letting go of Robyn at the same time – who pitched forwards. Robyn almost fell, tripped, but righted herself, knowing full well that if she ended up on the floor, on her back, she'd be like an upturned turtle. That she'd be done for.

Looking up she saw Simon was gone, but she made for the direction where he'd been standing. Needed to find a way out of the spa before Andersson caught up with her. She shouted after Robyn: 'You *slyna*! I'll kill you!'

It didn't seem like much of a threat, given she was about to do that anyway. Enough to get her moving, though, to get her away from there. But Robyn had no idea where she was going – not really. In the dark, and having only been shown round certain parts of this building the once, not to mention still suffering from the after-effects of the drugs and the Dark Room, she didn't trust herself one bit. Stumbling around, making all kinds of noises, Andersson would find her in no time at all.

Robyn banged into one of the walls, ricocheting off it like a pinball, then half-stumbled sideways through an open door. She

257

didn't recognise this room at all, but the light in here was better so that was something. It was better because of the huge window, letting in light from a silvery moon.

She could hear Andersson back there in the corridor, limping towards her. There was no point trying to hide in here, there weren't many places *to* hide, which left her just two options: head back out there again and pray the Swede hadn't caught up yet, though what little lead she'd had would have been decimated by her pit stop in this room. Or . . .

Her window of opportunity.

Robyn gritted her teeth. Looked pretty old, that window, as most of them did here – but the glass had probably been replaced during the renovations. She doubted it was toughened, however. Prayed it wasn't, because she couldn't open it without the use of her arms. There was no choice, in lieu of a door – some kind of escape hatch – Robyn had little option than to run towards it. Run *at* it, as fast as she could.

Might be doing their job for them. She had to live, Simon had told her, and this was suicide. The only good thing was they were on the ground level – imagine if she'd had a huge drop to deal with as well. Robyn angled her body so that her shoulder took the brunt of the impact and threw herself at that glass like a missile, noting her reflection only briefly as she did.

Like so many things the movies lie about, chucking yourself through a window really hurts, she found. It felt like she'd come up against a slab of concrete at first, thought she might have busted her shoulder as well, but the glass did eventually crack, her reflection shattering. And, as it did so, window shattering seconds later, she found herself falling onto the grass outside the building – the cold night air on her face. Now Robyn was grateful for whatever those drugs were they'd foisted on her, because it was numbing the serious injuries she must surely have.

Allowing her to crawl forward on her knees, somehow – more by luck than judgment, because she still didn't have her arms free

– shakily getting to her feet again to stumble forwards. Robyn heard the banging behind her – real banging this time – of Andersson catching up. '*Skit!*' the woman shouted, (which Robyn could only assume was a swear word) at the idiocy of doing such a thing, probably. Nevertheless, she was out. She'd escaped from Andersson and made it to the outside world. Sort of.

You've only escaped the woman temporarily, she said to herself. There was still time for her to catch up. To catch *her*. Just as she'd thrown herself at the window, Robyn threw herself across the grass – struggling to keep her balance again, but knowing what waited behind if she didn't move.

Running across the field, Robyn pointed herself in the direction she thought her car might be – though how she was going to drive it was anyone's guess. She should just find a hiding place out here, in some bushes or something. Wait it out till the morning, or until she could think straight.

But then she saw more figures up ahead. More ghosts . . . although these looked solid enough again. Those guards out here she'd managed to dodge, then? Except she recognised the closest. It wasn't Simon this time, not Sykes or any of those other projections.

It was Watts. Waiting for her out here, waiting to catch her and deliver her back to Andersson. To Boyd. He'd followed her and was waiting, was part of this whole thing somehow. Had let her down – just like every other guy she'd ever known. Apart from one, although even he had . . .

Watts' arms were out, running towards her, changing course so he could grab her. Which he did, finally, pitching them both to the ground.

Then there she was, Watts' boss not far behind. O'Brien standing over them and sneering. 'And where do you think you're going?' she asked. Nowhere apparently.

They all had to answer to someone. Watts to her, O'Brien to Boyd.

'Robyn! Robyn no,' Watts was whispering in her ear, gripping her, holding her down. 'Robyn!'

'You. Hey, you!' This was O'Brien again, but she was looking beyond them. Pointing. 'You! I said where do you think *you're* going?'

People were rushing past her, running to where she was indicating. Men and women in uniform. Policemen and women, rushing after . . . Andersson, they were going after Andersson!

Robyn looked from Watts, then back towards the spa. There were more dark figures, uniformed officers and cars – and, yes, now she could hear the sirens.

It took three or more coppers to bring down the big woman, but Andersson was finally on the grass, being handcuffed. Robyn squinted, spotted more people being brought out of the castle building including . . . a figure dressed in cream.

'Get up from there, you two,' snapped O'Brien, but there was a wry grin on her face. 'People will talk.'

Watts started to rise then, helping Robyn to her feet and starting to remove the straitjacket. She was still looking back, looking over at Sebastian Boyd, cuffed, with his hands behind his back, being led towards a police car.

She stared back at O'Brien, mouth open. 'What . . .'

'It's like I told you, Doctor,' replied the DI, still smirking. 'Nobody, absolutely *nobody* is above the law.'

Chapter 34

She'd been here before as well.

In the hospital, recovering after a case had wrapped. In that instance, it had been the ordeal with Sykes. Days, weeks of recuperating, of people bringing baskets of fruit, chocolate. All of them grateful, because she was . . .

'Lucky to be alive.' That's what doctors told her on both occasions. The first time because of Sykes, but technically her injuries at the castle had been 'self-inflicted'. She'd thrown herself through that window, although she'd had good reason – being stalked by a psychotic Andersson through the corridors and seeing no other way out. If she'd held on a bit longer, the cops would have been there, but she didn't know that at the time. At the time it was a choice between death at the massive Swede's hands – literally, around her throat – or a pane of glass. Robyn had chosen the latter, and luckily hit it at just the right spot.

Lucky to be alive . . .

A weak spot in the window that had given when she struck it, causing cuts and bruises and one dislocated shoulder, but it certainly could have been worse. Add to that the blow to the back of the head – calling for a scan, which thankfully came back clear – and those drugs in her system, it had all warranted a stay in Golden Sands' General. Days instead of weeks, but it had felt like much longer.

Cav had visited on a daily basis after the Oedipus business, but it was Watts who'd shown up every time that bell had rung during her time in this place. (*Had anyone even told Cav?* she wondered; probably not, and that was likely for the best, she guessed.)

Watts who'd brought the fruit and the chocolate, who'd brought her stuff from her hotel room – toiletries and the like – not to mention the company and conversation. Who'd brought the password-protected tablet so she could watch the interviews she hadn't been able to attend. Every evening she'd gaze at them, headphones on, deriving no small amount of satisfaction from seeing Boyd squirm in the hot seat, his very expensive lawyer whispering in his ear after each question.

'So, you're denying any participation in the deaths of Simon Carter and Kieran Thackery, Mr Boyd?' O'Brien had said during the grilling.

'I am,' was the only thing Boyd would say about that. The rest of it was simply 'no comment' on the advice of his brief.

'They didn't get a whiff of what was going on up there at the spa? Needed to be out of the picture, like Dr Adams?'

Boyd had wriggled about at that; they knew what he'd done to her, had found the chair in the Dark Room she'd been strapped to. They knew what he intended to do to her afterwards, or had a fair idea.

'No comment,' had been his reply in a barely audible voice.

It was more than they were getting from Andersson, that was for sure, the woman even less forthcoming than usual. But they'd caught her in the act, chasing Robyn across the grounds. There was no coming back from that. And they'd found enough inside the spa to be able to put Boyd away for quite a long time, to go after those investors as well – not to mention Graham Newton who'd been collared when he got back from his fishing trips for his role in supplying drugs. That man was currently singing like a canary about who was involved in the ring in their town, names who also had ties to the prostitutes Boyd had been using up at the castle.

Yet something still didn't sit right with Robyn about it all.

'How do you mean?' asked Watts during one of his trips to see her.

'Well,' said Robyn, in bed with the curtain drawn around them, her arm strapped up in a sling now her shoulder had been popped back into place, 'there's Cathy for starters.' The young girl from the spa, the one she'd encountered when she first went there and who was Kieran Thackery's girlfriend, had finally been questioned. She told the police that she had no idea what was happening up at the castle, let alone took part in any of it. Still devastated by the death of Kieran, she swore blind that he'd had no knowledge of any of it either. 'How could he,' she'd argued, in tears, 'when I didn't?'

Watts gave a shrug. 'Perhaps he found out about it some other way?'

'Hmm, bit tenuous,' Robyn had replied. 'He wasn't even the one who worked up there.'

'Or she could be lying,' Watts had suggested, which would fit with Robyn's whole 'no coincidences' thing, yet his face said he didn't believe that for a moment. A face she'd studied quite a bit while he'd been coming here, a kind face. Concerned. She trusted it, and trusted his judgement. However she could have thought he was involved in all this was anyone's guess.

Though there had been that one thing, hadn't there? The means by which they'd found her up at the spa. 'Bit stalkery,' she'd told him when she found out.

'It . . . it wasn't like that. I was just keeping an eye on you because—'

'Because I was acting like a loon?' she offered. 'Going on and on about the spa?'

'Er . . . I wouldn't put it exactly like that, but . . .' He'd looked cagey then, and admitted, 'Plus the psychic woman at the hotel kind of told me to.'

'Prescott?' Robyn's face screwed up at that thought, but she could hardly complain. She was here, and she was alive. It had taken Watts a bit of time to raise the alarm, to convince his DI to get a warrant to go into that place when he'd found Robyn's car empty, but O'Brien had listened in the end.

'Probable cause?' Robyn had said.

'I told her I could hear screaming coming from the place,' Watts admitted.

'From that distance? Really? And she bought it?'

Watts smirked. 'Not for a second. But she was starting to suspect something was going on up there too.'

'Christ, finally!'

'I mean, she knew from the start really. Just decided to ignore the pressure being put on her to turn a blind eye in the end, to ignore the victims' connection to that place. Like I said, she's a good copper.'

Robyn had smiled. 'Funny, she said the same thing about you.'

'She did?' Watts looked as pleased as punch.

It still didn't explain how Boyd had known about what was going on in Robyn's personal life, about Vicky and Simon. But when she raised this with Watts he also swore that he'd not said a word to anyone about it. 'Not even a little office gossip?'

He looked horrified. 'No. Never. I just wouldn't . . . Robyn, I'm not like that. Honest.'

And she believed him. It also made her think again about Boyd's words, how he hadn't come right out and said he specifically knew about her and Simon. That even if he did, there might have been other ways he'd found out. Vicky confiding in someone, say.

Speaking of which, she'd thought she spotted her on the way back from the toilets on her third day here. 'Vicky?' she'd called out, and her cousin had looked up – then looked away, turned around and started to walk off. 'Vicky, wait! Please wait . . .'

But by the time she'd caught up, her cousin had already left the hospital and she could see no sign of the woman outside. Had she got wind of what had happened on the grapevine, through Tracy? Had she even been there to see Robyn? Might have been visiting someone else entirely . . . Somehow Robyn doubted it. *Needed* to doubt it.

Because Vicky just showing up here meant there was hope. Meant they might be able to at least have a conversation like grown-ups instead of shouting at each other. Didn't it?

Don't kid yourself, Robyn thought. *Just because she's glad you're not dead doesn't mean she's forgiven you. Doesn't mean anything actually, other than Vicky's a good person. A better one than you.*

As if that hadn't been a surprise enough, there'd been another one. On the final day, when the doctors had been advising her not to stay on the painkillers too long for her shoulder – to only use them when absolutely necessary, because they could be addictive (yeah, no shit!) – Watts had visited again, his face a mixture of serious and excited.

'What?' she'd asked, sitting on the end of the bed this time with her feet dangling off. He'd made her wait, made her ask again – or had that just been her own impatience? 'Come on, what? Tell me, Ashley.'

'There's been a development,' he said.

'How do you mean?'

'In the murders,' he explained. 'One of them anyway.'

'All right, now you've got my undivided attention,' she replied.

'There's someone you really need to see,' Watts had told her then.

'Someone . . .? Not that fucking medium again?'

He'd shaken his head. 'A witness.'

'Jesus.'

'And you want to know something bizarre?'

Robyn frowned, hopping off the bed to join him standing up. 'I'm all ears.'

'We really don't need to go very far to talk to them.'

Chapter 35

Watts hadn't been wrong.

They hadn't needed to go far at all to see the person he'd been taking about, just a walk down the corridor and a ride in the lift. To a different level of the hospital, though the DS still hadn't said anything about where exactly they were going as they made their way. She could see which ward – which private room – they needed however, because of the uniforms posted outside. They were obviously not taking any chances with this witness, but just who the hell was it?

There had been another surprise as they'd neared the room, because waiting not far from the door was a person she immediately recognised. Stepping forward, Robyn said: 'Mr Platt?'

He smiled at that, obviously delighted that someone recognised him – or perhaps it was that somebody seemed pleased to see him? Because the last time she'd seen Jeremy Platt, the man who'd discovered Simon's buried body on the beach, he was being turned away from the desk at Golden Sands nick, his offer of help rejected. He stuck out his left hand to shake, but then realised Robyn's left arm was in a sling. To cover his awkwardness, she grabbed it with her free hand and gave it a kind of strange up and down shake instead. 'Do . . . do I know you?'

'Not sure that you do, but I know *you*,' she told him.

'This is Dr Adams,' Watts explained. 'She's been assisting us with this particular case.'

When Robyn let go, Jeremy clicked his fingers. 'The psychologist! Right, of course!'

Robyn nodded, then looked from Jeremy to Watts, confused. 'But I don't . . . I mean, how are you a witness, Mr Platt?'

'I'm not,' he said at the same time the DS said, 'He's not.' It just left Robyn even more puzzled.

'My father,' Jeremy went on, but stopped there. It did nothing to clear matters up.

'I'm sorry, I still don't . . .'

'He had a heart attack, you see. Not long before I found . . .' Jeremy looked down, though whether he was still upset by the memory of his father having the attack or finding the corpse was unclear. Then he looked up, suddenly happy and eager to say more: 'It was touch and go for a while, but he's a tough old bird. Took this long for him to recover enough to tell me . . . tell us though.'

'Tell you what?' asked Robyn.

'That he saw what happened,' Jeremy reported, smiling again. 'Actually, that's not strictly true. He saw some of it. He lives up on the cliffs there, you see. Just above where it happened. Line of sight's not brilliant but, well, he caught the edge of it. Likes to look out at the sea, watch the boats come and go. The surfers, swimmers, whatever.'

'And he saw what happened with Mr Carter?'

Jeremy nodded. 'He saw two guys having a row down there. Angle's not fantastic, as I say, so he didn't actually see what . . . But one of them was definitely . . . Well, it was the man I found.'

'Simon,' whispered Robyn. Then asked: 'Who was the other man?'

'That's just it,' Watts chipped in. 'He doesn't have a clue.'

'Do you mind if . . .' Robyn nodded towards the door. As eager as Jeremy was to be of use, she needed to hear all this from his father directly.

'Oh . . . oh yes, of course.' Jeremy stepped aside, and Robyn entered with Watts not far behind. She wasn't at all shocked to see O'Brien here – the first time she'd seen the woman since that night at the spa. Watts had passed on her regards, but she'd been way too busy untangling the mess Robyn had left them. Besides, the DI didn't really 'do visiting hours'. Except apparently when they had a new witness in a murder case.

'Doctor,' said the woman, who was sitting slumped in a chair at the end of the bed.

'Inspector,' replied Robyn with a curt nod.

'I trust you're feeling better?'

'I'm . . .' she began, suddenly switching her focus to the man lying down with all kinds of tubes and wires going in and out of him. A monitor on the far side of the bed displayed his vitals, including his heart rate, which for the moment was steady and strong. The man himself looked grey, however, his wrinkled skin hung limply from the bones on his face. Robyn had nothing to compare it to, hadn't known the fellow before he had his heart attack, but he certainly looked like someone who'd gone through a major life trauma. Compared with that, it seemed silly to complain about falling out of a window, so she replied: 'I'm fine.'

The old man spotted that there were more people in the room and looked over at Robyn. 'Hello there,' he said. 'You been in the wars, young lady?'

She gave a small laugh. 'Something like that. How are you feeling yourself, Mr Platt?'

'Oh, I'll be all right,' he promised her, but his voice wavered.

She stepped nearer. 'They tell me you saw something connected with our case.'

'I did, aye. Miss . . .'

'Robyn,' she told him. 'Just Robyn.'

'As in Batman and . . .' He grinned.

'Something like that,' she said again, then thought about Mia

268

and what she'd said to her. The promise she still needed to keep. 'These men you saw on the beach,' Robyn prompted now.

'Going at it they were. Really having a barney.'

'The kind that might lead to a fight?' she asked.

'Definitely,' the old man confirmed. 'The kind of fight that might lead to someone turning up dead.'

'But you didn't see them *actually* fighting?'

'As near as dammit. They moved out of sight before . . . And then, well, I was otherwise engaged.'

'He means having his heart attack,' Jeremy clarified from behind.

'Yeah, I got it,' said Robyn.

'First thing I did when I was well enough was tell Jeremy, got him to call the police.'

'I understand you've already identified Si . . . Mr Carter?'

Mr Platt snr nodded. 'From a photo they showed me. I needed my glasses to see it.'

'But you have no idea who the other man is?'

'Never seen him before in my life.'

'Can I just ask: how *is* your eyesight, Mr Platt?'

The old man pulled a face, as if she was questioning his very manhood. 'I get by.'

Robyn looked over her shoulder at Jeremy, who was about to say something then stopped. But his expression told her everything she needed to know.

'Listen,' said his dad, 'with the kind of binoculars I have, I can see a flea on a dog from twenty miles away.' It was an exaggeration, but Jeremy pointed out that they were the strongest on the market, even started to go into the specs, but O'Brien held up a hand to stop him.

'So, I guess the next step is to get some kind of e-photofit made up of the suspect,' said Robyn.

'Already in hand, we've organising a sketch artist to sit with Mr Platt.'

269

'Right.' A sketch artist, of course, thought Robyn who was used to the way they did it back in Hannerton. But it was better than nothing, would be something to go on.

'Not today you're not.' Everyone turned at the words, a female voice that was soft but at the same time carried weight. Robyn saw an oriental nurse standing at the open doorway, arms folded. 'Mr Platt's had quite enough excitement for now.' Then, to Jeremy: 'Your father needs his rest. Doctor's orders.'

'Yes,' said the man, blushing. 'Yes, of course. You're quite right, Bao.'

'Nonsense, I'm—'

'You'll do as you're told, Henry,' said the nurse to Jeremy's dad. He sighed. 'You see what I have to put up with,' he said, but did it with a sparkle in his eye. Robyn suspected he quite enjoyed all the fussing and attention. Like father, like . . .

'All right, all right. We'll clear out for now,' said O'Brien, getting to her feet. 'But we'll be back.'

'Thanks for all your help so far,' Watts chimed in, looking first at Mr Platt, then his son, and Robyn echoed that sentiment.

As they were leaving, Mr Platt called out after her, 'You watch your step now, Robyn. Aye?'

'Aye,' she replied. 'I will.'

Out in the corridor they gathered to mull all this new information over. 'Puts a slightly different perspective on things, don't you think?' said Robyn.

'Depends who our mystery man is,' O'Brien responded, hands jammed in her pockets.

'You think it might still be connected to the spa?' asked Watts. This was a bit of turnaround, pushing for there to be a link.

The DI gave a shrug. 'Who knows. There's very little we can do till we have that sketch. Watts, are you arranging for a lift for Dr Adams back to her hotel, once she's discharged?'

'Yep, on it. Oh, and while I think about it . . .' Watts fished around in her pocket, brought out her phone. 'It's been released now. Not really evidence as such, so . . .' She'd never got a chance to take any pictures, but in the end it hadn't really mattered.

'Thanks,' said Robyn, taking it from him. She keyed in the numbers that would open it, checking it was still working. There was no signal, obviously, but then what was new? She'd wait till she got back to the hotel and maybe give Cav a ring then, let him know what had been going on. 'If anything else happens—'

'You'll be the first to know, Doctor,' O'Brien assured her. And far from sounding like a fob-off or a threat this time, it sounded like a promise.

But more than that, it sounded like she'd been accepted as part of another team.

Or even a family.

Chapter 36

She wished she hadn't gone.

Hadn't been intending to, not even when she'd heard the news about what had happened. That Robyn had gone up to The Castle Spa, where Simon had worked, and got herself into all kinds of trouble trying to find out the truth. Trying to catch his killer. Part of Vicky was grateful to her for that, was worried when Tracy had told her that Robyn was in the hospital because of it, but there was also that little voice telling her that her cousin had done it for her late husband. Done it because of the way she'd felt about him, and might still feel about him.

But so much had happened in both their lives, they'd barely seen anything of Robyn – she'd stayed away on purpose because of what took place in the past. According to her because they didn't want to hurt Vicky (too late). But that choice *had* been made (yes, but who'd made it, Robyn or Simon?). Did Robyn still feel that way about her late husband, even after all these years?

You still did . . . do, Vicky reminded herself.

But Robyn had almost been killed, so she'd been told. Something to do with Sebastian Boyd being behind everything, ordering his bodyguard to do the same to Robyn that had been done to Simon. To Kieran Thackery, who'd ended up the same way.

In any event, her cousin had been injured, trying to get away. Was in hospital, recovering while the investigation continued. That had caused a stab of guilt, naturally. What if the last time she'd ever seen Robyn had been when they'd fought? When Vicky had told her to get the fuck out of her house? Had it been worth *that*?

Yes.

Probably. Maybe . . .

Vicky didn't know anymore. Life and death struggles tended to put things into perspective, didn't they? But was that still any reason to go and make her peace with Robyn, after everything that had happened? All the lies and betrayal? All the buried secrets. The sleepless nights picturing Robyn and Simon together, going behind her back. Hadn't lasted long and they'd all been young, but even so . . .

She'd made her mind up that she was just going to leave it all well enough alone. Not pick at that particular scab while it was healing. At some point in the future, perhaps, but not yet. Vicky wasn't ready for that, didn't feel like she had the strength or energy left.

That was when Julie had called up out of the blue, asked if she wanted to come round – an invitation she'd accepted gratefully.

'So, how're things?' Julie had asked, while the kids played upstairs.

'They're . . . Oh, I just don't know where to start.' She'd confided in Julie about what had been happening, because she trusted her friend not to say anything. Hadn't gone into the gruesome details, just the edited highlights, enough for her to understand why Vicky had told Robyn to leave. It wasn't as if Julie had liked her anyway after the stunt in the caravan, but she'd surprised Vicky at that point by saying that sometimes you have to try and forgive people for things that had happened long ago.

'I-I'm trying to do that myself,' she confided in Robyn. 'Face what happened all that time ago, get back in touch with Jay's father. It's not going to be easy but . . .'

273

'This is all too raw at the moment,' Vicky had told her. 'I'm just not sure.'

Julie had patted her hand then, saying, 'You know where I am.'

'Thanks. I mean that, Julie. And the same goes.'

She figured that was partly the reason Julie had got in touch in the first place, perhaps because something had happened at her end. She'd talked to Jay's dad and needed someone to chat to herself. But it was actually more to do with what Vicky was going through, and to do with Bella Prescott.

'She's sad that you've stopped coming to the meetings, but she understands.'

'I heard about what happened at The Majestic,' Vicky replied. 'Please tell her I'm very sorry.'

'That wasn't your fault – you didn't go for her.'

'No but . . . If I hadn't dragged Bella into all this . . .'

Julie laughed. 'Things happen for a reason, love. Don't worry about that; Bella's not. She did say to pass on a message, though. Said you needed to see her.'

'Who? Bella?'

There was a hesitation before Julie answered, then: 'Robyn.'

Vicky swallowed dryly. 'Did she say why?'

'She just said to see her, before it's too late.'

'Too late?' What did she mean by that? Surely the shit had already hit the fan up at the spa. Robyn was out of danger now, wasn't she? 'What did she mean?'

'No idea. That's all she said. I'm just the messenger really.'

And that had been that. Vicky had considered going to see Bella, to try and get more information about it, but if she'd wanted her to know more she would have said; Bella didn't strike her as someone who held things back, especially where a message like that was concerned.

See her . . . before it's too late.

All of which had tipped the balance, encouraged Vicky to eventually take the plunge and visit Robyn at the hospital. Not to forgive her, because she still wasn't sure she could, but just to . . . She didn't know what, actually. Talk? No, she didn't want to do that either. Warn her? Surely the worst had happened now, and she'd already failed to do that; Robyn wouldn't have listened to anything that had come from Bella anyway.

Just to see her, then. Make sure she was okay, not too badly hurt.

So she'd gone, had made it to the corridor after almost turning back at the entrance to the General. Breathed in and out, preparing herself to walk to the ward Robyn was in. But what she hadn't been prepared for was seeing her standing there in that corridor ahead. For her to see Vicky and start calling out.

No. No, I can't do this, she'd thought then, and this time had turned around and left. Ignored the cries of her name and got out of there as quickly as possible. Damn the consequences.

When she got home, Mia was waiting for her – Tracy was in the kitchen washing up (Vicky had already decided she was going to buy her a present or something for all that she'd done during this unpleasant time, for staying longer than she needed to and helping out). Mia had got over the whole snapping incident after Vicky had apologised, and it had been explained that Aunty Robyn had needed to be by herself for a while.

'To figure out what happened to Daddy?' the girl had asked and Vicky nodded. It seemed like the path of least resistance. Which was why Vicky was so surprised by what she had to say when she walked in through the door. Not the first bit, because she'd already told her that she was going to see Aunty Robyn, that she was in the hospital and not very well, but the second bit: the bit about Simon.

'Was she all right?' Mia enquired. She'd wanted to see her herself, but Vicky had said that it wouldn't be a very good idea, that she needed to get over her 'illness' first. 'Was she feeling better?'

Vicky felt awful lying to her – no, not lying, being economical with the truth – particularly given the mess they'd got into after hiding Simon's death from her. But she told herself that it was

275

in Mia's best interests, that it would only worry her to know what Robyn had gone through. 'She seemed . . . Yes, she was okay,' Vicky told her, which again wasn't strictly a lie. Though she hadn't been anywhere near close enough to see properly for herself, Robyn had been up and about. Okay, her arm was in a sling, but she looked well enough in herself (one of those stupid phrases people said that meant nothing at all). Was well enough to call out, follow her down that corridor to the hospital entrance – Vicky had seen her from her hiding place behind the bus stop shelter in the car park.

Mia had nodded, then said: 'Mum?'

'Yes,' Vicky replied cautiously, because in her experience something bad usually followed that tone.

'Aunty Robyn knew Daddy, didn't she?'

Vicky hesitated before answering, 'Yes. Yes, of course. You know she did.'

'I mean . . . She knew him really well, didn't she?'

Where was this going? Vicky wondered. 'Y-Yes.'

Mia looked down, then up again at her. 'Only, I heard you saying that she'd slept over with him when you were little. Younger I mean.'

Those words shook her. 'When did you hear that?'

'At Jay's. We both heard it.'

Shit. Mia and her creeping about. *Slept* with Simon, that's what she'd been saying – but of course a child would have equated that to sleeping over, like she did all the time with Jay.

Mia must have seen the shock on her face then, because she asked: 'What's wrong? It's okay, isn't it? It's not a secret or anything. Friends do that all the time – and we're family. Family's the most important thing, isn't it? *You* said that.'

She didn't know what she was talking about – family definitely didn't do what Robyn had done to her . . . to them both. One day Mia would be able to understand that, but at the moment she just thought this was no big deal. Which meant . . . 'Mia, who have you spoken to about this? Who have you told?' Then Vicky thought: *God, and* who *has Jay told?*

The girl looked guilty then, before replying, 'N-No . . . no one.' Which probably meant everyone and their pets. The whole bloody town probably knew by now.

'Mia . . .'

'I miss Aunty Rob-Rob, Mum. Don't you?'

It was then that Vicky really wished she hadn't gone to see her cousin. Wished again she'd never rung her and brought her here, regardless of the fact she'd been instrumental in bringing down the people who'd killed Simon.

Wished, although she felt guilty about this too, that she'd never clapped eyes on the woman.

Wished that they weren't family at all.

Chapter 37

Even before the face had started to take shape, he had a feeling he'd seen it before.

He'd returned to Golden Sands station after dropping Robyn off at her hotel the day before. His aim had been to catch up with work there, work he'd only half-heartedly been a part of lately because his attention had been divided. His time as well, spending every spare minute at the hospital with Robyn. Even when Ashley Watts was at the nick, he'd be thinking about her – something that hadn't gone unnoticed by his DI.

'Go on, head off early, will you. You're not much use to me mooning about like this.' Partly a joke, but also partly because he knew O'Brien felt bad about what had happened up at the spa. That if she'd acted sooner on all this, then maybe Robyn wouldn't have been injured in the first place. Wouldn't have been forced to head up there alone because she felt nobody had her back.

He'd had her back, and tried to get Robyn to see that. But when she wouldn't, he'd kept tabs on her instead. Had trailed her to the spa that evening, knowing full well what would happen – well, some of it. Knew she'd end up trespassing for sure. Knew she was in real danger as well, which was why he hadn't hesitated to make up the story about hearing the screams. It was only sort of made up. He'd convinced himself he could hear *something* . . . carried on the wind. Was convinced it was the right thing to do, even though it wasn't technically legal.

He'd almost gone after her himself – but then that really would have put a spoke in things if he'd been caught. Better to run it by O'Brien and wait for backup before going in, everything above board. 'Yeah, you're right. I can hear the screaming too, now you come to mention it,' she'd said on arrival – and off they'd gone. It had all worked out okay in the end; they'd saved Robyn before anything too serious could happen to her.

Like falling through a plate-glass window, you mean? Watts argued with himself whenever he thought about this, which was often.

If they'd been just a little earlier . . . But you had to be grateful for small mercies, didn't you? In this job, especially. Right now, Robyn was safe and in her hotel. Safe, well, and had no knowledge of what he was seeing, though that would change soon enough.

Because Watts had been left in charge of getting the sketch done, the artist having arrived around eleven or so the following morning – though it was closer to twelve before they'd been allowed in to sit with Mr Platt and get it done.

Jeremy had been there, naturally, to oversee things. Figured he was now an official part of the investigation, having discovered the first body and being the son of the man who'd seen the death occur. Or an altercation anyway; Mr Platt snr hadn't witnessed the actual murder – but what he'd said was enough to make them question whether Boyd and his employees even had anything to do with it at all. Unless that other guy Platt had seen turned out to be on their payroll, obviously.

'Eyes a bit bigger,' Mr Platt kept saying to the artist, who'd rub them out and draw them again. 'Nose a bit smaller. And eyebrows darker. But a square jawline, I remember that.'

And finally, bit by bit, that man's face had been revealed. They might have had cause to question whether he'd actually seen anything clearly at all before that, Watts wondering whether he'd simply nodded when they showed the old fellow that photo of Simon Carter. Perhaps Jeremy had said something beforehand, which would have skewed things massively. Might even have told his father roughly what Simon looked like. But this . . . no, this was undeniable.

Standing over his shoulder as he drew, once again marvelling at the artist's skill – his own speciality was stick men – Watts had become increasingly uneasy. It was a coincidence, he told himself to begin with; in the early stages of it all, certainly. Just looked vaguely like him . . . But once he was finished and Watts could see the drawing of the bloke, it was like he was standing right in front of him. As he had been once, not so long ago.

'Jesus!' he'd exclaimed.

'Language, young man,' Mr Platt admonished.

'But . . . Oh God, I *know* him,' Watts spluttered.

The artist was frowning, as was Jeremy. As were the uniforms still posted on guard outside, peering in and eavesdropping. 'What?' asked the old man, confused.

Watts tapped the paper then, in danger of smudging the work. 'I-I know him. I've *met* him!' He got the artist to hold the picture steady and took a photo of it using his phone camera. 'Get this to the DI, as quickly as you can. I need to go,' he told anyone who'd listen. The artist primarily, but also one of the uniforms.

If he'd been thinking clearly, Watts would have just sent the picture to her. She had good reception as a guest at the hotel, though the signal in the hospital was dodgy as hell. Instead, he'd hopped in his car. He needed to go to her, check for himself that she was okay.

Because he knew the man who'd been with Simon that fateful morning, the morning of his death. And so did she. Robyn knew him; she'd met him.

She could be in terrible danger.

Haring up one street and down another, he broke all the

speed limits getting to The Majestic and nearly knocked over a pedestrian or three. Pulling up sharply, he heard the tyres screech but took no notice.

Then he was racing through the entrance, the foyer, jabbing the button on the lift but not having the patience to wait for it. Tearing up the stairs instead until he found her floor, found her room and began pounding on her door.

Nobody answered and he was considering either getting someone to open it, or just breaking it down – when suddenly it was swinging inwards.

She was standing there, arm still in that sling, looking confused. 'I wasn't sure there'd be anyone . . . Ashley? Ashley, what is it?'

'I . .' He shook his head, pulled out his phone and showed her the sketch instead. Watts didn't need to explain – she knew exactly what was happening today. Knew what it meant as well.

'Oh my . . .' She put her good hand to her mouth.

'It's him, isn't it?'

Robyn nodded.

'I knew it. I'm not going mad then. We know who it is now!'

She held up a finger for him to wait, went into the bedroom and brought back her own phone. Opening it up, she began flicking her thumb across the screen. 'And,' she said then, before saying something he hadn't been expecting at all, 'I think I know where we can find him.'

Watts took the phone from her, stared at the screen.

Then he grinned.

Part Four

There has very rarely been a time when there hasn't been a funfair at Golden Sands, even if it was in the form of a small touring fair or fete which would visit the area. These days, however, there is a permanent site for the funfair near the pier, as previously mentioned. Entertainment for all the family; you can fill up on candyfloss, have your fortune told, go on the dodgems or teacups, even try the merry-go-round. There's definitely something for everyone . . .

And once you step inside you can always be guaranteed the time of your life.

Chapter 38

Chances were, he'd already done a runner.

But then, if he'd wanted to do that, why not go after he'd done the deed? *If* he'd committed the murders, that was. They still didn't know for sure. All Mr Platt's sighting and sketch ID did was put him in the right place at the right time – when Simon Carter was in exactly the wrong place at the wrong time.

Didn't prove anything, but it did mean they needed to have a chat with the guy. The one Robyn and Watts knew, the one who hopefully was still around now they were heading down to where he worked.

If she hadn't been bored, hadn't been going through it all again – the files she still had in her room, the rest of the case notes that had accumulated since she'd begun working with the team here – then she never would have spotted the connection. If she hadn't picked up the phone Watts had returned to her, been thinking about ringing Cav the previous evening and then decided against it again . . . she never would have woken up with it (in a sitting position because of the sling) still in her hand. Never would have thought about flicking through those photos she'd taken during those early recces here.

The beach, the amusements, the pier . . .

The funfair.

It had taken a couple of runs through those before she saw him, lurking in the background of one. Whether he'd spotted her too was another matter, and if he had, maybe that accounted for at least some of the feelings of being observed, but he'd been there. He worked there, judging from the hammer he was holding, the old work clothes. She might just have dropped lucky, caught him unawares – probably before he even knew who she was, or was working on the case at all. Just another visitor there, wandering around.

But she'd encountered him not long after that, hadn't she. Her *and* Watts. Wasn't likely to forget it anytime soon.

There he was, though, in those photos, large as life. Large all right; fit and strong, well-muscled. Alive, which was more than you could say for Simon. Just in a couple of them, too far away to see that scar on his eyebrow unless you zoomed in, but recognisably him. The man they knew only as John. There on that day, same as he'd been around later on in the pub. Definitely knew who she was by then. Definitely started chatting to her intentionally, was keeping tabs but in a very different way to Watts.

He'd be gone by now, surely? While they'd been focusing on the spa – looking in entirely the wrong place – here he'd been, someone who'd had an argument with Simon just prior to his death. Robyn hadn't known it at the time, of course. Not until Watts had shown up with that sketch, and they'd put two and two together. She'd been about to get in touch with the DS, actually, when he showed up at her room – out of breath and face etched with concern. Thought their suspect might have got to her first. Worried she was in danger, which was actually quite endearing.

As they approached and parked up, ready to go in mob-handed with uniform, Robyn was still shaking her head, though, saying to herself that he wouldn't be here. That he'd have done a runner.

Worth searching the place whatever the case, their first port of call before putting that sketch out into the world. It wasn't a huge area to comb through, but there were lots of places in there to hide. And the first he'd know about them coming would be when, or if, he saw them. They hadn't called ahead – wanted to catch him on the hop if he was there.

'But you, you're staying here in the station,' O'Brien had told her even before they set off.

'Like hell!' Robyn had replied, feeling more confident than she had in ages. Not to mention livid at the fact John had played her for a fool.

'I'll have enough to worry about looking for this bastard, without keeping an eye on bystanders.'

'I'm a bit more than that!' she'd argued, hoping they'd got past all this.

'The guv might have a point,' Watts had waded in at that juncture – and she knew he was only looking out for her, as he had been all along. As he had been back when they first encountered the man . . .

'What the fuck was all that about?'

'What?'

'That macho bullshit in there!'

'He looked like he was hassling you.'

'Believe it or not, I can look after myself.'

Hadn't been doing that back at the spa, when she'd needed help. But, as she said to them: 'I have to see this through. You owe me that much.'

Whether they owed her anything at all was debatable, but in the end O'Brien relented and said, 'Okay, okay. You can come with, but you stay well out of the way.'

That was all right: for one thing her arm was still in this bloody sling because of her shoulder; for another she had no great desire to put herself in the firing line. She'd done enough of that already. Bravery was one thing; downright stupidity was another. The cops knew what they were doing. She just wanted to see him get taken in . . .

If he was still there, *if* he hadn't run off.

So she'd stayed in the car, as O'Brien had talked to the people in the ticket office and they'd nodded. John was there then, if that really was his name. Still around. Robyn had swallowed dryly. As Watts and the uniforms had gone in, those guys tooled up with batons and tasers. Robyn had no way of knowing how the search was progressing, however. Waited in the car for what seemed like ages, before getting out, before making her way towards the funfair – to get a closer look. Still out of the way, not underfoot. Safe enough with those other uniforms guarding the exits, where families were being ushered out as quickly and quietly as possible by members of staff.

Here and there she spotted an officer entering a booth or checking out one of the rides, dodging those dodgems, so John hadn't been taken down yet. Of O'Brien and Watts there was no sign, but then they were coordinating all this so were understandably busy.

Robyn felt her pocket vibrate, and it gave her a start. For one thing, there was signal! She reached inside and brought out the phone – the one that had captured John, sadly only on the photos that had brought them all to this place. It was Watts . . . She thumbed the screen button across to answer the call.

'Ashley?'

'Not exactly,' came the reply, in a voice she recognised as well. That accent she hadn't been able to place the last time she'd heard it. 'But he's here with me. Aren't you . . . *Ashley*. We . . . *I* finished what he wanted to start in the pub that night.'

She heard a muffled grunt, which could have been anyone, but Robyn knew deep down was Watts. 'What do you want?'

'What do you think? I want you to come. I want out of here.'

'But I'm . . . I can't *get* you out. There are police everywhere.'

'Do you think I don't fucking know that? I saw them fucking arrive! Good job too, gave me a chance to get out from under them. To nab this twat as well.'

'Then how—'

'You're going to have to think of something. You're a clever lady. But you come alone, all right? You tell anyone, or I see you with any other coppers and this one'll be as dead as the others. I'll wring his neck.' The others . . .? Not just Simon, it looked like, but Kieran as well. Kieran who also worked here. 'Okay?'

'O-Okay,' said Robyn. What choice did she have? This man had already proved that he was *more* than capable of killing. Maybe if she could talk to him face-to-face again. 'Okay, just don't do anything rash.'

There was a gruff laugh at the other end. 'Too late for that, I reckon. Don't you?'

Almost certainly, Robyn thought to herself, but said: 'All right. Tell me where you are and I'll come to you.'

John hadn't done a runner, still hadn't got out of there. But she was beginning to wish he had.

And she was beginning to wish she had as well.

Chapter 39

Watts wasn't quite sure how he'd been incapacitated, because it had all happened so quickly.

He had no idea where John had come from or how that thug had got the drop on not only him, but the two officers that had been with him as well. But he'd certainly made mincemeat of them, putting them all down without even breaking a sweat. It hadn't been like that night in the pub, when Watts had fancied his chances – and hadn't wanted to look like a loser in front of Robyn (as it turned out, he had anyway). This time John had been waiting for them, had disarmed his colleagues in moments and knocked Watts out, dragged him into this place . . . wherever this was. Behind the scenes in one of the rides or something?

He was cuffed to some railings, using his own bloody cuffs! Had woken up to the sound of John calling Robyn, jamming the mobile into his face to get a mumble from him. Then John had wandered off, still speaking to her. Ironically, the signal was crystal clear at the fair even inside here.

Watts wished that it hadn't been, really. Didn't want Robyn in the middle of this. To be responsible for what happened to her. Wasn't exactly sure what the guy wanted Robyn to do! Watts tried calling out a couple of times, but that had just earned him a whack with a stolen baton when John got back: right across the face, opening up a cut at the corner of his lip.

'You. Shut it!'

'T-This place is surrounded, mate. There's no way you're getting out – whether Robyn comes or not.'

'I told you to shut it!' John snarled, but looked genuinely worried.

'You can't go through all of them out there, you know.'

John rubbed his face, then crouched down – dragging out a taser now. 'If you don't shut up, I'll fucking use *this* on you!'

'You should have buggered off when you got the chance,' said Watts – not knowing when to keep quiet, which had always been his problem.

'Would've looked more suspicious if I'd gone,' he said then. 'I was waiting it out. You lot would just have come after me if I'd gone. You or . . .'

Watts couldn't help laughing. 'What, and we won't now? You can add assault and kidnapping a policeman to the list.'

'Add it to murder? Have you heard yourself?'

Have you? thought Watts. 'And when Robyn gets here, then what? You think you're just going to walk out with her? You might as well take me.'

'She'll make a better hostage, if it comes to it. A civilian. Your lot will be more careful if I have her with me. Plus which, I can handle her better. Mind you,' said John smirking, 'you didn't exactly put up much of a fight, did you? Maybe she's got more balls than you after all.'

Watts ignored the jibe. 'What then, though?'

'I've got a plan,' John assured him. 'I know a few people who'll do anything for . . .' He was the one who shut up now, though, frightened he was giving too much away. But the guy was flailing around, wasn't thinking things through at all. Reacting, but perhaps he'd been doing that right from the very start? Perhaps that's what he'd been doing with Simon Carter, how he'd got into this mess in the first place? Lost his temper and—

'John?' said a voice and he whirled around, surprising them both.

Robyn, standing there in the corridor in the half-light, her arm still in that sling from the fall through the window. She'd obviously followed directions to get here, but none of them had noticed her until now. 'Robyn! Robyn get out of here!' shouted Watts.

'I *told* you!' snapped John.

'It's okay. It's okay,' she said, stepping forward. 'I came John. I'm here.'

Not that he'd realised, too busy arguing with Watts to keep a lookout for her. The DS hoped she'd brought half the bloody constabulary with her, ready to give this dickhead hell – but doubted very much she had. She'd be too worried about something happening to him. 'Get over here!' John ordered and she came tentatively forwards, eyes flicking over to Watts to see if he was all right.

'You can lose your phone now,' John told her, so she took it out and dropped it. Kicked it away when he ordered her to do that too.

'I'm not sure what you think's going to happen, but—'

'I told you. We're getting out of here.'

'I don't think we are, you know,' Robyn answered.

'Robyn, just go! You can—'

That was when he turned on Watts a final time, using the taser like he'd promised. Watts shook, jerked, felt those needle-tipped darts embedding themselves in him. Felt all that electricity passing through him – like having a terrible cramp all over his body, which was seizing up. But he also felt a certain satisfaction, because Robyn had gone – rushed back out through a doorway off to their left, so that when John looked back again she'd vanished. It all happened so quickly.

'Fucking bitch!' barked the man.

Watts just about had time to see where they were as the

door flapped back on its hinges. Behind the scenes, but not a ride. Then he passed out again, hoping that Robyn had made it back to safety.

Hoping those other coppers were out there, too, waiting to give John hell.

Chapter 40

She'd been here before.

In hell again and alone, the pressure on. Robyn had done as John requested, come here on her own – had to, or Watts was a dead man. Managed to get past the uniforms at the gate by using those brains John said she had. They'd been helping out with the 'evacuation' of the funfair, so she'd slipped through at a convenient moment while they were distracted. Robyn had managed to make it to this place without any of the others seeing her, though there had been a moment or two when she'd almost been spotted by O'Brien – cropping up at the worst possible time – but had gotten away with it. Thanks to her exploits up at the spa, she was becoming pretty good at sneaking around; getting as good as ninja 'I've been Cathy' when she'd first met her at the reception desk. Just so long as there was nobody behind her with a golf club this time ready to strike . . .

It had to be this place, didn't it – because history repeated itself, remember? She had to admit when John told her where they were, how to get inside through the fire door with the busted lock, she'd sighed.

Not again, she thought to herself.

But things were different this time. She wasn't tied up for

starters and John was a completely different prospect to the man who'd been with her that first time. Or was he? A killer was a killer when all was said and done; she just had no idea yet whether John enjoyed it. Whether he was doing this to fulfil some kind of twisted fantasy, or if there was something else behind it all. Robyn just hoped she'd get the chance to find out.

She should have stayed, made sure Watts was all right after he'd been tasered. But how could she? She knew full well she'd have been next. Captured, for sure. In the same shit she'd been in back when Sykes or Andersson had hold of her. At least this way there was a chance, and if she could get John to follow her instead . . . No point trying to lead him outside again, though – he'd just double back for Watts. She had to make John angry enough to chase her inside the heart of this place.

But what was she thinking, make him *angry*? She must be crazy herself! He could just as easily kill her in a frenzy like he had with—

'*This one'll be as dead as the others. I'll wring his neck.*'

Wouldn't even take that much effort to wring hers. Choke the life out of her in this dimly lit place of warped reflections that had been shut down for repairs (and the sensible part of her brain told her that was why he'd picked it, because it would be empty). Some of the surfaces were already cracked and splintered from the vandalism, which only added to the surrealness.

'Fucking bitch!' she heard him cry and knew he was coming; could even hear the banging, the knocking that she knew wasn't her imagination this time. Realised it wouldn't be long before he caught up with her. Before he found her, stalking round corner after corner – because, failing everything else, he needed her as a hostage to get out. 'You won't get far. I know this place like the back of my hand!' he shouted after Robyn.

You really do know how to pick 'em, she thought to herself – remembering when she'd first met this man back in the pub. How nice he'd seemed, how flattered she'd been by the attention. She could spot the patterns, tell you everything there was about a psychopath after the fact – but when it came to something like that, she had to confess her judgement was total shit. Always had been, probably always would be.

If there even *was* an 'always would be', if she got out of this. History repeating itself in more ways than one, except she was determined now not to let it. Not to be the victim, not to need saving again.

A flash of something out of the corner of her eye, and she turned just in time to see John behind her. He'd left the taser behind, and had a baton in his hand. So he was going to beat her into submission, was that it? But instead of coming for her, he smashed a mirror off to his right – seven years' bad luck! – one of the ones that was intact. It made her wonder whether he'd committed that vandalism here in the first place, perhaps knowing he'd need somewhere to hide out? The maniacal grin on his face just fractured and multiplied when he did that.

Robyn ducked around another corner, only to be confronted with an image that stretched her out beyond all recognition. Her breathing was coming in short gasps, nerves in tatters. She had no idea where she was going, or even how to get out now – just knew John would keep on coming.

Which he did, trailing her again: his reflection short and stocky; squat like that dwarf from the fantasy films everyone had gone nuts over when she was growing up. She rounded another corner, then another, only to find John standing inches away from her. Realising moments later it was just another reflection in this maze of them. That she had another chance to escape.

She ran, skirting around yet more of the recently smashed mirrors, but lost her balance, falling to the ground. 'Where do you think you're going?' her real stalker said, and his voice was echoing as badly in this place as his image. Echoing O'Brien's words back at the spa, as well. Robyn had no way of telling where he was now: ahead, behind, off to the side of her.

Scrambling to her feet, which wasn't easy with one hand, she narrowly avoided a blow from the baton – which hit the glass on her left and rained it down on her. Was this the fear Simon felt before he died, she wondered? Kieran too? As John bore down on them, as he did his worst.

Backing off, she heard him practically whisper: 'Boo!' It was at this point she realised that, yes, now he'd got over his initial anger he was indeed enjoying this . . . hunt. That was the only word for it. He was hunting her, and she wasn't even sure at this point whether he'd keep her alive or not.

'You can't get away.'

Robyn spun, thought she saw John, but it was just her own reflection once more. Shadows and reflections. This place was just confusing her; she had to trust herself. Trust her own instincts, use that clever brain of hers one more time. Use the darkness.

She closed her eyes. Waited. Sooner or later she'd sense it . . . And yes, there it was. Robyn felt him behind her, his own breathing. Another whisper: 'I told you, I know this place—'

'Like the back of your hand, yes I know,' she said through gritted teeth – at the same time using her free hand to pull out the piece of broken glass she'd hidden in her sling. Robyn whirled, opening her eyes and aiming for John's chest with the makeshift weapon. He raised the baton but was too slow, and it only served to throw off her strike, which went up and into his neck.

Robyn let out an exclamation. She'd only meant to force him back, to disarm him, but he was clutching that neck now, blood – which appeared black in here – pumping out through the wound. A wound he was actually making worse with his actions. He dropped the baton and then, seconds later, he backed up into a mirror and was sliding down it, knees buckling. John was making noises like someone trying to speak underwater.

Struggling to breathe, just like his victims had.

No . . . she thought to herself, *I'm no killer. Not even an accidental one. I refuse to be.*

'Hold still,' she told him, placing her own hand over the injury to help him stem the bleeding. None of which would make any difference if they didn't get him medical attention soon. But Watts was out of it, and nobody else even knew she was here. She'd made sure of that . . .

Only she hadn't been as stealthy as she'd thought. There was noise coming from somewhere, more banging, and again it was echoing. Then a voice that sounded vaguely irritated, called out, 'Dr Adams! Dr Adams, are you in here?'

O'Brien. She must have spotted Robyn after all, trailed her to find out where she was going, probably to give her a bollocking for not staying in the car. Thank Christ! 'Here. Over here.'

'Where?'

'Follow my voice,' Robyn called out. 'And call for an ambulance.' She kept the pressure on, hoping they'd get to her soon.

Relived now that she was no longer alone.

Now her new family was here.

Chapter 41

Things got sorted out pretty quickly after that.

Well, once John – second name, Bellamy – had recovered enough to talk to the police. Thankfully, it had looked worse than it was, hadn't even touched his vocal cords – but even so, by the time he was fit enough to be questioned in hospital, Robyn's shoulder had all but healed completely.

The first thing they'd asked him, when he finally saw that it was in his best interests to open up (as it was, he was in for a lot more than seven years' bad luck . . . in jail), was: why?

Sitting up in bed, with uniforms posted on either side of him, and a camera recording it all, he'd told them about the money they'd found that morning on the beach. 'We'd got into the routine of going for a run there, and wetter sand meant more resistance . . . Carter was the only other person who worked at the fair who was into fitness and whatnot,' their prisoner informed them. John had a served a bit of time in the army, even been posted abroad, which was where that eyebrow scar came from. That training explained how he could so easily incapacitate the uniformed officers at the fairground, who'd thankfully also now recovered. And working on the road at places like the fairground had only helped with his general level of physical fitness.

'Right, so the money?' O'Brien had encouraged, Robyn observing from the sidelines along with his court-appointed lawyer, who looked a bit like a fair-haired Danny DeVito.

'What the fuck were they doing burying it there in the first place? That's what I want to know!' John had growled, railing against the cuffs holding him in place at both wrists, which made the lawyer raise an eyebrow. He had no hope of getting John off, though, anyway.

'Easy now,' one of the officers on guard warned him, placing a hand on his chest.

'I mean, for fuck's sake! All that cash there, buried.' He was talking about the drugs money that had been left there, part of the operation they'd shut down at the spa. Money, sometimes drugs, were apparently left there on the beach at pre-arranged spots – probably a nod to the way smugglers used to do the same back in the day. Only on that morning, and after the storm, the metal tube had been uncovered. 'We wondered what it was, sticking up like that. Carter thought it was probably just junk, but I had a feeling about it. And inside there were all these fucking notes.'

'Fifty grand to be precise, which we recovered from your person after your arrest. Money you'd hidden in the Hall of Mirrors.'

'Yeah,' John admitted, hanging his head. 'Would've set me up nicely, that.'

Fifty grand, Robyn had thought to herself. The price of a life. Of Simon's life.

'*Had a stroke of luck. A windfall you might say.*'

'Carter wanted to split it, but I thought to myself – why should I?'

'Because he was your friend?' O'Brien suggested and John simply snarled. Simon, like her, had similar shit judgement when it came to people, apparently.

'That kind of money buys a lot of friends. And everything else.'

'So, you had an argument . . .' said O'Brien.

'You're leading, Inspector,' broke in the lawyer.

300

'Hardly. We have a witness to that,' O'Brien reminded the man.

John sighed, knowing he might as well come clean about everything by this stage. 'We argued, yeah. And, well, the next thing I knew he was on the ground, half in the water.'

'You'd strangled him.'

John nodded. 'When I realised he was . . . Well, I panicked. I started to bury him.'

O'Brien rubbed her forehead. 'You didn't do a very good job of it, though. Did you?'

'I got interrupted. I heard sirens and thought . . .'

'Those would be the ambulance sirens coming to Mr Platt's assistance up on the cliffs.'

John frowned, not privy to that information before. 'An ambulance? Fuck's sake.'

'So you killed Mr Carter for the money, buried him. Then . . . then you hung around Golden Sands. Why?' O'Brien enquired.

John let out a moan. 'I figured I'd wait till the heat died down. Like I told that other copper—'

'DS Watts, who you hit with a baton then tasered.'

Robyn couldn't help thinking back now to Ashley being stretchered out of the fairground, how she'd worried about whether he was okay. Visited him in hospital, returning the favour, until she knew for sure he was all right.

'Like I told him, it would have looked more suspicious if I'd just upped and left,' John continued. 'The fair had my real name, could describe me. I'd have been looking over my shoulder for the rest of my life.'

'Either for us, or the people you stole the money from. Danny Fellows' people, we suspect,' O'Brien reminded him, 'though as usual we can't really tie him to it.' Danny Fellows was the gangland boss of the region, known in a lot of circles as the Tony Soprano of nearby Granfield, his base of operations. That was also part of the deal: John would confess everything if they could offer him some sort of protection in jail . . . though good luck with that quite frankly. He'd spend the rest of his – probably quite short – life looking over his shoulder anyway for Fellows' men inside.

'It would have got me away, that money, overseas or something.'

'Bit of a gamble came right.'

O'Brien shook her head at his fantasy. 'So when you found out Dr Adams was attached to the investigation, you decided to approach her.'

'I was just buying her a drink,' John fired back. 'She's a looker.'

'Enough to see me right for a bit . . . Enough to buy a lady drinks.'

Robyn thought she was going to be sick.

'What a coincidence, buying her a drink *after* doing a little digging,' O'Brien continued, though had the good grace to look sheepish about the choice of words, 'finding out about the kinds of cases she'd worked on. The serial cases . . .' And he'd definitely planted the seeds that this might be one of those, including leaving that clipping for Robyn on her windscreen. Though, interestingly, not the original note: no, that had been down to desk sergeant Bob, they'd since discovered. Thinking he was doing O'Brien a favour, and hacked off at the newcomer himself, he'd got his grandson to slip that note about going home under Vicky's front door . . . So she hadn't imagined it after all! Needless to say he was now facing disciplinary action.

'All that information must have come in handy after Kieran Thackery discovered your little hiding place in that Hall of Mirrors, eh?' O'Brien folded her arms, leaning forwards. 'You could just make it look like he was the next victim in the sequence.'

'I kept telling the lad to keep out of there, that I was the one sorting out replacing those mirrors. It just made him more curious, more suspicious.'

'So you killed him in the same way as Mr Carter. Strangulation. Then waited till dark and took him down to the beach, had a half-hearted go at burying him as well. Didn't matter if he was found this time; in fact you were hoping he was, right?'

302

'I figured that would put you lot off the scent, give her . . .' He nodded over at Robyn. 'Give her something else to worry about. Something she was more at home with.' So Robyn had got that right, at least. The staging had been deliberate.

'Holy . . .' said O'Brien. 'You're a piece of work, aren't you?'

John had given her a lopsided grin at that, as if to say, 'I try my best'.

And basically that was that. They'd got to the bottom of the killings of both Simon Carter and young Kieran Thackery: both over money. Buried treasure, the kind Jeremy Platt had been searching for when he'd found Simon, as he'd told the journalists when they were so keen to interview him and his dad. Their moment in the spotlight.

The kind of treasure old-fashioned pirates fought over. The kind more modern pirates fought over as well.

The only upside to all of it was the operation up at the spa – the rings that were still being investigated. Stuff that was keeping both O'Brien and Watts busy, though Robyn had seen a lot more of the latter in the time she'd spent hanging on to see how all this panned out. While the DS was waiting to see how other things panned out, she suspected.

'You'll be heading back soon then, I guess?' he said to her as they eventually had dinner in a lobster place, which for Golden Sands was the height of haute cuisine. A thank you for what she'd done back in the Hall of Mirrors, though she insisted they were pretty much even now.

'I guess I will, yep.' Going home, finally.

He'd looked heartbroken then, that expression like a puppy about to be reprimanded. 'Back to Hannerton. To Cav.'

'Back to my colleague, DI Cavendish, yes. My friend.'

'Except he's more than that, isn't he? You'd like him to be.'

'Ash, please . . . He's . . . It's complicated. And he's married.'

'I know he is.' The silence hung over them for a little while, before she threw this particular puppy a bone.

'I reckon I've screwed up enough families, don't you? Mine included.'

Watts didn't reply, just took a drink of his lager.

'Besides, I think I'm going to swear off blokes for a while. See how that works out for me.'

'All men?' he asked.

'Maybe just the bad ones, if I can tell which are which . . . Ones who don't have my back.'

He looked down, began playing with his napkin. 'I'm . . . I'm not . . . I mean, I don't think I am anyway, one of those, but—'

Robyn laughed. 'You're not, Ash. Trust me. You're very sweet. And any time you fancy visiting *my* home . . .'

'Next week?' he said, and she couldn't tell if he was joking or not.

'Maybe give me a bit longer to settle back in.' Again, that puppy dog look, so she grabbed his hand and gave it a squeeze. 'But not *that* long, eh?'

He smiled and it lit up his entire face. Then a dark cloud passed over his features once more. 'Have you . . . I mean, tell me to mind my own business if you like but . . . Are you going to see them before you leave?'

The business he was referring to was of course Vicky and Mia. Something that really wasn't going to get sorted quickly at all. Didn't mean she shouldn't try. 'I haven't decided yet,' she told him. 'They probably won't want to see me anyway.'

'You might be surprised,' he said, giving her hand a squeeze in return.

'Well, I do like surprises.' Robyn smiled back at him. 'As long as they're the nice kind,' she added quickly.

Epilogue

It hadn't been a surprise. She'd been expecting the visit sooner or later. Knew she had to face Robyn, though it was the one of the most difficult things she'd ever done.

So, when the knock came and she answered the door – Tracy having gone off to her next assignment – Vicky said, 'I suppose you'd better come in.'

'Thanks,' Robyn told her, closing the door behind herself.

'How're . . . You've recovered now?' Vicky asked, facing her. She still wanted to know if she was okay, not just after the spa but all the other stuff at the funfair that had been major news for a while.

'I'm . . . I'm all right,' Robyn told her. 'Coming off the meds, and staying off them this time. Cutting down on the drink. I need to make a few changes in my life, I've decided. Get some proper help.'

'That's . . . well, I'm glad about that anyway.'

'Look, I just wanted to say again how sorry I—'

Vicky held up her hand to silence her. 'Please, I'm not . . . I don't think I'm there yet.' She'd been encouraged to get there, to accept that apology, not just by Bella but also Simon when he came through to her again, promising it wasn't what she thought . . . And Vicky knew exactly what the woman in front of her would say to that! Mediums and their nonsense. Either way, she just wasn't quite prepared to forgive her cousin right now.

'But . . . but you might be, one day?' Robyn pushed.

Before Vicky could answer, there was a thunderous noise from the stairs and Mia suddenly appeared. She ran straight for Robyn's legs, wrapping herself around them. It was the first time the girl had seen her since she'd moved out. 'Aunty Rob-Rob, I've *missed* you!'

'Hello trouble,' said Robyn, bending and hugging her back. 'I've missed you too.'

'But it's okay, I know you've been after the man who . . . did the bad thing to Daddy. Did you get him?'

Robyn looked Vicky in the eye then and said, 'I did, yeah. I got him.'

'Just like Batman!'

'Er . . . let's go with Batwoman, shall we?'

'*Thank you!*' said the little girl, stepping back and looking up at her aunty.

'That's all right. I did it for . . . Well, for you and your mum.'

The girl nodded, totally understanding in a way Vicky wasn't certain she ever could yet. 'I know about you and Daddy,' Mia stated then, which totally flummoxed the adults.

'What?' asked Robyn, searching Vicky's face to see exactly what had been said.

'About how you used to be friends when you were younger,' explained Mia.

'Oh,' said Robyn. 'Yeah. We did. But your mummy and daddy were better friends than we ever were. Than we could ever have been.' It was something that would have to be explained much better when Mia was older, and Vicky wondered again what she would think. Whether she'd be able to understand then. Whether *she'd* be able to forgive Robyn, either. Those were reflections of the future, though, not the past . . .

'*Such a long time ago.*'

'But still family?' asked the little girl.

306

Robyn looked again at Vicky, probably wondering what to say. Then offered, 'We're all we've got. We're family; we should stick together.'

Not fair, turning her own words against her like that. But she did kind of have a point. 'Anyway, you'll be heading off back soon, I'd imagine,' said Vicky suddenly.

'Noooo!' sang Mia, tugging Robyn's hand. 'Please don't go. Not yet!'

'I . . .' Robyn stared at Vicky. 'I should probably be off. Long drive ahead.' Mia pouted. 'But hey, I almost forgot . . .' She went into her bag and brought out a book, the latest Walliams she'd been assured.

'Oh wow! Thank you!' shouted Mia, taking it gratefully and hugging it to her chest. 'Are you sure you need to go? You can't just read a bit to me?'

Robyn looked at Vicky a final time and she relented. 'I guess if your aunty has time for a tea or something . . .'

Her cousin smiled then, relief and happiness shining out of her. 'I think that can be arranged.'

'Yay!' screamed the little girl and hugged Robyn again. It would be selfish of Vicky to keep her from her family any more than she had been already – obviously Mia loved Robyn to bits. But they'd talk about that over time.

For now, what harm could some reading do? thought Vicky. *Some reading, a cup of tea.*

And perhaps, someday, though she couldn't see it now, once the tears had finally stopped for good . . .

A chance to put all the bad parts of the past behind them.

A chance to start again.

Acknowledgements

As usual with these, if I start to thank folk, I'm inevitably going to miss someone out – so I'll just say a massive 'much appreciated' to everyone who's supported and helped me in my journey as a writer so far. But there are a few people I'd especially like to single out for this publication. Firstly, my wonderful editor Belinda Toor who I can't thank enough for everything. Her faith in me and my characters are really what's driving these books forward. I owe a massive debt of gratitude to Abigail Fenton and everyone on the HQ Digital/HarperCollins team, not to mention my fellow authors. I know it's said a lot, but it really does feel like a family. Also thank you to those writers who took the time and trouble to read *Her Last Secret* and offer a quote. Finally, I need to thank my whole family for their support, help and encouragement whilst writing this novel, especially my Marie who never fails to amaze and inspire me every single day; love you more than words can say, sweetheart.

Keep reading for an excerpt from *Her Last Secret* . . .

Prologue

As the girl stumbled forward, she had one name on her mind.

She'd lost her mobile back there on the street and didn't have time to stop and search for it; didn't have the strength. She just needed to get to some help, maybe make it to the clubbing part of town – though that seemed like a very long way away. And she was getting tired now, breath misting in the autumn air, hardly able to focus. Little wonder – because as she touched the wounds on her chest, brushing the handle of the knife that was still sticking out, that had been left in there as she'd attempted to escape, her hands came away wet. Totally black in the moonlight.

Blood . . . so much blood.

Pain that had been unbearable only minutes before was dulling now, making her numb. She clutched at a wall, leaving a hand-print behind her. There'd be someone soon, she'd find someone who could help her. In fact, yes, there up ahead the street was opening out. Even in her confused state, she knew where she was: the market square. Ahead of her were the stalls, empty now at night-time – not that many were used in the waking hours, either, apart from on certain days – rows of wooden skeletons, looking like the carcasses of long-dead monsters.

Monsters like the ones she'd been so afraid of when she was

little. Silly really, being scared of imaginary things like that, when there were so many real things to be frightened of after you grew up. She wished more than anything at that moment – as she slipped on her own blood, righted herself and lunged towards the stalls – that she could go back in time to those days. Back when make-believe creatures under the bed were the only things to worry about. Back when life was so much simpler.

She used the stalls to drag herself along, still searching the space for . . . there! Someone was waiting in the middle. Or at least she thought it was someone, only to get there and realise it was just tarpaulin hanging down on yet another frame. Things were getting hazy now, her vision blurred. Time was running out. If the monsters here were dead, then she wouldn't be far behind them. And wasn't there a part of her that felt relief at that, because living was so, so hard? She'd always assumed it would get better, but it never really did; always thought there would be a brighter day to come. Instead, it was getting darker by the second.

She flopped onto that stall with the canvas sheeting, pain shooting through her again and waking her up momentarily. Forcing her onto her back, because the knife wouldn't let her lie down on her front.

If I could just go back. If I could just see him one more time.

The man who'd always chased away those monsters back when she was tiny, who'd picked her up and put her on his shoulders when they'd go for walks in the park. Who'd tried to teach her right from wrong, set an example. And whom she'd treated so, so badly.

That's why the name that had been on her mind, the name that came out – as she finally went blind, as the last of her vital lifeblood seeped out – wasn't that of the person who'd done this to her. Their name was as far from her thoughts as possible.

No, the name she uttered with her last breath was that of the man she thought might come, as if they shared some kind of psychic bond and she was sending out a distress call. It was the person, when all was said and done, that she still trusted most in this world; the irony being that he probably didn't even know that anymore, regardless of how true it was.

No, the name on her lips was simply this, uttered as if she was five again: 'Daddy.'

Then all she knew was the dark.

Part One

The historic town and borough of Redmarket is situated thirty miles west of Granfield, and is so called because of its association with the meat trade, dating back to its founding in 70–100 AD. Originally the site of a Roman fort, later on an Anglo-Saxon village grew up around the area. However, it wasn't until the early thirteenth century that it received its official market charter. Known for its friendly locals, Redmarket is surrounded by beautiful countryside and yet is only a stone's throw away from a number of other thriving towns and cities.

Chapter 1

It always had been, and remained, the worst part of this job.

Some coppers called it the 'Death Knock' or delivering the 'Death Message' – but whatever name you gave it, the result was the same. You were delivering news that would devastate a family, changing their lives forever. Once the words were out, there was no taking them back again. The knowledge would have an impact on everything, from doing the groceries to whether you even wanted to get up out of bed in the morning.

So, DC Mathew Newcomb paused before rapping on the wood of that door. It wasn't simply the gravity of what he was about to impart, although it was the worst thing anyone could ever tell another human being; the worst thing they could possibly hear, as well. It wasn't even the effect on him; that wasn't – *shouldn't* be – what this was about. He'd done this dozens of times, although selfishly on this occasion he knew it would upset him more than any of the others. For the same reason he'd volunteered to come here in the first place, along with the Family Liaison Officer Linda Fergusson. Because he owed this family, knew them personally.

Because he knew the victim.

Linda was looking at him, those brown eyes of hers questioning. Mathew couldn't put the moment off any longer. He brought his knuckles down on the wood, hard, a couple of times. It was ridiculous, but he didn't want the knock to sound flippant – he wanted it to somehow convey the seriousness of his business. Wanted it to have told them some of what he needed to impart even before the people inside had answered the call.

Sadly, when the door opened, and standing there was the one person he would have gone to the ends of the earth not to see, she only frowned momentarily, then was suddenly smiling. 'Matt?' said Julie, and it was as if the decades hadn't really passed at all. They were still at school together. She had been his first crush – those freckles and that flaming red hair. Both had faded in the intervening years, the latter to an auburn colour. But in spite of a few wrinkles here and there, the beginnings of crow's feet at the eyes, she was still beautiful – even in those jeans and a loose shirt. She was still Julie Brent . . . Jules. How could he have thought he'd ever stood a chance with her? She'd only had eyes for one bloke, right from the start. 'I can't believe it. What are you doing . . .? I haven't seen you since the reunion a few . . .' Her gaze flitted from Mathew to his companion, but now she was frowning again. 'Mathew, what . . .?'

He opened his mouth to speak, but nothing came out. Mathew realised he was standing there like an idiot, yet there was nothing he could do about it. The words simply wouldn't come.

This had been a bad idea, he said to himself. He'd wanted to . . . what, break the news to Julie gently, make sure it was delivered in the right way? *Was* there even a right way? Didn't feel like it at the moment. Not at all. Wanted to be there for Julie, then? Even after all these years. But he was making such a cockup of it, leaving the poor woman just standing there, wondering what was going on. Looking from him to Linda, then back again. All Mathew could do was shake his head.

'Matt? Matt, you're scaring me.'

You should *be scared*, he couldn't help thinking. He opened and closed his mouth again, looking for all the world like a ventriloquist's dummy whose owner had laryngitis. In the end, he managed a strangled, 'I'm so sorry.'

But, as it turned out, he didn't need to say any more than that. She'd already realised he was here in an official capacity, from his expression, from the fact he wasn't alone; knew what his job entailed. There were really only three people this could be about – and Mathew had heard that Julie's dad was in a home somewhere, so if something had happened to him, she would have received a phone call from there. That left a choice of two, and probably only one of them hadn't been in the house all night. Wasn't an uncommon thing, if what he'd heard about the girl was correct – which was why Julie hadn't been worried . . .

Until now.

It was Julie's turn to shake her head, going into denial: 'No . . . no, it can't . . .' Mathew had seen this on more than one occasion as well. Julie's hand was going to her mouth, tears were already welling in her eyes.

'Who the bloody hell is . . .' The voice drifted through even before this newcomer followed, dressed in a vest and pyjama bottoms. Mathew recognised him as Greg Allaway, Julie's husband. Hair closely cropped to hide the fact he was going bald, and with a well-cultivated beer belly – even more so than the last time he'd seen the man – he was totally the opposite of what Mathew would have expected Julie to end up with. Mathew might not have stood a chance back in school, but he could run rings around Greg Allaway as it stood today. If he hadn't been married himself, of course. The thought made him uncomfortable, and wasn't welcome in any way, shape or form. But when Greg snapped, 'What the bloody hell is all this? I was just getting ready for work!' it surfaced again momentarily, and just for a second Mathew wanted to punch him squarely in the face.

Julie couldn't speak, was having trouble even standing. She toppled sideways against the open front door, and it was only when Mathew moved forwards to try and catch her that Greg did something to help – getting there first and grabbing her by the arm to steady her. Grabbing a little too forcefully for Mathew's liking.

Greg looked from his wife, back to Linda and Mathew. And was there a hint of recognition now that he could take the latter in properly? Did he remember him from the last time they'd met? Remember his vocation? Even if he didn't, Mathew had been told after all these years on the force he definitely looked like a policeman; didn't even matter that he was plain-clothes. 'What's happened now?' Julie's husband asked gruffly.

Linda spoke up this time, doing the job that she'd been trained for. 'I think it might be best if we came in off the street to talk about it.'

Greg looked back at his wife, who was on the verge of collapsing altogether – her green eyes rolling back into her head – and nodded.

Twenty minutes later, and they were all sitting in the living room: Greg and Julie on the couch, him with his arm around her; Mathew and Linda on the chairs opposite. Linda had made them all a tea, after asking where the kitchen was. An especially sweet one for Julie because she was in shock, although the woman hadn't touched a drop yet, kept staring at the mug in front of her on the coffee table.

'I just . . . I just can't believe it,' she kept on saying. 'Not our Jordan.'

All Mathew could do was shake his head in reply. Not that he hadn't done all the talking he needed to for now, hoping that what he'd said had helped a little. Of course, hearing that your daughter had been stabbed to death was never going to be easy to take in. But the fact that they had a suspect in custody, that he'd been picked up covered in blood not too far from the crime scene, must have been some sort of comfort to her. He left out the fact that they'd found fingerprints on the handle of the murder weapon for now, because it was currently being tested, but Mathew had no doubt whatsoever that they would end up belonging to one Robert 'Bobby' Bannister: Jordan's boyfriend.

'But . . . but why?' Julie asked again, gazing up at him with eyes that looked like they'd been scrubbed raw. All he could do in answer to that was give another shake of the head, because Mathew Newcomb didn't have the first clue. What he did know was that it was only a matter of time before it all come out in the wash. Things usually did.

'That young lass was always getting herself into some kind of trouble,' was Greg's reply. 'I've . . . *we've* done our best to try and help her, but, well, some people just don't seem to want to be helped, do they?' Before anyone could say anything to that, he added, 'Oh, Christ – work! I need to give them a call and tell them I'll be late in.' When he saw the look Julie cast him, he changed that to: 'Tell them I *won't* be in, I mean.'

He let go of his wife then and went out into the hallway to use the phone on the table there. It was only now that Mathew got up, went over and sat down next to Julie as she broke into another fresh bout of tears. 'Hey, hey . . . it's okay, Jules. Everything's going to be okay.' Hollow words and they both knew it. Nothing would ever be okay again as far as Julie Allaway was concerned.

The sound of Greg's voice on the phone wafted through to them and it was suddenly as if a light bulb had gone on in Julie's head. 'Has . . . has anyone let him know?'

Mathew was puzzled for a second or two, then realised who she meant. 'Someone's contacting him, from the station.'

As Julie nodded slowly, Mathew caught the look of confusion on Linda's face. 'Greg is Jordan's stepfather,' he told her, and she nodded.

'He . . . he'll be in bits,' Julie mumbled, as if she hadn't even heard Mathew's words to the FLO.

'I know,' said Mathew, patting her knee. 'I know.' She broke down once more, leaning across and sobbing into his shoulder.

There were words, but he couldn't really make them out at first. Then Mathew realised what she was saying.

'What are we going to do?' Julie was repeating over and over. 'What are we going to do?'

Jacob Radcliffe yawned as he sat waiting for the other members of his team to get their act together, to get *there*. It was like trying to herd cats, getting the producer, reporter and sound person all in one place at the same time so they could set off to their destination – this time to do a thrilling piece about an old married couple who'd been together for seventy years. Lucky them. Typical kind of thing for the local news sections on TV. Jake was *so* looking forward to pointing the camera at them and listening as they gave sage advice like: 'Never go to bed on an argument' or 'Try not to worry about things you can't control'. Jesus.

Where was all the big news? he had to ask himself. He'd been on more exciting gigs when he'd been a photographer for *The Granfield Gazette* back in the day. There was even that report about mob boss Danny Fellows and his operations that Jake's old colleague Dave Harris had been lining up until it got squashed. It had been exciting though, going round and taking pictures of the places Fellows owned, like that casino or the strip joint. Felt like they were doing something important, something worthwhile . . . Probably a good idea it stopped where it did though, if Fellows' rep was anything to go by, Jake often thought to himself. At least when you were interviewing old married couples there was no chance of ending up at the bottom of the river wearing concrete slippers.

He looked at his watch again, then out across at the newsroom at the various people who were in at this hour: only a handful so far, checking emails, answering or making calls. Jake yawned again. What was the point of arranging a time to set off on their long drive when nobody was going to show up but him? He had been hoping they could get this in the bag and out of the way before lunch, so he could sneak off and do some more editing on the short film he'd been making in his spare time. It was just something he was doing for fun at the moment, not really thinking it would go anywhere – and certainly not thinking along the lines of BAFTAs or Oscars – but maybe if he could get it up to scratch he could hit the festivals with it. Jake had mostly recruited students from the local unis and colleges to help with it all, people who'd work just for credits over several weekends. And it wasn't shaping up too badly at all, if he said so himself: a film about young people today and their thoughts about the future, where everything was heading. Fiction, but in a documentary style.

But he was never going to get it finished at this rate, not if Sarah, Phil and Howard didn't get their arses in gear so they could get this over and done with. 'For God's sake,' he said, stifling yet another yawn.

They were lucky he was in at all, the restless night he'd had. It had taken him ages to actually get to sleep and he'd only been in the land of nod a short while when he'd woken up, panicking and sweating. He could have sworn someone had been calling out his name, but when he turned on the light he felt quite silly for answering. Jake had struggled to get back off, tossing and turning, rolling onto his front, his sides. Thank Christ he didn't share a bed with anyone anymore, because they probably would have kicked him out onto the couch. In the end, he'd got up at stupid o'clock and made himself several cups of coffee – which was probably why he'd got here so early that morning, and why it seemed like he'd been waiting ages. Couldn't blame the others for staying tucked up in bed a little while longer, he supposed, but all the same . . .

Jake was relieved when he saw Sarah, their reporter, come through the doors, looking immaculate as usual (he'd once joked that she probably got out of bed looking like that, and she'd scowled and filled him in at great length about all the prep it took). She held up a hand in greeting, then pointed to indicate she was going to grab a drink before coming over. He sighed . . . but then neither of the others had even shown their faces yet.

Phil and Howard turned up together, laughing and joking as usual – not a care in the world – and Jake was just rising to go and join them when someone actually did call his name. It was their IT person, Alison, holding up a phone for him to come over. Jake touched his chest and she nodded, face quite serious.

'Who's calling me here?' he asked her as he trotted over. He had his work mobile on him, so why not use that? 'What's it about?'

Alison shrugged. 'Wouldn't say. Sounded official, though.'

Jake took the phone from her, his brow creasing. 'H-Hello?' He nodded when they asked if they were speaking to the right person, before realising they couldn't see him. 'Yes, that's me.'

Then, as the words came through the receiver, it was as if time stood still. Jake tried and failed to process them. Instead, he dropped the phone which hung down the side of Alison's desk by its cord. Then he walked away, leaving Alison and everyone else mystified, ignoring their calls.

He had somewhere to be.

He had something to do.

Want more? Order now!

326

Dear Reader,

We hope you enjoyed reading this book. If you did, we'd be so appreciative if you left a review. It really helps us and the author to bring more books like this to you.

Here at HQ Digital we are dedicated to publishing fiction that will keep you turning the pages into the early hours. Don't want to miss a thing? To find out more about our books, promotions, discover exclusive content and enter competitions you can keep in touch in the following ways:

JOIN OUR COMMUNITY:
Sign up to our new email newsletter: hyperurl.co/hqnewsletter
Read our new blog: www.hqstories.co.uk
🐦 : https://twitter.com/HQStories
📘 : www.facebook.com/HQStories

BUDDING WRITER?
We're also looking for authors to join the HQ Digital family!
Find out more here:
https://www.hqstories.co.uk/want-to-write-for-us/
Thanks for reading, from the HQ Digital team

ONE PLACE. MANY STORIES

If you enjoyed *Her Husband's Grave*, then why not try
another gripping crime thriller from HQ Digital?